MW01109373

A PLACE for ME

COLBY CHASE

A PLACE for ME

International street life to spiritual insight

iUniverse, Inc.
New York   Bloomington

A Place for Me
International Street Life to Spiritual Insight

iUniverse books may be ordered through booksellers or by contacting:
iUniverse
1663 Liberty Drive
Bloomington, IN 47403
www.iuniverse.com
1-800-Authors (1-800-288-4677)

ISBN: 978-1-4502-3134-3 (pbk)
ISBN: 978-1-4502-3136-7 (ebk)
ISBN: 978-1-4502-3135-0 (hbk)

Library of Congress Control Number: 2010907423

Printed in the United States of America
iUniverse rev. date: 5/24/10

To all the Twelve Step Programs and the faith, spiritual freedom and recovery they inspire in so many

"Sometimes, going left is the only way to get right."

Eddie Plummer

Contents

I gratefully wish to acknowledge first my, Higher Power, the people, Program and Principles of the Anonymous Twelve Step Programs, AA, NA, and CA in general, who I have had the pleasure of sharing and caring with over the years and without whom I quite probably would not still be alive, much less free of narcotics long enough to have written this book.

A very special thanks to my Grandparents, who gave me all they had. God bless them and may they rest in peace.

Thanks to Mon Cheri O. for always believing in me and being there for me.

A particular thanks to my special friends, C. J. and Cardo, who have loved and supported me unconditionally in, what at first seemed to be, one of my darkest hours and along with several others on multiple occasions, urged me to write this book.

Thanks to my long term long distance gal pal and spiritual cohort, B.C.C., who has reached out to befriend me since we first met long ago.

Last but certainly not least thanks to my mother and father for the gift of my creation.

Prologue

He has two thoroughbred white hoes that are renowned for getting money all over the world, a fast young black broad, and a down mixed blood that are all hard down for him. His alter ego suggests, *are we not an international player of sorts? So where they're really coming from, is out of jealousy and envy.*

Mitch rides by Dean's pool hall and discusses it all with him. Dean suggests, "Pretty, man, you need to take those hoes and get out of this little fucking town. These old niggas hate you, man, and if you knock that one girl, what's her name?"

"Her name is Denise, Dean."

"Yeah, whatever the fuck her name is, all hell is going to break loose if you do. Mitch, you're young and inexperienced. Most people, even some hoes, hate pimps because either they're envious and jealous, or because some family member, mother, sister, daughter, wife or girlfriend has been affiliated in some negative way with flamboyant, high siding niggas like you. I couldn't be no pimp with all that shit going against me. Plus, I'm too busy trying to get at a nigga's dick for myself anyway," and he laughs. Mitch doesn't find any of this stuff at all funny. "Pretty, you know that statement all you pimp niggas use, 'Pimping ain't easy,' well it really ain't. I'm going to call an old partner of mine from the Army named Lawrence. He now resides in San Francisco, and I'll see if he can put you in touch with some of the local talent there, so you can get up out of here."

"Dean, I like the Monterey Peninsula, and I plan to buy a house and live here because it's perfect for my game, and picking up fresh new game."

"None of that will matter Mitch if you're dead or in prison. This isn't a dress rehearsal or a military mission in the bush. There is a whole different down and dirty set of rules out here in these streets. I'll tell you something else, if not for me talking to Ward, you might have had a run in with him about his wife, Bobbie.

"Pretty, you can't just run around taking folks wives and girlfriends and expecting no repercussions. You've become a big time pimping nigga now, so you need the camaraderie and tutelage of other big time pimping niggas. Also, wherever you find yourself, you had better learn to watch your back, especially if you stay in that pimp game."

Mitch heeds both his partner's words after his stable begins to feel the heat. A lot of cops are on the take, especially in the little rural areas. The cops start harassing and busting Mitch's girls exclusively, so he finally gets the message that he and they are no longer welcome. He and Lana make plans to leave for San Francisco, but not before knocking Denise and claiming the number five girl for his stable. Mitch's alter ego amuses him with, *Hanks should have never doubted us.*

The spot Dean uses as his after-hours joint was once a house converted into a church that got converted back into a house. It has a paved parking lot that sit's off to the left rear of the closed in garage with a tall wooden gate to avoid police seeing how many cars are parked in there at any given time. There are two entry ways into the parking lot; one from the rear of the house and another used to drive in and out of the vacant lot driveway next to the house. Once inside the parking lot, one is secluded and not visible from the street or to people in the house.

Usually Dean has a guy at the gate to open and close it as traffic comes and goes. The night before Mitch and his crew are to leave town, Mitch is going to his car inside the parking lot as he is leaving. He notices no one is manning the gate, so he opens it and leaves it open so he can drive out. Mitch has picked up a couple of phone numbers from Dean. One for a guy named Fillmore Slim, who is supposed to be a big time pimp in San Francisco, and the other, Lawrence, the acquaintance Dean has previously mentioned to Mitch.

As Mitch reaches his car, he notices Broadway Sam (who he didn't even know was in the house) come into the parking lot from the rear of the house and close the gate behind him. Sam snarls, "Hey you little punk ass nigga, that was some foul shit you did snatching my partner's broad," as he menacingly heads towards Mitch's position. Mitch has the door of his Lac open and his right leg inside already. There is a car parked on either side of Mitch's car so he calculates the best vantage point to avoid physical contact with Broadway.

"Broadway, man, I don't want no trouble." As Mitch speaks he eases his 45 from the small of his back while using the darkness, the Lac door, and his body to conceal the move. Then he eases the silencer from his front left trouser pocket, because he realizes that the loud sound of the weapon discharging will draw attention to the parking lot and to him.

"Well, little motherfucker, it's too late for that, because that's just what you got now, trouble, and you won't fast talk your way out of this, either." Some of the things Mitch learned during his tour of duty in Nam, are that moving decisively and with the element of surprise in his favor gives him an edge. So as Broadway approaches, oblivious that Mitch is a threat of any kind, Mitch slowly backs away as if he is intimidated by the much larger man. Mitch *is* intimidated but his combat experience steadies his nerves. In the darkness of night, Broadway's profile keeps looming larger the closer he gets to Mitch, as Broadway is swiftly closing the distance between them.

Mitch slows his breathing so his hand will be steadier and his aim surer. He is gauging the big man's range of distance from him. He feels that familiar dryness in his mouth and the palms of his hands become wet from nervous perspiration. His stomach flips as if he's on a roller coaster. He knows all too well the symptoms are a result of fear and adrenaline. *Shit,* he thinks, *seems like all my life I've been filled with fear of some menacing big nigga doing me something.*

Chapter I

End of the Beginning

When he is born on November15, 1946, in Memphis, Tennessee, his father is at sea. His mother names him Mitchell Stone Jr. Asked what is to be his middle name, she can only think of the North Fleet where the child's father is stationed in the Navy, so she proudly states, "North Fleet." Thank God her parents are present and won't let her put that on a birth certificate. Can you imagine a Mitchell North Fleet Stone Jr.? She ultimately decides there will be no middle name at all.

Mitchell Stone Junior's earliest memory is that of a one year old toddler. His house is dark, and the shades are pulled down. He hears the wind blowing through the trees overhanging the eaves, because the silence is so still in the living room where he and his mother are hiding. He feels his mother's fear as she clutches him close while sitting on the sofa. He hears her say, "Shh baby, we don't want him to know we're in here." Mitchell Junior watches the menacing silhouette on the window shade as it passes the side window, and he is afraid because he doesn't know who the "him" she mentions is outside that window.

The figure knocking on the back door and shouting turns out to be his father. "Bee, open the door. Open it now," he hollers as his fists continue pounding against the door.

Bee reluctantly unlocks the door, pulls it open and steps aside to allow Mitchell Stone Senior inside. "Mitchell, stop yelling, you'll upset the baby," she says. Mitchell Senior has been out with some female or another, again. It is considered within Negro communities to be the manly thing to do. Mitchell Senior is six feet two inches tall, dark and slender in build. He is one of nineteen sisters and brothers all by the same mother and father.

His nickname for his wife, Goldie B. Stone, is "Bee" (for honey bee). Mitchell senior is a sailor during this post wartime mid 1940's. Goldie B is the only child of Goldie Senior and Jo Myrtle Fischer. When Mitchell Junior is born, Goldie B is only seventeen years old, going on fourteen emotionally. Mitchell is her first and only child. He is conceived out of wedlock, and her marriage to Mitchell Stone Senior takes place only months before the child's birth. Goldie B is what's known as a 'high yellow' because of her lighter complexion.

Goldie B is of mixed blood, Creole, Indian, and Negro. She is short and thin, with fair features and long flowing locks. Goldie is intelligent, yet naïve, to the ways of love and relationships. Mitchell Senior and Goldie B meet while she is still in high school. He sweeps her off her feet with his charm, smooth talk and uniform. At sixteen she becomes pregnant with Mitchell Junior while Mitchell Senior is in town on furlough. Even though totally dedicated to her husband and child, this morning she has had enough and is not going to tolerate his behavior any longer. She intends to have it out with him, drunk or sober.

"Mitchell, where have you been until this hour of the morning?"

"Oh Bee, leave me alone. Can't you see I'm tired?"

"Tired? You mean drunk and tired. Well, I'm tired too and I'm leaving you, Mitchell, and this time it's for good." He is too drunk to offer much opposition. Once he passes out she packs up Junior's things along with what she can carry of her own. After one last look back, she turns her head, raises her chin and marches out the door.

Back living in her mother's house, Goldie B is finding a new sense of freedom. She is making up for all she's missed out on during her adolescence because of bearing a child and getting married. She sets out about the business of catching up on her social life, while leaving the burden of parenting to her mom and dad.

Goldie Senior, Mitchell Junior's grandfather, nicknames Lil' Mitchell "Snoopy" (after the cartoon character). It is a fitting name as Lil' Mitchell is always snooping around where he doesn't belong. Snoopy in turn, calls his grandfather "Dandy" because when his family tried to teach him to say granddad, all he could muster was Dandy. Dandy stands six feet tall and is of medium build with light brown skin, fair hair, and features of Negro and Indian mix. Snoopy learns to call his grand mom, Mama Jo, because she is more like a mother to him than grandmother. Jo is small, light skin, fair featured and good looking. She is a proud little woman, also known as a "high yellow".

Growing up in Memphis, Tennessee, in the little community of Douglass, Snoopy develops what is known as an alter ego. He learns to play alone with his thoughts and his toys imagining his alter ego as a playmate or family member playing with him. He is rarely allowed visitors unless they are heavily screened and approved by his grandparents and "Madea" (the name he calls his mother). Even then, playmates are allowed quite sparingly. If they are unacceptable to his mom and grand mom, he is made to come in the house or they have to leave.

Over the years, Lil' Mitchell sees his father only on a few occasions. Then, his father remarries and moves away to Chicago and he no longer sees him at all. Lil' Mitchell's world begins to fall apart when around age eight or nine, his Madea announces to him that she's getting remarried and also moving to Chicago. So Lil' Mitchell is left to be raised by Mama Jo and Dandy.

It is apparent that since his retirement, Dandy is ailing more and more. Lil' Mitchell observes Dandy suffering from severe asthma after all those years working in the oat mills. He is noticeably older, sicker, and weaker. Lil' Mitchell also observes that the bond between Dandy and Mama Jo seems to be diminishing. She seems to be upset and short with Dandy about one thing or another, much of the time.

There is a guy or two that Lil' Mitchell notices coming to the house on a fairly regular basis under the guise of giving Mama Jo rides to various places, sometimes with Lil' Mitchell going along. On this particular day Mama Jo tells Dandy, "John is picking me and Snoopy up to drive us to a picnic he is having at his house for his two boys."

When John comes into the house he speaks to Dandy, "How do, Mr. Fischer?"

Dandy looks at him intensely. "Just fine John, how you?"

"Fair to middling, Mr. Fisher, thanks for asking." Then John turns to Lil' Mitchell. "Are you hungry boy? We got a mess of ribs and chicken cooking over yonder at my place." Inconspicuously, John peeks at Mama Jo. "Mrs. Jo, y'all ready to go?" On the way out the door John waves to Dandy.

Mama Jo tells Dandy, "I'll bring you back some barbeque, Goldie."

In a cracked voice Dandy responds, "Ne'er you mind, Jo, I'll just fix up something here."

The look in Dandy's face and the tears in his eyes as he watches Mama Jo walk out the door speak louder to Lil' Mitchell's heart than any words ever could. At ten years old Lil' Mitchell is still quite naïve about the ways of the world, but he intuitively feels his grandfather's emotional pain and sadness. He knows that Dandy's pain has something to do with John coming to their house, so he asks him, "Dandy, you okay? Are you sick again or something?"

Dandy continues to stare out the door behind Mama Jo without looking at Snoopy, "I'm just fine Snoopy. I'm just old, sick and *tired*. Now you go 'head with yo grandma, son."

A few short years later Dandy dies, and now at thirteen years old things begin to move swiftly in Lil' Mitchell's life. He finds himself with too much time and opportunity to make his own decisions about who, what, and where he spends that time and energy. In spite of crooked front teeth with some decay in progress, he finds a whole new breed of friends. He is now running with the 'in crowd,' and enjoying it. He loves the newfound notoriety and popularity it affords him. Always with a seemingly cheerful expression on his face and a bright smile, he finds himself among other smiling faces that hide the traces of their sadness and sorrow within. Lil' Mitchell finds that the other members of the in crowd are from homes with absentee mothers, fathers, or both, just like him. Together they find acceptance and solace in becoming each other's family.

The combination of these new associations and Mama Jo starting to work outside the home brings about a new problem. In fact, it has become a constant problem. Mitchell is skipping school so he leaves his grandmother little choice. Mama Jo sits him down and explains, "Snoopy, I talked with Goldie B today, and we've decided that for your own good you will go live with her in Chicago. You're out of control here with me. You're on your own too much and you're hanging out with the wrong crowd, so it'll be better for everybody this way."

Mitchell's alter ego tells him, *it'll be better for everybody but us.*

So Mitchell responds, "No Mama Jo, I won't go to Chicago. I want to stay here with you, and I promise I'll do better."

"It's all been decided, Snoopy, and I'm putting you on the train this Friday evening."

Chapter II

Arriving in Chicago

In Chicago after coming from a community much like a Negro version of Andy Griffin's Mayberry RFD, Lil' Mitchell experiences culture shock and alienation with the neighborhood, his family, and integrated schools. Mitch doesn't feel a part of his new family unit. He doesn't feel comfortable or that he belongs. From the first moment Mitch meets Duke, his mother's third husband and father to their two daughters, Mitch senses that Duke is not very pleased with Mitch's presence being forced upon them.

Mitch sets out to become at least friends with Duke, but Duke doesn't even speak to Mitch on a regular basis. When he does, it's to put Mitch down or verbally chastise him for what seems to Mitch as very minor offenses. Mitch feels Duke is short for a grown man and he drinks too much.

Mitch's responsibility around the household is to babysit his sisters, Veronica and Sierra, at night and at least partially on most weekends. He rationalizes that the family needs him in that capacity, but it doesn't make him feel any better about missing out on so many of his partner's extracurricular activities. It also doesn't help matters that he gets suspended from school on a regular basis for getting caught fighting, gambling or committing other infractions. All of which he considers stupid rules.

Mitch overhears his mom and a very drunk Duke auguring about him one night. Duke says, "Ever since he got here he's been nothing but trouble. He does nothing to help out around here. He's lazy, good for nothing and I just don't like him. I've tried, but I do not like him."

"He's my son and he has nowhere else to go, but with me. And he does a lot to help out around here. If not for him being here, we'd have to pay for a baby sitter."

"I'd rather pay for a baby sitter than to have to keep looking at his face."

Then, his mom starts sobbing, "Lord, please help me. I don't know what to do."

Mitch decides that he knows what to do. *As soon as I can I'm out of here*, he thinks. It would be better for his mom, him, and everyone concerned. He ponders where a fourteen year old with no money and no means of support can go. For now, his plan is to simply avoid contact and confrontation with Duke as much as possible.

In the years to come Mitch will come to understand that Duke's problem is not about him, his mom or anyone else outside of Duke himself. Duke's problem is that Duke really doesn't like himself very much and since he doesn't like himself, he doesn't like anyone else either. However, during this time, even though he doesn't know it, Mitch blames himself for what's wrong between his mother, himself, and Duke.

The one highlight in Mitch's life is his girl, Gwen, who is a thirteen year old 'high yellow', born of a White mother and dark skin Puerto Rican father. She has light brown, shoulder length, wavy hair, hazel eyes, and a medium build. She is very pretty and dresses quite provocatively.

When Mitch learns of the upcoming relocation of his family to a bigger apartment he is livid. Even though he recognizes that the family needs more living space, he is concerned about being too far away from his Gwen. He thinks, *it's hard enough for Gwen and me to get quality time together with her living just across the street, so it'll be next to impossible if we move far away.* He begs his mom to please find someplace close. She explains that the family has limited money to work with, but she will do her very best. So he should not be disappointed if she can't find some place close by.

Mitch arranges with Gwen to cut school with him this day, so they can spend time together. He knows he will not be able to run across the street and kiss her good night or have her run to him when she needs to be near him. Mouse (his nickname for Gwen) stays home awaiting Mitch's arrival. They have done this together many times. It doesn't seem to Mitch that walking is carrying him to her swiftly enough so he begins running full speed down the alley lined with winter snow. At her back gate, he finds her standing out in the alleyway waiting for him with her arms folded from the chill of the brisk Chicago winter day. There is snow all around as Mitch rounds the last curve just before the back gate of her building. She sees him, and runs crying into his arms.

They embrace as if oblivious to the world or the cold of the day, while holding on as if for their dear lives. They kiss long and passionately as each of their tears touches the face of the other. This is that teenage love that causes an ache throughout their bodies; an ache of longing to hold and be held by each other. "Oh Mitchell, you can't move that far away. I'll just die without you near me. I just know I will," she cries.

"I know, Mouse, I feel the same way, but we can't let this keep us apart. I'll come to you my every free moment."

"You promise? I love you *so* much, Mitchell."

"I know, and I love you more, Mouse."

Once inside Gwen's apartment, Gwen clings onto Mitchell as if letting him go will be to lose him forever. As they make love, all the frustrations of Mitchell's moving away to Ogden Park slowly dissipate into blissful climax. Afterwards, they fall into deep slumber. Mitchell wakes up first and takes a moment to just stare at Mouse in awe, because he thinks that she is the most beautiful thing he's ever seen. He lets out a deep sigh for he cannot remember ever feeling this way about another human being. He gently brushes her hair from her face, and he kisses it softly as one would a tender young baby. They lay all day laughing and swearing their love and allegiance to each other. As he's getting dressed to leave, Mouse kisses him the last good bye kiss for the fifth time just before he runs down the back stairs yelling to her, "I love you, Mouse."

"I love you more, Mitchell.

Chapter III

Military Life

Although Mitch has the best of intentions, it becomes harder and harder for him to make the trip back to the old neighborhood to see Mouse as often as he wants or she needs. With the absence of Mitch's presence and the untimely death of her sixteen year old sister, Deidre, Mouse becomes increasingly more sullen and withdrawn. Over the next several months, her mood swings increase in both severity and length. Communication between them becomes as distant as their geographical locations. Finally, one afternoon Mitch tracks her down and finds her leaning up against a big red car in front of his old neighborhood community center. There is another girl standing beside Mouse that is dressed really sharp, also in all red. As he gets closer he sees that Mouse and the girl are talking to someone in the big car. Mitch calls out to Mouse, and she hesitatingly comes running to him. He asks her, "Mouse, why didn't you wait for me at your house?"

"I thought you weren't coming, Mitchell." Mouse points towards the big red car, "My girlfriend, Kathy, called me over to the car to meet her boyfriend. I was just hanging out at the community center. With my sis gone, I didn't want to be home alone."

As Mitch and Mouse are talking, the door of the big red car swings open and this older, tall, light skin guy gets out. Mitch notices that the guy is also dressed in red all the way down to his shoes, and his hair is conked.

"Mouse, are they entertainers or something?"

"I don't know Mitch, but they sure look sharp, don't they?"

"Yeah Mouse, they sure do, but come on, I'll walk you back to your house."

Mouse grabs Mitch's hand as she waves and shouts, "Bye Kathy, I've got to go with my boyfriend." As her and Mitch are walking away, Mouse looks back over her shoulder again, and shouts to the tall guy in the red outfit, "Nice meeting you, Ricky."

After returning home, Mitch begins to share with his mom Mouse's behavior and his concern about her fear of being alone. "Well," Madea begins to explain, "There are things that you don't know about Gwen, Deirdre, and their father." Mitch sits up and begins to pay strict attention as his mom continues, "When Gwen and Deirdre were much younger girls... oh, five and eight years old I think, their father and mother were married and living together. One night when their mother comes home she finds the police and paramedics there.

"Deirdre had stabbed their father in the back several times when she found him drunk and passed out in Gwen's bed after molesting her. He was really in bad condition, Snoopy. Anyway, he never recovered from those stab wounds, and he died. Apparently, he had been doing that to those little girls for years and their mom didn't know anything about it. So Snoopy, I understand about Gwen needing someone with Deirdre gone and her mom being gone so much at work."

Mitch can hardly believe his ears, and is noticeably crying. He can feel his true love's pain throughout her years of being molested as if it were his own pain. He even feels the pain that he imagines she must still feel as a result of that experience. Mitch thinks, *if I had known her back then and found out about what was happening I would have killed her father myself.* Following this conversation with his mother, Mitch is determined to spend as much time with Mouse as she needs. Oddly however, he begins to see less of her, even when he has time, because she's more unavailable for his calls and visits. Mitch feels confused, wondering how she could do this with all they mean to each other. *Isn't she dying inside from not seeing me just as I am from not seeing her?* he wonders. *After all*, he thinks, *she is my girl.* Since she's the one true love of his fourteen years of life, he decides he will find and confront her.

Mitch is hanging around on the corner of the block where Mouse lives hoping to catch her coming home when an old partner of his named Ben walks up. After they exchange cordial greetings, Ben asks Mitch, "Man, did you hear about your ex girl's sister, Deirdre, dying?" Before Mitch can respond, Ben continues, "Man, Gwen is into some heavy shit these..."

Mitch cuts Ben off by grabbing Ben's arms, shaking him, and asking, "What kind of heavy shit do you mean? And Mouse is still my girl."

"Aw Mitch, I didn't know, man, because..." Ben is hesitant to tell Mitch about Gwen now that he knows they are still involved. He looks away trying to avoid Mitch's stare and persistent inquiry.

Mitch feels an overwhelming uneasiness in the pit of his stomach and is now both curious and afraid. "Because what, Ben? Please tell me." Ben is much taller than him so as Mitch positions his body to look up into Ben's eyes, Ben turns a couple of times trying to avoid Mitch's stare. Mitch grabs his arms again, "Come on Ben, you're my partner, man, tell me what's going on with Mouse."

"Okay man, Gwen goes with older studs for money, Mitch." Oblivious to the bigger boy's stature, Mitch quickly grabs Ben's shirt with both hands as if it is all Ben's fault, then slowly releases his grasp. Ben feels for his smaller partner's obvious pain at the news, but reasons that he would want the news given to him if the roles were reversed.

Mitch can't believe his ears, and his mind is racing so fast with jealousy, rage, pain, and betrayal that his body recoils swiftly turning the opposite direction. Uncontrollable tears fill his eyes. He turns back to Ben, "No man, that's just impossible. It just can't be. Mouse wouldn't do that to me, to…to… our relationship."

"I'm sorry, Mitch, but you know I wouldn't make some shit like this up, man."

When Mitch finally hears from Mouse, she is apologetic about not being around for the past few weeks. "But Mitchell, I've had some things to work out."

He tries to maintain his cool and reserve but he just cannot. He blurts out, "What things, Mouse?" Then his hurt feelings lead him to ask all manner of questions about what he has heard.

Mouse tells him to come over to her house and they'll talk about it, but he explains that he has to baby sit. "Well, when your momma lets you out again, *little boy,* call me."

He finds that cruel and hurtful, especially coming from his beloved, but he says nothing. Even with hurt feelings he still asks if she is okay before hanging up. For the next few days, all he can think about is Mouse; not school, not eating, not even his partner's phone calls trying to distract him from thinking about her.

Mouse calls again later in the week and tells Mitch, "Don't bother calling me or coming over anymore. I'm tired of having a boyfriend that can't do nice things for me, and doesn't have a car. On top of that, I need my *man* to spend time with me like Kathy's man, Ricky, does with her." Mitch notes how she uses the word "man" with emphasis. As far as he can remember, this is the first time she has referred to him as her man, instead of boyfriend.

Mouse's words pierce his heart like a spear, because he loves her so much. He reflects back to the pain he felt when his mom left him that first time. He also remembers how, through betrayal, Mama Jo could break Dandy's heart causing him to shed tears on more than one occasion; all the while supposedly loving him. He wonders, *how could they all be so cruel, while professing to love someone?* Thus begins the process of a young boy learning to soothe the hurts of life by masking his pain in the bravado of his alter ego. Mitch reflects on the vow he made to his alter ego that he would never let his mom make him cry again. Yet, here he is feeling the same gut wrenching pain, but this time over Mouse. Then it comes to him as his alter ego consoles him, *while it is true that we are truly hurt, and perhaps worse than we have ever experienced, Mouse must never know just how deeply hurt we are.* He makes a vow to never again let another woman hear him cry or hurt him like Mouse has done.

So with tears in his eyes and a sinister smile on his face he manages to calmly say, "You know Gwen, I really love you, but you have to do whatever you have to do." These are such grown up words from such a not so grown up adolescent boy, but he finds it the only way to cope with his pain and save face.

His acceptance and calm catch her off guard, so her response is in a less aggressive and softer tone, "Well Mitchell, I guess there's nothing left to say then." He wants to plead with her not to leave him, but with a great deal of difficulty he manages, "No Gwen, I guess there isn't."

His heart is broken as he hangs up the phone. His alter ego urges him, *we must make a vow this day to never call Gwen or seek her out again, no matter what.*

Mitch wonders if she had noticed how, at the end of the conversation, he called her *Gwen,* not Mouse. He hasn't called her Gwen in longer than he can remember. He walks out of that apartment this day feeling, and being, very different inside. Mitch resolves to his alter ego that, now that he's done with Gwen, he's getting out of his family situation and Chicago, too, somehow, someway. Mitch adds Duke, his mom, their two daughters, and now Mouse to an already growing list of resentments that he doesn't even know he's accumulating. He must escape his family life, Duke, and his feelings.

He is sick and tired of fighting and always having to watch his and his partner's back. He's not in a gang, nor does he wish to be. Yet, he still has to watch his back because there's an upcoming gang war on the horizon in his community of Ogden Park. Mitch has seen several commercials on television asking young men to join and serve in the Armed Forces. At age sixteen he gets a Social Security Card and signs up to go into the Army after his seventeenth birthday. There's only one catch, his mom will have to sign.

There's a shooting incident involving Mitch and some of his partners in a confrontation with a gang. He gets probation and his record will be sealed upon his entry into the U.S. Army on or about his seventeenth birthday. As fate would have it, he finds a way out of Chicago, but not before he finds out that his Mouse is working the streets for some pimp named Ricky.

Over the next three years of exotic travel and military training, Mitch begins formulating intimate relationships with different types of women of the world, and different types of weapons. In Korea, out on pass with a few of his fellow GIs, a prostitute named Evelyn comes over to Mitch, grabs his hand and shouts, "Him cherry boy and that one over there cherry girl." She is pointing to a pretty moon faced Korean girl with no makeup on named Sonji Pak, who is sitting in the back of the bar in a booth.

Evelyn waves for Sonji Pak to come up front to meet Mitch. Sonji is fifteen years old, short, sleek and slender. She is pretty with long jet black silky hair that hangs well past her butt, and has little tiny features.

With neither her nor Mitch having any family financial support, they formulate a bond that leads Sonji to become very affectionate with, and subservient to, Mitch. He is not accustomed to such treatment, but feels like he could really get used to it. In October,

15

1964, just a month before his eighteenth birthday, Sonji Pak tells him she is pregnant. "It must be yours, *Mit-tell san,* because me use rubbers with every other GI me go with."

Even though he's little more than a kid himself, he is excited about having a child with Sonji. He is irresponsible at seventeen, going on fourteen emotionally, so the preparations of proper protocol he should be making within the military system in order to marry her, don't happen. After traveling to France, England, Germany, Guam, Manila and Hawaii, Mitch receives rotation orders for Viet Nam in June of 1965. From the bottom of Mitch's heart he swears by everything that he holds dear that he, Sonji, and the kid they have coming will be united, married, and live happily ever after one day.

After only four months in Nam, even though they feel like four years, Mitch is ending what was a projected thirteen month tour of duty. Mitch is out of the Nam and headed back to the world. Mitch can hardly believe his ears when he gets the news. Mitch's new orders are compliments of the "Sullivan Act," since he is the only son to carry on the family name. The bottom line for him, however, is that he's headed back to the real world after over seventeen months overseas.

Chapter IV

California Girls

Back in the world, Mitch spends a thirty day leave in Memphis, Tennessee. Then he heads for his new duty station. He is picked up by soldiers from the transit unit at Ft Ord, California, located just outside the city of Seaside, California near, Monterey. Mitch reflects that he has never been stationed in a permanent unit at a base in the States, so he is excited about that; plus, it's sunny California. On the jeep ride to the base Mitch listens to the two black soldiers in the front of the jeep talk about different girls in the towns of Seaside and Monterey. Anxious to find out about the women in the towns, Mitch inquires, "Hey man, what part of town do the fine ass sisters hang out?"

A tall, six feet three, light skin and solid built, Spec 4 Campbell responds, "Not to worry, Stone, I'll show you where the finest broads in town are once you're off restriction." Just like that, he and Mitch instantly become close. Of course, Campbell doesn't follow through on his promise, but Mitch feels that he doesn't need anyone to show him anything about women. He feels confident that he can hold his own when it comes to them.

Mitch is chomping at the bit to get to town and get busy drinking and partying with California girls. He feels like he has to make up for lost time from the states. He is in the best shape of his young life at nineteen years old, highly charged, oversexed, and easily excited. He is restricted to post pending assignment to his new unit, a weapon's experimentation and training unit. Their objective is testing new troop assault weapons and monitoring the training of new recruit's on firing ranges. Mitch finds that most of his nights will be free to run the neighboring towns for drinking and sexual conquests.

His mail finally catches up to him and among it is several letters from Sonji Pak with more photos of his son. He is starting to show pigment verifying his Black heritage, and Mitch is happy to see it. It's still too early for him to see any resemblance to himself. Mitch believes the child is his and that should be all that matters, but there is always that *but,* in the back of his mind. He writes Sonji back, "I'm finally at a permanent duty station so I'll get your letters faster now, and I'll be able to respond much faster. I have no money right now, but as soon as I get things going I will send some."

Even in late December, 1965, Mitch notices that the barracks are still segregated by Whites and other ethnicities on the ground floor and Blacks on the top floor. He could care less he tells himself, because it will not change what or how he will do here. His plan is to soldier hard so he can take care of his business and his kid.

It is the wee hours of the morning and throughout the barracks the sounds of soldiers snoring and heavy breathing in their slumber can be heard. Mitch begins sweating, tossing and turning, as he struggles with the bed covers. He hears the lieutenant shout, "Pull back, disengage and pull bac…" There is a gurgling sound as the lieutenant dies from a bullet to his throat. Mitch runs his bayonet into the chest of another approaching VC. The bayonet makes a thud sound as it sinks into a mixture of flesh and rib bones of the VC's chest. Mitch feels his rifle violently shaking in his hands from the struggling VC impaled on the bayonet wincing in pain.

Mitch mumbles aloud in his sleep, "Must block the bayonet thrust… I… No! No! Ugh." Mitch lets out a blood curdling scream, just as that VC had. Then, Mitch's body jerks him into consciousness. He awakens clutching his chest in pain so real that he can hardly breathe. It is that same nightmare again in which the bayonet is in his chest, not the VC's. Mitch trembles as the GI in the next bunk shakes him.

"Bro, you're okay. It was just a dream."

Mitch turns over in bed, and curls up into the fetal position as his alter ego assures him, *yeah, it's just a dream.* Still, Mitch rubs and inspects his chest once more before going back to sleep.

On his first pass, Mitch hitchhikes to Seaside with a black GI corporal headed to town. Mitch notes that he has not seen so many fine multi-complexioned sisters in one place in over two years. He is like a kid in a candy store and sets out about the business of getting his share of the confections. After about two weeks, Mitch knows his way around Seaside, Monterey, and even partially the neighboring town of Salinas. He can usually hitchhike his way to one or the other, although he makes it a point to become buddies with older soldiers that have cars.

One night as he's hitchhiking to Seaside, Mitch is picked up by an ex-soldier with reddish processed hair. Mitch asks him where he got his hair done that way, and he points to a barber shop as he drops Mitch off at a plaza on Broadway Street. The plaza is where Mitch usually hunts for action, because a lot of the local girls are in and out of the various shops, restaurants and hang outs there. Mitch walks over to the barber shop to find out how much it will cost to get his hair processed. He feels that there is no longer anyone that can tell him that he can't; not Madea, not Mama Jo, and not even the Army.

The hairstylist doing the processing of hair is a tall, light skin GI named Smith, called Smithy, who works in the shop part time to make ends meet. Smithy tells Mitch it will cost twelve dollars, but Mitch will need to let his hair grow out from his crew cut first. A few others sitting around laugh at Mitch and one named Rob asks him why he wants to get his hair conked. Mitch thinks for a moment and responds, "I've wanted to do this to my hair for years but first my mom wouldn't allow it, and then I was overseas for almost two years straight."

Rob asks, "Oh, so you're in the Army?"

"Yeah, I've been in for over two years."

Smithy asks Mitch, "Did you go to Nam?"

"Yeah man, I just got back from there a short time ago, but I was only there for four months."

Rob tells Mitch, "I own this joint, and you know what young blood? I was in the Nam myself once, so if you want credit until payday I'll front you a hair do." So Mitch gets what little hair he has fried, dyed and swooped to the side.

When Mitch leaves that shop a few hours later, he notices young girls that haven't paid him much attention before, winking and blinking at him. He meets a young fourteen year old mixed Filipina and Black girl named Tabitha, who has more Filipina features than Black and to Mitch, she is just too fine. They start hanging out, but she is so young it is hard for Mitch to connect with her in the hours he's in town (which is usually from five pm until dawn if he gets lucky). With his new hair style, he gets lucky more often than not now. Also most of his weekend days are free, unless he pulls guard duty or KP.

One night on base, a black soldier named Sgt Benjamin Lee turns Mitch on to a joint of weed and Mitch tells him, "No man, I tried that stuff and it doesn't do anything for me."

"What, it did nothing for you? Tell you what, you hit this shit and if it doesn't do anything for you, I'll kiss your black ass."

"Okay, let me see it."

When Mitch puffs on it as if it were a Winston, Lee starts coughing from laughing so hard. "Man, how old are you? And you mean to tell me, you been to all those exotic places around the world you talk about, and you don't know how to smoke a joint properly?"

Mitch is embarrassed and feels stupid so he angrily states, "No, I only tried it once. I mostly just drink, man."

With tears coming out of Lee's eyes from laughing so hard, he shows Mitch how to inhale and hold the cannabis smoke deep in his lungs. Mitch appears about to pass out when Lee hits his chest with the back of his open palm and says, "Stone, blow it out, man, before you start hyperventilating, man," and Lee starts cracking up laughing at Mitch again.

Suddenly, Mitch feels a rush to his head and a sensation of pressure in his ears and then everything seems to start moving in slow motion. He has never in his life felt anything even remotely similar to this. His dexterity seems to be affected as he reaches out his arm and hand in an awkward manner to get his balance. "Man, what the fuck is this shit you gave me?"

Lee is now laughing hysterically as he grabs Mitch's arm and asks him, "Stone, you okay, man?"

Mitch smiles and says, "Okay! I've never been more okay in my life, man." He hungrily sucks on the small joint again. "Stone, this is Panama Red. Powerful stuff. So you only need a couple of tokes on it, man."

Mitch proceeds to take three more deep pulls on the joint. He can hardly formulate words, as his body and functions have been altered in ways that at first, seem almost frightening. Mitch has become comfortable with the strange sensations and is way beyond alright. Lee is laughingly making fun of him, but it doesn't seem to matter to Mitch anymore.

Over the next several days Mitch starts smoking weed three or more times an evening, during after duty hours only. Then one night he's hanging out in the medical company located next to his own company, and Smithy, Rob, and another GI are in the barracks popping uppers and downers along with smoking weed and drinking booze. Mitch asks them what they're taking and they all laugh, and Smithy asks, "Man, where you come from? It can't be Chicago, because every dude I've ever met from Chicago is down."

Mitch begins to notice that he is a lot more comfortable and socially acceptable with his peers when he's high, and what they think of him seems to mean everything to him when he's not. So he starts popping pills along with the weed, and now even while on duty. This is the time of his real in depth introduction to Jazz music, and he finds that it really goes with getting high and being stoned. Mitch also finds that the different drugs are like sedatives that prevent the nightmares that he seems to have when he's not high or on the sleep aids prescribed for him.

His friend Lee is a heavyweight on the boxing team, and Mitch decides to join the squad, so he can have more free time to get high without duty interfering. They do road work together and even train together. Mitch's speed enables Lee to polish up his skills by sparring with a faster opponent. In turn, Lee's weight and bulk helps Mitch learn how to roll with heavy punches and to avoid them whenever he can.

Then Mitch meets Hanks, a six feet, thirtyish, medium built, black Corporal out of Texas. Hanks drives a 1959 Cadillac Sedan Deville and they become close and start hanging out a lot. Mitch's bud Lee has a redbone girlfriend in Salinas that he's shacking up with named Josie, so he's not around enough to supply the rides to and from town that Mitch needs. Hanks becomes Mitch's closet bud in place of Lee, and it serves both their purposes since Mitch is known as the young, popular, cute guy with fly hair among all the young, hot, teen age girls. Hanks figures riding Mitch around will reap him one or two of those fine young girls as Mitch runs through them, and it does. Mitch has a baby face, so at nineteen he looks to be fifteen. He has no body hair other than his pubic area and his small stature makes him look even younger, which is one reason he is so attractive to fine young girls like Tabitha.

Tabitha has a young, fifteen year old friend named Sherry who is a 'high yellow' cutie like Tabitha. Hanks gets Mitch to have Tabitha introduce them and the four of them start hanging out together. Hanks asks about Mitch sleeping with Tabitha one night, and when Mitch tells him he hasn't, Hanks replies, "Why not, Stone? That young bitch is crazy about you and will do anything you tell her."

Mitch feels ashamed because he hasn't, so he lies to save face, "I almost did once but she had to go home, man."

"Well, you will this night and I'll show you how, even if she's at home." The older, more experienced Hanks is intuitively aware of his younger partner's lack of knowledge and savvy in dealing with women (other than hookers). He knows Mitch gets by because he is a young, air headed, cutie pie guy with fly hair.

Mitch's relationships with women, for the most part, have been in dimly lit rooms during sex for hire with hookers, so he hadn't honed the skills of closing the deal with young virgins like Tabitha. With the four of them in the Cadillac, they pull up in front of Tabitha's house to drop her off first. Hanks turns and looks into the backseat at Tabitha and Mitch and asks, "Tabitha, do you have your own bedroom?"

"Yes," she responds shyly.

"Show Mitch where it's located," Hanks continues, "so when you get inside Mitch can crawl through the window and you two can have sex."

She blushes as she looks at Mitch, and points to a particular side of the house. Once she does, she tells Mitch, "I'll leave the light on until you get back to it. Then, I'll turn it off so no one will see you come in, okay?" She excitedly kisses Mitch, jumps out of the car and runs into her house. After a few minutes go by, Hanks tells Mitch to go for it.

"Man, what if I get caught?"

"Stone, what if you don't? But even if you do, you look twelve anyway, nigga, so what can they do to you? Just be real quiet and go get that young pussy, nigga." Mitch laughs and he and Hanks give each other five. Mitch sneaks to the back of Tabitha's house, crawls into her bedroom window and seals the deal. This will prove to be only the first of such trysts with sweet, young Tabitha. When he comes out, he is as excited as if he has been in a successful battle skirmish. Hanks mentions to Mitch, "You know you could turn her out if you wanted to."

Mitch is naïve to such things, so he asks, "What does that mean, Hanks?"

"Damn Stone with all of these too hot to trot, young girls you got chasing you, man, you could be four or five deep in the game, nigga." Mitch has no clue about what "deep" or "game" mean in this context, so he just stares at Hanks curiously. At this time, Hanks doesn't bother to go into detail about it, so they drop Sherry off and head back to base.

Mitch takes up with a married young gal named Bobbie and they start spending as much time as they can together between Mitch's obligations to military duties and her responsibilities with her family. Bobbie is a petite, light skin, pretty, little seventeen year old with freckles. She actually takes the lead role in pursuing Mitch in sexual matters. Bobbie already has a two year old son, so she's been around the block a few times. Her husband is a guy named Ward who is a big, muscular, medium brown skin, twenty four year old dude. Mitch views it as just another game of cat and mouse with yet another female conquest. He's oblivious as to what could happen if and when Ward catches him with his wife.

At this time, Mitch begins to note that there is a big difference in the attitudes of Black women, in comparison to that of Asian and Europeans females. While sex is great with both, Asian and European women seem to him to be more humble and less confrontational. Hanks tells Mitch, "That's because, for the past two years, you've been buying pussy, which requires no particular conversation or skills of seduction on your part. As a result, you haven't learned how to play the game in wooing and dating. With buying pussy, the only game you need is the cash." However, Mitch figures that, either way, he doesn't like most of the interactions with black women, other than sex. He hasn't met any white women in the states, so the jury is still out on them. He has also come to accept being high as a way of life because he feels so much more in control and less self conscious when he is high than when he isn't.

Sonji Pak continues to write but Mitch's replies to her letters are growing further in between. He realizes he has no intention whatsoever of reenlisting in the Army just to go back to Korea, marry her, and get her and his kid back to the states. His alter ego rationalizes, *how could we support her even if we did go get her? We don't even make enough money to support our self. If not for some chick or another buying us weed and booze, we wouldn't even be able to stay high.*

Mitch stays high every chance he gets. He considers dealing weed to make some extra money. He always has it and everyone comes to him for it, but he reasons that the Army barracks are too open and lack the privacy he'd need to store his product. In the bush, the Army didn't seem to care, but here it is a totally different story. Realizing that he can be prosecuted and perhaps even dishonorably discharged which could affect his ability to find work once he's out, dealing is not an attractive option.

One night Mitch has arranged with Bobbie for her to get away from her husband and meet him and Hanks at a party. Another soldier partner of Mitch's named Brown is married and living in off-base housing with his wife. Mitch talks Brown into letting him and Bobbie spend the night on his sofa. Mitch and Bobbie get drunk and stoned and Hanks drops them off at Brown's home. They smoke and have fantastic sex all night until Mitch passes out.

The next thing Mitch knows, Hanks and Smithy are shaking him to wake him up. He looks around and Bobbie is gone, so he jumps up, throws on his clothes and heads for the base with them. He is not charged with being AWOL, but he loses his last stripe as he is demoted from E3 down to E2, at which point he stops even caring what happens concerning his military status. He is restricted to post for three days and given hard labor. He works ten to twelve hours doing various different strenuous chores. He feels that his efforts to regain his rank are going in reverse and that depresses him, but he doesn't ask himself if getting high could have anything to do with it. Hanks and Mitch are getting high en route to Seaside one evening not long after that incident, and Hanks tells Mitch, "Stone, you got me doing all the driving while you hog most of the weed, man." He pulls the big Caddy over, walks around to the passenger side, and tells Mitch to slide under the wheel and drive. Mitch feels too much shame and embarrassment to tell Hanks that he doesn't know how to drive at nineteen years old. He slides over, gets behind the wheel, and does what he's closely watched others do, but he moves very methodically and slowly. Hanks notices Mitch's obvious difficulty and discomfort behind the wheel and inquires, "Stone, do you have a driver's license?"

Mitch mutters, "No."

Hanks asks, "How did you learn to drive, then?"

Mitch admits that he has learned through watching others and practicing driving jeeps at the motor pool while on guard duty. Hanks is laughing really hard and pointing at Mitch, "Well, it shows because you sure as hell can't drive worth a shit." It hurts Mitch's feelings that his older mentor could make fun of him, but he makes no comment. Instead, he's thinking he has no one to show him such things. Suddenly Mitch is consumed with anger and self pity, because it's not his fault that he doesn't get *it*, whatever *it* is at any given time. He reasons that it's not his fault that he is so uninformed. So he takes a big swig of whiskey and a couple of pulls on the joint to forget about it.

Mitch falls deeper into getting high, being irresponsible and screwing every young chick that he comes across. It's June, 1966, and he is broke right after payday. Again, he manages to get some chick or another to buy him weed and booze, and sleep with him; but he reasons that he absolutely cannot reenlist in the military. Yet, there are very few options for his future out of the military. He stops writing and calling his family, but every now and then, he writes Sonji. Basically, he's at an impasse in his life and stuck with no place to go to—either forward or back.

Tired of waiting for Bobbie to sneak away from her husband, Mitch hooks up with a young sixteen year old named Brandy. Tabitha can't move freely enough to supplement his needs since she is restricted by her youth. Brandy, he thinks, will work out perfectly to fill the void of the other two, when they are both absent. Brandy is a petite, medium brown skin cutie with long flowing hair and an older than sixteen year old body; and she worships Mitch. Brandy introduces Mitch to her friend Sandra and she, too, falls head over heels in lust with Mitch. Sandra is not attractive but has smooth, brown skin and is tall with a great body. She's sixteen, and available, so Mitch starts seeing her behind Brandy's back and adds her to his list of the optional young bodies at his disposal.

On any given night he beds two, sometimes three of them between five pm and sunrise. Mitch sets up his rendezvous to see the three young girls based on his own schedule and their availability. Even so, his alter ego has deep, fleeting feelings, *there should be more to our life than what we have going, but we stay too stoned to think clearly enough to seek out a different course for our life and affairs.*

Chapter V

Coming of Helena

Mitch is pleased to find weed mixed with Vin Rose wine is an intense aphrodisiac because he can no longer afford whiskey unless one of the girls buys it for him or steals it from their parents. Under the influence of drugs and alcohol, his sexual appetites are insatiable. Just thinking about it, he laughs out loud. He loves it and reasons: so must they or they wouldn't keep coming back. Mitch has picked up quite a reputation as a young lady's man, so older GIs with cars seek his favor. They know there'll be a string of young, hot, teeny boppers following his trail. His old bud Campbell, who picked him up when he first arrived in California, is one of them. Now he, too, wants to hang out with Mitch. No big deal to Mitch because he is not threatened by bigger men in competition for women.

He has come to feel that he's as good as any and better than most where women and sex are concerned. Then, one evening his old running partner, Sgt Benjamin Lee, invites Mitch to town with him to meet his wife. Mitch thinks, *Yea that's cool. I'll have a ride into town,* so he calls a couple of his girls and lines up some action for later. Mitch figures he'll get free booze and weed while paling around with Lee. That way, he'll already be good and high for his first romantic rendezvous. On the way, Lee explains that his wife, Helena, is a German girl who he met and married overseas when he was stationed in Heidelburg. Mitch is thinking, *yea okay, then what?* He has been with German women along with many other types of women of the world, so he thinks, *who cares?* Mitch is more impatient than attentive as Lee rambles on about this Helena.

Lee tells Mitch that Helena is staying with a girlfriend named Cheryl, a redbone who is also married to a GI currently serving a tour of duty in Germany. Mitch has developed a particular attitude about women. He views them as objects of lust; period. So when Cheryl comes to the door, Mitch instantly finds her attractive and doable. He sizes her up thinking, *I'll get at this one later, maybe?* Lee introduces Mitch to Cheryl and to break the ice with Cheryl, Mitch flirtatiously comments, "Damn Lee, I thought you were going to tell me that this was your wife, man, but I'm glad she's not," he says as he shamelessly eyes Cheryl's body up and down.

"I hope you meant that as a compliment, Stone."

"I meant it as way more than a compliment, Miss Lady."

"Lee, this little old, cutie pie ass nigga moves fast, doesn't he?" Cheryl's statement to Lee is more of a comment than question, while smiling approvingly.

Just then, this tall, blue eyed blonde glides into the room, and it's as if the whole room lights up for Mitch. Mitch thinks, *so this long legged, sexy drink of pure sensuality is Helena.* Helena runs and gives Lee a big hug and kiss, as Lee is trying to introduce Mitch.

When she disengages from her hug with Lee, she looks at Mitch. "Hi Stone, I'm Helena, what's your first name? I hate it when you military guys only use your last names. My husband, Ben, here," she says with a nod towards Lee, "had me calling him Lee back when we first met in Germany."

"My name is Mitchell. Nice meeting you." Mitch is so nervously excited that he can hardly let go of her hand. Mitch reflects on how

Lee has told him that, because Helena is an international prostitute, he no longer wants to be involved with her. Right about now, as Mitch stares at Helena, he's trying to figure out what is wrong with his bud, Lee. Mitch feels self conscious and uncomfortable, as Helena stares him up and down, because Lee is his partner. He reasons that it's that same discomfort that he instills in the young girls as he is undressing them with his eyes in the process of preying on them. Mitch fancies himself a hunter of young females, but he feels completely out of his element with Helena flipping the script on him.

Mitch is so busy wrapped up in his alter ego that he only half hears Lee and Helena discussing Lee's girlfriend, Josie. "Ben, what exactly is it that this Josie does for you?" Helena asks.

"Helena, I'm not with her for her to do anything for me; except being with *only* me."

It startles Mitch when Helena asks him, "What do you think *Fast Mitch?*"

Mitch thinks for a moment about the name she has just called him, having never been referred to as such, but he likes the sound of it. "Huh, aw…I didn't hear what the question was."

"The question I asked Ben is, why would he want to be with some square girl that isn't doing anything for him other than sex, when he can have a working girl like me that'll do everything for him? And my question to you Fast Mitch is what do you think of all this?"

Mitch thinks what she says makes all the sense in the world to him, but he tries to back his bud, Lee. "Hey, you know, it's not my call Helena."

"But if it were, which would you choose?"

Still trying to get out of answering, "It would really depend on who each of them are."

"Good answer, Fast Mitch. So let's just say the one that goes and gets money for you is me, and the other one that you have to support is Ben's girlfriend, Josie?"

Mitch thinks momentarily, having seen both and thinking that they are both truly fine in their own different ways, but for Mitch there is no contest. Josie is a redbone and stuck up with that sense of entitlement that Mitch hates. He laughs loud and looks at his partner. "Sorry man, I have to go with Helena on this one." All four of them laugh.

As Lee and Mitch are leaving Mitch notices that Helena continues staring at him. Then Helena shocks him with, "You know Fast Mitch, you are some kind of fine little thing. You know that?"

Cockily, he responds, "Yeah, I've been told." On the drive to Mitch's drop off point, Mitch asks, "Lee, man, what's wrong with you, not wanting a fine looking woman like that?"

"Stone, I don't want a wife that sleeps with other men for money."

"What, you'd rather her do it with other men for free?"

"No, I just want a regular wife, man."

"Man, there's definitely nothing regular about Helena."

"She tried to make me into her pimp."

"What the fuck is wrong with that, nigga?"

"Stone, you're the one who likes all those fast broads, man. I don't."

Mitch can tell his friend is getting irritated, so he drops it and says good night to Lee when they arrive at his destination. Even though he's excited about the rendezvous with one of his girls, he can't take his mind off Helena. He feels she has just flirted openly with him to get at Lee, so he goes on with his business at hand, sweet Tabitha. He notes that he really didn't know that his bud is that stupid.

The following day, broke and kicking back on post, there is a call for Mitch at the company headquarters office. It's Helena and before she can continue, Mitch tells her Lee is not on base. "Fast Mitch, I'm not looking for Ben. I'm looking for you."

Shocked and nervous Mitch asks, "What can I do you for?" He is immediately embarrassed by his mistake in words. "Aw… I meant what can I do…?"

She interrupts him with her hearty deep laugh, and even that arouses Mitch. "I know what you meant, Mitchell. Allow me to buy you a drink."

"Okay, when and where?"

"You know my roommate's boyfriend, Campbell, don't you?"

"Yeah, I know Campbell real well."

"Well, I'll have her tell him to pick you up at eight pm tonight if that's cool with you."

"Yeah, that's cool, see you then." Mitch gets out his olive green silk suit he had made in Paris along with a silk white ascot for his neck. He primps his hair and splashes on cheap Old Spice cologne. As he stares at his image in the mirror, he likes what he sees.

On the way to the girl's apartment, Campbell briefs Mitch on the situation. "Man, I don't know what you did, but this Helena broad is crazy about your little ass, nigga."

"She's crazy about me? Man, we just met yesterday. We haven't even really talked."

"Well, your little ass will get a chance to do a lot more than just talk this night." "What? She's my partner's wife, man. Are you crazy? Lee will kill me and you."

"Mitch, she didn't invite me out for a drink." Campbell laughs as he shares this with Mitch.

When Mitch and Campbell walk into the apartment, Helena shouts, "I'll be out in a minute, Mitchell." When she comes out of the bathroom she finds Mitch's mouth hanging open, as he's undressing her with his eyes. She looks nasty, whorish, and sexy to Mitch, and he likes all of that.

His alter ego thinks, *there goes our new rule of not messing with our partner's and family's girls.* Helena smiles approvingly of his obvious lust for her.

"Baby, are you thirsty for that drink or me?" Everyone laughs as Mitch is looking noticeably embarrassed.

Campbell tells Mitch, "Man, I never thought I'd see you lost for words."

Mitch figures she's just trying to pump him for information about Lee and Josie. Still, Mitch is a bit uncomfortable hanging out with Lee's wife, but only because Lee is a heavyweight and Mitch is a lightweight. He reasons that, if it ever came down to a fight he'd have to kill Lee, but for now he's going to enjoy the evening of dining, smoking weed, boozing and partying. Before entering the restaurant next to the Capri nightclub, Helena hands Mitch a one hundred dollar bill for dinner and drinks later, which is the first one hundred dollar bill Mitch has ever possessed. After dinner they all drink and dance a bit in the Capri, which helps Mitch to relax a bit more. After about three straight shots, Mitch becomes cool, calm and collected. He grabs her hand to go dance again and she stops him. "Fast Mitch, we need to talk." Mitch sits down thinking he has said or done something to offend her or that she is finally getting around to what she really wants, information about Lee.

"You know, Mitchell, you're a pretty classy young guy. I really like the way you carry yourself for a guy that looks so young. Have you ever been involved with a working girl?" Mitch tells her about Sonji Pak. "How did you feel about her working, other men and all?"

"She was my girl, and I still love her, and my kid."

"It's really incredible to meet such a young black guy that's seen and experienced all that you have. It's like one minute your face lights up and you do or say something that's like a sixteen year old. Then, the next minute, you're all poised and talking like a man of the world about having silk suits made in Paris." Mitch feels embarrassed, nervous, and the need to explain, so he starts to do so. Helena stops him from speaking by putting a finger over his lips, and follows it with a long, deep, wet kiss. When their mouths separate she explains, "Baby you don't ever have to explain anything to me. The reason I told you all the things I see in you, is because all of that really turns me the fuck on."

Mitch can hardly believe this is happening to him. It seems like one of the many scenes he's seen in movies. All four of them are at the same table, so everything that Helena and Mitch are saying can be heard by Campbell and Cheryl. Helena moves her chair so she can press her upper body into Mitch's. She half whispers into Mitch's ear as she kisses it and asks, "How would you feel about me working for you?"

"What about Lee?" Mitch's head is spinning from the music, booze, weed, and the intoxication of the moment with this tantalizing creature.

"Fast Mitch, let me handle the situation with Ben."

When Helena and Cheryl go to the wash room, Campbell leans over and tells Mitch, "Stone, Cheryl just told me that broad makes a ton of money, man, and will give it all to you if you play your cards right. You are the luckiest little nigga I've ever seen. Why couldn't that shit happen to me?"

"Because nigga, you ain't me." They laugh and slap five on it as the girls return.

When Helena and Cheryl return, Helena grabs Mitch's face in her hands, and whispers, "You are so fucking sweet and fine," and proceeds to tell him about the game and lifestyle she plays, and how they're going to do it together, now. "Mitch, do you want to hang out with me tonight?" Mitch doesn't know what hanging out with Helena may entail, but whatever it is, he's all for it.

He tells her, "Let's get out of here." The four of them go back to the apartment. It's only a two bedroom apartment and Cheryl's two kids are in the second bedroom, so Helena and Mitch get the living room sofa. Mitch has thought of himself as somewhat of a sexual aficionado and athlete. This night he finds out that he has been but a novice because, for his very first time, Helena teaches Mitch how to go down on a woman from a female perspective of pleasure. Based on his information, or the lack thereof, he finds it to be a strange but effective new procedure and he loves the power it appears to give him.

Mitch is a very willing student as she guides his movements with her body, almost without a single word. As her body responds to the pleasure and benefits that a woman gets from oral sex when it is performed properly, his excitement grows without bounds. He follows and then learns to lead all at the same time. She whispers, "What I love about you young fuckers is your stamina." In between their sessions throughout the night, she tells him that he's going to be her pimp, she'll buy him this and that and they will play the game around the globe together.

Mitch doesn't know about any of that, but right about now, he doesn't care either. When he comes to, he feels like he's been on a five mile forced march in the field. Helena is a big woman as are most German females that he has known. Helena is the same height as him, five feet nine without heels, so in heels she towers over Mitch by three or more inches. Mitch reasons that he won't need to be in the Army to stay in shape with this big bone, fine female in his life. They started on the sofa bed, but he comes to near the kitchen. As he reflects on an evening of the best sex he has ever had in his young life, he smells food cooking. He turns over and sees Helena fixing breakfast, at lunchtime. He looks at her big, long shapely legs that seem to go from the kitchen floor right up to *heaven,* and he sighs out loud. She asks, "Are you hungry, baby?"

He lays there looking at her curvaceous body as she moves about in that flimsy housecoat that seems to cling to her every sensuous move, and he feels jealous of that robe and stupid for thinking that way. He laughs and asks, "Can't we eat later?"

She laughs and tells him, "You're a pretty big boy for such a little guy. I'd like nothing better, but I have to work and I'm kind of stiff and sore from last night. You'd better let me rest if you expect me to get any money tonight."

He laughs and says, *"You're* sore and stiff," as he pulls out his member and shows her the cuts and bruises.

She comes over and looks. Reaching down, she kisses it as she asks, "Did I do that to you, baby? I'm sorry. I guess I got carried away, huh? I haven't been with a man other than for work in quite a while."

"Hey, there's no harm done. I've never been circumcised, so when I get carried away or a woman is too tight or sometimes just because, I get cut or bruised up."

"Well Fast Mitch, we'll have to be more careful, won't we?"

"No, we won't, thank you very much." They both laugh, as she kisses him. They eat, shower together and she gives him nine one hundred dollar bills, which is the most money he's ever had at one time in his nineteen years of life. He has been around the world, but being with Helena makes him feel perhaps it's been just the opposite; the world has been around him.

They spend all day talking until it's time for Helena to go out to work around nine pm. After Helena is gone, Mitch gets up and changes into the outfit he brought with him from base and goes out to party. He's at the Capri Club right off the junction of Fremont and Broadway Streets. The word has already traveled throughout the little military community about Mitch and Helena. At the bar Smithy tells Mitch, "Man, word is you knocked a bad white hoe from a partner of yours."

Mitch acts like he doesn't know what Smithy is talking about, but when he pulls out the wad of hundreds to pay for his drink, Smithy gives him five. "Nigga, I knew they were telling the truth. How else can you have a bankroll like that?"

"Smithy this dame is my partner's wife, man, and I don't want it to look like I got at her behind his back, man."

"Nigga, whether you got at her or she got at you, which is how I heard it went down, it doesn't matter. The bottom line is, you got that bitch, baby. You don't have the game to knock a broad like that, so she has to really like you." The two men give each other five and laugh.

Helena starts giving Mitch two to three hundred a day and she buys a 63 Chevy Impala, that she calls "just transportation." She may consider it temporary, but to Mitch this car is all that, because he has never owned a car. Also, she starts taking him to have suits and shirts made. "Your jewelry and attire must be unique to you only." She begins educating him with an understanding of who the principle players are in this new game, their interactive roles with each other, and the name of the game itself.

The first day Helena rides with Mitch driving, she is shocked that he is such a bad driver. "Baby, how did you ever pass the driving test for your license?" and she starts laughing, "because you're a terrible driver."

Her words cut Mitch like a knife, and he feels inadequate like she's putting him down. Angrily he snarls back, "I've never had a driver's license."

Noticing his anger over her trivial comment made in jest only, Helena intuitively knows that her young lover really needs to be handled with kid gloves. She realizes that emotionally, like most men, he is just that, a kid. His travels and experiences around the world may far surpass the average nineteen year old, but he is still just a nineteen year old.

She is worldly and knowledgeable enough about men's fragile egos and pride to know that his is perhaps the most fragile she has ever known, and she has seen and known many. She notes that, for whatever reasons, Mitch is ultra sensitive to criticism. So from this day forward she vows that she will play him just like she plays all men, to glorify him in his strengths and support him in his weaknesses, without him knowing it. Helena realizes that she must be to him all that he needs at this impressionable time in his life; lover, mentor, mother, friend, and source of his income. She smiles and she rubs his face, thinking she knew the job was hazardous when she took it. Of course that's part of why she took the job in the first place. She can mold him into becoming whatever she wants him to be.

Helena teaches her young lover to drive properly and urges him to get a driver's license. She explains to him that being in their line of work they need as little exposure to the law as possible, especially in the states because, here, what they do is illegal. She is subservient and agreeable with Mitch. She subtly, mentally and emotionally, nudges him into making what decisions she comes up with for their lives and affairs, as if they're his own, so as not to aggravate his fragile ego.

Before they go apartment hunting together, Helena first finds an appropriate dwelling. Then, she takes Mitch along and shows him the three possible choices of apartments and leads him into deciding on the one she has already selected. "Honey, this one is in the middle of the complex and our business will be too highly visible to other residents within the complex. Don't you think we need one that's more secluded, so our affairs as we are coming and going are less visible to the surrounding community?"

"Yeah Helena, that makes a lot of sense." So Mitch tells the landlord of that property, "This one won't be appropriate for our needs, but thanks for showing it to us."

Mitch is too excited because wherever the apartment is located it, too, will be his first. The next one just like the first, he loves it too. "Helena, this is a really nice joint, huh?"

"Yeah it is baby, but I know you're thinking of me in wanting this one, because I know you see that this one is also too exposed to visibility from up and down the street," as she waves her arm up and down the street to further drive home the point. She then leans over and whispers in his ear, "And daddy, remember what we do. Plus, I just know you want to at least look at the other one before you make your final decision. I mean, it is your decision, Mitchell."

"Yeah, we need to see all three first."

"That's a great idea honey."

Helena teaches Mitch how to go about renting the third apartment for them and he feels so proud and responsible in doing it. She allows him to handle all of their money, while helping him learn to put away stash cash for rainy days or speedy departures from a particular city or town. Mitch still won't get a driver's license, so she gives up trying to manipulate him towards that.

Mitch is growing more reliant and trusting of Helena as time and events continue. All his friends in and around the game are telling him that she is the real deal as far as the game goes, so hold onto her. During the weekdays when she is in town, she keeps the car and picks him up from base when he is free of military duty. When she leaves on road trips, Mitch drops her off at the airport and picks her up when she returns. He doesn't ask where she's going or when she'll be back, because every time she comes back she has jewelry, clothing, or something along with the cash for him.

On her first trip she brings him back a one carat pinky ring which is Mitch's first diamond ring.

Mitch is so excited about that ring that he wears it in bed and while taking showers. She tells Mitch that the time he has left in the

Army will give them time to put together a proper wardrobe, his jewelry and perhaps even add to his stable.

"Helena, what does stable mean?"

Careful not to irritate his sensitivities, Helena calmly responds, "Honey, it's your family of working girls."

Mitch's alter ego inquires of him, *what working girls, we only have her.* Even so, Mitch thinks better of pursuing the subject any further. He feels like whatever she says is just fine with him as she is becoming his all. His buds and everyone that sees or knows about what's going on with him are envious. Some are even bitter with jealousy and hating.

Helena arms Mitch with the facts about why all the players are all of a sudden trying to be his buddies. "They know you're new to the game, and they'll do and say anything in an effort to get at me, a money making white whore and the source of your newly found material success."

One afternoon as Mitch is getting dressed to leave the apartment, Helena rolls over in bed and asks, "Daddy, where you going?" As she notices what he is wearing, she sits up and asks, "Baby, what in the hell do you have on?" Mitch has on a green, black, and brown mixed knit and suede sweater with royal blue slacks and gray alligator shoes and matching belt. Helena chuckles slightly at first and tells him, "Baby your colors have to match," and she interrupts herself as she starts laughing uncontrollably at how silly he looks in all those colors.

It seems mocking and rude to Mitch and it hurts his feelings, so without thinking he turns and snaps, "Bitch, what's so funny?" He surprises himself and Helena as he stares at her for a reaction.

She intuitively realizes that she has hurt the feelings of her young, overly sensitive man, again. After apologizing, she jokingly tells him, "I'm just having a silly bitch moment, daddy." In the process of commending him for putting her in check, she says,

"You do know that old saying, daddy, you give a whore an inch, and the bitch will try to take a whole mile." Mitch understands and they both laugh, but Helena still makes him promise not to leave the house again without her checking out the outfit he's wearing.

Helena explains to Mitch that colors go with like colors for shoes, suits, silk underwear, socks, the belt and the whole outfit. So she starts getting up and laying out what he is to wear the next day and what to change into for mid day or night time attire. He now changes outfits two or three times a day when he's in town. Mitch loves all the attention, and feels pampered, as his friends have come to call him, 'kept man.'

Mitch dresses and wears jewelry like a movie star or some other form of celebrity, and he begins to notice that girls who had previously been standoffish towards him are now seeking his favor. Wherever he goes in the various clubs and joints in Seaside, people know him, even some that he has never seen before. He loves the notoriety and sudden accelerated popularity.

One night while Helena is out of town, Mitch is hanging out at a local after-hours joint where all the pimps, hustlers, drug dealers, and street people hang out and gamble, drink and get at loose broads. Through Hanks, Mitch meets the houseman, a big, dark skin, ex Army sergeant, hustler, and homosexual named Dean. Dean likes Mitch, and the fact that they have both served tours of duty in Nam helps to cement their association. When Dean first lays eyes on Mitch, Mitch's hair is fried, dyed and swooped to the side. He is wearing an all light green matching ensemble including his alligator shoes and belt. Dean runs an after-hours joint featuring gambling, food and illegal after-hours booze.

One night, around the 4, 5, 6 dice table Dean approaches Mitch in open forum and asks, "Little old fine ass nigga, I'd ask you how much you want for that dick, but you're that nigga with that money getting white hoe, so I know I can't afford it."

Mitch is noticeably embarrassed, but other players are standing around looking, so he feels he has to respond in some way or another. Mitch has heard of Dean and the rep he has for being a hell of a hustler, dope dealer and killer, in spite of being a homosexual. Mitch is silent as he carefully thinks of a proper response. The game has come to a standstill awaiting Mitch's response to Dean. It is quiet as all eyes are upon him when he pulls out a bankroll of about fifteen hundred dollars to lay a bet on the table. Finally, he breaks the silence, "Tell you what, houseman, out of respect for this being your joint and all, I'll only charge you ten grand for this dick."

Dean is a big, six five, solid built, dark skinned man with an imposing presence. He is reputed to be good with his hands and is not hesitant to get busy with a weapon either. There is silence for what seems to Mitch to be forever. Dean stares into Mitch's eyes and Mitch stares back into Dean's. Mitch begins to wonder if he said the wrong thing, but feels confident because he has his 45 on him. His alter ego reassures him, *we may not know about this new game, the right things to do or say, but we do know weapons and how to get busy with them if or when need be.* Everyone around the dice table is staring quietly back and forth between Mitch and the Dean.

Suddenly the grim expression on Dean's face turns to a smile as he responds, "Like I said young blood, I knew I couldn't afford that dick, but I can afford to buy you a drink little ole nigga. What are all the rest of you niggas staring at? I'm running a 4, 5, 6 game here." Everyone goes back to doing what they were, and Mitch joins his bud, Hanks, and Dean at his bar in the kitchen. From that night on Mitch is cool with Dean.

Attitudes around town begin to change somewhat about Mitch. At least, it is known that short or tall, Mitch will stand up to them all. Still, there is a lot of unrest among the local players because Mitch is the only young up and coming pimp in town that's really doing well. However, since Mitch is still doing essentially what he has always done, they feel no immediate threat. All Mitch does is stay really high now that he has plenty of money, but his modus operandi is still the same with women. The exception is that now it is he that wines them, dines them, screws them and leaves them, and not the other way around; that is when Helena isn't in town.

Helena returns from her second road trip and brings Mitch a diamond face Longines watch. He is so excited that he picks her up at the waist and spins around with her as he thanks her. She explains to him, "Saying 'thank you' is not a required part of a pimp's protocol with a prostitute, and we need to talk, anyway. Come here honey and sit down with me for a minute." Mitch follows her directions as he excitedly admires his watch and counts the money she just gave him. Helena places her hand over his to get his undivided attention. "Mitchell, you know I love and respect you very much, right?" As he nods his head that he does while still admiring his new watch, he wonders why it is when women get serious or angry with him, they seem to always call him Mitchell. First his mom, then Mouse, even Sonji Pak, and now Helena, seem to think what they say will have more impact.

He's trying to figure out what he's done and… Helena breaks his mental chatter as she shakes his hand, and asks, "Mitchell, are you listening to me?"

"Yeah, I'm listening, mama."

Being careful with Mitch's fragile feelings, Helena explains, "I don't want you to take this the wrong way Mitchell, but *your* free fucking every stray bitch in town makes for a bad rep for *you.* It's one thing to fuck a bitch you're trying to turn out, but just fucking for the sake of fucking makes you a common whore, unless it's with a girl that's paying you." Mitch remains silent as he listens attentively. "If you're sexing up every bitch in town for free, there is no exclusivity for a woman that's either paying you, or is contemplating paying you.

"If you need to get off and you can't find me or a bitch that's at least talking about paying you, take matters into your own hands, with your hot little ass." She then smiles at him to prevent her scolding from hurting his overly sensitive feelings. They both laugh because they realize that along with schooling him, Helena is running interference from a bunch of young females being with her young lover, especially for free.

Mitch smiles as he kisses her gently on the mouth. Then, he looks into her eyes and asks, "So big mama gets jealous too, huh?"

She laughs that sensual hearty laugh of hers that turns Mitch on every time. "Don't worry daddy. One day there'll be more pussy around us than even your hot little ass can handle." Mitch isn't concerned about that day or those that may come, he is totally consumed with this sexy ass blonde female in front of him right now, as he disrobes her and takes her right on the kitchen table and floor.

At a club one night having heard of Mitch's success with his ex wife, Lee confronts Mitch at the bar. Mitch stays strapped because he has learned quickly that his stature is even more of a liability in the game than in the real world, and he will be among the first to be challenged in a misunderstanding because of it. After nineteen years of it he stills doesn't like it, but he recognizes that it's just the way it is in his life. Lee asks Mitch, "Did you think about us being partners when you got at my wife, Stone?"

Mitch measures his distance between Lee and the time it will take him to reach his 45. After positioning his body to maneuver away from Lee's possible lunge, "First of all Lee, I didn't initiate this relationship that I'm in with Helena, man."

"Yeah, so she tells me."

"And second, she told me when she discussed it with you, your response was, 'Whatever,' and that she should do what she wants to do."

"Oh, so you trust what she tells you, huh Stone?"

He stares into Lee's eyes and responds, "I trust her with my life, man." Mitch figures that there is no more to say, and will let Lee's next move dictate what and how it will be.

"All I can say, Stone, is it's lucky for you that I don't want her anymore." With that being said, Lee reaches out his hand to Mitch. Mitch uses his left hand to shake hands in order to keep his right hand free to reach his 45, just in case, and vows to watch Lee's hands from this day forward.

Over the next couple of months, Helena schools Mitch on how to walk, talk, act, dress and manage money. She tells him, "If you can't do a better job than a bitch can of managing her money, then you have no real purpose. Women are born knowing how to manipulate men to get what they want out of them, but the same things that motivate a whore to be a whore in the first place, are the very same things, more often than not, that make them bad money managers." Mitch feels in awe of Helena and how she thinks. With all the money and new toys, he views Helena as the mother he feels he lost, as well as his lover and mentor. She teaches him things that he has not learned about being a man, playing on women's weaknesses through finding out their vulnerabilities, and becoming their strength in those areas.

Helena tells him that the very first basic thing to understand is, "One can control a woman's body for periods of time, but the key is to control her mind. Once he is in control of her mind, the money, body and heart usually will follow." Mitch worships Helena unlike he has any other woman, including his mom and grand mom. They spend countless hours freaking, talking and role playing.

Since the little discussion with Helena, Mitch is more actively getting at different girls to work for him, instead of just freaking with them. Now, he becomes a threat to the much older hustlers in town, because the girls that Mitch gets at are now among theirs. Mitch is quiet, reserve and somewhat self conscious around and about the various spots that players frequent, because he is not surefooted in this new arena. He decides to do more listening than talking to see how these old men ply their skills to the game that he is being introduced to by Helena. He remembers her telling him, "If you learn to let a person do all the talking, they'll tell you all they know and all they don't know." So he reasons that he'd rather people think him unknowledgeable about the game, than to open up his mouth and prove them right.

An older local gambler that has a couple of hoes and goes by the name of Red Walker tries to play Mitch into gambling. Walker is a retired Army sergeant who knows that Mitch has a white hoe that makes a lot of money. It seems everybody in the little town of Seaside, who is about or around the game, knows about Mitch and his white hoe. One night Walker invites Mitch over to his house for an after-hours gambling party. Mitch views it as an opportunity to get better acquainted with the local older players. When Mitch arrives with his partner Hanks, all of Walker's little click are there. Mitch joins in the regular crap game, but notices that most of them are aiming their bets at him because he is anything but proficient at gambling.

Mitch drops a quick hundred bucks and quits, at which time Walker starts in on him by saying, "Well, you aren't a gambler, and near as I can tell you don't sell drugs, so what is your claim to fame, young blood?"

Mitch is unsure if Walker is talking to him or not, so when he turns to look around and sees Walker and a few others staring at him, he inquires, "Are you talking to me, man? If you are, my name is Mitchell, not young blood."

"Okay then young…aw… I mean, Mitchell, what's your angle? You're no gambler and you don't…" Mitch interrupts Walker with, "Yea, yea, I heard that part. Well not that it's your business, but if by angle you mean, what I do, I'm in the military." All Walker's little group starts to snicker and whisper among themselves.

"No man, I mean what is your hustle?"

Now Mitch gets really irritated at Walker for questioning him and snarls, "Primarily to mind my own business and stay out of the business of others, you know what I mean?"

Mitch's inexperience in such situations is evident to his old bud Hanks, who tells Walker, "Nigga, you already know what my partner's hustle is. He only has the best hoe on the Monterey Peninsula." Walker is taken back as everyone cracks up at that, and it lets Mitch off the hook, for now.

Hanks consoles Mitch. "Mitch, fuck these country, jealous ass, old niggas. I grew up in a little town just like this one, so I know how they think. They're just trying to rile you, because they feel threatened. You're a young nigga, half their age or less, that's having money and nice things that it's taken them all their lives to get. Just stick with that fine ass white bitch you've got, and you'll go far in this game." Mitch doesn't get it and wonders how his older partner can understand and know all of these things.

Mitch is growing more accustomed to the new arena of pimping, playing and parlaying in the game. As he comes to be referred to by his peers as a shaker and mover, his response is, "Hey, I resemble that remark." He is more verbal and less self conscious than ever before in his life, because he has a new and more purposeful agenda as directed by Lana (his nickname for Helena), who works like a woman possessed to get his money. He frets not about what, where, or how she's doing, because, as she has taught him, she's in the business of laying down first and getting up last for the cash.

He is responsible with the money, and makes plans about coming up. He pursues and knocks different females that he and Lana turn out into the game. First is Bobbie, the married girl that he kicked it with prior to Lana. Bobbie approaches him one night in the Capri Club, and tells him, "Mitch, you look so fine and act so grown up lately in your matched up threads, diamonds, and pretty car."

"Hey, check this out baby, all this you see costs money, and what happened to that love affair we shared?" Then, he pays for his drink as he flashes his large bankroll, and asks, "I mean, Bobbie, where is the love?"

"I've never done anything like that before Mitchell. I don't know what to do."

"Do? All I need you to do girl, is be willing. Where there is a will there is a way."

Bobbie tells Mitch that she really never stopped loving him, and she is no longer with her husband, so there is nothing to stop them from being together. "Yes, I'll work for you Mitchell," she states emphatically.

Mitch takes her to his decked out apartment, and is planning to bed her, when in walks Lana. Mitch and Bobbie are sitting on the sofa cuddled up and Lana inquires, "So, I have a new sister, huh?" Seeing the look of uncertainty on Bobbie's face, Lana introduces herself. Afterwards, she tells Mitch, "I'm only here to change clothes and hair, babe. Here," she says as she hands Mitch two hundred in cash. Lana, like most working girls, changes clothes and wears wigs along with their own hair for different styles and looks of seduction for obvious attraction and promotional purposes. Once Lana has changed outfits and is leaving, she tells Bobbie, "Nice meeting you Bobbie, I look forward to getting at it with you girl. Bye daddy."

Mitch counts the money and waves the roll in the face of Bobbie as he's *high siding,* "Can you do this for me Bobbie?"

"I don't know Mitchell, but I'll try."

"You do that baby and all will be well." It never dawns on Mitch to have her get some of her own clothes; instead, he takes her shopping that next morning for a real fly outfit to work in and drops her off at the house she rents. As he's leaving he tells her, "I'll be back to pick you up at eight pm," and gives her a kiss and a swat on the butt. When Mitch returns to his apartment, Lana quizzes him about who and what this Bobbie is about, and why he feels the necessity to buy her clothes before she goes to work for him.

After he briefs Lana, she responds, "Mitch, turn Bobbie over to me and I'll make a money maker out of her." So Mitch reasons that it's set and he's got two hoes now, but Bobbie goes sideways, and the word around town is that Mitch is buying square broads clothes with his working girl's money. He is too pissed, so he goes on the hunt for Bobbie with his 45 automatic, just in case there is a problem with some dude when he runs up on her. His pride is hurt, so he has bad intentions for Bobbie. Lana tells him, "Keep your composure daddy, because it was your idea to make the investment in her. You'll learn that sometimes those investments work out and sometimes they don't. Bobbie has been your girlfriend and that's always a difficult situation to turn around into what we do."

While driving around town like a maniac Mitch runs into Dean at his pool hall. Dean has a barbershop, pool hall and a restaurant in the main plaza on Broadway Street. This is where all the mellow fellows frequent because that's where all the young hot teeny bopper girls frequent as well. Dean proceeds to talk Mitch out of doing something stupid concerning Bobbie. "Mitch, you have too much to lose by doing something stupid to that little girl. Use your head, boy." As they are talking, Hanks walks in and joins in what is turning out to be a Mitch roast session. Dean tells Hanks, "You try to talk some sense into this crazy ass, little ole pimp nigga."

When Hanks hears the details he bursts into laughter. "Stone, are you totally insane? You got it like all of us are trying to get it, a young, fast money getting white woman that will die and go to hell twice over for your crazy little ass, man, and you're trying to throw all that away over a broke, tack head bitch." Then he grabs Mitch's left hand with a diamond watch and two diamond rings on it. "Young nigga, you better get a clue." Then he points to Mitch's feet and continues with, "Your shoes cost more than the average nigga's whole entire outfit in this town, so you better get that shit in your head straight, man."

By now Mitch is laughing as he realizes how stupid he would have been to do what he had in mind, and thanks Dean and Hanks for pulling his coat. With that, the three of them exchange five and Mitch plays the juke box and sits down to get his gators polished, thinking just how much he has to learn about this game, and life in general.

There will be many such episodes as Mitch goes about the business of honing his newly acquired skills. One thing he learns from Hanks is, "Pimping isn't personal, it's just business. You have to spend money sometimes in order to make money. And some of those times you'll lose your money, because great hoes like your Helena don't grow on trees."

At least he's stopped wining, dining and screwing square broads for free. Like Lana continues to tell him, "Like life, pimping is a process not an event. It will take more than one hoe, along with time, energy, and effort to get where I know you will one day be." Mitch finds Lana, and all she tells him to be mystical somehow, because he can't figure out how she knows all this stuff before it happens. Then when it happens, he's reluctant to ask her why or how she knew it would, because he doesn't want to appear too inexperienced in her eyes. Of course, she already knows who he is and who he isn't, but he doesn't know that. In Mitch's mind, he questions why Lana is so good to him, because he doesn't feel worthy. He doesn't share those doubts with anyone for fear they will think less of him because of them, including Lana. He is literally clueless that she already knows he doesn't know any of the things she's teaching him.

From Lana's standpoint, it is glaringly obvious that Mitch doesn't understand that what he knows or doesn't know is not the reason she's with him. It's just him, those innocent, sometimes naïve, little boy eyes, and lustful looks that he gives her that she finds so attractive. Also, with the potential of who he can become in the game through her love, support and tutelage, she's down with him for the long haul. There are many things that attracted her to him in the beginning, but these are by far the most significant in her heart and mind. It is these things that have become her driving force in life. She embraces her young lover in her heart, not only as his lover, but somehow perversely as a proud mother emotionally embraces her son. They even act out sexually in role play as mother and son, while fantasizing incestuously, as Lana has no maternal off springs, nor does she desire any.

She teaches Mitch everything he'll need to know. "Always pay tribute to your women, for it is they that wage the daily battle of wits and sex for your money. It is that very same money and sacrifice that makes a pimp who and what he is. Inside every woman is a whore, it's just a matter of a pimp finding out what tune brings it out of her, and playing it to perfection. For now, until you get your bearing in this new arena, older women will serve you best, because you are a hot, young freak and cutie pie, and that'll just tickle the hell out of old bitches fancy. Always be mindful around women wherever you may be, because you could miss an opportunity at a new bitch if you aren't."

Mitch has until November 17, 1966, for his military discharge date, and it is now late August, 1966. Lana agrees with him that it is a great idea to send money for the son in Korea that he is now sure is his. Mitch's father has a birth mark around his left eye, which is a darker pigmentation than the skin on rest of his face. As the boy gets older there is a similar section of different pigment coloration around his left eye, amazingly, as well.

Lana believes that good things happen to people that do good things for family, and shares those sentiments with Mitch. Mitch is developing a certain indifference to that principle for some reason that he doesn't understand. However, everything else that she tells him is cool with him, as he grows in worship of her.

Finding his Army schedule interfering with his pimping career Mitch declares to Lana, "I'm going to desert from the Army and become like a guy I once met in Saigon named Troy, who had a strip joint. That will enable me to focus full time on learning to better ply my craft in the game."

Lana almost laughs, but thinks better of it because this is not the first ridiculous idea that her young lover has come up with, and she's sure it won't be the last. "Honey, is it okay if we talk about this a little bit first?" Mitch sees no reason why they cannot, so he agrees. By the time the conversation is over Mitch sees the stupidity of his decision and agrees that he should just stick out the last few months.

Chapter VI

A Place for Me

In early September, Lana leaves on one of her road trips, and after about three weeks she's ready to come home. She calls Mitch at the apartment one night, and gives him the time of her flight arrival. "And guess what, Daddy? I have a super surprise for you," she says. Mitch is elated as he can hardly wait to see what it may be. He finds it hard to sleep that next night so he smokes a fat doobie to relax and calm his nervous excitement from thinking about the new shoes, jewelry or whatever item Lana is bringing him, and of course more money. When he goes to pick her up at the airport the following day, to his surprise, Lana has brought a drop dead gorgeous, statuesque blonde of about Mitch's height with blue eyes.

If that isn't enough, when Mitch says, "Hello, I'm…"

The new girl interrupts him, stating, "You are Mitchell, and I am Brigit."

It's not what she says or how fine she is that almost stops Mitch's heart, it's the French accent that drips of sensuality that gets him. She is not the first French female he has met, so it takes his mind back to his brief stay in Paris. His eyes are wide and nostrils flared like a stallion about to come in first at the Kentucky Derby. Lana jumps in his arms and kisses him wet and hard, as Brigit observes them. The airport is in a buzz as people stare and make comments about the three of them when they walk by together, arm and arm. Mitch just loves the attention they get. It makes him feel in control, powerful and bigger somehow. On the drive to their apartment, Lana explains how she and Brigit came to meet in Miami, Florida, on the last leg of her trip.

"We were both working a country club that caters to the Rolex caliber clientele."

Mitch interrupts, "Lana, what is a Rolex?"

Brigit laughs and Lana reaches into the back seat and touches Brigit's face gently explaining, "Brigit, Daddy doesn't like for his girls to poke fun at him, okay?"

"I'm sorry Mitchell. I didn't mean any harm by it."

Mitch tells her it's all good, but because of his complexes he had been ready to over react. Lana turns her attention back to Mitch. "Honey, a Rolex is an expensive watch. Generally when worn in certain circles it insinuates cash, and usually lots of it. What we do is slip them a Mickey and roll them." Mitch is aware of what a Mickey is from watching old movies. "It's referred to as the Rolex Circuit, Mitch."

Mitch just drives in silence, and again wonders, *from where and how does Lana know all this stuff?*

Lana continues, "Anyway Daddy, Brigit and I are going for this same trick and we decide to join forces, freak with him and split the take." Both the women are cracking up. "Daddy, Brigit is riding this old white guy's face for dear life to keep him busy, while I'm cleaning out his wallet, dresser or wherever he may have cash stashed. Then when I make too much noise going through the rest of his things and he tries to get up, Brigit screams, 'Wait a minute honey, I'm cuming.' As the guy is trying to get up to see what's going on and starts mumbling, she grabs his ears and buries that sweet pussy of hers in his face so hard that when I look around all I see is his legs, wiggling in the air from struggling to breathe."

Mitch is amazed at how much fun these girls seem to have in tricking and playing men out of money, as well as straight out robbing them whenever possible. He falls deeper in love with them and this game. Talk about the ultimate game of cat and mouse, this seems to be it for him. They stop on the way and eat an early dinner, then on to the apartment.

Brigit tells Mitch, "I had a black boyfriend named Darrin, who isn't a pimp. I met Darrin while I was working in Germany and he was stationed there in the Army. We stayed in touch, so when I came to the states working, I looked him up and we were together for a while. But then, he tries to change me into a housewife, and a housewife, I am not nor do I aspire to be. I'm a whore," she concedes and then she laughs.

Mitch lights a joint and makes a drink for Brigit and himself and he passes the joint to her. She hits the joint and sips her drink as she further explains, "Helena and I started hustling together and we freaked with each other on dates, so we decided we liked it, and became lovers. The rest is history, and here I am."

Brigit and Mitch are laughing as Lana comes into the living room from putting her things away. She nonchalantly hands Mitch a bank envelope with six thousand cash in it, and says, "Partial compliments of that little old white gentleman, and us" as she and Brigit burst into laughter, again. Then Lana inquires, "So what did I miss, you guys?" Lana makes herself a drink and grabs the joint from Brigit. Mitch is so busy, excitedly fumbling through the envelope of cash, that he hardly hears what Lana has said.

Brigit tells her, "I was just explaining to Mitchell about Darrin and how we met."

"Never mind that, bitch, what do you think of our daddy?"

"I like him. He's cute and sexy like you said." She leans over and sniffs Mitch's neck and rubs his face with her hand, "And he smells sweet and his skin is really soft, also like you said, too. So Mitchell, do you also taste as good as Helena said you do?" All three of them laugh.

"How about you judge that for yourself," he responds as he slides his fingers gently into Brigit's long blonde mane and settles them at the back of her head. He grabs a hand full of her hair gently, tilts her head slightly back to the side and his tongue traces along her neck to her earlobe, and on down the back of her neck. As Brigit moans slightly, Mitch kisses her open, waiting lips softly, but hungrily.

Lana joins them as the booze, weed and sheer lust fuels the fires of their passion again and again. This is not Mitch's first time having sex with more than one working girl at a time, but by far the most significant in his mind, because these two are *his* working girls, and it's not just sex. They're making love to each other's body for the sake of passion, alone. The three of them explore each other's bodies and Mitch feels ecstasy and passion unlike any he has ever known to a point where he feels as if he has died and been reborn into one continuous rhythmic orgasm. Spent and now laying back, Mitch watches the bodies of these two lustfully insatiable creatures of the night writhing around, entwined, moaning and groaning towards completion, yet again. While watching he smiles. He experiences voyeuristic pleasure while smoking weed, drinking, gloating and feeling confidently self assured at the fact that now they are three.

With Brigit still asleep in bed, Lana begins to lace Mitch up with how to best play Brigit. "For now, daddy, she is my woman but your bitch because that's how I knocked her. As you can see, she isn't the sharpest knife in the drawer, but my intuition tells me she'll be loyal to me, therefore, to you too, okay?"

Right about now Mitch is a believer, so whatever Lana says is alright with him. "Whatever you say mother, if that's how we need to play it, so be it."

"Daddy, I need you to know that this bitch has real bad mood swings though, or something like that. I found out right after we started hustling together. It's almost like she has two personalities or something. All I know is one of those bitches in her is a money making whore, but the other one we'll need to give a lot of tender loving care and maintenance. What I should say is that you will have to because I'm a whore and I can't get wrapped up in another bitch's crazy ass bullshit. I mean, fuck that. I'm crazy enough on my own, on any given day."

With a curious expression on his face, he asks, "What do you mean, Lana? This bitch is like the broad in that old movie Cybil, where she has multiple personalities?"

"Daddy, I don't know about all that, but you'll see what I mean." Then Brigit enters the room so Lana discontinues the conversation about her.

"Wake up sleepy head," Lana says as she walks over and gives Brigit a kiss. While she's holding Brigit, Lana looks over Brigit's shoulder and continues with Mitch, "Honey, what I was about to say is that you'll see what I mean."

Brigit asks, "Helena, are you guys talking about me?"

Mitch walks over and joins his bottom in hugging Brigit and he responds, "As a matter of fact, Brigit, we were talking about how good of a money maker you are." While still holding Brigit's face in her bosom, Lana winks and holds up her thumb to Mitch. She then makes her lips move silently to form the word "perfect," and shakes her head from side to side insinuating how fast her young lover catches on to this new game of cat and mouse, or in this case, cat and new girl.

One week before Mitch's scheduled discharge from military service his two girls pick him up from post and he notices that they are all stoned on weed and giggly. Mitch high sides in front of his Army buddies that are standing by watching. "You two vampires are driving around in my automobile stoned, huh?"

The two girls jump out of the car and are all over Mitch, as Lana giggles, "Well, Daddy, if we wreck this one, you already know we'll make the money to buy you a new one." As she says that, the two women look at each other and burst into laughter. Mitch realizes that it's because they like playing and showcasing for the public as much as he does, maybe more.

As Mitch crawls into the backseat, a white buddy of his named Brent asks for a word with him. Brent is a big, southern, fun loving, brown eyed guy in Mitch's platoon. Brent and Mitch get high smoking weed on base together sometimes. Mitch turned him on to his very first joint, so now Mitch is like his hero, and if there's anything that Mitch eats up, it's hero worship from his peers.

Brent asks Mitch if he can get a discount with one of Mitch's girls, and Mitch responds arrogantly, "Man, I don't have a pussy on my body, so ask them." He smiles, winks, and gives Brent a hand slap for five. "Yeah, you're one of my getting high buds, Brent, so I'll put in a word for you, man. Alright?" Brent smiles and sets up a rendezvous with Brigit for later that evening.

As they drive off Mitch notices the soldiers drooling over his girls and looking enviously at him. He can just imagine them thinking what he has been asked several times in the past, 'How in the fuck does that little fucker do that?'

As he settles back and begins pulling on the joint that Brigit has handed him, his alter ego answers within him, *if they have to ask how we do it, then they'll never understand it, even if we tried to explain it to them.*

Actually, Mitch doesn't quite understand it himself yet, but his soldier buddies don't know that. Lana interrupts Mitch's day dreaming and tripping, "Daddy, we have a wonderful surprise for you." Lana likes doing things that surprise Mitch because she enjoys watching his face light up like a little boy on Christmas Day.

"Bitch, don't start that teasing me shit again, what is it?" When Lana won't give in, Mitch asks Brigit, "What the fuck is it she talking about, Brigit?" Brigit and Mitch have become like incestuous siblings under Lana's parenting and rule, but Mitch knows Brigit can't keep secrets from him, because she gets too excited about them herself.

"Bitch, if you tell Mitchell, I am so fucking done with you."

"Daddy, I can't tell you, but don't worry, it's right in front of our apartment…aw… I mean, it's at the apartment."

All three of them laugh, as Mitch tells Lana, "Don't be mad, mother, you know this bitch can't hold ice water on her stomach." As Mitch thinks about it, he realizes that Brigit is immature like he is, and they have grown closer because of it.

Brigit feels self conscious so she asks, "Mitch, are you laughing at me?"

"No baby, I'm not laughing at you. You're my baby." Brigit now laughs approvingly. "Anyway Brigit, even if I was laughing at you bitch, you don't need to be all up in a pimp's business about it."

"Yes sir," she says as she mockingly salutes him and the three of them start really cracking up. Mitch notes that everything just seems to be a lot funnier when one is stoned on weed.

Pulling up at the apartment, Mitch sees a royal blue 1967 Eldorado Cadillac with a royal blue vinyl top and royal blue leather interior with a blue ribbon wrapped around it. Lana knows that Mitch's favorite color is blue. Mitch is so excited that he is jumping around kissing and hugging the two women. Lana tells him, "Baby, there's more," and she hands him three one-way tickets to her home town of Heidelberg, Germany.

Brigit kisses him and she kids him, "We're leaving three days after you get discharged from purgatory, Daddy." They all laugh and stand in the alley next to their apartment hugging each other and laughing at how excited Mitch and Brigit can get. Mitch fights back the tears of happiness and joy. He feels he can't very well let them see him crying, because it wouldn't be appropriate for what he feels is his current station in their lives.

Mitch calls his mom and grand mom to tell them about all his newfound success and the upcoming trip to Germany. Goldie asks him what he's doing. Proudly, he tells her he's a pimp, and has a couple of white working girls. Goldie is shocked and lost for words. At this point in Mitch's life, tact and diplomacy aren't his strong suits.

All Goldie can think to say is, "Be careful Snoopy. When will you be coming home?"

"I am home, Madea."

"Snoopy, me, Mama Jo and your two sisters have to move from where we are now, which is staying in Mama Jo's little one bedroom flat." She doesn't give any other details and Mitch doesn't ask. He feels much alienation between him and his mom. Mitch has for years, and is totally puzzled as to why. He just can't figure out what he could have said or did to cause it. Nothing he does seems to be right or good enough for her to view him favorably. Mitch reasons that he cannot get caught up in all that right now. He doesn't think to ask if they need money. Either that or he just doesn't care if she does because he is too much into himself and his own selfish interests and agendas.

After being with Lana for only a short time and getting laced up with the game, Mitch sees Tabitha and tries to turn her out on his own. However, he is too new to the game to know the right things to say or what moves to make. So when he purposes that she leave town and work for him abroad, she refuses and won't say why, except that she is afraid.

That night Mitch is kicking back watching television as the girls are working the different bars in the city of Monterey. The phone rings and its Lana, "Mitchell, you need to come get your bitch before she gets us both busted."

"Whoa, mama, what's up?"

"What's up is that this bitch has flipped the fuck out, and I don't know what to do with her."

"Send her home to me, Lana."

"No Mitchell, she's too crazy to drive, take a cab, or go anywhere on her own. Please, just come get her because she can't work like this, and she's hanging onto me so close and tight that I can't work either."

"Okay, where are you?" Once she tells him they're at a bar by the name of the Keg in Monterey, Mitch tells Lana, "Keep her there until I get there." Mitch jumps in his *Rado* and heads to Monterey. He parks behind their Impala, goes to the passenger side where Brigit is sitting, and knocks on the window. Brigit jumps into Lana's arms like a frightened little child.

After much coaching between Lana and Mitch, Brigit finally looks at Lana and asks, "Is it okay for me to go with him?" Lana kisses her and assures her one last time that it is, so she gets out of the car and goes with Mitch. Mitch is amazed how the seemingly confident, assertive and sexy female that *chose him,* is not present in this frightened little creature that cowers before him. Brigit keeps saying to him, "Please don't hurt me," over and over again until it begins to irritate Mitch. Somehow, though, he intuitively knows that getting upset will only make matters worse with her.

Mitch slows the monotone of his voice, exhibiting no aggression or excitement that might frighten Brigit further. Once home he gets out and tells her, "Brigit come to me," as he holds his arms out to her. He has to say it twice, but she finally gets it and goes to him. She flinches when he reaches to hold her, and he reassuringly tells her, "It's all okay little one, I got you." As she trembles and cries in his arms, he's thinking, *what the fuck is this shit all about?*

Then as she clings tightly to him, she whispers, "Your voice. Talk to me please, and hold me." Mitch is clueless as to what she means by 'your voice,' but he complies as best he can. She won't let Mitch out of her sight and grasp. When he goes to the bathroom, he has to take her. As he makes himself a drink and rolls himself a joint, she holds onto him, begging him not to stop talking to her. After a couple of hours she slightly begins coming around, and starts to talk to him. She starts off apologetically, "I'm sorry, it's just that sometimes I feel so afraid, lost and alone." As he holds and rubs her face and long pretty hair, he instinctively inquires, "Brigit, when was the first time you remember feeling these things?"

"I don't know, maybe a long time ago when people hurt me," she replies and then starts to cry again. "My mom got sick and there was nobody else to take me. They put me in these different houses, and the men…" Too upset to continue, she sobs and trembles as she grasps tightly on to Mitch again, and whispers, "Mitchell, make love to me, please."

Mitch finds himself aroused by her vulnerability, neediness, and the power it gives him over her. She is sexy as hell anyway, so he obliges her while Herbie Hancock's jazz hit of 1965, "Maiden Voyage," plays softly in the background. From the sounds of Brigit's garbled ranting and raving during their sexual encounter, Mitch manages to make out Brigit's different experiences or fantasies involving rape and all manner of other perversities that may or may not have occurred. One thing he does know for certain is that his senses become totally lost and submerged in the intensity of her passion as a result of whatever is going on within her mind. In the intense heat of the moment, Mitch's alter ego suggests to him, *we may not know what it is or why it is that makes her do what she does, but we're loving every minute of it, and hope that at least this part of her never changes.* When it is over and Brigit lies smoking a joint, Mitch is looking in the bathroom mirror thinking, *what the fuck was that?* As he nurses the bite and scratch marks on his arms, thighs, neck and back, he can't determine if they were just fucking or if they were fighting.

Brigit walks into the bathroom and tells Mitch, "Something about you and your voice makes me feel safe and unafraid."

Mitch laughs and points to his abrasions. "Brigit, if this is an example of your feeling safe and unafraid, I'd sure as hell hate to see you feeling unsafe and afraid." They laugh and hug as she tends to his scratches and bruises.

"No really Mitchell, I wanted to tell you that first day. The sound of your voice makes me feel safe like you somehow understand, but I didn't want you and Helena to think I was some kind of nut job, freak, or something," and she laughs at herself for making such a statement.

Mitch's alter ego adds, *it's too late for that, because crazy is exactly what we think she is.* However, intuitively, Mitch lies as he responds, "I do understand, Brigit."

She believes him and abruptly turns serious again. Taking Mitch's face in her hands, and looking deep into his eyes, she says, "Mitchell, you and Lana are all the family I have, and I will never leave you. You own me."

From that night on, it is his voice and touch that she needs to hear and feel, even more so than Lana, on the occasions when she gets like that. He thinks back to Lana telling him, "Brigit is my woman, but your bitch, for now." He and Lana find that scenario is short lived, because he becomes the most comforting force in Brigit's sometimes troubled spirit and mind. Sometimes it takes but a look from him, or he will find that he can talk Brigit through the episodes by phone. Sometimes he simply has to go bring her home, but still other times it takes days for her to come out of it, or she just wants sex with him in different naughty ways and in different conspicuous locations. It all just depends on how bad she gets at any given time. Mitch has to play it by ear as each occurrence arises. Mitch is all good with the sex part, even though he is clueless about exactly how he seems to usually say or do what calms her. All he knows is that there are times when she acts like she can conquer the world and sets about the business of doing it getting at his money. Then, there are other times when she needs to just be held, comforted and reassured like a frightened little child.

Mitch is growing to feel so powerful and in control that his ego and sense of self is becoming bigger than all three of them. The next few days seem to fly by for Mitch, and he is almost living in his new car. The 63 Impala becomes his girl's work vehicle so he doesn't have to share his new *hog*. Mitch feels sadness that he must be torn away from his new car for the trip abroad. It has become a part of his identity, like his jewelry, matching attire, and of course, his girls.

Lana has explained to Mitch on more than one occasion, "The wardrobe, cars, jewelry and bankroll are all part of what distinguishes one pimp's status from other pimps. Also, a hoe's decision to choose a pimp is based upon these things along with how he looks, acts, and carries himself. How his girls represent his game also depicts whether he is a bona fide player or not." On the plane for Germany, Mitch finally tells Lana about trying to get Tabitha to come with them and explains what happened. Lana is pissed, and exclaims, "What! Why did you wait until now to tell me?" Before he can answer, she continues with, "Please don't blow another opportunity like that. Had you gotten me involved, that young bitch would be on this plane with us right now, and if you do the math, that equals you'd have another whore, which equals more money, which compounds into more stuff for you, capiche pisano?"

"Lana, what the fuck does that mean?"

"It means, 'do you totally understand.' It's Italian."

"Yeah, I get it. Now, you get this in English, bitch, I have no problem with you pulling my coat to all this stuff, but watch how the fuck you talk to me, hoe." They look directly into each other's eyes and both start laughing.

"Yes sir, I get it and I see somebody else is starting to get it as well."

Chapter VII

Coping with Jealousy

In Heidelberg, Mitch meets Lana's mom and dad, Ralf and Meike Kaufman, who own a string of pubs. He also meets her uncle, Andreas, and her older brother, Sebastian. Mitch notices that Lana and her family seem to have that bond that he has lacked in his own family. Lana explains to Mitch, "Our family name, Kaufman, derives from us being merchants and tradesmen. Most of the pubs my family now owns have been in our family for years." Mitch chuckles as he thinks merchant and tradesman are definitive titles for Lana. On top of that, it also just happens to be what she does extremely well. Mitch finds that her family overall are positive and receptive to his relationship with their only daughter.

Seeing that Lana's family is fairly well off and obviously knowing what Lana does for a living, Mitch is curious as to what would make a woman as beautiful, smart and savvy as Lana turn to prostitution. He decides to satisfy his curiosities about that along with his curiosities about how she knows so much about the life and the game. To his surprise, she is more than willing to discuss it with him. "I was formally turned out at the age of fifteen by a black GI pimp, who married me underage and took me to live in New

York City. I have always liked mostly women, about ninety percent of the time. The GI's name was Malcolm, and he accepted me being like that and being a whore, so I married him. I whored for him for four years at different locations around the globe where he was stationed, and wherever he sent me. It was him that taught me to play the Rolex Circuit and rob tricks and the other formalities of the game."

Mitch is somewhat astonished and his male sexual ego is a bit dampened by her admission of her sexuality. He asks, "So you started selling pussy at fifteen?"

"No, I started long before that, Daddy. My uncle started molesting me when I was ten, eleven, or maybe twelve. I don't remember exactly. He always bought me something nice or gave me money afterwards. I began to go to him and get whatever I wanted, whenever I wanted it, by threatening to tell my father." Then she laughs, "It would scare him so bad that he'd always get whatever I asked for if he didn't have it already." As she tells her story, Mitch listens and watches his girl's mood go from tears of pain to one of joy and triumph over her mastery of playing men. He feels rage and sadness for the anguish of her experiences. He even thinks about killing her uncle, as she continues. "By the time I was fourteen, I was turning dates with a lot of my uncle and father's friends, and soon after that I started turning dates with GIs.

"I found that white men repulsed me since my molestations first began, so the very first black GI I met, Malcolm, I fucked for free. Since then, I have only been with brothers and women unless I'm being paid. I figure if men are going to use my body anyway, I might just as well get paid for it." Then she laughs that deep hearty laugh of hers. "But I can tell you this—it is so different with you because before you, I never had an orgasm with a man."

Mitch's male sexual ego and insecurities pop up, "Yeah right, I am just so sure that I'm the first."

As she smiles seductively, she reaches over and pinches Mitch's face cheek and asks, "Well honey, the proof is in the money, isn't it? You are just so fucking hot and sexy that I get on fire from just kissing and caressing this tight little black ass of yours." She grabs Mitch's butt cheek in her hand and squeezes it, as she sucks in her breath through her teeth making that hissing sound that makes him lustfully insane. She tells him, "I have to have you right now, right here, in the pub." As she starts undoing his fly at the table, Mitch is pleasantly surprised, embarrassed, and looking around to see who's looking at them, while Lana is oblivious to seemingly the rest of the world at that moment. He quickly forgets his male sexual pride and ego and loses himself to this very freakish white girl. She leads him to the men's bathroom and locks the door. From the sink, to the floor, to the stalls and through several knocks at the door, they ravish each other. As the knocks and inquiries come through the door, Lana laughs deeply from her chest and shouts, "Out of order!"

Mitch feels so caught up in the abandoned passion of the moment that he feels almost as stoned as if he is smoking a joint. He feels nasty and perverse as he whispers, "You liked it when your uncle took you, didn't you?" She moans as he asks the question and he grabs her hair hard, and pulls her head back so her face is up to his. "Didn't you, you fucking bitch? You loved it when he took you?"

She whispers, "Yes, I loved it, I wanted it. I am fantasizing about it now, and it makes me hot just thinking about it." He takes her savagely and once they are done, she tells him, "We must have these little talks more often, Daddy. You're really some kind of little freak." They laugh hearty and embrace as they walk through the pub looking at the curious and knowing stares from the patrons. "Mitch, *fuck,* I love it when you talk to me about that sick, dirty, nasty shit while you're fucking me. You are a dirty little bastard, you know that?"

However, with the heat of the moment passing, Mitch's fragile male sexual ego and pride kick in again, as he starts thinking, *she's just playing me to prevent me from being jealous. She really does like sex with other people as much as she does with me. Maybe even more.* His alter ego encourages him, *yeah so what, we get the money damn fool, which is the important thing. What do we care if she or Brigit get off with other people?* Mitch still reasons that he can't help it, but he does care, as the inner conflict escalates within him.

Up until this point the money has, for the most part, bought off Mitch's jealousies and insecurities about his two girls. Mitch reflects, *I hate it when they come home to me, in the wee hours of the morning, and tell me about who they dated for how much, what position they did it in, and how it felt with this one or that one.* He gets so mad that he wants to beat the shit out of both of them, so he's learning to just get high, spend money, or play with his new toys instead.

He tries to rationalize that he lives like a celebrity, goes where he wants when he wants, wears tailor made suits and reptile shoes, has lots of diamonds and gold, and has phenomenal sex. For a little black country boy that comes from where he comes from, he is a monumental success story. Still, he feels alone and lonely, wondering what good it does to have all this money and stuff, when Lana and Brigit are either working or sleeping all the time. Once a week, every now and then, he gets to go out with them, play, and high side. Otherwise, he feels all alone.

Somehow he feels when the girls aren't with him, people don't recognize who and what he has become. He doesn't understand why, without them, he just doesn't feel adequate in this new lifestyle and role. They have become the source of everything; how he feels, thinks, and what he does. So when they're not around him, he feels a certain emptiness and alienation from the stares he gets, and he doesn't feel like he's 'all that' for some reason. He tries to talk about it with Lana while she and Brigit are dressing for work one evening, but she asks, "Honey, you have everything, what in the fuck are you talking about?"

Brigit just goes with the flow and laughs, "Yeah Daddy, pimping ain't easy, huh?"

Half serious but jokingly, he responds, "Both of you bitches need to stop playing shrinks with me, and get at the business of getting a pimp's dough."

Lana says, "Yes sir. Now that sounds more like our daddy."

Mitch decides that discussing such things with his girls is of little consequence, but wonders who he can talk to about what he is feeling. Mitch is roaming around the city's different red light districts. He sees GIs on pass and it takes him back to his days in the Army. He thinks, *how simple my life seemed then compared to now, even with all this stuff I have acquired. Then, someone else told me when to eat, sleep and even when I was free to screw. There was a certain security in all of that.* Suddenly, he feels overwhelmed by it all, so he takes a couple of pulls on a joint and all the questions in his mind and heart seem to dissipate until he can hardly remember what he was uptight and self conscious about in the first place. He has come to appreciate that weed is not only a great aphrodisiac, but a powerful sedative in his life and affairs.

Mitch is having too much fun when he's not lost inside his own pessimistic negative thinking. Entering a jazz club one night with his two girls, he notices there are several other pimps present with their girls as well. Very few are Black. Instead, most are either Anglo or Spanish looking. As Mitch tips the maitre de and they head for a table down front, a few of the other players raise their glasses to him as he passes. It makes Mitch feel like he's all that and belongs some place, finally. After they get seated, an older white pimp named Christian sends a bottle of Dom Perignon champagne to his table with his compliments.

As the waitress tells Mitch the bottle is compliments of Christian, she points him out to Mitch. When Mitch looks at him, Christian waves his glass in the air in a gesture of a salute to Mitch. Then Christian waves his other hand around in the air admiringly of Mitch's girls. The recognition makes Mitch grow about a foot and a half and his head becomes too big for the burgundy fedora he is wearing. Lana has matched the fedora with his tailor made silk and wool blend suit, burgundy crocodile shoes and matching belt, a pink silk shirt, and pink and burgundy silk tie with matching kerchief. Lana has Mitch dressed like an upscale department store mannequin. Lana is wearing a burgundy knit suit with a mink collar, matching crocodile pumps, and bag. Brigit has a different style pink knit suit with matching crocodile pumps and bag. The three of them look like they should be on the cover of GQ or Vogue magazines.

Christian comes over to Mitch's table and introduces himself. He and Mitch shake hands, and when Christian goes to introduce himself to Brigit and Lana, the girls just stare at Mitch without even looking up or acknowledging Christian's presence. So Christian apologizes to Mitch for trying to introduce himself to Mitch's girls without Mitch's permission, and invites Mitch for a drink at the bar. Mitch is exalting in the feelings of the moment, so he tells the girls, "I'll be right back," and starts to walk away.

With well intentions, and being the proverbial nurturing mother hen to her young lover, Lana cautions Mitch of the older pimp, Christian's, motives, "Honey, if he starts asking you a bunch of questions about your business do not engage him in conversation about it, okay? He has several girls working for him, so he knows he was out of line trying to get us to talk to him. I don't trust him and you…."

Mitch cuts her words off with a kiss, because he has become accustomed to his overly protective bottom girl watching his back and being suspicious of any and everyone he encounters. He eases her nervousness by letting her know that he is on top of Christian's move. He whispers in her ear, "Don't worry big mama. I may have been born late to the game, but it wasn't late last night. I'm all over this," and he winks at her.

Lana strokes his face gently and acts like everything is all good, but after Mitch walks off, she tells Brigit, "Switch seats with me." Lana wants to sit where she has a better view of her young lover. When the three of them are out together, Lana always sits to Mitch's right and Brigit is always on Mitch's left, which signifies that she is second in seniority. In this particular case, Mitch's right side seat has Lana's back to the door and bar.

Brigit doesn't get it so she asks, "Lana, why do you want to switch seats?"

"Bitch, I'll tell you later. Right now just move your ass." Brigit leaps out of the chair, for she knows better than to get on Lana's bad side when she's nervous or upset.

As Mitch heads for the bar he's thinking that a few months ago he would have been offended and embarrassed by his bottom girl acting like he can't handle himself in any given situation. Since then, he has come to realize that Lana only has his best interest at heart. Now, he has come to realize that Lana is all the way down for him.

Mitch joins Christian at the bar and, this time, Mitch buys the drinks. Mitch notices that Christian is about his own height but a bit heavier with sandy blonde hair and blue eyes. They talk about where they are each from, how they came to be in the game and admiringly, of the girls at each of their respective tables. Christian has three girls at his table with him and Mitch learns that he has twenty to thirty others throughout Heidelberg. Mitch respectfully compliments him on his senior status in the game and proceeds to listen more than he talks. Mitch learns that Christian is French and German and has been affiliated with working girls in some capacity or another since before he was Mitch's age. He explains to Mitch, "There is easy availability of fresh young working girls all over Europe since the last war left so many countries and regions in destitution. Therefore, young, pretty, White, Asian, mixed breeds, and even Black girls are plentiful for the plucking. And, unlike your

America, here it is all legal and neat and tidy, and even when it isn't, there are ways," he confides as he bobs his head from side to side. They both laugh in understanding of those ways.

As Mitch leans into the bar sideways while laughing, he notices Lana on the edge of her seat waiting and looking anxiously. She knows Mitch has a gun on him but she also knows other things that Mitch doesn't know. As Mitch throws her a kiss she tilts her head to the side questioningly. Mitch throws up his hands in front of his body as if to say everything is cool. Christian points over Mitch's shoulder at Lana and asks, "That one watching us is your wife?"

Mitch looks back over his shoulder at Lana and responds, "You might say she's my partner."

"She is a very valuable asset to you Mitchell, yes?" Mitch looks into Christian's eyes without responding, as Christian continues, "She is extremely protective of you my young friend. I know the good ones like that when I see them from years of practice." Christian puts his forefinger against his own temple and states, "It is like a sixth sense with me after all these years in this business." With that he bids Mitch much success, gives him his card with his phone number and address on it, and goes back to his table.

When Mitch gets back to his table Lana hurriedly tells him, "Daddy, you don't know how things are over here and all the things these men with working girls are involved in. It's not just regular pimping; it's kidnapping, extortion, drugs, and even murder to get working girls to do what they want. People like that will have no problem killing you and making girls like me and Brigit work for them, especially since you are a foreigner and not knowing your way around and all." Mitch carefully considers all that Lana says, becks for a waitress and orders two bottles of Dom to send to Christian's table. Once they're delivered and Mitch sees Christian looking his way he holds up his glass in a salute to Christian, and waves his other hand in the air, as if to give Christian compliments on his girls.

Christian bursts into loud laughter and holds his glass high in the air and has his girls do the same, as they all toast Mitch's reciprocal gift. Lana goes from a look of shock and amazement at Mitch's antics to laughter along with Brigit. Lana tells Mitch, "Daddy, you are insanely impossible," as she hugs him. Of course Brigit joins in the hugging, too.

As they leave the club, Mitch feels like he has held up under his first mediocre challenge from another pimp, and it happened on the world stage. He feels confident as his alter ego encourages him with, *Christian had tried us on for size, and all things considered, we held our own.* Mitch receives even more confidence from the looks that he and his girls get. He is sure Christian feels his actions much louder and clearer than any words he might have said. Once outside, Mitch walks up next to a trash can, hands Lana Christian's card, and removes the lid. Lana rips the card into tiny pieces as she smiles sinisterly while throwing the small pieces of the card into the trash. The three of them laugh and catch a cab home.

Chapter VIII

Finding Comfort in New Success

Mitch and the girls are moving whenever and wherever Lana says, so within a few days of the incident with Christian, they leave for Amsterdam, Holland. Mitch is excited about getting to their next destination because Lana and Brea (his nickname for Brigit) have been telling him that Amsterdam is wide open with all kinds of exotic drugs, music and sex. It all seems weird to Mitch because prostitution is legal, at least everywhere he has been abroad, and lots of drugs flow freely without a lot of hassles from the police.

When they arrive in Amsterdam in January, 1967, they rent an apartment with a living room patio overlooking one of the waterways and charming bridges, as well as a magnificent view of parts of the city. The weather is chilly, but nothing like what Mitch has known in places like Korea and Chicago, and here he learns it rarely dips below zero. The first night, there is a foggy mist that brings a bit colder temperature, but it doesn't stop them from getting out and getting around to the night life.

As they sightsee, he notices that a good deal of the white people here are either blonde or platinum blondes with blue or green eyes. Lana tells him it's because, in the Netherlands there are mixtures of Danish and Scandinavian descent, and like New York, a European version of a melting pot of ethnicities. Mitch doesn't really care what they are. He just knows that the females are just too fine. They have a great lobster dinner and the girls take Mitch to buy some blow for a little after dinner social high before heading to the Casablanca Jazz Club to party. The Casablanca is located in the heart of the world renowned Amsterdam Red Light District. The extraordinary scenery of old crooked houses along the cobbled streets of the tree-lined canals flood Mitch's senses. He is blissful about Brea and Lana taking some time off to enjoy showing him around before starting to work in the Red Light District.

Everything is just too exciting, new, and different for him to be doing it alone. There is no comparison to when he was on weekend furlough here while still in the Army. Back then, he was on a very limited time frame and budget. He had to get right to the business of getting laid and getting on. At the Casablanca they first catch a local Danish jazz quartet, and to Mitch's surprise and joy the jazz 'Dynamic Duo' of Jimmy Smith and Wes Montgomery take to the stage. They have an album released in 1966 by that same name, and are simply two of Mitch's favorite jazz musicians of all time. They play cuts from one of their latest albums, *Further Adventures,* featuring the single *Round Midnight,* as it is just around midnight in Amsterdam. When they mention the song they are about to perform, Lana looks at Mitch and comments, "How avant-garde and with such perfect timing."

Mitch leans over and asks Lana, "What does avant-garde mean?"

She smiles empathetically, kisses him on the lips and responds, "It means daring, radical in pushing the artistic needle of their craft."

The next afternoon they go for a water taxi ride on one of the waterways near their one bedroom apartment. They are told by the water taxi operator that they are lucky that the waterways haven't frozen over so far this year. They have lunch with coffee and hot chocolate just inside the doorway of a sidewalk cafe to avoid the chill, as Mitch's alter ego suggests to him, *it would be just fine with us if we stay here to live from now on.*

The girls leave Mitch for a while to get hooked up for work at the start of the upcoming week. Mitch does more shopping, hanging out, sightseeing and getting at local females. He has a little guide book and ponders that he will probably not be able to see all that there is to see here, even in his entire lifetime, as he is totally engrossed in it all. Lana and Brea get a spot in the Red Light District to work, and take Mitch to show it to him. Mitch loves that all the windows in the buildings they pass are filled with different types of females displaying their bodies, fetishes, and assets, making him feel like a kid in a candy store. However, with the availability of so much candy, it becomes repetitious after fifteen to twenty windows.

Lana explains to Mitch, "The Black and exotic females are more of a commodity here, because every other female working the district is a blonde with blue or green eyes. What do you think about me and Brea working together in one suite window? It'll give us somewhat of an edge as we will work as a two girl team. By doing so, we will have a somewhat uniquely different eye catching appeal to get more dates. After all, it's about what men or women see here before they purchase that counts. Brea and I are always thrilled to do each other or anybody, anywhere, anytime, male, female, or midgets." She and Brea laugh at her comment.

Mitch is thinking they should keep that kind of information to themselves. Still, he agrees with the logic of her suggestion because while they may not make as much money per date, they'll have a lot more dates, theoretically, than the average girl. Plus, all the money they make goes to the same place anyway—his pocket. With that thought in mind, he props his crossed legs up on one of the other chairs at his little table and clasps his hands behind his head with a huge smile and a look of contentment on his face. When the waiter comes back and asks if he can get Mitch anything else, Mitch orders a hot chocolate laced with a shot of Cognac, and a small pack of marijuana and papers. He thinks, *there is nowhere in the states where one could do what I just did,* and he laughs out loud.

The waiter, Peter, sees Mitch laughing with no one else at the table and asks, "Is everything alright, sir?"

"Peter, I have never been more alright in my life, man. But please, call me Mitch. Are you Danish?"

"Okay, Mitch. I am Norwegian and you have very pretty girlfriends."

"You know what Peter? You are absolutely right about that, and here's for your good taste." Mitch rolls a joint, smokes it and leaves a ten dollar American currency tip for Peter. Then, he walks off down the cobble street skipping, window shopping and taking in the sights.

The girls are way too excited about going to work, for Mitch's comfort. Brea even says out loud, "I'm so horny just thinking about getting to work and sampling all those different new bodies." Then Lana gives her a high five on it.

Mitch feels like kicking both their asses because of his jealousy, but his alter ego asks, *what excuse could we possibly use? They are absolutely perfect with us and to us.* It doesn't change the fact that Mitch still feels pangs of jealousy about his girls enjoying sex openly with other people, outside of the three of them. So later in the evening while Brea is showering, Mitch tells Lana, "We never did finish our conversation."

"About what Daddy? You already know who I first fucked, or at least who first fucked me, and that I love fucking and all the money you get." She laughs as she continues, "So, what is it that you want of me now sir, blood?"

"I'm serious L, (another nickname for Lana)."

Her demeanor changes to one of concern. "What's the matter, baby?"

"You never told me how you know all the stuff you do. Who taught you all this stuff about money, budgeting, and just everything?"

"Okay Daddy, I get it. I was raised in the pub business from like age five or so. When I would be around my dad while he was doing his books or ordering new stock, he would always tell me exactly what and why he was doing whatever he was doing in the business. He even taught me the bartering games that he would play with liquor and food sales people.

"Then, I lived in New York from fifteen years old until I was almost twenty while working for Malcolm, in between traveling all over getting money for him. When I left him I went back home to Heidelberg and still sold pussy, but I also managed one of my family's pubs for about five years. I met Ben and we were married two years later. We were together for three years until he introduced me to you, but, I never stopped loving selling pussy and playing and hustling men out of money, so I've applied myself at being what you might call a student of this game."

"Why do you and Brea find it necessary to share the vivid details of your work with me?"

"You're our daddy and you need to know everything about us; what we do, how we feel, what we think and what we are capable of in any given area. If you don't, you are leaving yourself open for the unexpected."

"What do you mean, unexpected?"

"By the game's standards I'm an old bitch; therefore, I don't play a lot of little girl games with you, but that will not be the case as you start having other hoes, younger or older. As you get with pursuing very young bitches, fifteen to seventeen or so, depending on their mentality, you will find they are the most vulnerable, gullible and impressionable. They're easily molded into good long term whores, like me and Brea. Look at it this way it's a lot easier to write *your* message on a blank blackboard than on one that has traces of the writings of others.

"And baby, you must learn to have thicker skin when it comes to sex and your women, because that's what we do, sell fantasy and sex. You should be happy we're at least not doing a job that we hate. Also, you need to know every night whenever possible what a bitch is doing with their hands in reference to the other pimps and stealing from you. Remember honey, when the cats away the mice will play, and that holds true for whores too, especially."

After they are gone to work Mitch is left again with his negative, pessimistic thinking. His mind is racing over all manners of carnal pleasures that his women are performing and enjoying with strangers. He drinks and smokes bud, and then does lines of blow. Somewhere in that mixture he again realizes that he is the envy of most men, and he reflects on the looks of jealousy and envy that he always gets when out with Lana and Brea. His alter ego reminds him, *we have everything we could ever have imagined wanting in our possession or at very worse a phone call or a brief stroll away.*

As the drugs and booze continue to subdue Mitch's rational thinking, illusions of grandeur make his personal sacrifice of his women's bodies and souls a tribute to his worthiness, and it all again begins to make sense to him. He reasons that he, too, like his main, will have to become a student of this game and that he, too, loves it. Who wouldn't? Alone in the little apartment that night, as he's listening to jazz and tripping off the combination of stimulants that he has taken, he comes to the realization that, for better or worse, the game is that which he has sought for the better part of the last twenty years of his life, *a place for me.*

Mitch and the girls, who he continues to consider more like his family than his own blood family, work their way through

Copenhagen and Paris in Europe, and the island cities of Honolulu and San Juan, then finally Miami, on their four month trek at the money. Lana tells him, "In order to ply skills as a man of the world in the game, you must have worldly experiences." In almost every place they stop, Mitch gets acquainted with one or two different players before the girls and he move on to the next location.

Along the shores of Waikiki beach in Honolulu, while Lana and Brea ply their crafts on Kalakaua Avenue, Mitch sets out to meet other local players in his rental car. This is what's known as the money strip; like Fifth Avenue in New York, Rodeo Drive in Beverly Hills or even the Strip in Las Vegas. At a local bar in the early evening, Mitch meets a pimp named Sweet Wally. Sweet Wally is about Mitch's height and size. For that reason, and in the name of the game, they hit it off.

Wally is a late-twentyish dude out of Washington D.C. with three white hoes and a 1967 midnight blue on blue Cadillac Brougham. Wally puts Mitch down with the happenings on the island along with a few after-hours gambling joints. As they cruise Kalakaua Avenue, Wally familiarizes Mitch with the turf. "Yeah Mitch, the island is like a haven for hoes, man. I mean, it's still not legal here and the cops still get at hoes just like they do on the mainland, but a pimp can get real proper dough here, man. I've been back and forth to the island a few different times, but the island is like home base for me and my game, man. One of my broads will rip off some oriental trick or another for a bank. They run hot to the tracks here and we head back to the mainland to work different tracks there until it cools down here. Then, we come back here and to do it all over again, man." With that, the two men laugh and slap hands for jive five, as Wally continues, "Man, on this track hoes have to be swift and aggressive to get at a nigga's cash."

"Wally, I'm not concerned about all that, because I got two world class white girls that have gotten it on tracks all over the world, including this one." Mitch observes the heavy concentration of hoes walking the avenue. "Wally, man, there are more hoes concentrated in this one area than I have ever seen, except maybe in Amsterdam. But there, hoes work out of certain areas, where building after building of large plate glass windows have nothing but wall to wall hoes. They're not on the street, and it's all legal, man."

"Damn Mitch, you been to Amsterdam, man?"

Mitch feels his head swell in pride as he decides to high side for his peer in the game with his world travels. "Yeah Sweet, we spent the last four months globetrotting through Amsterdam and Germany, France, England, Copenhagen and a few other spots around the globe, while getting at my dough, man."

"Man, you look too young to have done all that stuff, Mitch."

"Sweet, looks can be deceiving. I'm twenty years old, man."

After their girls are off from work that morning, Mitch follows Wally to an after-hours spot on the island run by a big time pimp named Boss Big. In the after-hours Mitch observes pimps talking shit to each other in high siding, flashing their girls, cash, and capping on each other. Mitch hasn't seen this many black pimps in one place in his short career span.

Wally introduces Mitch to Boss Big, who is a tall, huge man of a Black GI father and a Hawaiian mother. The first thing out of Boss's mouth when he's introduced to Mitch is, "Mitch, you got to be the youngest motherfucker with hoes I've ever seen. How old are you nigga, twelve?" The big man and the others laugh.

Mitch has pretty much learned everything that he knows up to this point in his life from his observations watching how others carry themselves, and picking up on it from them. He eyeballs Boss Big and mimicking his peers as he says, "Nigga, I'm not just a young motherfucker, I'm a young motherfucking pimp named Fast Mitch." Boss Big is a well known influence in the game on the island, so everybody stops their conversation and whatever else they're doing and starts watching and laughing at the exchange that's starting between Big and Mitch.

"Hey Mitch, little nigga I was just giving you your props, man."

"Well, Big, nigga I was just helping you to give me all my props, properly, because nigga I got five hundred dollar bills," Mitch says as he flashes his wad of about two g's in both one and five hundred dollar bills at Big. Then, while holding his hands in the air and wiggling all the fingers on both hands with two diamond rings on each hand, Mitch shouts, "I got diamonds, gold, rings and things, along with multiple hoes and Lac just like every other real live Mack."

While laughing hysterically, Wally tells Big, "Looks like you met your match, Boss, baby, somebody that can talk as much shit as you man," and he gives Mitch five.

Mitch is thinking, *I'm way over my head in this cap session.* Still, he isn't backing down, especially in front of Lana and Brea.

It reminds Mitch of an old saying Dandy used all the time, "If you can't take the heat, stay out of the kitchen." So Mitch feels, as a student of the game, all this is part of the kitchen.

By this time pimps, hustlers and hoes are giving high fives and laughing loud. Afterwards, Big tells Mitch, "You alright nigga for such a young cat. The average nigga would have become too defensive and probably ran up out of this joint from that kind of pressure I bring high siding. I like your style, Pretty." Big introduces Mitch to a couple of other pimps that he doesn't know already, and still others come up and introduce themselves, while Mitch and Big exchange contact numbers. Mitch gives Big the number to Hanks apartment back in Monterey.

Big starts calling Mitch, 'Baby Face' or 'Baby' for short (after gangster Baby Face Nelson), and takes Mitch under his wing for the remaining few weeks that Mitch and his crew are on the island. Mitch isn't all that fond of the new handle, but he realizes it's out of respect and admiration from his new older pimp partner. In years to come Mitch will contact Big when he or some of his game are headed to the Pineapple State, and vice versa, Big and his game will come and spend time wherever Mitch is set up, at any given time. Over the years, Mitch will come to realize that hustlers get shot and killed behind high siding and embarrassing or shaming another in front of their peers and game, and realizes he got lucky.

Staying in one place gets boring so it's on to Miami, where Lana and Brea tag team a trick and sting him for three g's during the first two days in town. Obviously, plans change and they leave ahead of schedule for Monterey. As the plane lands in Monterey, Mitch feels excited and happy to be back in the states and the familiarity of the Monterey Peninsula. He feels a lot like he did coming home from the bush, but this time instead of being a battle tested war veteran, he fancies himself a world tested international player. After gathering their bags, Mitch is insistent about going to get their cars from storage before going to a motel.

On the road again, cruising the boulevard in his hog with the personalized license plate *PAY2LAY,* he sees a couple of people he knows, and can't wait to high side his new wears, ride, and jewelry. Wherever he goes he stands out, because among the local young teen age girls he is treated like royalty.

He leaves his girls to get a new apartment and their furniture out of storage because, in these times, Black applicants are still not welcomed in some upscale neighborhoods like Monterey. He reasons that he has a way around that though. With two gorgeous white prostitutes clocking large dollars for him, no proprietor will refuse them entry. Once they're in and Mitch shows up, oops, it's too late to turn him down. He has a good laugh while riding along as he gets a lot of pleasure out of that thought, and the projected look on the proprietor's face when he sees Mitch show up.

The girls rent a townhouse style apartment in between Monterey and Carmel. Every few months or so, Mitch has to sit down with Lana and go over their itemized budget of things to be paid, and their Profit & Loss Statement (P&L) up to that particular point.

She has so far entrusted Mitch to do it, as she coaches him on how to prioritize and allocate cash to the appropriate creditors like their car loans. At the beginning of the month of May, 1967, Mitch is going over the budget with Lana and he doesn't mention Sonji Pak's allotment. She inquires, "Mitch, where is the allocation for that girl and her kid in Korea?" Not wanting to disappoint her, he shrugs his shoulders upwards, as if to say he doesn't know. "Daddy, when did you send that girl money, last?"

"I haven't sent any money since we left for Germany, L. I figured I'd catch it up when we got back here," he replies.

"Honey, that's not right. Don't you remember how happy you were telling me that her kid is undeniably yours and how you knew it, and you wanted to go get them one day? Why haven't you sent that girl money for them in over four months?"

"I don't know. I forgot." Then, he thinks better of it. "I just didn't feel like it."

"Is that what Brea and I are to expect if something happens to one of us, you just might not feel like helping us? Baby, you must learn to take care of the people that take care of you. There are so many dog ass men in this game that dog out their people, man. Nothing good ever becomes of them. Honey, do you understand that Brea and I are accountable to you? If we don't work our asses off getting at your money, we know what to expect. In order to be a great pimp, you must have as great a sense of accountability in all your affairs with all your people. Your women will follow your lead."

Mitch does not agree, but for the sake of peace and his future cash he pretends that he does agree, and sets aside the money as she requests for Sonji Pak and Lil' Mitch. As he reflects back, he concedes that he has always left different women, whether family or not, or they left him; and eventually he abandoned all thoughts and connections with them all, completely. It has even been that way with male associates. He has no answer as to why that is. He just knows that it is that way.

Shortly after this conversation, Lana decides to trade in the Impala for a new vehicle. Hustlers can walk into certain dealerships with enough cash and clout (i.e., hoes to show as to their ability to pay), and drive out with whatever they want. Of course, they usually get fleeced with interest and penalty payments by the dealers, just because the dealers can get away with it. Not so with Lana, she barters and threatens to take their business elsewhere, and they get a much better deal. Mitch just takes it all in and files it away under things to remember, so when it's time for him to do it he can make himself and his big mama proud. They buy Lana a 1967 Pontiac Bonneville using this exact method, and of course for his main, Mitch gets her the license plates *LAY2PAY.*

One early evening as Mitch is leaving the apartment, Lana and Brea are standing in the front door watching him walk to his Rado. Lana shouts, "Fast Mitch, come through the bar tonight so we can show off that little tight, black, sexy ass of yours, okay?" Brea comments, "Daddy, you are just too fine with all that pretty hair."

"Brea, our pretty little daddy is all hair and dick," says Lana as the two women burst into laughter. Then, Lana abruptly stops laughing, grabs Brea and says, "Yeah, he's a little pretty boy, *Pretty Mitchell.*"

Mitch turns as he hears the girls say the name a few times over and all three of them start laughing. As he gets in his car to leave the two women run out of the apartment half naked to his car window. Lana tells him, "Daddy, that name is a keeper." From that day forward his street handle becomes Pretty Mitch. Mitch is shaking and moving in and around the neighboring areas of Seaside, Monterey and Salinas, and the name Pretty Mitch is becoming associated with who he is and how he performs his craft. He knocks a new girl here and there, so his notoriety and acclaim in the area becomes increasingly more threatening to the older more established hustlers.

Lana continues to tutor and help Mitch hone his pimping skills by teaching him to interview a prospective *turn out*. She explains, "Usually, in every whore's life like mine, there has been some form of sexual molestation or physical or emotional abuse. It just seems to go with what motivates the average female to turn to prostitution and work for a pimp in the first place. Daddy, it's like the idea you came up with for my license plates, 'LAY2PAY,' it's all about money and sex.

"Sex is the weapon that women use to control men. In it, a woman feels that she's somehow taking back the power that was taken from her when whatever happened to her, happened. Mitch, you need to figure out how to become a bitch's everything and they'll do everything to make sure that you have everything, just like me and Brea. That's why we lie, cheat, steal, kill or risk being killed for assholes like you." She smiles playfully and rubs his face.

"Daddy, Brea is a perfect example of that. Look at how dependent she is on us, especially you because I don't have the patience to deal with her when she's flipping the fuck out. You, however, will sit or lay with her for hours, bringing her around. Fuck all that shit. I couldn't be a motherfucking pimp. Just let me go sell some pussy or rob a motherfucker, and you do all the rest, and I'm good with that," and she laughs at herself.

Sometimes, when he and Lana finish with one of their sessions of OJT, Mitch feels both enlightened and frustrated because he questions, how in the hell he'll ever remember it all. As he settles back in his recliner chair he ponders it all, and in times like this he reasons that it would have been simpler to have just stayed in the Army. However, a couple lines of blow, a pull or two on a joint, and a stiff double shot of booze makes him remember what his primary purpose in life is, the money. Then, after admiring all his stuff, his alter ego reminds him, *look at how big and powerful it all makes us feel.* Mitch is then good to go again. He reflects on how the world looks at him wearing Brea and Lana on his arm. It's as if he's bigger than life itself, and he vows that he's willing to pimp or die for that feeling.

Chapter IX

Accountability

While riding and hunting fresh game one day, Mitch runs across Brandy, who had been one of his little girlfriends while he was still in the Army. When he sees her he whips a U turn in a busy intersection because his alter ego reminds him, *Brandy was our baby back then.* Mitch pulls along the side of the curb and calls out the window, "Hey sexy, what's up?"

Brandy smiles flirtatiously and responds, "Mitchell, I heard you were back in town." As she looks admiringly at Mitch's Lac, she asks, "Where are you headed, Mitchell?"

"I'm headed wherever you are little mama. Get in. You know, Brandy, I've thought an awful lot about me and you since I left for *abroad."* Mitch accentuates the word abroad, because he has learned that all young girls are impressed with not only his attire, car, jewelry and his new demeanor manufactured by Lana, but also that he is now a world traveled player. He laughs inappropriately as he damn near turns himself on just thinking about it all.

"I've thought a lot about you too, Mitchell, and I never stopped caring for you."

Mitch thinks, *gotcha, you bitch,* as he puts in a Temptations eight track tape and flips to the song, *Ain't to proud to beg,* to set the mood for his appeal. "Baby, I know I lost probably the best thing I ever had when I foolishly left you for Tabitha. I know now how wrong I was to let you go. Can you find it in your heart to please forgive me?"

Brandy's eyes well up with tears. "Oh Mitchell, you have no idea how I've longed to hear those very words come from your lips. I just knew you cared for me like I do for you. But, Mitchell, what about those white girls you got working for you now?"

"Mama, that's just business, you know, my game, but you're still my baby. Check this out little one. They're really cool, and I want you to meet them, okay?"

"I don't know Mitchell, do you think…."

"…They'll love you because I do. Just relax baby, you're back where you belong now, with Pretty Mitch." He turns up the volume and speeds towards his spot and Lana. He is so excited that his heart is racing. "B Mama (he nicknames Brandy on the spot), pour your daddy a drink baby, the bottle and cups are in the glove box."

As she reaches for the cups she states, "Mitch, you sure talk real different these days."

"B Mama, I am real different these days. Now, look back in the glove compartment and get that bag of grass and roll us a doobie."

He knows that he has no clue where or how to start turning B or any other female out properly at this point, so he knows to follow instructions and get her to L. Upon arriving at his spot, Brea and Lana happen to be driving up from the grocery store. Mitch winks at Lana, and introduces B. "This is Brandy, better known as my B mama. B mama, this is my big Mama, Lana, and the crazy one there is Brea," he tells Brandy as he points to Brea.

As Brea and B sit downstairs kicking it, Mitch is upstairs coordinating the game plan for flipping B with Lana. Lana tells

Mitch, "Daddy, its hard turning a boyfriend/girlfriend relationship into a pimp and whore relationship, which is part of what happened with my husband, Ben, and me. But this one at least seems willing to do whatever you say, judging by the way her eyes glaze over when she looks at you." Lana laughs suspiciously, and asks, "Daddy did you fuck her?"

"No Lana, we haven't kicked it like that since long before I met you."

Lana laughs again. "Well, did you suck her pussy, then, Mitch?"

"I did nothing with her, L, yet."

"Good, then let's get to it. Just follow my lead, Daddy," Lana instructs Mitch as they head back downstairs. Sensing the young black girl's discomfort, Lana tells her, "Honey, why don't you go over there and sit by your man," as she points to Mitch. "We know you two want to be alone, but first we have some business to discuss, okay?"

Lana turns her attention to Mitch. "Mitch, how much did you say it was going to cost you for that attorney?" Mitch starts to speak, but Lana interrupts him. "Oh yeah, five thousand, right? Damn, that's a lot of money right now, man, but we have to come up with it or you'll go to *jail.*" Lana's tone goes up as she emphasizes the word 'jail' for maximum effect on B.

B has been silent up until then, but now with shock on her face from being concerned for Mitch, she asks, "Mitchell, what did you do, baby?"

As Mitch looks between B and Lana, Lana responds, "Mitchell doesn't want to worry you now that you two are back together, but he had to shoot a guy when we first came back from abroad." Mitch almost laughs and with the rush of adrenaline surging to his head he finds it difficult to keep a straight face, so he gets up, putting his back to B, as he makes himself another drink. After belting down the shot he turns with a look of being troubled and stares into his drink glass.

Lana continues supplying cheese to the mouse. "Let's see, we've got thirty five hundred so we'll have to come up with the rest by Monday. That'll give the three of us girls five days to come up with fifteen hundred. Thank God this is military pay weekend coming up. So between tourists and those little horny soldier boys I believe we can make enough to keep you from going to *prison*, Mitchell." Lana walks over to B, kneels down in front of her and looks directly into her eyes. "Honey, you do want to do all you can to help keep Mitchell out of prison, don't you?"

B looks from Lana to Mitch, who is still standing by the bar looking glum. "I'll do anything I can to help you, Mitchell." Then looking back at Lana, B says, "I really don't know how to… I mean, I never done…"

Lana hugs B and comforts her. 'Sweetie, let me worry about all that. Now, go give Daddy a big hug and come with me, we've got a lot of work to do before tonight.' B runs and jumps into Mitch's open arms. As he kisses her tears away she starts to smile.

"They can't send your ass to prison, nigga, after I just got back with your ass." As B holds onto Mitch and shakes her head from side to side, "Uh uh, no, no, I waited too long for this." Mitch looks over her shoulder and gives his main the thumbs up.

Mitch takes B to get a fake driver's license, like his own. Then Lana and Brea sort through their things and find an appropriate outfit for B. Lana and Mitch give B a crash course in things to do and not do on the stroll and in bars, concerning police, other pimps and hoes, and with tricks. As the three women leave for work they each kiss Mitch for luck. Mitch thinks, *superstitious bitches that believe in stuff like my kiss for luck and mercy money.* Mitch sits nervously by the phone in his apartment, as he is decked out in navy blue silk pajamas, a monogrammed 'Pretty Mitch' navy blue crushed velvet robe and matching crushed velvet slippers, a drink in one hand, and a joint in the other. The suspense is killing him about how his new girl, B, is doing, as he keeps checking his watch and mentally conferring with his alter ego.

Finally, at around ten thirty the phone rings and he is relieved that it is Lana. "Bitch, I thought I told you ten o'clock sharp." Mitch finds it disrespectful that his main girl laughs at his comment. "Bitch, what is your major malfunction? I'm talking about my motherfucking business, and you find it funny."

"Of course not, daddy I'm just laughing at how pleased you're going to be with this new young turnout of yours. These soldier boys are eating that young, pretty, brown pussy up. B has been nonstop since we got to the stroll, and I can't wait to get at that fine young ass of hers, myself."

Almost too excited for words, Mitch tries to act poised. "Lana, that's great news, but what about checking in on time next time, please?"

"I'm sorry, Daddy, but would you rather a phone call on time or your money right on time?" Then she laughs, realizing she has left her young lover only one response. It is her way of keeping him on his psychological toes.

Mitch is learning to recognize Lana's moves easier and quicker now, and without his complexes getting involved. "Okay, real slick hoe, you get a pass this time, bitch," he concedes as he laughs, knowing she got him again. As he hangs up he jumps up on the sofa and starts jumping up and down. Then he jumps off the sofa and begins dancing around the floor, all the while yelling, "There's pimping going on up in here, and a young nigga is three deep up in Monterey." He cannot contain himself, knowing his new turnout is getting at his money. He feels it's on and popping with his crew of three. He can do lines of blow and drink comfortably now, not that he hasn't already been doing just that all night long anyway, but now he feels much more relaxed and can get high worry free.

Mitch spends the better part of the week riding and looking in on his new girl, B, as his alter ego muses, *it may be difficult for some niggas to turn a boyfriend/girlfriend relationship around, but we're Pretty Pimping Mitch. Pimping is our game and hoes are our claim to fame, so we can bust any hoe before she go.* Mitch reflects that his rebirth into the game in Seaside is his calling, and he again vows that if he doesn't get hoe money, then he wants no money. He will soon have an opportunity to fulfill that very same vow of pimp or die. It begins one night at Dean's after-hours joint. Mitch shows up with his three girls after working in the wee hours of the morning. He picks up a buck and a half from B along with his other traps from his two main stays. B is clocking bank on a regular basis, so Mitch feels comfortable, fat in the pockets, and happy.

Mitch has always been obnoxious, pretentious, and flamboyant, but now, with money, position, and the pimping, he is unbearably opinionated. He's wearing a tailor made powder blue silk and wool blend suit with a matching powder blue knit and suede sweater complimented by Navy blue on powder blue gators and belt. His diamonds and gold jewelry are sparkling and every strand of his process is perfectly in place, worn in a popular style called the JFK. Lana is dressed in a powder blue ensemble and Brea and B are dressed in ensembles of Navy blue with all three showing plenty of legs and flesh. They are dressed exclusively for this late morning player gathering because it is the favorite spot of the local hustlers and street people to converge after a night of plying their various skills in the streets. They all come dressed to impress and to high side on each other in attempts to impress each other and each other's girls for possible action at knocking one or more from a rival's stable.

As the four of them strut up in the joint, it is obvious to everyone that Mitch and crew are the stars of this show. Heads and eyes turn, as a certain momentary hush comes over the living room. Mitch simply points to the living room as he walks through it, and his girls sit to become his neon signs of advertisement for other working girls, as they come in and out. Mitch continues on into the kitchen. He stops at the bar briefly and orders drinks for his girls and pays for them. Then he proceeds to the garage where the 4, 5, 6 dice game is being played on a pool table green.

Mitch's girls are responsible for watching and listening to see which females are watching and talking about him. Lana and B notice one particular young, 'high yellow' sister with freckles named Denise. She can't take her eyes off Mitch. Once Mitch's girls are seated together, Denise comes over to them and whispers to B, "Brandy, is that pretty black motherfucker there your man, girl?"

"Yeah girl, his name is Pretty Mitchell."

"Ooh shit girl, that little nigga is so fine he makes me wet. I need to go to the bathroom and change my underwear, girl," and Denise and B crack up laughing. Denise has gone to school with B and has been turned out long before B. Denise is also sixteen years old and long legged with big brown eyes and a slamming body for a girl her age. She belongs to one of the good old boys in Seaside named Paul, who sees her talking to Mitch's girls and gets in her face about kicking it with them. Paul is a tall, mid to late thirtyish, dark skin gambler that has just one girl, Denise. His thing is actually gambling, but he is also known for having different hoes from time to time. When he forbids Denise from talking with Mitch's girls, she sets out to find Mitch so she can just gaze upon him in the flesh.

At the 4, 5, 6 table Mitch sees another old squeeze of his, Tabitha, looking gorgeous and appetizing as always, staring at him seductively, but he notices that she's standing by a light skin, well dressed, tall cat in his late twenties who carries himself like a player. Mitch hears Dean refer to the guy by his street handle of 'Fast Walking Cuzz.' Mitch doesn't remember him from being on the set before he left town, but reasons that's how it is in the military towns, 'hustlers and hoes come and go.' Being full of blow, weed and booze, Mitch decides to get at her by trying Cuzz on for size.

So right in front of everyone he addresses Cuzz, "Say man, you do know that's my girl there," as he points to Tabitha.

"Nah Mitch, I know she used to be your girl, but now she's my woman." There's a bunch of players and hustlers in that garage and some laugh, while others back quietly away from the table to see what's really going on between Mitch and Cuzz. It is not uncommon for such a situation to end in gun play, with someone being shot or killed from issues erupting over money, hoes or simply disrespect.

Mitch notes that there seems to be no malice in Cuzz's comments. He figures him to be a player of at least a rudimentary knowledge of how the game goes, instead of just another fool ass nigga who he'll have to shoot. However Mitch reasons, *if it does come to that, then I'll be the one who gets his shot off first.*

Cuzz throws the ball back into Mitch's court. "What is a nigga that's got hoes doing with a girlfriend in the first place, Mitch?"

Dean tells Mitch, "Dice on Pretty Mitch."

Before responding, Mitch throws 4, 5, 6 as he's looking around the table, seeing the jealousy, envy, and animosity from the majority of the older hustlers. He nervously smiles while shaking the dice in the cup. His alter ego questions, *what have we talked our self into here?* Realizing he's in too deep in the capping session that he, himself initiated, Mitch responds, "Nigga, I'm a world class pimp. And in the words of the late great Malcolm X, 'I've sold white pussy to black men and black pussy to white men,' all across the globe. I'm Pretty Mitch, which means you need to watch your bitch. I got two pockets of fresh hoe money and three of the fastest hoes on this Peninsula sitting right out there," as he points towards the living room.

"Yeah, I heard of you Mitch, but they call me Fast Walking Cuzz, and it's all about straight pimping on mine."

"Nigga, pimps don't walk anywhere, we let our hoes do the walking." The action at that table literally stops, as the two young players cap and high side on each other until Dean interrupts.

"Both you young pimp ass niggas are stopping my action, so take that high siding and pimp shit talking out of my game here."

Cuzz responds, "No harm meant house, just two young players excited about this pimping and getting acquainted."

Mitch throws out a twenty dollar bill on the table. "I meant no disrespect Dean, to you or Cuzz, man. The drinks are on me."

Cuzz throws out a ten. "Yeah but, Mitch, your drink is on me."

Mitch responds, "Okay, let's do this then," while all the time Mitch is feeling Tabitha's eyes going up and down him. Mitch and Cuzz laugh and give each other five, as they go out to the kitchen bar to kick it. On the way out of the garage, Mitch notices Denise staring at him. He just figures lots of women stare at him, and he gives it no more thought. Mitch and Cuzz exchange where they're from, how they turned out, and small talk about the game. Mitch finds out that Cuzz is from L.A. Also, Cuzz has three other hoes in town with him from L.A. and Tabitha makes four.

"You know Mitch, if you had gotten at one of these old niggas like you got at me just now, you would've had to kill them. These small town niggas have serious complexes about young niggas having hoes."

"You know what, Cuzz? I thought about that halfway into it with you, man, but I was committed by then." They both laugh and give each other five again. Over the next few days, Cuzz and Mitch kick it and put in work getting at fresh game together. Other than Hanks, who is still in the Army, Cuzz becomes the one riding bud Mitch has in the whole town. For Mitch all is fair in love and war, and especially the game, so one night Mitch serves Cuzz notice that Tabitha 'chose' him. Even as Mitch is telling him, he reflects that they have grown close, and hopes Cuzz understands it's nothing personal, just business. He pulls his Rado into the business plaza lot, driver's window to driver's window with Cuzz's green on green 67 Cadillac Coupe Deville convertible to give him the news. Mitch keeps his 45 in his lap as he talks to Cuzz, just in case Cuzz has a different agenda in mind.

The exchange of clothes and information go okay and now Mitch's crew is four. After picking up Tabitha's clothes and personal items, Mitch is driving out of the apartment complex where Cuzz has her staying. Before pulling through the gate he hears, "Hey, Mitchell," and it's Denise.

Mitch responds, "Hey you, what're you up to girl?" B and Lana have told Mitch all about what Denise has been saying about him since that night at Dean's. He's been looking for her since, but is only just now catching up with her. Denise knows she's out of line being up in another pimp's face unless it's about the choosing. So he presses the matter. "Denise, take a ride with me, baby."

"I don't know Mitch, that nigga, Paul, will kill me."

"Not if he doesn't know about it. Come on, please, you already know what's up with you and me. Promise, I'll bring you right back."

She looks up and down the apartment parking lot, runs and jumps in the car with Mitch, and slides down in the seat, so no one can see her, especially Paul. Mitch speeds off and heads for the City of Salinas. "Where are you taking me, Mitchell?"

"I'm taking you where you and I both want you to be." Mitch takes the route to Salinas through the Army base at Ft Ord where he was stationed. They don't make it through the base before she grabs his crouch with one hand, while holding a finger of her other hand just inside her lips, as if she's a nasty shy girl. The very idea of all this drives Mitch lustfully insane, but his alter ego reminds him, *for females that are already hoes, it's about them having to pay2lay with us, read our license plates.* However, Mitch finds himself in uncontrollable lust over this sexy and nasty young black seductress. His alter ego loses the mental jousting, as he pulls over and gets busy with Denise. During sex she moans and groans about how much she wants to be with him, and will be as soon as she gets her money together. Mitch thinks quite frankly she's just playing him for sex, but even so, right about now his mission statement is a bit fuzzy. He's lost in the lust of the moment with this luscious, young, smooth 'high yellow' body.

When they arrive back to her apartment she tells him, "Mitch, wait in the parking lot for me for just a minute, okay?"

As Mitch waits for Denise he's thinking, *if that old nigga, Paul, shows up I'll have to shoot him about a bitch that hasn't given me a dime.* Just as he starts up his car she comes running down the back stairs, runs over to the driver's window and hands Mitch one hundred and ten dollars and kisses him.

"I know this isn't enough for you Mitch, but I'll get the rest, I swear. I want to be with you *so* bad. I'll let Brandy know when I got the rest," and she runs back up the stairs. Mitch feels that a buck ten is plenty enough for her to choose him. He reasons that, if Lana and his other girls find out about this little interlude, he did get paid for it, even if it was after the fact.

When Mitch gets to the apartment and excitedly starts describing the incident to Lana, he finds out that Lana has had B tell Denise that she needs at least three bills to choose Mitch. *Ah, so that's why Denise thinks she needs more money before choosing becomes official,* he thinks. So Mitch decides to omit the part about sexing up Denise on the Army base. Mitch is feeling at ease and financially secure with a nice piece of stash cash put away, four hoes down getting at his money, and a new one in the making. However, as he has been taught, he continues to stay down for fresh game nevertheless.

Chapter X

Kill or be Killed

"Hard to believe, isn't it Hanks?" Mitch is laid back smoking a joint high siding. "I've gone from dead broke to five hoes in under a year."

"You must be counting Denise as part of that equation. I'm not so sure you should do that just yet," Hanks responds in between puffs before passing the joint back to Mitch.

"Oh yeah, why is that?"

"Don't seem like Paul's gonna let her go. He's been making a point of bad mouthing you, and he's not the only one."

"Who else?" Mitch inquires.

"Red Walker," replies Hanks. "You remember Red. You had a slight run in with him before you went abroad."

"Yeah, I remember Red. What's Paul been saying about me?"

"Paul said to me, 'If that little Mitch nigga doesn't stay away from my girl, Denise, I'll plant dope in one of his cars and cross him into the penitentiary.' He knows how tight you and I are, so I'm sure he wanted me to tell you."

Mitch asks, "What kind of a pimp is that? Why doesn't he use game to keep his bitch from me?"

"Mitch, you don't get it, man. For these small town niggas, that is game. And just so you know, Paul, Red Walker and Broadway Sam are all in this thing together about you, so watch your back."

Mitch knows all three of these men. He knows Walker from trying to front on him at the after-hours gambling joint before he left for abroad. Broadway Sam is a big, dark skin dude with a gap in his front teeth who is known to carry a razor. Mitch is thinking, *he's too big for me to fight straight up, with or without a razor, so like Hanks said, I'll watch my back real close.* Sam has a couple of older hoes, but his claim to fame is also gambling, just like most of the older local hustlers that have hoes here. "Hanks," Mitch asks, "I understand why Walker and Paul are in this against me, but why the fuck is Broadway mixed up in this, man? I haven't had a problem or run in with Broadway. In fact, Broadway always smiles, shakes my hand, and is cordial and complimentary to me."

"Mitch, Dean and I were talking, man, and we both feel that you've outgrown this town and this area. Plus, if you weren't my partner, I probably wouldn't like you either because of your high siding and shit talking. It pisses the people off that aren't rolling like you. It's like your attitude is, 'it's all about me, and fuck everybody else.' I understand that you're just a young nigga excited about pimping hoes and getting money, but these are small town country niggas that aren't with that bro. Still, my man, I'd be down with you in this stuff, but I have to hustle with, and around, these niggas."

Mitch understands and thanks his old friend for the heads up. When he gets home he puts a 45 under his car seat and vows to continue packing the one on his person as well. Mitch reasons that he is just about straight pimping, which makes him far superior to his counterparts in this town. Some of them have hoes but straight pimping isn't really their best game. He has two thoroughbred white hoes that are renowned for getting money all over the world, a fast young black broad, and a down mixed blood that are all hard down for him. His alter ego suggests, *are we not an international player of sorts? So where they're really coming from, is out of jealousy and envy.*

Mitch rides by Dean's pool hall and discusses it all with him. Dean suggests, "Pretty, man, you need to take those hoes and get out of this little fucking town. These old niggas hate you, man, and if you knock that one girl, what's her name?"

"Her name is Denise, Dean."

"Yeah, whatever the fuck her name is, all hell is going to break loose if you do. Mitch, you're young and inexperienced. Most people, even some hoes, hate pimps because either they're envious and jealous, or because some family member, mother, sister, daughter, wife or girlfriend has been affiliated in some negative way with flamboyant, high siding niggas like you. I couldn't be no pimp with all that shit going against me. Plus, I'm too busy trying to get at a nigga's dick for myself anyway," and he laughs. Mitch doesn't find any of this stuff at all funny. "Pretty, you know that statement all you pimp niggas use, 'Pimping ain't easy,' well it really ain't. I'm going to call an old partner of mine from the Army named Lawrence. He now resides in San Francisco, and I'll see if he can put you in touch with some of the local talent there, so you can get up out of here."

"Dean, I like the Monterey Peninsula, and I plan to buy a house and live here because it's perfect for my game, and picking up fresh new game."

"None of that will matter Mitch if you're dead or in prison. This isn't a dress rehearsal or a military mission in the bush. There is a whole different down and dirty set of rules out here in these streets. I'll tell you something else, if not for me talking to Ward, you might have had a run in with him about his wife, Bobbie.

"Pretty, you can't just run around taking folks wives and girlfriends and expecting no repercussions. You've become a big time pimping nigga now, so you need the camaraderie and tutelage of other big time pimping niggas. Also, wherever you find yourself, you had better learn to watch your back, especially if you stay in that pimp game."

Mitch heeds both his partners' words after his stable begins to feel the heat. A lot of cops are on the take, especially in the little rural areas. The cops start harassing and busting Mitch's girls exclusively, so he finally gets the message that he and they are no longer welcome. He and Lana make plans to leave for San Francisco, but not before knocking Denise and claiming the number five girl for his stable. Mitch's alter ego amuses him with, *Hanks should have never doubted us.*

The spot Dean uses as his after-hours joint was once a house converted into a church that got converted back into a house. It has a paved parking lot that sit's off to the left rear of the closed in garage with a tall wooden gate to avoid police seeing how many cars are parked in there at any given time. There are two entry ways into the parking lot; one from the rear of the house and another used to drive in and out of the vacant lot driveway next to the house. Once inside the parking lot, one is secluded and not visible from the street or to people in the house. Usually Dean has a guy at the gate to open and close it as traffic comes and goes. The night before Mitch and his crew are to leave town, Mitch is going to his car inside the parking lot as he is leaving. He notices no one is manning the gate, so he opens it and leaves it open so he can drive out. Mitch has picked up a couple of phone numbers from Dean. One for a guy named Fillmore Slim, who is supposed to be a big time pimp in San Francisco, and the other, Lawrence, the acquaintance Dean has previously mentioned to Mitch.

As Mitch reaches his car, he notices Broadway Sam (who he didn't even know was in the house) come into the parking lot from the rear of the house and close the gate behind him. Sam snarls, "Hey you little punk ass nigga, that was some foul shit you did snatching my partner's broad," as he menacingly heads towards Mitch's position. Mitch has the door of his Lac open and his right leg inside already. There is a car parked on either side of Mitch's car so he calculates the best vantage point to avoid physical contact with Broadway.

"Broadway, man, I don't want no trouble." Mitch starts talking as he eases his 45 from the small of his back while using the darkness, the Lac door, and his body to conceal the move. Then he eases the silencer from his front left trouser pocket, because he realizes that the loud sound of the weapon discharging will draw attention to the parking lot and to him.

"Well, little motherfucker, it's too late for that, because that's just what you got now, trouble, and you won't fast talk your way out of this, either." Some of the things Mitch learned during his tour of duty in Nam, are that moving decisively and with the element of surprise in his favor gives him an edge. So as Broadway approaches, oblivious that Mitch is a threat of any kind, Mitch slowly backs away as if he is intimidated by the much larger man. Mitch *is* intimidated but his combat experience steadies his nerves. In the darkness of night, Broadway's profile keeps looming larger the closer he gets to Mitch, as Broadway is swiftly closing the distance between them.

Mitch slows his breathing so his hand will be steadier and his aim surer. He is gauging the big man's range of distance from him. He feels that familiar dryness in his mouth and the palms of his hands become wet from nervous perspiration. His stomach flips as if he's on a roller coaster. He knows all too well the symptoms are a result of fear and adrenaline. *Shit,* he thinks, *seems like all my life I've been filled with fear of some menacing big nigga doing me something.* Mitch holds the 45 just out of sight behind his right leg as Broadway starts into the front of the row between Mitch's car and the car next to his driver's side. Mitch stops at the rear of the opening as he feels his back touch the tall wooden fence. He calculates that Broadway is now in the most opportune range for accuracy. Moving quickly towards Broadway, Mitch puts two back to back rounds into Broadway's chest, whoosh… whoosh, and then

Broadway's body thrusts backwards onto the ground. Still moving forward, Mitch looks around and sees no one. Now standing over Broadway, Mitch puts two in his head, whoosh...whoosh. He cautiously looks around again, and still seeing no one he gets in his car and forces himself to drive off slowly and methodically.

As Mitch is driving home, he dismantles the 45 wiping the parts clean of his prints. He stops at different locations and throws those parts into the ocean up and down the nearby Seaside and Monterey coastline. Mitch reflects how, the whole time Broadway was stalking him, he could only see Broadway's lips moving. His mind was so focused on not getting beat to death that he didn't remember hearing a word coming from Broadway after his initial verbal threat. Somehow it is now after the fact that Mitch recalls the words that Broadway was saying to him. Mitch smiles nervously as he thinks, *that nigga's size doesn't mean a lot now.*

The incident brings to mind a mission back in Nam when Mitch was the only GI among his recon unit small enough to fit down into one of Charlie's little spider holes. Mitch had attached the silencer to his 45, pulled out his flashlight, and worked his way into the small hole as a couple of troopers initially held onto his boots, just in case. Crawling inside he left the flashlight off as he used his elbows to creep along, listening carefully along the way. It was dark, still, and quiet once his whole body was inside. A good distance inside he heard sounds, so he positioned his body to allow both arms to be straight out in front of his body. The flashlight was still off, but it was pointed before him along with the 45 in his other hand. His stomach was doing flips, the palms of his hands were sweaty, and his mouth went bone dry as he swallowed desperately to get the much needed moisture to his palate and lips.

Mitch lied perfectly still as he clicked on the flashlight. The light shined on the faces of two shocked VC. Mitch opened fire and he heard those familiar grunting and thud sounds of men, as their bodies were hit by rounds. He also heard bullets hit the walls around him and saw the flashes of light coming from both his and their weapons being discharged. He clicked off the flashlight, emptied that clip, and reloaded another. There were moaning sounds as Mitch clicked on the flashlight. The light shined directly into the open eyes of the closest VC, seemingly staring back at him. Mitch had thought he was still alive and a threat, so he had put several more rounds into his body and the other one as well. Then, after the longest few seconds, Mitch finally realized they were both either dead or unthreateningly disabled.

Mitch's alter ego had reasoned, *Lady Luck has smiled upon us once again. Had we not turned on the flashlight when we did and momentarily blinded the two VC, they would certainly have hit us with at least one of those rounds they fired at us.* As Mitch crawled over the motionless bodies of the two VC, out of fear and caution he put two in each of their heads just to make sure. When he came up out of that hole he noticed the looks on the faces of his fellow troopers. They seemed to look at him differently as if he were bigger and more powerful, because of what he had just done. So he began to reason that, *if I want to be treated bigger then I must act bigger, and do bigger things.*

About two hours later Mitch calls Dean and asks if there is any action at his gambling joint. Dean tells him there isn't much going on inside, but there's quite a bit going on outside. Mitch pauses and asks what kind of action. Mitch can tell in Dean's voice that he believes Mitch already knows what's going on outside, but neither of the two men say anything about it. Instead, Dean asks Mitch what time he and his girls are leaving in the morning. Mitch tells him they are leaving Monterey at first light.

What Dean says next conveys that he does indeed know that Mitch was involved in the event in the parking lot. "They will now know that there is bite in your bark. So they will come at you real hard, and given the opportunity, those niggas will kill you, Mitch.

But, between Hanks and I, we'll work all this out somehow, so keep us posted about where you land."

As Mitch hangs up the phone, Lana and Tabby (his nickname for Tabitha) walk into the bedroom. Lana hugs him and she hands Mitch her and Tabby's take for the night. "Hey Daddy, here is two of your checks." When she sees Mitch nonchalantly fold the bills and stuff them into his pocket, she senses something is going on with her man. She reflects that Mitch is usually overly enthusiastic when any woman gives him money at anytime, so whatever is happening with him must be a big deal. "Tabby, I need to talk to daddy alone for a minute, so be a sweetheart, go downstairs and make the three of us a drink, okay?" Tabby leaves and Lana closes the bedroom door. "What's the matter, baby?"

Mitch sits on the bed and leans over with his face in his hands. "Fuck, I blew it L. I killed that nigga, Broadway."

"What? Honey what are you saying, you *shot* Broadway, Broadway Sam?"

With his face still in his hands, "Yeah L, he's dead."

Lana pulls Mitch's head to her bosom and near hysteria she begins to rant "Oh my God baby, what happened? When? Does anyone else know? Oh Mitchell, you just can't go to jail, baby. I'll go fucking nuts without you."

Mitch stands and holds his main woman. "Lana, only Dean knows, and you, so far."

"Mitch, will he tell on you? God, I swear I'll kill him if he does."

"Shh L, Dean's cool with me and has my back. We just need to get the fuck out of here."

"We will baby and we should leave early; like as soon as Brea and the other girls get here. Oh by the way honey, I hate to add insult to injury, but Tabby is four going on five months pregnant.

Daddy, don't you think that since we'll need to travel light and fast, she'll only be excess baggage? Especially, with us having to relocate, get situated and all. We need to leave her here at least until she drops this kid."

"Tabby pregnant, then that bitch knew she was pregnant when she chose me." Hearing the laughter and chatter of Brea and the other two girls arriving, Mitch instructs Lana, "Tell Tabby to get her fat ass up here and, L, get the rest of my checks and bring them up here to me."

When Lana comes back up with Tabby, she points out to Mitch that the larger stack that she lays on the dresser is Brea's, and is wrapped in a rubber band as always. Then she lays B and Denise's checks on the dresser on either side of Brea's, while specifying which is whose. Then, she abruptly leaves the room and closes the door behind her.

"Sit down bitch. When I asked you a week or so ago why your belly was getting so fucking big and you told me it was just water, you lied to me, didn't you?"

"Daddy, I'm sorry, but I didn't think you'd take me back pregnant. I know it was the wrong thing to do, but I really want to be with you Mitchell. And I needed to be with you then. I would have left town and went to work for you when you first asked me to before you left, but I didn't know how these two white girls would treat me."

"You should have asked me, bitch."

"Ask you what Mitchell? Hoes will pretend to be alright with another bitch to please the man, and then stab her in her back like Cuzz's other hoes tried to do when I first got with him. I didn't know what they might have done to me once we were somewhere on the other side of the world. Now I know that Brea and Lana are cool as fuck, but I didn't know it back then. I can still work for a few more months and then when it's time to pop, you can just send me back home to my momma until I'm up and running again. Then, I can come back home to you."

As she pleads her case, Mitch is thinking, *I'm way too fly and have much too much going on to have some big bellied bitch cramping my style on the road.* He reasons that pimping is all about the right appearances. He has enough to deal with, maybe a warrant for his arrest, niggas looking to maybe kill him, and this whole relocation trip. "Pass Tabby, you should've told me up front, and I'd have let you come to me after you had the kid. The last thing I need is you popping out a kid on the road with us. Get your shit together. I'm dropping you at your mama's house, so we can get up out of here." Tabby's things are already packed, as they are headed out in a short while anyway. She cries as she gathers her things with Lana and B helping, and they try to console her. Mitch has Brea drive him and Tabby in the Bonneville to drop Tabby off, and help her take her bags into her mom's house. As he's leaving he tells the other girls, "Be ready to roll when I return." So they begin loading the Rado with their things and his. Dean and Hanks have agreed to get Mitch's furniture and accessories into storage for him. Mitch is in the back seat, as they pull up in front of Tabby's mom's house. Tabby is still crying and turns to face Mitch and makes one final plea. "Mitchell please, I am so sorry, I didn't mean to deceive you."

"Well you did bitch. After tonight, you'll be lucky if you ever see me again."

"Please daddy, I'm so sorry and I swear I'll never lie to you again. At least, let me make it up to you. If you won't take me with you now, then let me come home to you after I drop this baby. I'll make your money right, I swear it Mitchell."

With mixed feelings Mitch agrees, "Okay baby, you do that."

She hurries and gives Mitch her mom's phone number and address. "Just call me daddy from wherever you are and I'll come to you, okay?" After her things are in the house, she walks with Brea back out to the car where Mitch awaits them. "Well, I guess that's it for awhile, daddy. Can a bitch get a goodbye hug and kiss?"

Mitch kisses her soft and tenderly, as he caresses her butt cheeks. Once their lips are apart he grabs her hand and puts five rolled up one hundred dollar bills into her hand, per Lana's instructions. She cries and thanks him. As Brea drives off, he notices in the side rear view mirror that Tabby is standing in the street watching after them until they turn the corner. On the drive back to the apartment, Mitch does a few lines of coke as he finds it difficult to define all that he feels. He knows that he feels love for Tabby and even now, misses her. However, he is unable to identify the animosity and anger he feels as feelings of betrayal and jealousy about her pregnancy, and with another man's kid especially, after him being her first. His alter ego convinces him through false pride and vanity, *Tabby shouldn't have dared get pregnant by another man. Did she not know that she is our girl?*

As they hit the road that morning, Mitch throws the address and phone number Tabby has given him away while they head down the freeway. Having had no sleep at all, Mitch and his crew stop in Salinas and rent two motel rooms so they can all crash. They sleep all day until around four pm. Then they go for breakfast near one of the tracks. While they're eating, Lana mentions, "Daddy, things are jumping around here, so don't you think it's a good idea for us to get down at your money here for three or four hours before we head on to San Francisco?" As far as Mitch is concerned, almost anytime, anyplace is a good time to get money, so he sends his girls to work the track and bars, as he goes hunting for women to recruit. While they're working, he figures that he might as well work too for the four to five hours until mid evening. Then they can head on into San Francisco.

Mitch is cruising around meddling different young Mexican females when he sees a real fine little Mexican girl coming out of a grocery store. He pulls the Lac over and toots the horn, as he notices how pretty she is, and perhaps the first young Mexican female he's ever seen with short hair. Her hair is styled with her bangs hanging in her face just above her eyes and short in the back and on the sides. Mitch is into long hair, but on this little Latina, short hair seems to work quite well.

"What's happening girl? What's your name and can I keep you?"

"You have to get me first, and someone already has me."

"Yeah, but that's a mistake little mama. I'm that short, dark stranger you dreamed about since you were a little girl, who's finally come to sweep you off your feet. Well, I'm here now, live and in living color. So we can be together forever. Plus, I think I'm in love with you."

"You talk a lot of shit, but you sure have a pretty car."

"I'm Pretty Mitch which means I'm supposed to have pretty cars, Mexican stars, and rings and things. Please, tell me you name."

"My name is Margo."

"Will you marry me, Margo?" She laughs and looks up and down the street, but she doesn't leave, so Mitch thinks maybe, just maybe.

"Take a ride with me so I can propose properly. Come on, you and I both know you want to." "Oh yeah, well... will you bring me back here?"

"I swear on our first child." To that she really laughs and reaches for the door. Mitch thinks, *gotcha, you bitch*. As she gets in the car, Mitch notices that her little mini skirt can hardly cover her butt. She keeps adjusting it down and it is arousing the hell out of him. She has on a tight, little low cut, short sleeved blouse with no bra. It barely holds the ample breasts of a girl her size. She is about five six or seven, which is actually tall for a Latina, her sexy legs are long and shapely, and her skin has the look of being slightly tan, but natural. Mitch's alter ego suggests to him, *she is so sweet that she makes our tongue hard.*

"With a name like Pretty Mitch, you're a pimp, huh?"

"Do you want me to be?"

"It really doesn't matter to me, because I'm with a pimp now."

"Who, what's his name?"

"Salinas Red, do you know him?"

"Yeah, I met him once in a joint in Seaside. He's an old nigga, so what are you doing with an old man like that?"

"I don't know, he was supposed to be teaching me to work the streets, but I haven't done anything yet. That's why I got with him, because I knew he was a pimp."

Mitch starts salivating, as his alter ego figures, *that old nigga, Red, fell in love with this young, hot, sixteen year old, Mexican pussy.* Not that Mitch can blame Red, because Margo just exudes raw sexuality. "You got him hooked on that sweet, little Mexican pussy didn't you, you, sexy little bitch?"

"I don't know, I guess something like that, because that's all we do is fuck, all the time."

As they ride kicking it, she leans her back against the door and comfortably props her left leg up on the seat displaying a perfect little pussy, aimed right at Mitch. He stares at her. She's wearing no makeup at all, but still drop dead gorgeous and just begging for the pimping. Right about now, however, a part of him is thinking, *she's begging for something else.*

It takes Mitch all of about two hours of riding and kicking game at her, before she submits. "I think you're cute so, yeah, I'll leave town with you, but you have to fuck me first."

Mitch starts praying to the pimp God in his mind, *please, work with me here.* It takes all Mitch has in him to not pull over and get busy with this little Spanish freak, but he remembers the game comes first. "Of course I'll fuck you, but you have to pay me first."

"I have about thirty dollars."

Mitch laughs and tells her, "Okay, give me that," as he sticks out his hand. After she hands him the money, "No baby, this won't cut it, but not to worry, I will teach you all you need to know about getting money (meaning Lana will). Then, I'll fuck you until you can't walk."

"Oh my God, you're making me all wet on your car seat."

"Not to worry baby, its leather, and patience anyway, hot little bitch." He's half talking to her and half to himself.

"You better stop talking nasty to me like that, then."

Back at the track, Mitch turns Margo over to Lana and tells Brea to get in his car. Mitch is so turned on by Margo that he pulls around in back of a bar that his girls are working to relieve his sexual tensions. Brea already knows what time it is, because this is not the first time she and her man have done it like this. Smiling and giggling, Brea frantically pulls up her skirt so she can get with Mitch. When he parks his car, Brea is all over him. From inside to against the back of his ride and ending up against the wall of the bar, Mitch relieves himself with Brea.

When Brea and Mitch come out of the bathroom from washing up, Lana walks over to them smiling, "Daddy, you want that young Mexican pussy real bad, don't you?"

Brea and Lana both crack up at the incident. Mitch is standing there knowing he's cold busted, but he momentarily considers trying to deny it. Brea hugs him to ease his self consciousness. "Daddy, it's all good, you can use me like that anytime you want." After she says that, he manages a slight smile of embarrassment. As they load up at the motel to leave, Lana tells Mitch in private, "I'm so proud of you, because you're beginning to think with the pimping and not with your dick. Plus, there'll be plenty of time for freaking with this one, she's a keeper."

Her compliments make Mitch feel good, kind of like a young boy that just got approval from his mother, mentor, or favorite teacher. As Lana continues with her comments, Mitch thinks, *L is all that and even more to me, she is my family.*

Chapter XI

Small Fish in a Big Pond

With his crew now five again, they set out for San Francisco. He doesn't bother with the courtesy pimps usually adhere to with other pimps because Red never turned Margo out, therefore she's fair game. Mitch's alter ego adds, *shame on that nigga for putting his dick before the pimping. This young bitch came looking for the pimping. It's just like us taking some guy's girlfriend. Now, she's going to get this pimping served up raw. Let Red find out when and however he finds out.* As they hit the freeway, Lana is driving and starting to school Margo about the game for him. They are both in the front seat and Mitch is in the back of the Rado. Brea is driving Denise and B, as they follow in the Bonneville. As Mitch listens to Lana lacing up Margo he thinks, *Margo has no clothes, make up, or anything. How perfect, a sixteen year old impressionable Mexican bitch without a place to belong. We will become her family.*

When Mitch pulls onto Fillmore Street off the Fell Street freeway exit, he and his girls see that there are hoes everywhere. They're on both sides of the street all the way up and down Fillmore. He can't reach Fillmore Slim by phone, so he arranges a rendezvous with Lawrence at the intersection of Webster and McAllister Streets. They exchange car descriptions by phone and Mitch sets out to rendezvous with him. Lawrence drives up in a 1966 white on white Cadillac Sedan Deville and Mitch is in his 1967 Eldorado, so Mitch already starts feeling like a big dog.

When Lawrence gets out of his Lac, Mitch notices that he is a tall, dark, unimposing man. Mitch feels that he can trust him, up to a point, because of who introduced them. When Mitch gets out of his ride, Lawrence looks him up and down and with a shocked expression on his face, "Man, how old are you, fifteen or sixteen? You have to be the youngest pimp I've ever seen."

Mitch feels offended because his baby face and stature is always the first thing people seem to notice about him, so he doesn't respond. He just stares up at the much taller Lawrence. Mitch feels that he'll just let Lawrence think whatever he wants. Then Mitch smiles that little smile of his and chuckles as he thinks, *well at least he didn't say I'm the smallest.*

Lawrence senses Mitch's tension over his comments, and says, "Hey man, I wish I had gotten in the pimp game when I was your age, instead of the Army. I'd be rich by now. I mean, I've had hoes here and there, but I'm no pimp. I'm a hustler, dope dealer, and retired Army Sgt E7. That's why I was trying to get you hooked up with a pimp like Fillmore Slim. He's doing it big, like I heard you are."

After getting his girls checked into the Lombard Plaza Motel on Lombard Street, Mitch proceeds to put them down in strategic areas as guided by Lawrence. He has Lana drive Brea and Margo to the Tenderloin. They follow him and Lawrence to the area of the San Francisco Hilton, which at the time is right across the street from Pam Pam's restaurant (a hangout for mostly white and exotic hoes, tricks and players). Then Mitch drops B and Neicy, (his nickname for Denise) off on the corner of Fillmore and Eddy Streets. There are hotels and rooms available all over town as trick pads, but, all of Mitch's girls are well versed in the improvisation of what places and spaces they can perform their skills. With his game down, Mitch is free to roll and get the 411 from Lawrence about the city.

Lawrence asks, "Mitch, where are you from, man?"

"I'm out of Memphis via Chicago, abroad, and most recently the Monterey Peninsula."

"Oh, you're an international young nigga, then?"

Mitch pushes his chest out, and brags, "Yeah, you could say that I am an international player."

Lawrence takes Mitch around to a couple of different after-hours joints and introduces him to different hustlers, dealers, and pimps. One such person is Larry Coffee, known as Fast Larry, who is not only a pimp, dealer and hustler but also a known killer. Larry is forty two years old, stands about six four, medium built, light skin, and wears his hair in the JFK style process. Larry and Mitch seem to hit it right off, as he tells Mitch, "So you're another of those pretty boy niggas, huh Pretty Mitch? Well check this out Mitch, I got hoes and you got hoes, so why don't you lose this lame and let's ride and kick around this pimp game." He says it right in front of Lawrence's face, and Lawrence doesn't respond. So Mitch thanks Lawrence for the info and help, and goes to roll with Larry.

Larry has a black on black, 1967, Cadillac Fleetwood Brougham. Larry's a big man, so he has the seat way back from the dash. Mitch doesn't like Broughams, because he feels they are just too big, especially for a guy of his stature. They ride while exchanging info on each other, as Larry checks a few of his traps. As Mitch observes Larry's expertise with his girls, Mitch recognizes that he has a whole lot to learn about the pimp game. Larry seems to intuitively know that Mitch is relatively new to this level of the game just by talking with Mitch.

Then it is Mitch's turn to show his own prowess with his girls, so he rides through where he has his game down, oblivious to any possible motives on Larry's part for plucking him for one of his girls. First he breaks B and Neicy, then on to the Tenderloin on O'Farrell Street right off Powell Street. It's almost three am and that's the designated time and place to rendezvous with Lana and the other two girls.

When Mitch sees Lana and Brea, he tells Larry, "Pull over here for a minute, man." As the black Ham pulls up in front of Lana and Brea, they see two unidentified black men inside the Ham, turn their faces away quickly, back away from the curb and start walking further down the sidewalk. Mitch is bursting with pride, as he feels Larry watching the mannerisms between him and his two women. Mitch lets down the window and calls Lana's name just loud enough for her to hear him. When she turns, he winks at her.

Lana smiles and calls Brea, who is already further down the sidewalk. As Brea starts back to the car, Lana asks Mitch, "Do you want just me, or do you want both of us to come with you now."

"Nah mama, I'm just looking for pretty white girls."

As Brea gets back to the vehicle, Lana is still kicking it with Mitch and responds, "Well baby, you got two pretty white girls right here." Then she, Brea and Mitch crack up about it. The three of them know it's all about high siding for another pimp.

Mitch feels confident as Lana and Brea have responded like pros. As all down working girls know, if a car pulls up with players inside, and their man isn't one of them, they walk away. They're out of line for reckless eyeballing another pimp or his car, unless of course they're looking to choose or break themselves. When Mitch asks where Margo is, Lana responds, "That little Mexican bitch is getting at your check, daddy."

Larry waits until Mitch dismisses his game. "Mitch, you got game other than the four I've seen, man?"

"I got a little Mexican bitch I knocked in Salinas on the way up here, man. Those two, there," Mitch says with a nod of his head in Brea and Lana's direction, "are the very top of my game."

"Damn Mitch, young nigga, you got White girls, Black girls and a Mexican, and you got those bitches marching like soldiers, man."

While he doesn't say it, Mitch thinks, *actually the orchestration of my broads is played to Lana's tune, and I'm good with that. For now.*

Mitch hears from his old partner Hanks, and the word on the street in Seaside is that the cops suspect Mitch in the Broadway Sam deal. Someone gave his name as a probable person of interest, but the authorities apparently have no proof, so no arrest warrant has been issued. Mitch is relieved to hear that, and asks that Hanks keep him in the loop for any info that he or Dean might come by concerning the incident. Mitch feels that for now, no news is good news.

Trying to adjust to his new surroundings along with all the success, money, and new toys, Mitch realizes how very little he truly knows about this pimp game from a male perspective. After all, hoes turned him out, and white hoes at that. He begins to pay close attention when around older, wiser and successful pimps and players of longevity. As a student of the game, he learns to listen and listens to learn. Fast (his nickname for Fast Larry), shows him various facilities around town for players; like after-hours joints, hair and nail salons, speakeasies, bars, and hotels. Fast introduces Mitch to other pimps, dope dealers, hustlers, pick pockets, boosters, and street people that Fast figures Mitch might need the services of at some point.

Another thing that's becoming increasingly apparent to Mitch is that the most successful pimps are big, tall dudes, and a good deal of them are light, bright and damn near white cats. He realizes that he needs to acquire a competitive edge, something unique to him. At only five nine and one hundred and forty five pounds (including all his jewelry and his 45), he feels somewhat outclassed getting action at fresh game. He realizes that he overcame his size disadvantage on the peninsula because he had more style, charisma, and youth, than did the competition there. However he is no longer a big fish in a little pond. Here, it's a whole new ball game, as he finds himself just one of many young, fast, sharp pimps and players. He's not enjoying all the stiff competition.

A lot of the major players that he hangs out with are more interested in knocking his women than in pulling his coat and helping him become down with the game. He also notices that all street people adopt street handles, usually a name after some notorious criminal figure out of history, or ones that insinuate being hip, slick, and cool. *So that's why Big in Hawaii named me after the gangster, Baby Face Nelson,* he reflects. *Umm, guess I'm catching on.*

Mitch and Fast become close riding and trapping buds. Mitch's awareness of Fast as a no nonsense killer is reinforced. Coming out of Adel's barber shop one day, with hair and nails perfectly done, they find that a drunken wino has spilled spaghetti on the brand new red Rado that Fast has recently purchased. Fast proceeds to punch the guy unmercifully until he drops. Then he really shocks Mitch by purposely kicking the wino's eye out, while cursing at him. As Mitch and Fast are walking back from the barber shop after getting something to clean off Fast's Rado, Mitch inquires, "Fast that was a bit much, man, don't you think?"

Fast snarls at Mitch, "Everything seems like a bit much for guys like you Mitch, because you little fellows are real sensitive." The comment cuts Mitch to the core, because it aggravates his Napoleonic Complex, which he is not yet even aware that he possesses. To Mitch it seems to be a deliberate insult. He doesn't comment. Instead, he keeps his eyes down towards the sidewalk, while distancing himself far enough from Fast to be able to get to his 45 before Fast can get his hands on him. He has seen how unmercifully vicious Fast can be.

Once Mitch reaches what he thinks is a safe distance from Fast, his body tenses as his throat goes dry and the palms of his hands sweat. However, to Mitch's dismay, he looks up and finds the bigger man, Fast, has kept close in stride to him and is now staring down directly into his eyes and watching his every move. The stare between the two men becomes so intense that they stop walking, and stand face to face gauging each other for a hint of what's to come next. Mitch contemplates bolting back to a safer distance and firing his 45 at Fast. Instead, for what seems like the longest moment he just stares into Fast's eyes. Mitch feels sure that even at this distance he can still draw and discharge his 45 before Fast can get his hands on him. He reasons that if he runs it'll only make his shot less accurate.

Finally, Fast's facial expression and posture relaxes as he allows a half smile to come on his face. "Mitch, I came pretty close to buying the ranch, didn't I?"

Mitch looks at Fast confused as he thinks, *Fast must be crazy. We have just come to within a hair of a mere moment of being involved in a permanent solution for a temporary problem, and here Fast stands half smiling.*

Fast interrupts Mitch's thoughts. "Mitch, you're alright with me, my young brother. I wasn't referring to your stature when I called you a little fellow. I was referring to your lack of credentials and experience in the game. I mean you've done and seen a lot and even been a lot in this game up to this point, but you're on the real fast track now, my brother. You need to learn not to get mad, but to get even. Most men will approach you with their fists in a misunderstanding, because they'll under estimate your size. That will put the element of surprise in your favor, but you need a rep. Do you understand why I came down so hard on that wino back there?"

"You did it to make a point to him?" Mitch half asks a question and makes a statement.

"My young brother, that wino is harmless, the point I'm making is for these other niggas that saw what went down or will hear about it. Niggas will figure if I'd do that to someone that I know is harmless, imagine what I'd do to a motherfucker that I feel is a real threat. You see, where I'm coming from?" Mitch acknowledges that he understands by nodding his head and saying, "Capiche, Pisano." At that, both men laugh. Fast continues schooling his young partner with, "Bro, if we're going to continue kicking it like we've been doing, you'll need to acquire thicker skin, man. You need to understand that when we have to make a move in a situation, we move decisively and hard to leave a lasting impression, like I did with that wino back there. The element of surprise must always be in our favor, so always make sure you have the edge by being the one that dictates when, where, and how the situation will play out."

As Mitch and Fast are getting into Fast's Rado, Mitch is taking it all in, but it seems to him that Fast has had tactical training. Mitch is perplexed as to where Fast learned all this stuff. "Fast, man, were you in the Army or Nam?"

"Yeah Mitch, I have lived my whole life in the Army and Viet Nam. Can you dig it?" They laugh and give each other five. "They call this life the game, because it's all about playing, but some niggas out here in these streets haven't read the book. And even some of those that have read the book sometimes don't adhere to the rules, and will try you if you show weakness of any kind. Even down niggas will bend those rules if they can get away with it. Rules are only as worthwhile as the strength of whoever is applying them to carry them out. So, there *will* be times, not *may* be times, that one has to govern oneself accordingly."

In the course of their relationship as road dogs, Mitch learns a lot from Fast as he becomes Mitch's mentor. Even Lana likes how Fast is down with, and for Mitch. Lana suggests to Mitch, "Fast is a keeper because he is truly interested in your well being and success." That's saying a lot for Lana. She doesn't trust anyone around Mitch, male or female, other than Margo, Brea and Niecy.

Lana doesn't include B in this mix because she feels, "B isn't commitment oriented to hang with just one man," as she's telling him one night after B had been flirting with another pimp. Mitch and Lana have to continually check her for being flirtatious or out of line with different pimps from time to time. She develops into what is known as a fly by night broad. Almost like a premonition, B chooses Johnny Valentine, a pimp partner of Mitch's. Johnny is the usual tall, light skin, good looking guy. He is only a few years older than Mitch, but at this point, far more experienced in the game. When he serves Mitch about B, Mitch rolls with it and they remain buds. After all, hoes come and go as all pimps know, and even though Johnny will never be like Fast, he's still down.

Fast has a driver and personal bodyguard named *Grave Digger Jones,* who is a large, six feet six, dark, muscular man of about forty, nobody knows Digger's age for sure including him. He was left at birth in a laundry mat and abandoned by his hype mom. Mitch feels uncomfortable around Digger because he seems to always be in a bad mood and, at this stage of Mitch's development, he takes it, and everything very personal.

Mitch and Fast make a pact that they won't get at or accept each other's girls choosing between the two of them, at any level. Of course, if a broad hasn't been with either of them in a long time, then they understand that all bets are off. They reason that there's plenty of fresh game in the streets, and their bond is bigger than any one broad. Mitch notices that Fast maintains a stable of mostly Black girls, except for a fine ass little Mexican broad named Cookie. Cookie and Mitch's Margo meet at an after-hours joint one night when Fast and Mitch are out high siding and flashing their girls. The two Spanish girls are about the same age so they hit it off really well, and they start hustling together. It works, so Mitch and Fast don't fix it.

Fast's primary income is drug dealing and when Mitch inquires about it, he simply explains, "Straight pimping is a whole lot easier than being a drug dealer. There are lots of dope sellers, but not many dope dealers, just like there's lots of niggas with hoes, but not a lot of real down pimps. Pimping isn't just getting a bitch to go sell pussy and steal trick's money. A bitch can do that without a man, though usually with no degree of consistency.

"Pimping is about protecting the investment and the organization of a hoe's efforts, and the management of the proceeds. This shit is done like a business to where a bitch's mind is free to perform her main job description, which is getting money. Then her pimp takes care of her personal needs; family where necessary, and everything else like cases, attorneys, and other affairs." Then Fast gets really serious. "Now the dope game is something totally different Mitch. You must be ready to cripple, maim, kill, be killed, or perhaps spend the rest of your life in prison. The rewards are many times greater than hoe money, but so are the liabilities. Anyway man, you got all kinds of hoes clocking bank for you on a daily basis, so stay with what works and always remember, today's dealers are potentially tomorrow's buyers."

It's late Saturday night in San Francisco and Mitch and Fast are rolling with Elmore, a tall medium built, dark skin pimp about Mitch's age that's from San Francisco. Elmore is driving a brand new black on red 1967 Cadillac Coupe Deville. Fast and Elmore are in the front seat, while Johnny Valentine, the guy that knocked Mitch for B, and Mitch are in back. They are riding, kicking the pimp game around, and capping and high siding on each other as they do lines of blow. Suddenly, Elmore tells Fast, "This nigga, Johnny Valentine, shot me and then went and shot, himself." All four of the men start laughing. Mitch doesn't know what Elmore means and learns later from Fast that Elmore and Johnny had a run in before Mitch met either of them, during which time Johnny shot Elmore over some broad and disrespect. Also, Mitch learns what Elmore meant by 'Johnny shot himself.' Johnny started shooting heroin back then.

While still laughing, Johnny hunches Mitch and tells Elmore, "Nigga, I'm going to shoot you again if you don't pass that blow back here so Mitch and I can get at it." Mitch and Johnny laugh and give each other five.

Mitch is feeling good from the blow, weed and booze so he comments, "Yeah Fast, you're my main man and you're up there hogging the coke with Elmore, what's up with that, man?"

Elmore cuts in, "Mitch, with what I been hearing about the way you do your pimping, you need all the blow and flow you can get to keep jumping up and down in all those hoes of yours pussy damn near every morning after they get home from work, nigga. It's all over the streets Mitch, so when you finish with yours tonight, why don't you come over and do mine, too." All of them start cracking up and slapping hands for five, except Mitch.

Seeing he's getting to Mitch, Elmore continues, "I heard that Mitch's hoes spend more time parked in alleys and side streets fucking him than they do tricks." Fast, Elmore and Johnny burst into laughter again, but Mitch doesn't find it funny at all, in fact, it embarrasses him.

Then Johnny joins in, "Yeah, and if it's not too late for you Mitch, after you do his, you can come do mine as well. Nigga, I'll even pay you."

Laughter is really going on now. Mitch feels that the tone of things has become about roasting him, and he gets defensive because it hurts his feelings. He aims his anger towards Elmore. "I see why you got shot nigga, you talk too much shit."

Elmore responds, "Mitch, you should talk, man? Nigga, you're the original shit talker, man." Then he smiles at Mitch in the rear view mirror and sticks his hand back to Mitch for five.

Fast jumps in, sensing Mitch's anger. "That's why Pretty knocks you nigga's for your bitches, because not only is he a hell of a Mack, but he's a hell of a young freak as well." He manipulates the situation and helps his young protégé off the hook. With Fast's intervention

Mitch begins to recognize it's nothing personal. It's just how pimps keep each other on their toes.

"Fast, I don't pay these old niggas no never mind. They're just jealous because they can't keep up with me. I can do two, three or four bitches a night and still stay hard, because I'm a young *Mac*adamia Nut."

Johnny adds, "Yeah young nigga, those hoes will have fucked and sucked you dry in six months to a year. You'd better get with this psychological pimping. Can you dig it?" Mitch smiles as he and Johnny exchange hand slaps. "That's what happens when hoes turn a nigga out. They make sure they teach him to give up as much dick as they want." Mitch now laughs heartily with the other three men.

After Fast and Mitch are dropped off at Mitch's ride, Fast starts right in with Mitch. "That's what I was talking about concerning your thin skin, Mitch. There is a time to get busy and there is a time to just go with the flow. Mitch, what a bitch does with her pussy isn't our business beyond handling our business. You're going to find that hoes run into dudes or other hoes that they just want to fuck, and will, whether we like it or not. "There are all kinds of broads with different sexual appetites and some of those appetites don't include the pimp they're paying, because pimping isn't about the pussy, it's about the mind and the money. You know how there are certain of your hoes you like to freak with, and them with you? Then, there are those that you really don't prefer sexually. I mean you'll do them, but they're not your particular preference.

"Well, the same holds true for them, but that won't stop them from still being down ass bitches to you and for you. A pimp's mind must work independently of his dick or jealousies over a bitch's body, because if we don't, we'll go fucking nuts worrying about this or that bitch doing it with someone else. We're not in the love game, we're in the money game, so the one who cares the least, or has the best illusion of caring the least in the relationship, controls the relationship. As long as a bitch is getting your correct dough, man, who cares who or when she has fuck buddies? One thing is for damn sure, no one Mack, or man, can keep up with one hoe's sexual appetites, never mind a whole stable of them." He and Mitch laugh at the logic in that. "So be grateful for any help you get bro when they get it elsewhere. Man, you better come on in and get this shit right, nigga, huh?" With that Fast smiles and offers his hand to Mitch for five.

Mitch continues learning that a really big part of the pimping is showing off for other pimp's and their girls, as well as his own; that's why all the slick names, jewelry, flashy clothes, cars, and smooth talk and walk. One never knows when they'll get the opportunity to knock one or more of someone else's working girls. Mitch observes that a lot of hoes do their hoeing when they're in designated locations like strolls or bars. He figures real hoes should wake up hoes and go to sleep hoes, which should mean that a bitch's mind and instincts need to be conditioned to always be about the business of getting money. They should think 'money' whether it's at the beauty parlor, having a meal in a restaurant, at a gas station, or any other situation. He has even had some of his girls turning dates with some of their 'baby's daddies.'

Hanging out with Fast, Mitch begins acquiring the male perspective of the cultivation of fresh young game. In addition, two big time old school pimps and players enter his life. The first is a fifty year old small man of Mitch's stature that goes by the street handle Mickey Cohen. Mickey is a light skin guy with reddish processed hair and has been in the game since he was a teenager growing up New York. He is a master at turning out young underage White, Mexican, Asian and other non Black females into the game. Tony Goshay, the second old player, is a forty year old, tall, heavy built, light skin guy out of Baton Rouge, Louisiana. Tony has been in the game of flipping underage Black females for forever. Mitch is in the barbershop one day getting his hair and nails done and listening in on these two older pimps high siding, talking about their game.

Sitting perfectly quiet and attentively, he is awe struck by these two legendary masters of deception in the pimp game. The barbershops are where all the players come through and hang out at one time or another throughout their day, because when one has a process it requires daily comb outs (restyle) to look sharp and freshly done at all times. Today, Mitch is finished with his business in the shop, but he hangs out, watches, and listens. The shop is located right across the street from the old Manor Plaza Hotel and Big Daddy's Pool Hall, right off McAllister and Fillmore Streets. Adel is a short, medium brown skin man, and the main hair stylist in the shop. He also loves to snort dog food, (heroin). He is so good at doing processes that a lot of players fly him to different cities just to style their hair. The joint is buzzing all day and into the late evenings with pimps, hoes, dope dealers, boosters, shot broads, hustlers, and hypes selling miscellaneous clothing and merchandise from leathers, suede, minks, reptile wear, guns, cameras, or simply anything that will turn a buck.

Tony and Mickey are high siding for the crowd as they cap on each other. Tony starts out, "Mickey, nigga, what did you end up doing with that fine, young, fifteen year old blonde bitch you just knocked?"

Mickey responds, "Nigga, what do pimps do with hoes? She's out selling pussy."

Tony laughs and says, "Well, you'd better hope the cops don't knock that bitch."

Mickey starts talking louder, "Man, I got that young bitch's mind locked up so tight that a nigga could use it as a safety deposit box, and I got her proper id. Plus, she keeps me eating pork chops and steaks every day." Everyone starts laughing and slapping each other's hands for five.

Tony flashes a wad of one hundred dollar bills. "Yeah nigga, but can she get it like this?"

Mickey pulls out an even bigger wad of one hundred dollar bills. "I don't know nigga, you tell me, what cha see is what cha get."

After the capping session between the two old players, Mitch introduces himself to Mickey and Tony and tells them a little about how he's playing the game himself. Mickey is astonished at how young Mitch looks so he asks, "How old are you young blood?"

Defensively, Mitch responds, "What difference does that make? I got five hundred dollar bills, a Lac and jewelry just like any other true to life player in this game."

Mickey is looking up and down at Mitch's attire, jewelry and overall appearance. "Hold on young blood. I just love seeing you young niggas coming into this game, especially with the way you look like you're doing it. Why don't you take a ride with me and Tony? I like your style, Mitch."

The three of them ride to Mickey's home located in a part of Frisco known as the Avenues. As they roll into Mickey's garage, Mickey starts high siding and explaining to Mitch, "Mitch, hoes come and go, but real estate is here to stay." Mickey knocks on the wall of his garage to illustrate saying, "This is forever. Get enough of these and the cop and blow of hoes in the game won't matter. A nigga can always attract more money when he's already got money. Mitch, always remember hoes are damaged goods from abuse issues usually, from which they form low self esteem and animosities against men in general.

"With a pimp, these women find acceptance, a source of self esteem in that man, security in his aura of invincibility, guidance and direction, along with financial planning and management. Through their man, they get the illusion of their own invincibility and pride, as long as they pay for it, which is why they pay for it in the first place. Can you dig it?"

Mitch reflects that it is amazing how he is hearing some of the exact same things from people that don't even know each other in

129

the game. From then on every chance Mitch gets to hang around with Mickey or Tony he does. Through them, he will learn to hone the skills of preying on young broads and turning them out.

Mickey ends up with white slavery, pimping and pandering, and statutory rape beefs with some fifteen year old white girl. She won't testify against Mickey, but he is a well known black pimp and he knows he can't beat the white slavery, so he takes a deal from the courts for a lesser sentence. Mickey and Tony just fade off the set. That's how it is in street life. People disappear from the different street sets to prison, drugs, insanity, or just come up missing. Every now and then one may get lucky and live through it all and square up. It's a more dangerous game preying on young white girls— more so than other ethnicities—because they draw more heat and consequence if a player is caught, especially if he happens to be Black.

The world is not color blind so, even in this game, race plays a major role. However, young white girls are the most profitable merchandise, so Mitch is prepared to pay whatever the cost to be the boss. He reasons that the money and lifestyle are just too good. Mitch is riding in the Mission District prowling early one afternoon. There is a high concentration of Chicanos that live there, and where there are Chicanos there will be young Latinas. As he turns off Mission Street he sees a real fine redbone wearing red short shorts with matching red Go Go boots and a white blouse buttoned up above the naval.

Mitch honks his horn with the familiar hustler style of the bay area, which is two short beeps followed immediately by three short, three more short, and ending with two short. Everybody that is remotely affiliated with the game knows about it, so it gets their attention when they hear it. The redbone turns and looks admiringly at Mitch's ride, then at Mitch as he gets out getting right at her. "Girl, you are just too sexy for your own good." He's thinking she's about as whorish looking as she could possibly be. "Baby what's your name? Can I claim you as my dame? My name is Pretty Mitch and…"

She interrupts Mitch. "I'm Ernestine, Mitchell, you don't remember me?" Mitch searches his memory banks and can't place her, so he plays it off.

"Oh yeah, now I remember mama. It's just that I am so stunned with your presence and beauty, forgive me. Where you going with all of that prime time merchandise?"

Smiling from Mitch's flirtatious complimentary remarks, she responds, "I'm headed to Mission Street to catch a cab to the Tenderloin." Mitch steps to his passenger door, opens it and says, "Sexy redbone mama, I got your cab right here."

"Thanks Mitch," she says flirtatiously as she slides into the seat of Mitch's Rado.

Mitch's alter ego thinks, *gotcha, you bitch.* "So little mama, you obviously don't have a man or you wouldn't be hopping up in a pimp's ride and kicking it like you're doing. What's up with that?"

"I know you're a pimp, Mitch, and I wouldn't be in your car if I didn't have getting down with you in mind."

"Well check this out baby, how can I tell? I mean, America is the land of milk and honey, but a nigga can't taste it without any money."

"Mitch, I've seen how you're doing it, and I don't want to disrespect you with chump change. I only have about half a bill on me right now, but I'm on the way to work in the Tenderloin right now."

Mitch thinks, *I need something from Ernestine right now to at least begin sealing this deal.* "Why don't you let me worry about how much or how little money is enough, and break yourself." Ernestine reaches in her boot and pulls out two twenty dollar bills and two ten dollar bills, peels off fifty of it, and hands it to Mitch, while starting to put a ten back in her boot. Mitch sticks out his hand and becks for the ten spot. "Hold on little mama, now you don't want to start our relationship off on a sour note do you? Is there a man that I need to talk to about this move?"

"Mitch, a bitch can't go to work broke, this is for mercy money. And no, there is no man, well… no other pimp, anyway."

Noticeably aggravated, Mitch turns deadly serious. "Well first of all, a bitch needs to leave when and how much mercy money she gets to a pimp's discretion." As he turns to face her showing his displeasure, he asks, "Can you dig it?"

"Yeah daddy, I can dig it. I'm sorry. I didn't mean to be out of line or nothing."

"Not to worry little mama, we'll kick it more in detail after you get this cool," as he waves the money she just gave him in her face. "I'll put you down with my rules and regulations as to how to advocate my business correctly at that time. Can you dig it?"

"I can dig it, Mitch."

Mitch gives Ernestine four one dollar bills as mercy money, and drops her off on the corner of Eddy and Leavenworth Streets with instructions as to what time they'll rendezvous in the wee hours of the morning. As he pulls away from the curb, Ernestine waves and shouts, "I'll get the money right Daddy," as she proudly turns and struts pass the other working girls that just saw her get dropped off by her new daddy, Pretty Mitch.

After two weeks to the day that Ernestine starts paying him, Mitch pulls up to the curb where Ernestine is working and finally agrees to make love to her. "If you have a great night tonight little mama, you might get lucky with me after work." She is so excited that she jumps around like a little girl that's been told she's going to see the circus when it comes to town. The power of being able to instill that kind of anticipation in a woman gives Mitch a sense of indescribable control.

Mitch hears Lana's words ringing in his mind, "For those hoes that you knock who aspire to freak with you, and believe me most will, you need to have them in such a mental and emotional state of surrender that by the time you touch them, it'll be your pleasure that's in the forefront of those whore's minds, like it is in Brea's and mine." Mitch has learned all the right questions to ask in his probing process to find the buttons of control or to enslave the minds of his different girls. He remembers Lana also saying "It doesn't matter what color they are, how pretty or even how intuitively gifted they are, they are all damaged goods, including me, so you must learn to prey on those weaknesses."

The stage is set this morning for Bonnie Parker (nickname for Ernestine). It's about four am and he has just picked her up from the stroll. He puts on R & B love songs that he knows 'pull on young black girl's heart strings.' After she fixes them a drink, they do a few lines of blow and smoke a joint. Mitch thinks, *now the table is set to start the interview process.* He has continually denied him and her, her advances to sleep with him.

Mitch probes her mind and history this early morning, and he finds that Bonnie Parker is like ninety nine percent of the hoes he has known up to this point in his brief career. Not all of the females that are molested become hoes, but as Lana has taught him about hoes psychological profiles, "Ninety percent of all whores have been abused or molested."

As he lay on the bed in the apartment that Bonnie Parker shares with Niecy, he chuckles to himself as he thinks, *how I have longed for this fine ass, young, redbone bitch's body.* As she comes in the room after showering and doing what hoes do right after working, she asks, "Mitch, what's so funny?

Nigga, you've been smiling since you picked me up this morning."

He can't tell her that he is as excited, maybe even more excited than she is, about finally getting at that ass of hers. "You know,

Bonnie, I don't see you as just another hoe of mine. I feel more permanence between us like you're my woman, baby. I mean, I know it sounds crazy, but I feel you in here," he says pointing to his heart. "I knew when we first met that we were destined to be about so much more than just the pimping."

"Mitch, I feel the same way about you. I understand that I'm not supposed to be all wrapped up in you and all, but I really am, and have been since that very first night at the club that you grabbed my chin in your hand and told me how pretty I am."

As she snuggles her nude body up under Mitch, he goes to work. "So who was it, your father, brother, relative, or family acquaintance?"

Disarmed by the weed, booze and because she feels comfortable with Mitch as her daddy, Bonnie openly explains, "My body has been developed like this since I was thirteen, Mitch." Then she lays back so he can get a good long look at her. Seeing this tight, young, cocoa butter complexioned sixteen year old body that he observes is smooth and blemish free, Mitch falls deeper into lust, but remembers his primary purpose, and he tells her to proceed.

"My mom used to be a hoe and she always had a bunch of different boyfriends around our apartment. I started getting fucked by various ones of them even before I was thirteen. My mother never believed me when I told her about it, so I started making the men pay me. At fifteen, I moved out of her house and lived with the old man that I lived with when I got with you. I didn't have to work or anything, except screw him once a week." Then she gets excited and sits up on her elbows so her face can be close to Mitch's face. "But Daddy, I love selling my pussy. So I'd go sell pussy on the weekends and go to clubs and meet fine ass niggas like you and freak with them, but when I met you I knew I wanted to work for you."

All this time Mitch is thinking Bonnie is a prime candidate for a predatory pimp like him. It's like Lana says, "Damaged females and young girls that fall in love, lust, or fascination with guys like you are tailor made for the pimping, because sometimes these hoes are just there for the money, pimping, the game of street life, and the excitement of it all." Mitch reasons that such is the case with Bonnie Parker. They spend the remainder of the morning getting high and freaking.

Mitch is at a soul food joint one afternoon on Fillmore Street. It belongs to Fast and is appropriately named, 'Fast Food.' Along with Mitch, is Fast, Johnny Valentine and another guy named Riviera Red. They're hanging out at a table always reserved for Fast whenever he comes to eat or talk business there. The men are at the front of the diner kicking it about the wild, wild, wide open the West Coast. Picking up on young runaways as a source of fresh turnouts in these times of the hippies and free love couldn't be easier. Mitch and Red are seated with their backs to the front door, as Fast and Johnny are seated across from them. The table is just inside the door and next to the front window. People are passing as they come and go, so neither of the men seated at Mitch's table notice anything out of the ordinary when the woman stops behind Mitch's seat, until it is too late.

The woman pushes the muzzle of the snub nose 38, Saturday night special, against the back of Mitch's head. "You low down dirty bastard. You got my baby working the streets and I'm going to kill your punk ass, nigga." Mitch is so scared that he keeps his hands flat on top of the table and stares straight into Fast's eyes, unconsciously soliciting help.

Fast shifts his eyes down to in front of him just under the table. As Mitch recognizes Fast is going for his piece, Mitch starts talking to the woman to distract her from seeing the move Fast is making concealed by the table and table cloth. Very softly Mitch responds, "Miss, I don't know your daughter." He immediately knows that was the wrong thing to say. The woman pushes the muzzle of the gun harder against Mitch's head. "You're a lying son of a bitch, nigga. You do know her, and nigga you also know she's only sixteen."

Mitch is puzzled because he doesn't know who she is and from the looks in his partners' eyes, neither do they. "I'm going to blow your brains out, nigga."

It feels like an out of body experience to Mitch. In a very low whisper he hears himself say, "Miss, that won't do you or your daughter any good. Is taking my life really worth sacrificing your own, and your daughter not having a mother?" Mitch's mind is running through different scenarios of how this will all play out, other than him dying this way. His alter ego reasons, *this is all or nothing now, and we have just one shot.* At that exact moment he hears muffled sniffles of crying coming from the woman, as the muzzle starts to shake against his head. "Miss, you really don't want to do this." Mitch feels the pressure of the muzzle ease up a bit from against his head.

When he no longer feels the muzzle against his head, he slowly turns to face the woman, who is now, crying hysterically. "I am so sorry, Miss, please believe me. You're absolutely right and I'll bring her back home to you." Seeing her, Mitch recognizes the redbone as Eva, the mother of Bonnie Parker, because he has seen her once before. By now Mitch is thinking, *people that are capable of pulling the trigger don't spend five or ten minutes talking about doing it, they just do it.* Fast nods his head to the side, as if to tell Mitch to shift his body to the side so he can get a clear shot at the woman. Mitch slowly gets up while positioning his body between Eva and Fast, because he knows that Fast will kill her. Mitch continues, "Eva, don't do something that'll only bring more harm to you and your daughter."

Hearing Mitch use her name, Eva cries harder and lowers the gun to her side. Mitch moves slowly and cautiously towards Eva, as he's thinking just how fine she is for a thirtyish year old female. Mitch reaches for the gun and she releases her grip on it, and all but collapses into Mitch's arms. She cries out, "Oh my God, I'm to blame for this. I should have believed her." Even as Mitch holds her, he feels her supple breast and body press back and forth against his body as her body convulses from sobbing. Then she cries out, "I just want my baby back home."

Mitch feels almost aroused from it all as he holds her tightly to him. He has to fight back a chuckle as his alter ego insinuates, *damn, that's really fucked up; we get an erection from just manipulating a bitch. How much we love this game.* In the coming weeks, Mitch will add Eva to his stable creating his first mother and daughter combination in his stable at the same time. There will be many other such combinations over the years, including blood sisters on a couple of occasions. After all, Mitch determines, *all is fair in love, war, blood, and pimping.*

Chapter XII

Expanding Horizons

Margo has been consistently getting at Mitch's money for over six months now, and she averages about two bills a day, six or seven days a week without giving Mitch any problems. She tells Mitch of problems with her younger thirteen year old sister, Lucinda, in Salinas. Lucinda is being molested by her alcoholic dad and her brother who is a *hype*. Mitch discusses it with his bottom woman first, before making a decision. Lana feels the same way Mitch does about it so she explains, "It's like the same scenario that Margo went through with their father and brother, and of course you must go to aid Margo with her family problems. That's what pimps do, Mitch. Margo is a down young hoe, whose sole focus is getting it for you, daddy. Daddy, Margo is only sixteen, so she will serve you diligently for many years to come, especially once you show her that you're all the way down for her and hers, like she's all the way down for you."

Mitch leaves Lana, Brea and Eva in Frisco and he is on the freeway to Salinas that next morning. He takes Margo, Niecy and Bonnie Parker to Salinas, so he can not only take care of Margo's business, but the girls can take care of his business while he's there.

Margo's mother, Mable, has been getting beat down by Margo's father for years, so she needs to be out of that situation as well. After they get Mable and Lucinda's personal belongings, Mitch and Margo promise they'll both have everything they need with him and Margo. Mitch puts Mable and Lucinda away at the motel where he and his girls are staying so they'll be safe from the father and brother. Then, Mitch sets about his hoe business. Mitch notices that Lucinda, even though only thirteen, is fine and sexy as hell. "What's up with Lucy?" he asks Margo.

"Lucy has been asking me questions about working like I do, but she's only thirteen, Poppy. She's my kid sister, but I'll let her decide what she wants to do, okay Poppy?"

"That's cool Margo, so we'll just see how it plays out." However, Mitch is thinking, *the situation is going to play out sooner than later because of the way Lucy's eyes light up when she scopes me out along with my threads, ride and jewelry.* She also gets so excited with how sharply dressed Margo and his other two girls he brought with him are, she'll want those things for herself soon.

Margo has been telling Mitch about all the Mexicans that work the farm and fruit fields around the Salinas area, and how much money her, Niecy and Bonnie Parker could make out there. So Mitch decides to check it out the first night, instead of the regular tracks. He finds that what Margo told him is an understatement. Droves of Mexican field workers line up to date his girls. Margo speaks Spanish, so she helps Mitch orchestrate the whole thing. The first night Mitch has only his Rado and a rental car. His plans are to drive Mable and Lucy to Sacramento, get an apartment there for them and his game, and expand his horizons to include Sacramento. There's been a buzz throughout the streets of San Francisco about Sac jumping for hoes.

Mitch has Margo using the front seat of the rental car, Niecy is using the back seat, and Bonnie Parker (being lowest in the pecking order) using a stack of blankets that Margo has a couple of the

Mexicans bring. At first Bonnie wants to turn tricks in Mitch's Rado until he threatens to make her go on the ground without blankets. Margo explains to her poppy, "These wetbacks aren't going to spend over ten to fifteen dollars, maybe twenty on very rare occasions, but they will buy pussy all night long." The girls either do straight blow jobs or *trick fuck* most of the men and, while it makes their job easier, it's still work. Most men with a condom on, drunk or sober can't tell the difference between a wet pussy and a lubed up hand, especially drunk, including Mitch. Mitch chuckles as the field workers go in one door and out the other as he collects their money with his two 45s in his double holster in plain sight. As soon as one man is done, he goes and drinks some more and gets back in line to go again. Mitch's three girls turn back-to-back tricks all night long until daybreak. It's the hardest fast money a working girl will ever have to make.

By the time morning comes those three hoes are so exhausted that they look rode hard and put away wet. Wigs are hanging off their heads every which way, and all three girls are half dressed and not wearing shoes. However, Margo is a Mexican stud, and she tells Mitch she'll drive the other two girls back to the motel, since they are already unconscious in the rental car. "Poppy, when it comes down to it, Mexican women are stronger than other types of women."

Mitch gets the Salinas field worker's game down to an exact science with the help of Margo. He rents a van along with the rental car on Saturday so he won't have to get his Rado dirty from the muddy roads while driving out there. The Mexican field workers usually only last ten to fifteen minutes, and if any take longer than that the hoes make them get back in the line and pay, again. Each broad will turn twenty five to thirty tricks or more a night. That's times three broads over three days, that's some serious *grip,* (cash) of three to four thousand. This will become one of Mitch's watering holes for when he absolutely has to have some cash in a hurry. It will be especially useful in motivating lazy bitches to run hard and fast, like race horses, to make enough money to keep from going back out there. Strolls, bars, hotels or anywhere will be a piece of cake to broads after working this track.

With the weekend behind them, Mitch hits Sacramento with Margo, her mom and sister, Niecy and Bonnie. He drops them all at a motel as he goes to rent an apartment close to one of the tracks in the 4th and S Streets area of the city. Margo gets three motel rooms, one for Lucy and Mable, one for Bonnie and Neicy, and another for her and Mitch. Once Mitch gets the apartment for Margo and her family, he fully furnishes it with all the accessories they need by having Margo use stolen credit cards and cashing stolen checks with fake id. Margo has all the furniture and appliances delivered to a vacant apartment. Then Mitch pays a couple of local cats to move it from there to the actual apartment because he's never going to finish paying for any of it anyway.

Finally, Mitch meets the famous Fillmore Slim. One night at the pool hall, soul food, gambling shack all in one, on the corner of 4th and S Streets, Mitch is parked sitting in his Rado doing lines of blow and kicking it with an old school pimp named L.A. Freddy. Freddy is a tall, dark skin dude, with a blonde streak in his processed hair. Freddy has a brown on beige, 1967, Ham that's parked right behind Mitch's Rado. Fillmore passes by in his gold on gold, 1966, Eldorado Cadillac. Freddy lets the window down and shouts for Fillmore to stop and come over to Mitch's Lac. When Fillmore gets out, Mitch notices that he is about six four, maybe taller, thin, light brown skin, and a knock kneed dude with a baby face like his. Freddy introduces Mitch to Fillmore and they exchange cordialities about cars, clothes, and the game, like players do out of respect. Mitch appreciates that Fillmore, like Freddy, never asks him how old he is or makes any comments or insinuations about Mitch's stature.

Mitch, Freddy and Fillmore decide to go into the pool hall and kick it over dinner. Mitch mostly listens to the two older pimps. Having been around in enough circles to have heard about Fillmore's reputation as a down pimp, he wants to pick up on it all as Fillmore and Freddy kick it.

Sacramento is a small town, much like Seaside, but during this period of *Reaganomics* there are players from all over California and even the rest of the country in Sac. That's because Sac is wide open for hoes getting money. While Frisco has become smoking hot on working girls, Mitch finds the state capital is wide open; go figure. Mitch sends for Lana, Brea and Eva from Frisco and he makes Sac his home base for the time being. However, Sacramento is much too small of a game for Lana and Brea, so they hit the road periodically. From Salt Lake City Utah, Vancouver, BC, Las Vegas, Hawaii, and other places abroad, they work the Rolex Circuit while he stays in Sac with Margo, Niecy, Bonnie and her mom, Eva. Mitch usually gets his money from Lana and Brea over the wire. Sometimes, however, he flies out to kick it with them wherever they are or flies them into Sac to kick it with him. Mitch has come to understand that different hoes run hot on different strolls for one reason or another, but usually because they take some trick off for cash. Different strolls run hot from time to time routinely as cops start sweating the area by taking hoes to jail and harassing them. That's why a crew always needs several little watering holes to get some quick relatively trouble free cash.

Meanwhile, he starts knocking Mexican females, as he learns the psychology of how to deal with them. Having Margo is a big help in his strategy as she teaches him. "Poppy, we Mexican women are idealistic in our approach to our men, romance and relationships. We believe once we give ourselves to a man its forever with that man in our hearts and minds, because we are extremely loyal. Mexican women are usually quite shy and humble at first, except for me, but I'm a freak." She laughs at her own comment. "We love to tease and tempt men and we are suckers for smooth talk from a guy we like, because it pulls on our heart strings." In a short period of time at the end of 1967, Mitch has a stable of five Latinas including Margo. Mitch loses Bonnie Parker to another pimp, and in this case, like daughter like mother, as Eva quits the game again, and goes back to Frisco.

Mitch reasons that she is an old bitch anyway, and has way too much down time from female problems and mood swings. Mitch is beginning to understand why Lana told him, "Stick with young broads because older broads have too many opinions and require too much maintenance." Mitch has the other four Mexican girls living and working out of the same apartment. He notes that it is the best set of stabled broads in one place that he has had in his brief tenure. They range in ages from fifteen to seventeen with Margo being the only seventeen year old and his acting bottom, with Lana and Brea roving. Mitch thinks of just how much Margo is like Lana, and justifiably so, Lana did raise her. As their numbers grow, Margo moves from the motel suite with Mitch into the apartment with the girls. She tells Mitch that she needs to be among them to stay up on top of their minds and to monitor what they're doing with their hands.

Niecy is happy to live with Mitch by herself, except when Mitch is entertaining one or more of the others. One early morning after all the girls are in, Mitch is laid up with Neicy when Margo calls. "Poppy, we have to do something about Lucy. Momma is telling me that she is running around half naked with all kinds of old men like a little tramp. Will you talk to her with me?"

"Yea Margo, go pick Lucy up and bring her by here before you go to work tonight and we'll handle that. Right now, y'all crash and get some sleep so you're fresh for tonight." Mitch is thinking, *of course I'll talk to Lucy because if she's going to run around screwing everybody in town anyway, I might just as well get paid for it. This is the 'sooner than later' I had contemplated it would be with Lucy.*

He sends Niecy to work in a cab, so he can wait for Lucy and Margo. Mitch just lost his first mother and daughter members of his stable, and now he is about to have his first blood sisters in his stable. Lucy walks in the door first, wearing near nothing. It is the age of the braless, no panties, free love, reveal more flesh generation, and Mitch loves it because most young broads are running around looking slutty and whorish.

Lucy is smiling flirtatiously with Mitch as usual, and sits on the side of the bed facing him, legs wide open with her right leg propped up on top of her left, while licking her lips seductively. Mitch is thinking how cute and tiny she is, as most Latinas are. Chronologically, she may be only thirteen; however, nothing else about this little creature sitting in front of him is that age. "So little one, I've been hearing about your escapades. What's really going on with you, 'Little Lulu'?"

Lulu laughs appreciatively about Mitch nicknaming her and asks, "What did you call me?" I like that. She's a naughty little cartoon girl, Mitchell. You know what Mitch? I want to work for you, but my mom and sister are tripping the fuck out on me about it. What do you think about it?"

Margo walks over to Lulu and points in her face. "Lucy, watch your mouth in front of my poppy, okay? And you can't do what I do you little bitch."

"Fuck you bitch, I can say and do whatever the fuck I want."

Margo slaps Lulu's face. "You little bitch; you can't talk to me like that."

Mitch pulls the two Latina sisters apart and sends Margo to get dinner for the three of them from the bowling alley and restaurant next door. "Lulu, you shouldn't talk to your family like that, baby."

"I know Mitchell, but Margo and my mom make me so mad, acting like I'm a baby and shit. My mom knows what Margo does with you and I want to do it with you too," as she smiles at Mitch, deviously insinuating.

Mitch is already down with Lulu joining his stable and he puts Margo down with it too. After all, Lulu is already hoeing anyway. The three of them eat dinner together. "Margo, Lulu is going to give or sell her pussy as she sees fit regardless of what you or Mable may say, do, or think. So she might as well be with someone that is down for her best interest, like me and you. Here's the deal, explain it to your mama. Just tell her that Lulu is with family. Plus, it'll increase Mable's allotment each month too," he says and Margo and Lulu laugh along with him.

All of a sudden Margo stops laughing and gets serious. "Why is it that my kid sis and all these different other bitches get pet names and I'm still just Margo, Poppy?"

"Because your name fits you just like you fit with me—perfectly." Margo smiles her approval of that answer, as they finish diner while giving Lulu a crash course in the proper ways of doing what she's already doing anyway. Lulu has already been in the hunt, so now it's just a matter of honing her skills. Who better to do that with Lulu, but him through Margo? Plus, Mitch remembers learning that women are born with the skills to play men, while men have to learn how to play women. That's just the way nature planned it.

One night Mitch is gathered at the joint on the corner of 4th and S Streets with a few other pimps, including Fillmore Slim, Diamond Guyman out of Sac, Mel Salsbury out of Frisco, Clayton out of Seattle, and, another pimp named Tommy Benton, out of Vancouver, B.C. Tall, six five, and light skin, Tommy has a stable of eleven, consisting of a mixture of white and Mexican girls. Tommy, Mitch and Fillmore are shooting pool at one table, and Clayton, Mel and Diamond are playing at the other. They're all drinking, doing lines of blow, high siding and trash talking about the game. Just outside the door is one of the strolls and all six of Mitch's Mexican game are scattered throughout that track, including his latest addition, Lulu, who is now getting at it without Margo's aid. Margo and Lulu communicate in Spanish when plotting on tricks and getting at other pimp's Mexican game for Mitch.

Margo comes through the door of the pool hall that leads directly to the sidewalk, and gets Mitch's attention. "Excuse me, may I speak to you a minute please."

"What bitch, you got a pimp's money?" It is common knowledge in the game that pimps love to show off for other pimps by displaying their prowess and control over their girls, and the girls love it too.

"I'm getting at it Poppy. *Uno minuto por favor?*"

"Alright baby, but this had better be good." Still holding the pool cue in his hand, Mitch sticks his head halfway out the door, "What's up baby?"

"I need you to come down the street here a minute," she says as she points.

Mitch places his pool cue against the wall and says, "Fillmore, shoot by me, man. I got hoe business." He follows Margo down about three or four houses, and there *she* is standing next to a tree.

"Poppy, this is Debra. Debra, this is my man, Pretty Mitch."

Mitch rubs Debra's pretty face with the back of his hand, and he uses what little Spanish he has learned, "*Hola bonita chica?*" Mitch looks from Margo's features to Debra's and he thinks, next to Margo, Debra has to be the prettiest Mexican broad he'd ever seen. He also notices that Debra has that long thick jet black hair classically noted with Latinas. She is a petite four eleven, slender, sixteen years old with a lighter complexion than the average Mexican; obviously mixed with some Anglo Saxon blood. She has on a black mini skirt about the size of a large handkerchief on this little girl, with black patent leather buccaneer boots, huge tits with no bra, and a sheer black see through blouse that is barely enough to keep her breasts in, tied above her navel.

Her eyes are like half open slits, as if she is about to climax or is slightly high. Mitch will come to understand that's just the way her eyes are naturally. Her lips are slightly apart displaying her pretty white teeth. Add to all that her accent and she has Mitch falling in greed and lust all at the same time. Margo interrupts Mitch's thoughts. "Mitch, Debra is with Tommy."

"Tommy who? You mean Tommy Benton? He's right inside."

"Yeah Poppy, that's why I couldn't tell you about it in there."

Then Debra tells Mitch, "Umm…. I want come home, you."

"Whoa, wait a minute, we can't talk here. Margo, take her to the apartment in the Bonneville, and I'll meet you there in a hot minute." Excited at the prospect of knocking a new broad, Mitch tells Margo to hurry before Tommy comes out.

Once inside the apartment, Debra tells Margo something in Spanish. Mitch doesn't get what it is, but he does notice it ends with, *dinero,* and if he's learned nothing else in Spanish, he knows, money. Debra takes one hundred and fifty dollars out of her boot and hands it to Mitch. "I no like Tommy and no have more money, he beat me. Can I stay here, you?"

"Little mama you don't have to worry about anybody beating you ever again," and Mitch checks his 45 and heads back to the spot to serve Tommy notice. It's not that Mitch expects any trouble; it's just that Tommy is a big guy. He also has somewhat of a reputation for beating at least a couple of niggas down that served him on a couple of occasions.

As Mitch climbs into his Rado, he reflects that he and Tommy are cool, but better safe than sorry. Also, he remembers that the element of surprise always has to be in his favor. When Mitch walks into the pool hall, he positions himself by range and distance to reach his piece, by approximately how long it'll take Tommy to close the distance between them. There are several players still in the pool hall, so Mitch decides to serve Tommy in front of everyone to appeal to his professional pride. Mitch really likes it in Sacramento, and reasons that he doesn't want to be forced to have to kill this big ole nigga if at all possible.

Mitch orders a round of drinks for everyone in the pool hall, on him. When the waitress brings the drinks Mitch hands her a twenty dollar bill, tells her to keep the change, and holds his glass up in the air. "These drinks are by way of Tommy's ex bitch, he toasts."

Tommy is so surprised that he almost chokes. "What the fuck are you talking about, Mitch?"

There is silence for what seems like an eternity, then Mitch responds, "I'm talking about that fine ass little Mexican bitch, Debra. She chose me not half an hour ago." Mitch looks around at the other men and then back to lock eyes with Tommy. Mitch notices that Tommy's posture is relaxed but still there is that look of indecisiveness in his eyes.

The other players start clowning, heckling, and rubbing it in. Every pimp knows how it feels to be served. It's embarrassing and sometimes pisses one off, but it's all part of the game. The few times it has happened to Mitch, he recalls he didn't like it either, but pimping isn't personal.

Mitch's alter ego reminds him, we *have no family or back up out here, all the way across the country from our humble beginnings. Being the new kid on the block and considerably smaller than all the men present, this will perhaps be our defining moment in Sacramento.* It seems to Mitch that everywhere he goes he has to prove himself in some form or fashion.

Only a brief moment has passed since Mitch gave Tommy notice, but it seems much longer, to Mitch. Finally, Tommy finishes his drink, and responds, "Nigga a bitch can't choose without money. I just broke that bitch for sixty bucks less than two hours ago."

"Well, I guess what you're telling me Tommy, is I got at least a two hundred dollar a night bitch in Debra, because I just broke her for a buck fifty a little over thirty minutes ago. Now Tommy I'm coming at you out of respect, man, and I hope a bitch isn't going to come between me, you, and this pimping."

As Tommy looks around at the other major players on the scene, no matter what he feels or thinks right about now, if he's a down nigga in this game he has to fad what just went down with style and grace. "Alright Mitch, since you brought it correct and with respect, let's have another drink at the bar, so I can tell you what I know about that bitch, and make arrangements for you to get her things." Tommy and Mitch go to the bar and go through the exchange of information. Afterwards, "Mitch you can have what little stuff Debra has." Mitch follows him to a motel room and gets her stuff without incident.

As Mitch is back in his Lac about to leave, he asks Tommy, "Then, we're all straight?"

"Well, that bitch did owe me two hundred that you should cover, Mitch."

Mitch laughs, "Nigga please, don't go there," as he sticks his left hand out the window with the palms face up for five from Tommy.

Tommy laughs and slaps Mitch's hand. "Had to take a shot my brother, but it's all good. We're straight." As Mitch watches Tommy walking to his 1967 green on green Ham, he takes the 45 from between his legs, lets up his window, and drives off thinking, *Tommy bears watching.*

Chapter XIII

Experiments with Different Drugs

Mitch is beginning to have negative side effects when he smokes weed. It makes him too paranoid and uneasy, so he stops smoking it altogether. Then the dreams and nightmares become more frequent again, so he starts snorting more coke. To keep from being so jittery and paranoid from doing the coke, he begins drinking excessively. It's like a 'catch twenty two.' He just can't seem to find that perfect high that weed once gave him. He remembers an episode he went through on the plane leaving Vietnam. He had three quick shots of straight whiskey, as he felt safe for the first time in four months. He dozed off, but woke up when his body jerked from a nightmare in which he was being closed into a small space and stabbed to death. It was so real that he woke up trembling and sweating as he grabbed his chest and grunted that same sound that he had heard too many times from dying or wounded men.

As he stared out the window only half seeing the sky, he remembered the eyes of a particular VC he'd killed up close and personal, and that horrible last look in his eyes. However, in his dream, that look was in his own eyes and he felt the pain of the thrust of the bayonet in his own chest. That VC had to be about his own age, probably had a family, loved ones, and a purpose for being there, just like him. Only he was the one going home to his family while that VC and many other VCs and GIs would never go home to theirs.

Mitch remembers observing the coffins of fallen comrades lined up at the airport in Saigon ready to be shipped back to the world. He remembers thinking, *who or what had decided which of us would live or die, and why, and what had it all meant?* The stewardess had brought Mitch a glass of water, which he gulped down and then ordered another straight shot of whiskey. He found some peace in taking out his 45 and laying it concealed between his legs, under his small carryon bag, but the dream was still disturbing to him. He remembers his alter ego having asked him, *why are we having this kind of dream now, and not back in the bush?*

At Oakland Terminal he had asked to see a doctor for sleeping pills to ward off the demons of his dreams, or what was actually nightmares. After a series of tests, the shrink had diagnosed Mitch as claustrophobic and having post combat stress related nightmares. "It's all part of the trauma associated with combat son. It will lessen over time, and it will eventually pass altogether. It is customary that some GIs have such dreams that may not begin until they get to a place where they feel physically and psychologically safe, which is why you had your first dream of that nature on the plane while safely heading home. Otherwise, it's over, so get over it, because it's all part of war."

Mitch remembers thinking, *but how do I just get over it?* Yet, he hadn't voiced those sentiments. The shrink had prescribed pills for the nightmares and to help Mitch sleep. They had worked for a time, but lately it's a different story. Not only have the nightmares returned but daytime delusions are becoming more and more common.

Rolling with a pimp partner, Mel Salsbury, Mitch does lines of crystal one evening. After he gets dropped back off at his car, Mitch becomes so paranoid and jittery that he shoots out the window of his own Lac thinking he sees a threatening shadowy figure. There will be many different incidents involving drugs over the years for him. It seems that sometimes Mitch just can't figure out what's going on with him. He feels like there is more of something, someplace or someone missing from his life. He has some of the most drop dead gorgeous females on the planet who quibble with each other just to be in his presence. He has grown in the game to a point that when he is out alone in public now, people know who and what he is without his girls being visible. When a bunch of his girls are out with him, he receives looks of love and hate, admiration and aversion, but he knows deep down inside of everyone with those looks they wish they could do what he does.

Yet, still there is something missing inside him. He is free and lives outside of it all. His attire is always expensive, prime time, unique to him and far beyond proper. No one tells him what to do or not do. He fancies himself a prince among thieves as he reflects on what Tony Goshay told him, "Pimps are the chosen ones because among all the different types of hustlers, 'pimps are the crème del la crème'." Still, there are those times when he doesn't feel like he's really about what it is that he's being about. It makes no sense to him to feel this way, so he tells no one about it. Even if he did want to discuss it with someone, who would that be? *I have an image to uphold,* he reasons.

He tries different stimulants, barbiturates and sedatives like red devils, yellow jackets and tuinals. He finds that they all work, but make him too irritable, rambunctious and violent. He laughs about that as his alter ego expounds, *we're all of those things without anything in our system.* When he takes any combination of these pills and adds booze, he feels like all of that and six feet eleven on steroids. So he takes them only sparingly.

About a month after knocking Debra, Mitch is on full with red devils, coke and booze when he runs into Tommy at a bar down by the greyhound bus terminal. Tommy offers to buy Mitch a drink and he accepts. While they're drinking and kicking it, Tommy asks Mitch if he's ever been hunting. Mitch laughs loudly, "Yeah, I hunted for four straight months once."

"Really, Mitch, what kind of game were you hunting?"

Mitch is really cracking up now. "I hunted the biggest game there is, man, in the bush of Southeast Asia."

They both share that laugh, as Tommy inquires, "Mitch, I can't even imagine being in all that shit, man. What was it like?"

"You know what, Tommy I'm really not looking to go into all of that, man. Just know that there was nothing glamorous about it, unlike the old war movies I once watched as a kid."

"I can dig it Mitch, so why don't you go pheasant hunting with me tomorrow morning?"

"Nigga, I don't hunt birds, I hunt niggas that get out of line with me." They both really laugh to that. Mitch remembers that he has just purchased a brand new stolen pistol, a 38 snub nose, so he agrees to tag along to do some target practice. It's common knowledge that Tommy is an outdoorsman of sorts. Mitch has heard several players talk about going hunting or fishing with Tommy, so he makes nothing more of it than a friendly invitation.

The next morning Mitch has on a set of his old military fatigues, and a short leather jacket because it is a brisk winter morning around Sacramento. They stop at a gun shop where Tommy picks up shotgun rounds and Mitch picks up a box of rounds for his new 38 and they're on their way. When they get to the location to hunt pheasants, they each do a couple of lines of blow and down a quick shot of Remy Martin Cognac. Tommy is parked on a long ridge road that has a ravine on either side. The side Mitch is on has a lake about fifty yards from the ridge. On the other side, the ravine is laced with thick bushes. Tommy is on that side stalking pheasants.

Mitch is firing off rounds at a dead pheasant lying next to a piece of a dead tree sticking up out of the water. After going through a half box of rounds, Mitch reloads, puts the safety on his 38, and places it in the shoulder holster he purchased with it. He goes back up on the ridge closer to the side that Tommy is on to check Tommy's progress with the hunt. It has taken Mitch about an hour and a half of carefully aiming and firing to become accustomed to the handling of his new weapon. As Mitch is looking down into the brush of the ravine where Tommy is, he spots Tommy stalking a pheasant's location. Just then, a pheasant flies up from Tommy's right and continues across in front of him to his left. Tommy fires up at the pheasant, which now just happens to be directly between him and Mitch.

Almost instantly, Mitch experiences a rush that feels like a gust of wind with sharp darts in it. Then he realizes that what he's feeling is shotgun pellets striking his face, neck, hands, legs and fingers. The impact of the blast isn't enough to knock Mitch off of his feet, but the shock of being shot causes him to fall backwards hard. He instinctively grabs his 38, takes the safety off, and lays there trying to get his focus with the gun at his side. Mitch is in shock and is dazed from hitting his head hard against the ground. When Mitch sees Tommy running up the hill out of the ravine with the shotgun up across his body in a position of port arms, Mitch's alter ego tells him, *Tommy shot us intentionally, and is coming to finish us off.*

For an ever so brief moment, Mitch's mind is running on pure adrenaline and combat training, as if he is back in the bush. With Mitch's head spinning, it is hard for him to focus enough to get a clear view of Tommy. Mitch's gauge of Tommy's range of distance is also distorted, so he shakes his head from side to side and rubs his eyes with his left hand to try and clear his vision. Then he sits up, resting on his left elbow while still lying down. When the blurry image of Tommy is as close as Mitch dare allow, he quickly raises the weapon, aims, and fires off three quick rounds in the direction of the center mass of the blurry image, as best he can make it out, pop...pop...pop.

One round goes clean through Tommy's forearm and out the other side without hitting his body. The metal of the rifle deflected it. Another round goes into that same forearm, hitting the metal of the shotgun, and stays inside his arm just under the skin closest to his body. The third apparently goes into space.

As Mitch's vision clears he sees the shotgun knocked out of Tommy's hands, and he hears him scream out in obvious pain. Mitch sits further up on his left elbow, so he can get a good shot at Tommy, when he sees Tommy bent over holding his right arm. "Mitch, what the fuck, nigga? You shot me."

While still aiming the pistol at Tommy, Mitch shouts back, "Nigga, you shot me! What the fuck is wrong with you?" Tommy slowly stands up relatively straight, so Mitch gets to his feet and cautiously walks over to Tommy. "Where you hit, man? Let me see," says Mitch as he grabs the taller man's arm to access the damage. As Mitch turns Tommy's right arm over with his left hand, he still has the 38 at the ready in his right hand. Tommy grimaces and groans in pain as Mitch points and tells him, "See, this one went straight through, and this other one is right under the skin here. They're just flesh wounds, I think."

As Tommy starts to snarl at Mitch, he sees small traces of blood running down Mitch's face and neck from the shotgun pellets. "Mitch, I didn't know I shot you, man."

"Nah nigga, I was just laying there sun bathing. Nigga, of course you fucking shot me," he shouts as he wipes blood from his face and neck. The two men's eyes meet and they both realize that, with all the events that led them up to this very moment, it's easy for either of them to assume what they had. Mitch helps Tommy into the car and they drive to the town doctor that caters to hustlers.

"How bad are you hit, Mitch?"

"Man, I'm kind of numb in a few places, but I don't think it's bad, because everything seems to work, but it still burns like a son of a bitch."

As Tommy cradles his right arm with his left hand and hisses through clenched teeth out of pain, "Mitch, I had eleven hoes when you knocked me for that Debra bitch, man, which means I still got ten, so what in the fuck makes you think I'd shoot you over one bitch?"

"Tommy, I'm laying on the ground shot and dazed, and all I see is the nigga that shot me running up on me with the gun he just shot me with at port arms. Now you do the math." As Mitch drives, he holds lines of coke under Tommy's nose and makes him drink a couple of big swigs of cognac as they are en route to the black doctor's office.

The doctor tells Tommy, "It's good this fellow is a lousy shot, because a bit lower or higher, and it probably would have done some serious damage."

Mitch laughs inappropriately and notices the doctor, his nurse, and Tommy looking at him strangely for laughing. Mitch cleans up how his laughter must look to them. "I was just thinking how lucky we both are, Doc."

However, Mitch's alter ego reasons, *we are about as accurate as they come with firearms. Had it not been for using a new pistol and our vision being screwed up when we discharged those three rounds, all three would have been in exactly the right place. And Tommy wouldn't need a doctor.*

The nurse removes buckshot from Mitch's face, neck, hands, and clothing while he's lying on the next table over from Tommy's. She tells Mitch, "It's a good thing that he was so far away when the blast hit you or it might have done more damage to you, as well. The leather jacket and heavy military fatigues absorbed most of the pellets that hit your body and you're lucky not to have lost an eye."

Tommy and Mitch agree that the whole thing has been one big unfortunate accident. "Mitch, under the circumstances, if I were in your position, I would have shot me too."

"Yeah, it was an unfortunate accident Tommy, and I'm just glad neither of us got seriously injured, unless that damn pheasant was in on it with you, nigga." The doctor, Tommy, the nurse and Mitch all laugh.

Of course that's not the way the grapevine gets it. What circulates around is "Tommy Benton and Pretty Mitch had a shoot out over some Mexican bitch." Still, Mitch and Tommy move on from that to become good partners. They will kick it in a couple of different cities throughout the U.S. and Canada over the years to come. During this time, Mitch also hooks up with a superb mouthpiece named Ronald Thurman, who will serve him and his different crews in different cities, states, and capacities throughout the sixties. Ron is fascinated with pimps and hustlers and is a down attorney.

One weekend Mitch and Clayton ride up to the Marysville and Yuba City area just outside Sacramento. Clayton is a tall, dark skin pimp that has three white girls working for him. Clayton drives a red, 1967, Eldorado. Mitch has been kicking the game with him in Sac, on different occasions. Mitch has Clay and his three hoes follow him en route to Marysville because another partner of theirs named Bo Pete, also has three white hoes operating in the Marysville area. Bo Pete is a medium height and build, old school player out of Texas that drives a 1967, black on black Ham, has been working Marysville for about two months, and ranting and raving about the money he's making.

Mitch has Lana and Brea with him so, between the three pimps, there are eight white hoes. Bo Pete has an apartment in the neighboring town of Yuba City. It's after-hours, so Pete's hoes are off work just as Mitch and Clay's are. They're kicking it at Pete's apartment after surveying Marysville and finding it a one horse town that's too small for their big city working girls or them. The three of them are high siding about the kind of money their girls made that night just before Mitch and Clay hit the road heading back to Sac. Pete asks Mitch to leave him some blow, but all Mitch has left is half an ounce stashed in the trunk of his Rado. Mitch and Pete go downstairs to get the blow and come back upstairs to take out a bit for Pete; blow and go.

The eight broads are all in the living room and kitchen drinking and kicking it with each other while waiting on the three men so they can do a couple of lines too. It's about three to four am, they got jazz playing low and mellow, and the three men are feelings real cool up in that joint doing lines and drinking. Mitch, Pete and Clay are in the bedroom with the door closed kicking it as Mitch breaks down the package in portions to leave some with Pete, give the girls a couple of lines each and enough for the three of them to do.

The three men hear a loud crash coming from the living room. Clay snatches the bedroom door open, and there's a flood of cops coming into the apartment. Before they can adjust, the cops are in the bedroom, guns drawn, yelling, "All you niggers get face down on the floor with your arms behind your head and legs spread."

Pete asks, "What's the problem officer, this is my apartment."

One cop hits him in the gut with the butt of a shotgun, and yells, "Boy, one more word and I'll blow your black ass head off."

Mitch and his two partners look at each other realizing what time this is, and lay perfectly still and silent. Being the smallest guy has its advantages in situations like this, because cops always go after the bigger sized or better armed suspect to neutralize the greater threat first. Finally the police get the broads in cars, and Mitch and his buds in different cars en route to jail.

At the jail one of the two cops named Malloy, is playing the good cop and asking most of the questions. The other, named Bozeman, is playing the hard, bad cop. Mitch, Pete and Clay still have their hands cuffed behind their backs in the little room. Malloy is a big burly Caucasian guy of about six feet tall with reddish hair. Bozeman is a taller blonde cop with a heavy southern accent and just as stout of build. Malloy tells Mitch and his buds, "We got the drugs and the pistols, all of your personal property, cars, jewelry, belts, shoes, and money, which is about three grand between y'all."

Then Bozeman adds, "Where y'all get this here kind of cash from? You ole boys think y'all some kinda hot shit, don't cha? Y'all got that pressed hare, them big cars, all dis money, and a gang a white women. Boy I believe y'all some of them there pimps, ain't cha? Who are them gals y'all got wit cha, and how old y'all figures they is?"

Between Mitch, Pete and Clayton, Pete is the oldest, most experienced, and the only one of them who actually has an address in the area, so Pete responds, "Officer, one of those women is my wife and the others are family and friends of hers from out of town visiting us at our apartment."

"Yeah, right. Of course they are," Malloy comments.

As the two policemen are about to leave the room, Mitch asks, "Can you officers take these cuffs off, please?"

Malloy takes out his key and starts taking the cuffs off Mitch and his two partners, as Bozeman asks Malloy, "Do ya think it's safe to let these here boys outta them cuffs? I mean, they wuz armed with firearms which insinuates, given the opportunity, they wuz probably prepared to use em." Then Bozeman nods his approval for Malloy to continue taking the cuffs off.

The police still have the girls down the hall separated from the three men, and Mitch can barely hear their voices as they are also being questioned. He tells Pete and Clayton, "If either one of us hasn't done a thorough job of pimping on even one of those broad's minds, we're going to be in more serious trouble than we already are. I'm talking statutory rape, pimping and pandering, contributing to the delinquency of a minor, and who knows what the fuck else?"

Mitch is relieved when, after about two hours of sitting in that little room, the cops finally bring a phone in and let him make a call. So the three of them figure none of the broads have cracked. Mitch feels more confident that they will get out of this alive now, so he starts high siding. "It will take more than a small hick town cop to break my well trained thoroughbreds, but I had my fingers crossed, because only two of them are mine."

Not to be outdone, Clay responds, "Nigga, you see we're getting our phone call don't you, so it must be more than just you that's put down some real pimping. And I got three of them that they got out there." They all laugh nervously out of relief.

Mitch calls his lawyer, Ron, wakes him up, and frantically tells him where, who, how many and what's going on with the eleven of them. "Holy shit, Mitch, I need to hurry and spring you guys."

Pete tells Mitch, "Man, tell the lawyer to please hurry because these rednecks are acting real crazy."

They are only given their car keys, cars, belts, shoes, and ids from their property being held. Jewelry and cash are kept for evidence, so they have no money to give the bondsman or the attorney. Once they are bailed out and standing out by their cars, Mitch asks Ron, "How much is this going to cost us, man?"

Ron answers, "The bonds are five grand for each of you three guys and two grand for each of the girls, so, for the bondsman alone, the cost is thirty one hundred, plus a two hundred and fifty dollar service charge. We're talking a total of thirty three hundred and fifty dollars for him." Then, after Ron talks with the cops inside, he pulls Mitch to the side. "With all of what you guys got going on here, I figure seven g's and none of this ever happened and I'll only take a thousand."

Mitch is shocked at the figure Ron gives him. "Damn Ron, that's eleven thousand three fifty, what about the three g's they already kept, man? That's a lot of bread, man."

"Mitch, the money they kept counts toward the seven thousand so all you need for them is another four thousand. What price do you put on your asses?" The question puts it all more in perspective for Mitch and the other two men. Mitch is just happy to still be alive and in one piece. He reflects that he grew up in the deep south in times when to be seen intimately talking to or touching a white woman would have meant, at best, a near death experience, so he accepts the losses.

Mitch gladly tells Ron, "I'll get the money to you once we're back in Sac."

"I'm not worried about it, Mitch." As they're all getting in their cars to leave, Ron waves at Mitch and says, "Do us all a favor from here on out, Mitch, and stay out of these small towns with your white women."

"Ron, I will. I swear."

Clay and Pete give Mitch their share of the bill and Mitch pays the debt. There will be several other incidents when Ron will come to Mitch or his people's rescue over the years, in different cities and states. However, between drugs and being constantly on the move, like so many other things, Mitch's accumulated debts with Ron will eventually slip through the cracks.

After moving his base of operations back to the city by the bay with only Margo and Lulu left of his Latinas, Mitch's stable continuously changes its face beyond Lana, Brea, Niecy, Margo and Lulu, as hoes come and go. Other than Lulu, the other four are maturing in their respective position in the pecking order. Lulu is wild and prone towards severe mood swings like Brea, but she's not near as mature as Brea. Plus, Mitch can't possibly spend as much time with Lulu as maintaining her will come to require. Mitch has Niecy staying at the Booker T. Washington Hotel on O'Farrell. Margo and Lulu have a hotel suite in the Tenderloin and Lana and Brea are in another suite in the Tenderloin. All the while, Mitch and Lana look for a house for them to buy.

Back in Frisco only a few weeks, and hooked back up with Fast, Mitch is in the process of knocking a petite, light skin, little seventeen year old sister named Christine. She has been trying to choose Mitch since he got back. Christine works for a gangster pimp named Frank Jennings, who is notorious for just taking nigga's hoes and bulldogging different hustlers around town out of their drugs or whatever else he may want.

In fact, Mitch has avoided officially knocking Christine for so long because he doesn't want to tangle with Frank. Frank is a six four, large, muscular, menacing looking, very dark skin dude with a long razor scar on his right forearm and an appropriate resume for his overbearing temperament. When Mitch first gets money from Christine, she tells him that she is afraid of what Frank might do if she outright chooses Mitch, but she still really likes Mitch's style, and will kick him down whenever she can. Mitch goes to Fast for advice about the situation. Fast informs Mitch, "Pretty, you will have to kill Frank to have Christine or any other bitch of his, but if you don't serve him and word gets out that you're charging one of Frank's hoes you will still have to kill that nigga." Then, Fast laughs with that deep voice of his.

"So Fast, what you're telling me is I'm damned if I do and I'm damned if I don't?"

"That's pretty much it, Mitch. However, on a more positive note, you really have no choice, because if you back away from this, you might just as well back away from the game at the level you're representing it now. You're a pimp and pimps have hoes, anybody's hoes that choose them. If you can't protect her or yourself, then you leave yourself open for all manner of challenges from all different directions. Everybody that knows you respects your game expertise, Pretty, but it's like we kicked it when we first met, man. Niggas like Frank don't adhere to the rules and regulations of the game if and when he can get around them. Justifiably so, because if a nigga isn't down enough to fad adversity in handling his business, then someone else will take it over and handle it for him."

"Then Fast, I'll just leave the Chris bitch alone."

"It's too late Mitch. You're in it now, so you might as well be in it to win it. Also, remember what I've taught you, and never fight the same fight twice."

Mitch is thinking that all sounds well and good, but he doesn't want any part of Frank. However, Mitch's alter ego suggests, *if we are to think of our self as a down pimp and player in this game, then we must do whatever we must do to represent that, pimp or die.*

Mitch is accompanied by Fast and Digger on the night that he serves Frank the news about Chris. Fast has told Mitch to expect anything from a nigga, like Frank, so Mitch wears both 45s. Fast and Digger have Mitch's back as Frank usually has one or two dudes rolling with him. It all goes down according to *Hoyle*. However, Fast and Mitch both know it all goes that way because of Fast's reputation and presence.

A few nights later, with Mitch and Fast riding in the back of Fast's Ham, Digger pulls up in front of an after-hours run by a big time gangster dealer named Wimpy. Fast takes out a balloon of heroin and a capsule of cocaine and passes Mitch the coke so he can take a blow. Fast proceeds to mix the rest of the coke and heroin together, and starts doing lines of the mixture. Mitch watches in curiosity as he always does when his older pimp friend and mentor does this. Having always been curious as to what it is about heroin that seems to enslave its users, Mitch decides that this night he will finally find out for himself. "Fast, let me get with some of that shit, man."

"Pretty, this is the most powerful thing you'll ever encounter in your life, and if your shit isn't together up here," Fast points to Mitch's head with his finger, "you'll get stuck fucking with this shit, man." Mitch is insistent, so Fast reluctantly passes the mixture to him. When Mitch tries to pull the hundred dollar bill that the mixture is on from Fast's hand, Fast holds onto it until Mitch makes eye contact with him again.

Fast cautions his young protégé one last time. Mitch laughs and tells him, "Fast, you're worse than my bottom bitch, nigga. I can handle this shit and anything else that I need to, because I'm Pretty Pimping Mitch. You better recognize nigga." Mitch and Fast slap five with each other's free hands and laugh, as Fast releases his grasp on the dope covered bill.

For the very first time Mitch snorts heroin, acting as if it's just coke. Fast grabs Mitch's arm. "Hey man, easy with this shit partner, let the first couple of lines take effect before your little greedy ass dives right back in. This is my private cut, Mitch. This shit will knock you on your ass." No sooner than Fast says it, and after just two quick lines, the effects seem almost magical and like nothing Mitch has ever felt before.

He gets a warm sensation in his gut as the heroin makes its way through his blood stream. It causes his flesh to heat up to a point of itching, and he bolts from the car throwing up. After that it puts him in a state that's like a dream world. He nods and scratches and his mind races back to when he'd watched his partners in Nam using this stuff. Mitch finds that heroin makes him feel unbelievably mellow and free of any and all concerns. Mitch is nodding and scratching, first his face and neck, then his arms and legs, and then everywhere. His voice becomes scratchy and hoarse, as he goes from nodding out to speeding up in a split second. As the three of them head up the stairs of the after-hours joint, Mitch feels a sense of freedom and a self assured composure and confidence in a way unknown to him before now.

Mitch and Fast are involved in the game as Digger watches them. In walks Frank with one of his boys named George, a big, dark skin cat about Frank's height, but thinner. Mitch becomes instantly on guard, because he knows who, and exactly what he's dealing with in Frank. Frank starts talking loud like he always does, as he comments, "Well Wimpy, I see you got little pimps and big pimps up in this joint tonight, huh," as he glances from the eyes of Fast to those of Mitch.

Mitch ignores Frank's comment and looks into Fast's eyes as Fast gives Mitch that look that Mitch has come to understand means something is about to go down. Fast turns and looks over his shoulder at Digger in a manner that insinuates the same to him. Mitch begins gauging the distance and time factors for Frank to get to him, versus Mitch getting to his 45 and busting on Frank. Mitch slides another foot further down the table away from Frank, as Frank throws 4, 5, 6 and gets the dice. After a couple of rounds of dealing the dice, Frank intentionally doesn't pay Mitch, so Mitch reminds him. "Frank, you didn't pay me for that roll, man."

"Yea Mitch, I paid you." There are two men between Frank and Mitch, and they both stand up from their hunched position over the table because they sense tension in the air.

Mitch notices that Digger has positioned himself at the side of Frank's man, George. Once Fast sees that, he adds, "Frank, I was watching, man, and you really did forget to pay Mitch, man." Being full of dog food, Mitch feels no particular dryness in his mouth, nervousness, or sweaty palms, only resolute calmness as he focuses.

All of a sudden Frank stands up straight, makes eye contact with George, then looks in Mitch's eyes as Mitch stares back into his. Frank obviously feels that Fast is the greater threat between him and Mitch, so Frank's eyes only glance at Mitch, before quickly shifting to Fast. Then, while staring at Fast, Frank snarls, "What Larry, is this little nigga your bitch now, or....?" The roar of Mitch's 45 in the room cuts off Frank's last words, boo yow... boo yow... boo yow... as the other men around the table bolt back out of the way and some run out of the room. In a split second Mitch puts three in Frank's torso. The first strikes Frank in the left side of his upper chest in the area of his heart. Mitch hears the grunts as the impact of the first round causes Franks body to turn facing him. The next two go directly into his frontal chest cavity also in the area of his heart. Frank's body slams into the back wall. Then Mitch watches as Frank's lifeless body slides to the floor making a thud sound like a huge sack of potatoes dropping.

At this range, Mitch is more than confident that the first shot probably killed Frank, but with the other two, Mitch knows for sure Frank is dead. Mitch has momentarily been oblivious to anything else around him. As Mitch's mind focuses back on the rest of the people in the room, he notices that Fast is drawn down, and Digger is lowering his 357 magnum from the side of George's head, while holding George's gun in his left hand.

Fast says, "Everybody just stay real calm and easy baby; just a little misunderstanding here."

Wimpy is irate. "Nigga, what's wrong with you niggas, doing that shit up in my motherfucking joint and costing me money?"

Fast responds, "Wimpy, that wasn't on *Big* Mitch. That was on that piece of shit nigga there," as he points his 357 at the body of Frank. Fast spreads ten one hundred dollar bills on the table and tells Wimpy, "If the damage is more than that, man, it's on me, and you know where to find me, Wimpy."

Wimpy scoops up the money and has a couple of his boys take care of the body. "Larry, what about my pool table, carpet, and …?"

Fast cuts Wimpy off, "Like I just said Wimpy, give me the bill, man." As Mitch, Fast and Digger leave, Fast compliments Mitch on moving swiftly and decisively. "It had to come from you, Big Mitch, so 'to the victor go the spoils.' This is your defining moment, Big Mitch. Don't sweat this, this is the wild, wild, west and shit like this happens all the time in our circles. It is common place for niggas to get killed and dope fiends overdose on drugs and get fleeced for whatever they have on them, while their bodies are left by, or in, dumpsters. This particular nigga was a terror. A lot of people were afraid of him and will be glad to see his punk ass gone, including *some* cops. In fact, most of the district cops are on the take anyway, and the ones that aren't don't step on the toes of their partners that are. For a grand or two, this never even happened. Killing a nigga can be paid off like a traffic ticket without doing a day, especially a dope dealing, pimping ass nigga with a history of raw dogging like that nigga. All you need is money, Big."

Mitch has felt privy to fast money and now basks in the glory of a reputation as well. He is no longer referred to as that little ole pimping nigga, but that pimping nigga that shot Frank Jennings. He begins to notice all of a sudden that it doesn't matter that he is five nine. Also, Fast now calls him Big Mitch. That means an awful lot to Mitch, as he reflects back to Lana's words, "Always look at what one is doing with their hands, their body language and their eyes. What one does will speak so loudly you won't hear a word they say." What Fast's actions are saying is, he's all the way down with Mitch.

Mitch feels confident about representing himself among true to life players in an all or nothing situation. Plus, he beams with pride as his mentor pays tribute to his show of heart and courage. After Mitch and Fast are in the back seat of Fast's Lac, they do more lines of speedballs.

Several months later Fast comes to Mitch to back him in a move on another occasion when Digger is in L.A. on business. Mitch is so proud and enthusiastic about his mentor having that kind of confidence in him that he readily and anxiously agrees, while not even knowing what the move is about. Mitch meets Fast at his home in Daly City. As Fast gives Mitch a sawed off shotgun with extra shells to carry, he asks, "Mitch, you have your 45 on you?"

"Nigga, is seven up?" They laugh and slap hands and set off to do the deal.

Fast briefs Mitch on the two dope fiend twins named Ron and Don, two big, dark skin hypes that deal drugs for Fast in the Fillmore district. They have screwed off a package that Fast has given them and are now hiding out in a hotel in, of all places, the Tenderloin. That is about as stupid as popping someone in your backyard and hiding out from the cops in your front yard.

Mitch thinks they must both be complete idiots, knowing what Fast is like and only running one neighborhood away. He further reasons that dog food makes niggas do stupid shit. Then, he vows that stupid like that will never happen to him; even though, he now snorts coke and heroin throughout each day.

Fast and Mitch are on either side of the hotel door, as Fast has his Mexican broad, Cookie, knock on the door saying, "Room Service."

"Just a minute," Ron answers. Fast waves Cookie away to go down and get in the driver's seat of Fast's Lac parked in the back alley. Then Mitch and Fast hear muffled voices from inside the room and believe that both the twins are inside. They see Don open the door slightly and peep through. Seeing no one, Don is fumbling to release the chain on the door. Fast kicks in the partially open door before Don can react. The door slams open knocking Don, to the floor. Mitch draws down on Ron and slams the muzzle of the shotgun hard into Ron's mouth, busting his lip and knocking out most of his front teeth.

Ron shrieks in pain and mumbles, "Please don't kill me, man."

Fast shouts to Mitch, "Don't kill him, Mitch." While keeping an eye on Ron, Mitch checks the bathroom to make sure there is no one else in the hotel room. Mitch notices that Fast doesn't even have a gun in his hand. Fast snarls at Don, "Get up nigga."

Don starts pleading as he stands, "Larry, we'll make up that money, man, I swear it."

Fast hits Don with a left hook that breaks his jaw and knocks him out, then he turns to Ron. Ron is now standing and holding his mouth. He gets on his knees to try to avoid getting knocked out by Fast and begs, "Larry, please don't kill me and my brother, man, we'll make it right."

Fast kicks Ron in the groin and spits on him. "I know you will nigga, because we're going to sit on you niggas until you do. Now, where is whatever is left of my money and package?" After Ron recovers from the pain of the kick, he hands over the remaining drugs and money, which is nowhere near what they owe. Mitch pours a pitcher of water in Don's face and they take the two men to a cut and bag pad, and set them up with balloons of dog food to sell.

Fast has a smoke shop with a big plate glass window in the block between Ellis and Eddy Streets on Fillmore Street. Just inside is a bar and counter for the sale of various cigars, cigarettes, and smoking paraphernalia. Fast makes the two twins stand just outside the window with a couple of his boys to watch over them selling drugs. They stay there until they work off the money they owe for the package Fast had given them and his profits.

Fast makes Don work the whole time with his jaw broken and once they have worked their debt off, Fast breaks Ron's jaw too. The twins beg for a fix, and Fast tosses two dime balloons of heroin into the gutter and threatens that if he ever lays eyes on either of them again, he'll kill them. Mitch is embarrassed for the twins, as he watches them shamelessly fish the balloons out of the gutter.

Mitch asks Fast, "Didn't you tell me to only fight the same fight once?"

"Yeah, I did Big, but those two niggas won't bust a grape with steel toe boots on, and walking around with broken jaws is better advertisement than them just disappearing." Mitch recognizes the logic in that, as he and Fast slap hands.

Chapter XIV

Put Up or Shut Up

Hanging out with Fast on this particular night, Mitch and Fast come across a tall Sicilian cat named Carmine. Carmine is a thick, six one, wise guy who loves black prostitutes of all shades of color, shapes and sizes, which is one of the reasons he frequents some of the neighborhood clubs. Another reason is, he is fascinated with black pimps. However, Mitch observes that even beyond those reasons, Carmine seems to be an intricate figure in at least some of Fast's business, although in what ways Mitch isn't sure. Mitch simply hasn't asked the how, what or why of it all, until now. Mitch has noticed that Fast seems to spend a good deal of time with Italians, so he inquires, "Fast, where do you know all these Italian dudes from?"

Fast just plays it off, "Me, Carmine and the Italians have a few business ventures that we oversee together." Mitch understands that Fast's evasiveness isn't personal. It's just about business. Fast is real old school. He came up at a time when it was truly all or nothing. Take this mixed, light, bright, damn near white, fine ass dame with green eyes and long curly brownish blonde hair named Precious. All the pimps are after her to choose them. Fast and Mitch are no exceptions, so she's playing them both, back and forth with her in the middle.

At least she thinks she's playing them. One moment she'll give Fast a hundred or two with the promise of choosing him, and the next minute she'll do the same with Mitch. They both sex her up and wait on her to make the next move, which doesn't happen. Then, she's all up in the after-hours and hustler hangouts talking about, "I'm playing not one but two major players out of their dicks for chump change. Am I a bad bitch or what?"

When Fast and Mitch kick it with each other after hearing about her blatant disrespect, Fast explains, "What that bitch doesn't understand is, real down pimps communicate without inhibition about little poop butt bitches like her. Big, you already got a rep that you'll check any man, any size that gets out of line with you. But either you're an all the way down nigga and are willing to prove that nobody, male or female, fucks with you, or you'll become known as a nigga that a bitch can play and be out of pocket with, without consequences. I have a plan that'll send a message that nobody, hoes or niggas fucks with you."

That same night of this discussion, Mitch and Fast are en route to the stroll located in Hayes Valley on the corner of Webster and Hayes Streets. They are in a stolen vehicle wearing all black with black leather gloves in search of Precious, who usually works off that corner. The two men do lines of blow and heroin as they are en route. From a distance, Mitch and Fast spot Precious getting out of a car, obviously coming back from turning a trick. About a half block away they put on black ski masks. Precious is standing on the corner as the two men move swiftly getting out of the vehicle. Mitch throws the three quarters full bucket of gasoline on Precious and Fast lights a book of matches and throws it on her.

The two other hoes named Mattie and Clara that are standing close by run screaming, as Precious runs screaming the other way in flames. Mitch tosses the bucket to the ground and as he and Fast get back into the car, Fast shouts to Mattie and Clara, "Do either you hoes know who we are?"

Mattie shouts back, "No," as she continues running.

Fast yells, back "Well, we know who both you bitches are and who your men are."

Mitch has a hard time with this move, but he justifies it by thinking about something his commanding officer had said to them before a mission one morning back in Nam, "No matter who, what, how old, or how young, if they are perceived as a threat we do them before they can do us. I'd much rather explain the untimely death of a Vietnamese National, than have to explain one of you trooper's death to your family." Deep down inside, Mitch feels it was an unnecessary and stupid thing to do. He reflects on how such a beautiful young girl is now forever scarred. His alter ego suggests, *yeah, now no one will get the money she would have made.* Even now, a part of Mitch is more concerned about the money than the sacrifice of a human being. He remembers being trained in the bush, "They are not people, but targets, the enemy, and what we do is simply another mission that must be carried out."

Cops pick Fast and Mitch up, and harass and question them. Unofficially, they are considered as possible suspects in what the police describe as mayhem, assault with intent to do great bodily harm, and attempted murder. Detective Seymour, the big, white, known racist homicide cop questions Mitch. "We know it was a big man and a small man, which fits the description of you two. We have an eye witness that recognized one of your voices, and we got motive."

Mitch stares straight ahead and asks to call his attorney as the two detectives leave the room. When the two detectives return into the little sound proof room the second detective named Fritz, who is also a big white guy with dark hair speaks saying, "Well, your pal already gave us the information we need to save his own ass and fry yours. What I suggest you do Mitchell, is cover your own ass likewise by giving us your side of why and how it all went down."

Then Seymour adds, "If she had been a white girl we would have just blown you two coon's brains out before we even got this far and, case closed," as he swipes his hands back and forth together insinuating wiping Mitch and Fast off their hands.

Mitch thinks the two cops have nothing and are clutching at straws, so he again asks to call his attorney. Seymour snarls at Mitch, "You don't need a fucking attorney; not just yet asshole. You're free to go, but mark my words *pimp,* I swear I'm going to nail your nigger ass and you can bet your ass on that." He snatches Mitch up from the chair and slams him against a cushioned wall. "No matter how long it takes me I will get you." Then he draws his face close to Mitch's and snarls, "You're a real tough guy aren't you when it comes to women?" With that, he shoves Mitch towards the door.

Polson and Coley, two white narcotics detectives that are on the take with Fast, (by way of Fast's Italian connections), inform Fast about who is feeding the homicide cops info. Their alleged witness is Clara's pimp, a hype named Spoon trying to snitch his was out of, of all things, a petty ass forgery beef. He wasn't even there, so his broad, Clara, had to have been the one to tell him about it.

Spoon comes up hot shot, and his girl, Clara, just disappears from the set, so Fast and Mitch move on with business as usual. Fast assures Mitch, "Now, niggas and hoes alike will not only respect you, but fear you, and both will think twice about trying you." As time passes, Mitch will become aware that Fast is right. When word gets out that it is presumed to be them, and they get away with it, Mitch notices that all he has to do is look hard at any girl of his and they cringe in fear.

Mitch is now shaking and moving hard and fast. He is having seven or eight hoes on a regular basis. He's getting one fifty to two bills a night, average per broad. The name Pretty Mitch is ringing bells throughout the bay and he's looking to make half a million this year easy. He buys a house in Daly City for his main two girls and himself, in his name only. He feels that now, when they're on the road talking about coming home, they'll actually be able to come to a real home. San Francisco has truly become their home base. He has learned that owning property gives good solid hoes feelings of stability and encourages would be potential hoes to strive for the same in their future.

One night at The Booker T. Washington Hotel on Ellis Street, Mitch and a bunch of pimps and hustlers are at the bar roasting and high siding on this kid from out of town named Cochise. Cochise is a tall, light skin guy in his mid to late twenties. Cochise gets mad because his three black girls are seated at the booth table in the bar with him as the roasting is going down. Cochise singles Mitch out of the four men roasting him. "Little ole nigga you ain't all that, I'm about to knock one of your bitches any minute now."

Mitch takes exception to it, feeling that Cochise singles him out because of his stature, instead of one of the other three men roasting him. Mitch is still extremely sensitive to taunts, jokes or put downs concerning his stature. Since the early days with Fast, everybody in town that knows Mitch, or knows of Mitch, knows that he has a little man's complex, and he's a loose cannon because of it. Mitch reasons that Cochise is new in town and apparently not aware that Mitch just looks five feet nine, but operates well over six feet in all the areas that count.

So Mitch sheds the attitude of fun and playful roasting and adopts one of intense seriousness, "Who are you talking to, man?"

"I'm talking to you, Mitch, nigga."

"Nigga, you don't have enough money to talk back when we're roasting you. You need to fuck with little fellows on your level," and he turns back to the bar and slaps five with Fast.

"Well Mitch, how about I fuck with you? You're a little fellow."

At first Mitch thinks about shooting Cochise, but he decides to shoot him down verbally, instead. "Motherfucker, little fellows don't drive twenty thousand dollar custom Rados, or pimp world class white women who keep them eating steaks and lobster every day." Then Mitch starts really clowning, "Big one picks up the little one, nigga." Cochise pulls out a bankroll of about six to seven hundred. Mitch pulls out his diamond money clip of twenty five to thirty, one hundred dollar bills. Everybody in the joint is laughing and slapping hands as Mitch is clowning.

Fast, sensing the cap session is getting out of hand, tells Cochise, "Mitch beat you young blood, so why don't you cool down and let's have a drink and keep it pimping."

In an effort to save face in front of his girls, Cochise asserts himself, "Let's take it outside, Mitch."

Fast laughs and makes light of what Cochise says, because he knows where his young partner's head will take it next. "Big Mitch, fuck that dumb shit, show this nigga how you rolling, man." Mitch's group of four, Cochise, his three girls and other amused parties head outside. Fast whispers to Mitch, "Don't worry about this nigga doing something stupid Big, I got him."

Mitch walks over to his Rado and pulls across the street blocking the street with the headlights shining on the front door of the hotel and the gathering group, and he jumps out. As Mitch reaches the front of his Lac he hears Fast telling Cochise, "Young blood, we're pimps, not boxers we kick game for ours."

Mitch figures that Cochise must have said something about fighting for Fast to say that. Cochise then responds, "I can kick game for mine, too."

Mitch continues clowning, "Well nigga let your ride speak since we already know your bankroll can't speak for the level of game you're trying to represent."

Fast points at a 1965 Chevy Impala parked just up the street from the Booker T. Washington Hotel and shouts, "Big, that Chevy right down there is Cochise's ride."

Hearing that, Mitch starts really high siding. "Nigga you're all up in a real pimp's face talking shit, and driving a Chevy! Nigga, pimps roll Lacs, hoes choose Macks, and those are the motherfucking facts. And as a matter of fact, since you can't fade anything else about a real pimp, what kind of drawers are you wearing, nigga?"

By now, hoes working the track, hustlers passing by and cocktail waitresses are outside looking at the show. Mitch's group is urging him to continue clowning Cochise. Mitch knows Fast has his back just in case Cochise does try something stupid. Mitch is standing in front of the headlights of his Rado in a tailor made midnight blue suit with sky blue pinstripes, midnight blue gators and belt, a midnight blue fedora with a sky blue hat band, and a midnight blue and sky blue leather and double knit double breasted sweater.

"Nigga show me yours and I'll show you and your hoes mine, better yet check this out." Mitch pulls his slacks down to just above his knees, bends backwards pushing his pubic area towards the hotel crowd, and flashing the Navy blue sheer see through briefs he's wearing. The crowd loses it, laughing.

Wimpy, the guy that runs the after-hours where Mitch was involved in the shooting is cracking up while telling Fast Larry, "Larry, that nigga, Mitch, is out of his motherfucking mind, man."

Even Cochise's hoes are laughing at Mitch clowning, as Cochise's main broad, comments, "Uh, uh, nah, that little nigga didn't do that."

Cochise loses the cap session, and over the next several days, Fast knocks one of Cochise's girls, which adds to the fuel that makes him jack (rob) Niecy, and almost fuck off his life. Mitch figures he has invited Cochise's actions upon himself by high siding that hard on him, which obviously humiliated Cochise in front of his game and other major players in the game.

Fast advises Mitch to leave town for a bit behind popping Cochise, just in case Cochise tells on him. Mitch agrees, so he hits the road with his crew in tow. First they hit Sac again and work the circuit of strolls between Sac and the Monterey Peninsula. Money is money and money doesn't know or care where it comes from.

Mitch takes a flight from Sac to Frisco to stop over to get his hair and nails done, because no one styles hair like Adel, especially in little towns like Sac or Monterey. While Mitch is at the shop getting his hair done, Fillmore Slim comes through so they start kicking it. Slim fancies, himself, a hell of a pool shooter, and lures Mitch into a game of nine-ball. It's probably not that Slim is such a great pool shooter. It's more like Mitch is such a bad pool shooter.

Mitch drops thirty or forty bucks to Slim at Big Daddy's Pool hall while they're hanging out. They kick it about the game, people they've kicked it with in Sac, Fresno and a few other spots where Mitch and Slim have pimped together. After a couple of games at the pool hall, Mitch is on the way out to get a taxi to the airport for his flight to Monterey, when Slim offers to drive him instead. Slim has a new driver, some older guy that Slim knows from way back in the day before he was in the game. Mitch sits in the back seat of his 1969 Brown on gold Ham. This guy is driving them to the airport, and Slim is riding shotgun. Fillmore starts shouting orders at his driver to turn left here, right there, or drive faster or slower. "Pretty Mitch has a flight to catch nigga, and I don't want him to be late because of your fucked up driving."

Then Slim asks Mitch, "Pretty, how old are you, now?"

Mitch is thinking, *well so much for Slim never making comments about my age and baby face.* Noticeably irritated, he replies, "Slim, how old do I look, man?"

"Nah Mitch, it ain't no thing, I'm just trying to make a point to this nigga, here. He wants me to teach him this pimp game at thirty some years old, and here you are a young teenage nigga with four or five hoes already." As Slim waves his hand towards his driver, he continues, "See nigga, it's like I told you, pimps are born, not made." Mitch recounts that this is the first and only time he's ever seen the legendary pimp disrespectful in the least bit to anyone.

Mitch rides in silence as he thinks how glad he is that he got turned out into the game the way he did, because he couldn't be a nigga's flunky or driver to get it. He reasons that he would have shot Slim or any other nigga that talked to him like that. Then, his alter ego reminds him, *we need to understand that this must be what the hand that Slim's driver is playing calls for.*

After only a few days back in Monterey, in early 1969, Mitch hits the road again from Seaside with Niecy, Margo and Lulu. They work through Fresno, Sac, Seattle, on Pacific Coast Highway, Salt Lake City, Vancouver, on the Las Vegas Strip and down town, L.A., then finally to Honolulu, Hawaii. Mitch calls Boss Big in Honolulu to get the low down about the streets. Hoes are hitting so Mitch and his six hoes set off for Hawaii. Along Kalakaua, Mitch again cruises with Big in his new 1969 blue on blue Bentley. Mitch doesn't know what a Bentley is, so he asks, "Big, why do you have this kind of a car, instead of a Lac?"

Big explains, "Baby Face, most niggas don't even know what a Bentley is. It's in the double RR family of automobiles, and I say *automobile* because when you get to this level of vehicle it's no longer just a car. Can you dig it?" The two men slap hands and laugh about it. Big tells Mitch, "The street game is undergoing a drastic change all over Hawaii and in parts of the mainland since last seeing you, Mitch. Where there was once many strolls and hoes on them, they are dissipating because of law enforcement scrutiny." Mitch thinks about what Big is saying and thinks that it has even changed in Frisco during the couple of years that he has been in and out of the bay.

"Boss there'll always be enough street hoes to keep a pimp like me rolling and fat. Plus, I don't have as much upkeep as you." In jest he pokes Big's belly to illustrate what he means. The two of them laugh and slap hands.

"Pretty, what I mean is, we got some good years of pimping left like the old days, but mark my words times are changing." "Big, fuck all that shit, man. I'll be pimping until I die." They laugh and slap five again. Big thinks that his younger energetic partner, Mitch, isn't hearing him, and if he is he doesn't want to hear it.

Mitch still lacks the vision of his experiences. He doesn't get it because he feels if one stroll isn't happening, just find another, or in some cases (like he did in Salinas), just create another. He has not yet learned the message that old adage conveys, 'everything must change nothing stays the same.'

Mitch wakes up in his eighth floor hotel suite with a surfside view of the ocean to Margo shaking his shoulder and saying, "Poppy, Larry is dead."

Half asleep and hung over from blow, booze, and pills, and having been passed out for almost twenty four hours, Mitch asks in a hoarse voice, "What did you say, Margo?"

"Cookie just told me that Larry had a real bad car wreck and he's dead." Margo and Cookie have remained real tight and no matter where either of them may be at any given time, they make time to call and gossip.

"Get me a blow and a drink," he orders. As the drugs and booze calm and awaken Mitch's senses all at the same time, the news Margo gave him sinks in, so he calls Fast's square wife and Adel at the shop to find out for himself. It is true, so Mitch flies back to pay his last respects to the man that had become like his family, father, big brother, mentor and the closest male confidant that Mitch has ever known. He will miss the rides, talks by phone and walk of life they shared.

When Mitch flies into San Francisco to attend the services, he notices that there are Rolls Royces, Lacs and other exotic vehicles for blocks. Minnesota Fats, who is a pudgy heavy set light skin hustler and dealer that Mitch has known for some time, walks up to Mitch and tells him, "Even though Fast Larry was hooked on shooting that shit he never stopped having money." Then he touches Mitch's shoulder to get his full attention as he continues. "I mean hundreds of thousands into the millions of dollars, Mitch. But I know you know that, though, because he was your boy."

As Mitch unthinkingly says, "I know," what he really means is he knew Fast was having big money all along, but because Mitch is still quite naive to such things, he didn't realize that Fast was hooked or shooting heroin until just now. Seems he has to hear someone else say it. Fast was such a hard case that no one would have said it to his face even if they did know. Then Mitch reflects that he and Fast had always joked and kidded about when and how they wanted to go out when their time comes.

Mitch reflects back to a night that he and Fast were parked in North Beach kicking it full of coke and heroin. Fast told Mitch, "You know Big, when I go I want to go out fast and hard just the way I've lived my life."

It was almost like they were so close that they would complete each other's sentences. "Yeah right, Fast, and become a legendary whisper on the lips of street people." The two of them had slapped hands and laughed to near tears.

Mitch learns Fast was full of heroin coming into San Francisco from his home in Daly City and crashed into the freeway embankment. Mitch hears that it took them quite a long time separating parts of him and his Lincoln Continental out of that cement. Fats tells Mitch, "The paramedics said that, 'with that kind of impact, death was instantaneous,'" so Mitch is pleased that his partner hadn't suffered.

Before flying back to Waikiki, Mitch is getting his hair and nails done at the barbershop on an early Friday evening when in walks Digger. Mitch saw Digger at Fast's funeral, but he didn't have the opportunity to give Digger his condolences. The two of them exchange greetings and Digger asks to speak to Mitch in private. After Mitch finishes his nails he steps into the back of the shop and sits down with Digger. "What's up Digger, man? You know I never did thank you for watching my back that night, so thanks man."

"It's all good Mitch, but man, I need some work Mitch. Things have been hard since Larry… and all. Mitch, man, I'll cover your ass, man, like no other nigga will. I mean, I'll sleep outside your bedroom door, like I did with Larry, man."

"Hey Digger, I know who and what you are, man, but I'm straight pimping, and I don't really have a need for your services, man." As Digger thanks Mitch anyway, and starts to walk out of the back room Mitch asks, "Digger, how you fixed for cash, man?"

"I got a few bucks Mitch, is all." "Well, listen man, I'll keep you in mind and when I come back off the road I'll see what I can do, alright?" As Mitch shakes hands with Digger he puts three hundred dollar bills in his hand.

"Nah Mitch, I don't…"

"Digger, I know, man, and I'm serious. I'll get back at you. Consider this an advance, okay?"

As Mitch boards his flight back to the Pineapple State he ponders that one hell of a player has left this game, and him. Back in Waikiki, Mitch puts in a call to Tommy Benton in Vancouver, B.C., to find out how things look in the streets there. After getting the green light from Tommy, Mitch puts Lana, Niecy, Margo and Lulu on a flight to Seattle so they can cross the border into Canada. He flies back to Frisco with Brea and Chris (the girl he knocked from the guy he had to kill). There, he picks up his Rado from their house in Daly City. Then the three of them drive up to B.C., working the road as they go.

Once in Vancouver, Mitch hooks up with Tommy, and they get hunting for fresh game together. Mitch seems to always come up with at least one new dame on his trips to Canada, but that's when he's hunting solo. So he plans to kick it with Tommy only a couple of hours and do his own main hunting alone. While they're cruising in Mitch's Rado, they encounter an abundance of fine young French Canadian white girls everywhere, and unlike Mitch has experienced in the states, white people in Canada are much like those abroad. They could care less if a person is Black, White, or clear, for the most part. In fact, Mitch has found that being Black in Canada is an asset in knocking young White girls as opposed to a liability.

Tommy gets hungry and since they don't want to completely stop working and do a formal sit down meal they pull up in front of a McDonalds and park on the street just in front of the order window. Mitch is the first to spot her, a sixteen year old with short hair like Margo's, but blonde with blue eyes and long legs. He and Tommy couldn't hope for a prettier or more naïve young girl. As they approach the window, she is smiling and excitedly giggling, "Are you guy's singers or musicians?"

Tommy and Mitch look at each other and Tommy comments to Mitch, "I think we got one here."

Mitch tells her, "Yea, we're entertainers and I'm looking to make you the star of my next show."

Tommy cuts in, "But if you become the star of his show you'll make me really jealous, because I need you to be the star in mine."

She is so excited that she can hardly contain herself. "Oh my God, you guys sure dress nice, and have pretty hair, and nice jewelry, and that car is just gorgeous, man."

Mitch jumps right in on that. "That's my chariot and I am your black night in blue armor come to fetch you away to paradise." Then after reading her name tag, he says, "Kelly, have you ever been in love, or lust?" Her face flushes red as she blushes and averts her eyes from Mitch's. "Well Kelly, I am in both with you right now. What time do you *get off...?* From work, I mean?"

Kelly stares at the floor out of embarrassment of how brazenly bold Mitch speaks and acts with her. "I get of...aw...I mean my shift is over at four pm."

Mitch looks at his diamond faced watch. "Your chariot will await you in two hours my lady, at exactly four pm. Alright, are we on?"

"Yeah, that'll be okay."

Tommy, not to be out done, jumps in, "Wait a minute, I've got a bigger and newer chariot than Mitch's and..."

Kelly interrupts Tommy and smiles flirtatiously at Mitch while responding, "I don't like big cars. I like the smaller sportier ones."

Tommy laughs at her comment and concedes, "Well Mitch, I guess that's pretty much that." He and Mitch laugh and exchange hand slaps. Mitch notes that this is one of those rare occasions that he gets the girl, instead of one of his taller pimp associates, but he is the driver, and the driver of the vehicle usually has a slight edge, regardless of stature. Either way, he is pleased with the outcome this time.

The two men order as Mitch continues complimenting, wooing and wowing Kelly the whole time. He drops Tommy back off at his car, and doubles back to pick up Kelly. It is a courtship process over the next few days of getting at Kelly. He exposes her to his girls in order to leave nothing to Kelly's imagination about whom and what he really is and is about. At first he has her believing that he's a talent scout and agent, but she senses what's really going on with Mitch. Kelly falls hard and fast, so Mitch tries her on sooner than he perhaps normally would since he and his crew are pulling out in a couple of days. "Kat, (his immediate nickname for Kelly), I know it's only been a short time, but in these few days I've gotten my feelings involved with you. You're all I think and dream about girl, and I have never, ever, known and felt this way about another woman before.""Oh Mitch, I think about you that way too. How long will you be gone from here?"

"Well Kat, in my business we travel a lot. We go everywhere, abroad, Hawaii; you know we do it all, Maine to Spain and Tokyo to Frisco. I'm very tempted to ask you to come with me, but I know you probably can't or won't." Mitch drops his head and begins to fumble with his hands. "I will be leaving Vancouver in a couple of days and losing what we've found will be so hard for me. I just don't want it to end here, like this."

"Mitch, you are so different than anyone I've ever known, and the way you talk to me and touch me makes me all tingly inside just thinking about you." As he drops his head faking devastating sorrow, she grabs his head in her arms and presses his face into her ample bosom. "Mitch, I could come with you….aw… I mean I want to be with you wherever you go."

"But, what about your family, won't they be concerned about you, with you only being sixteen and…" In actuality Mitch is unconcerned about any of that.

Kat cuts his words off with a kiss. "I'm going with you Mitch, and I'll just call my mom and dad when we get wherever we're going and let them know I'm okay." Mitch explains to her that they will need money and she lets him know that she has two hundred dollars saved. He laughs and tells her, "It'll take a lot more than that baby, but I know a way that we can get all the money we need, still party just like we've been doing these past few days, and see the world in the process."

Kelly is all ears, willing and teachable. With some tender loving physical, mental and emotional care, Mitch sends Kat across the border into the states with Lana and Margo, as he drives Brea, Niecy, Lulu and Chris. It is the age of runaways and free love, so such incidents happen frequently. Young girls are looking for fun and alternative ways of living outside of the old, conventional structures of society, and Mitch definitely has a whole host of alternate ways.

Chapter XV

Seduction of More

After a few days of getting money in Seattle and getting Kat's feet wet in the game, Mitch flies Lana, Kat, Niecy and Chris to Frisco. He takes Brea, Margo, and Lulu back with him, stopping at a couple of little spots along the way. In San Francisco Mitch runs into a wise guy and old associate of Fast's named Carmine. Carmine is indulging in one of his favorite pastimes, chasing some fresh, young, black female bodies. Mitch is in a group drinking and kicking it. The group includes Honey Bear and Lil' Butch, a local kid that Honey Bear has made his driver, and is raising in the ways of the game. Honey Bear is a large, dark skin, older east coast pimp and hustler out of Detroit. Mitch likes Lil' Butch because he is one of the few pimps that he has met that's even smaller in stature than him. Mitch has gotten into the mode of checking people that call him little or small, and he no longer allows hoes to refer to him as honey or sweetie. He feels that those are classically names used by hoes in conversing with tricks.

Carmine is sitting with one other Italian guy named Pauley. He always has one or two men with him that Mitch can remember. Carmine sends over a bottle of bubbly to Mitch's table. Mitch and the crew with him hold up a toast to Carmine and Pauley. As Mitch and his partners are laughing and picking between the young cuties that come throwing themselves at the five of them, Pauley comes over to Mitch and asks that he join Carmine and him for a drink, just the three of them. Mitch is feeling no pain from the booze and coke, so he goes over. After brief small talk to break the ice, Carmine asks Mitch, "Do you know who I am?"

Mitch smiles saying, "Yeah, you're an old business associate of Fast's. No pun intended with the use of the word old."

"None taken Mitch, do you know what business that was?"

Mitch gets serious because he doesn't know where this conversation is going. "Yeah, I know what kind of business it was. It was none of my business kind of business," and Mitch and the two Italian men laugh at that. Before Carmine can respond, Mitch continues, "Seriously Carmine that was between you and Larry, man. I'm not into gossip or people that are."

Carmine and Pauley look at each other approvingly, and Carmine turns back to Mitch. "That's real good Mitch, because gossiping only hurts the gossiper. You know what I mean?" Mitch looks up from his drink into Carmine's eyes and nods that he does. They stare into each other's eyes in silence for a brief moment. "You know Mitch, I asked Larry once, 'if there was one guy that you knew that you would go down with, if it's all on the line, who would it be?' And you know what he said?"

Mitch remains silent, intuitively knowing that Carmine expects him to ask who Larry had said it would be. "Larry said to me, and I quote, 'if I had to pick just one nigger to go down with, with it all on the line, it would be Big Mitch'." The shock shows on Mitch's face, because he had always felt that way about Fast, but he had no idea that Fast had come to feel that way about him as well.

"So Mitch, I gotta ask myself, what the fuck is it that would make a man like Larry chose a little fucking guy like you, if it's for all the marbles. Hey Mitch, no pun intended about the little guy remark. I mean, Larry told me how you are about that."

Mitch takes a sip of his drink, and responds, "None taken, Carmine."

"Anyway, so Larry tells me about the night at the dice game, and this fucking guy, Frank, what's his face and, enough said."

"What does all this have to do with me, Carmine?"

"You know, Mitch, we had a little bit to do with handling the aftermath of that situation from that night in question for Larry, indirectly for you Mitch, because that's how Larry was by you. I mean, he explained that you were one of his, and being that Larry was one of ours…" Carmine leaves the sentence dangling as he makes circular motions with his hands. "Are you catching my drift here, Mitch?" Mitch remains silent, and nods his understanding of what Carmine is saying.

"Now Mitch, we got three or four different fucking guys in the Fillmore, and we still can't duplicate Larry's production." Mitch notices that Carmine uses his hands a lot in expressing himself, just as Italian guys that Mitch has known in the Army did. "Anyway Mitch, so I'm thinking, how about you handling this for us?"

Mitch is looking at Carmine as if he doesn't know what he's suggesting, as Carmine persists. "Will you consider taking over the Fillmore District for us? You will be the main guy in the district for us, everything will come through you. Of course, I'll have to okay it with my dad as a formality. So, what do you say, Mitch?"

"Carmine, in all due respects to you and the memory of my late partner, Fast, I'm a pimp, and all I do is rest, dress, and break hoes with finesse." Carmine explains how much money Mitch can make, but what really gets Mitch is the part about being fully protected from the cops in this business and with his girls as well. Plus, their other dealers in the Fillmore will work for him.

Mitch does the math. As he does, Carmine does, and Carmine's father does as well, and so it's on. Lana is furious when she hears of Mitch's decision and she cautions, "Mitchell, please, no, you're a pimp, not a drug dealer, and I've even heard you say yourself before, today's dealers are tomorrow's buyers."

"Lana this is different, you'll see. All of us will be protected from the cops and other niggas in these streets with these people backing us. The possibilities are unlimited here." Lured and intoxicated with the thought of a license to deal and steal for him and his girls, the potential power, money, control and notoriety, Mitch will not be denied. "Come on L. I need you all the way down in this with me." When all is said and done Lana reluctantly submits.

Closing out 1969, there are a lot of new and old faces in the game in the bay area. Between what Mitch has learned from hanging with Fast and now from the Italians, he begins to structure his regime based on their tried, tested, and proven family structure. Mitch is twenty three years old as he starts putting together a dependable crew.

First, he needs at least one, go to guy like Fast, but Fast is gone. Then it dawns on him that Grave Digger Jones is about as good a go to as there is anywhere. Mitch reflects back to Fast telling him, "Digger is a killer, and will go all the way down with you no matter what, but Digger is not the sharpest knife in the drawer."

Meanwhile, Carmine introduces Mitch to Walter, who is a mixed Italian and Black illegitimate son of Don Vincent Di Stefano. Don V (as Mitch comes to call him) is also Carmine's dad and Mitch's connection from which Mitch's marching orders come, usually indirectly through Carmine. Walter has a spot in the Fillmore District, but his actual house is in Daly City.

Before Mitch is introduced to Walter, he asks Carmine, "Why don't you have Walter head up things for you in the Fillmore, being that he is blood?"

Carmine shakes his head as he's driving them to meet Walter. "Mitch, Walter's Achilles heel, the thing that has been holding him back from being in the position that Larry was in the first place, is that he isn't too bright with organizational skills." As Carmine moves his free hand to express himself, he continues, "Now dependable, loyal and following simple directions he can, and will, do for you, just like he did with Larry."

When they arrive at Walter's house, Mitch instantly sees what Carmine meant. Walter is a great looking cat, that Mitch figures hoes probably just eat up, but with a near childlike mentality. Walter is big, tall and muscular, like Carmine, and Mitch can readily see the blood resemblance between them. Mitch's alter ego causes him to chuckle with, *it would appear that at least where black women are concerned, we obviously have a situation here of like father like son.* Walter is twenty nine years old and, because of his genetic mix, he looks more Spanish with thick black curly locks, than Italian or Black. Mitch's alter ego infers as Mitch shakes Walter's hand, *if we had this dude's looks and stature with our attitude and mind we'd be the terror of all the other pimps.* Walter has been in the drug game and carrying out tasks in some capacity or another for Don V and Carmine since he was fifteen or younger. Walter will be Mitch's main lieutenant, for now. Mitch will come to find that Carmine was also right when he said that Walter will kill or die for him. Little does Mitch know that both will come to pass. Walter has a half brother on his mother's side named Stack of Dollars. Their mother was in the game and is now deceased. Stack has never known his father, which isn't uncommon for some people in the ghettos in and around the game.

Mitch finds Digger staying in a room at the Manor Plaza hotel, and asks him if he still wants a job. Digger calmly agrees. He never shows too much emotion, good or bad, about anything, but Mitch has come to understand that's just Digger's demeanor. Digger becomes Mitch's driver, personal bodyguard and confidant, as he knows the dope game in and out, after years of working for Fast. Mitch will come to trust Digger with his very life on a daily basis.

Between Digger, Carmine, Stack and Walter (who in spite of his mental handicap, knows weight, count, and protocol in the streets in the dope game), Mitch gets a crash course in this new game. Carmine tells Mitch, "I asked you to do this because you've got heart and you're smart." To illustrate his point Carmine points to his own head. "The weight, count and the rest is just a matter of the semantics in this game. For a guy like you, it'll all come instinctively natural for you. Plus, I know you got a lot of wisdom and street smarts from Larry, who God rest his soul, was the very best."

Mitch thought pimping took a strong stomach and insensitivity, but he is in for a very rude awakening. Now, he realizes what Fast tried to tell him about dealing being a totally different kind of thing than pimping. Still, Mitch finds that the end justifies the means, so he is quite willing to again pay the price to roll the dice, and pay the cost to be the boss. Mitch notices that the streets are increasingly going from dozens of working girls in just about every block up and down the Fillmore, Tenderloin and Broadway to now just isolated little groups of prostitutes here and there around town and across the bay in Oakland. When Mitch first hit Frisco, for as far as he could see down Fillmore Street, there was the game going down. Now, there are more dope strolls that hoe strolls.

In the beginning of this new quest for power and money, Mitch actually likes being involved in the hands-on selling of the drugs. It's all part of his cultivation and OJT. What better way to learn about the modus operandi of hypes, than by dealing with them direct for a period of time. It also makes him feel superior and powerful. He stays on full of dog food, coke or whatever on a regular basis himself, since he has abundant and easy access to it all by simply making a phone call or sending someone to get it for him. Not to mention, he keeps an overly unhealthy supply on hand wherever he may be for extended periods of time.

Mitch neither collects money or hands out drugs he just orchestrates it all. That way, the cops can never say Mitch is dealing. Sometimes, the hypes bring short money to cop. He'll demean them and make them do tricks to amuse him, especially the broads. He learned this from watching Fast do it in the past on many an occasion. Once, a guy he knows that had been a pretty good pimp named Mike Mack comes up to cop with only fifteen dollars for two dime bags. "Come on Mitch for old time sake, man. You remember when we were pimping all up and down the West Coast together, don't you, Mitch? I swear I'll make up the five next time."

"Nigga, if I give in to every junkie that comes with short money to cop I'll go broke. I got the very best dope out here, and that's a fact." Mitch can see that Mike is real sick and decides to have fun with him. "Mike, you got any jewelry left or anything else to trade, man?"

"Man, if I had jewelry or anything else, Mitch, I wouldn't be short."

Mitch has learned that hypes will say or do anything to get over on dealers for a few bucks. Mitch feels, however, that he is not the one. He believes what Mike is saying is quite probably untrue. "Mike, come up with the five bucks, or buy just one bag, or cop from one of these other niggas out here."

Totally disgusted with Mike as he begs and pleads, and is drawing too much attention, Mitch's alter ego suggests, *we should just have one of our crew give this Mike nigga a hot shot* (mixture with battery acid). Instead, Mitch has Stack of Dollars throw the two dime bags into the gutter, as Mitch tells Mike, "Nigga crawl like the maggot you've become. Look at yourself. You're a disgrace to the pimping, nigga." The call of heroin supersedes all self respect and pride, so Mike does just as Mitch says and begins sifting through the crude in the gutter to get the two bags of dope. Mitch gloats at him as his alter ego reminds him, *we never liked Mike anyway, and now he's just another big mouthed, big man brought to his knees by heroin.* As Mitch watches Mike scurrying through the gutter, Mitch thinks how much he loathes hypes.

Members of Mitch's crew work a few different spots up and down Fillmore Street. A great deal of pimps, hoes and hustlers are falling prey to the lure of heroin. Where money had been their primary goal, now drugs is becoming their reason. Mitch feels they just have weak wills. His old pimp bud, Fillmore, rolls through the dope stroll and sees Mitch one day, so he parks and gets out of his Ham to talk with Mitch. Noticeably on full with dog food, Mitch, exchanges cordialities with Slim. "Yeah Mitch, I just got back from New York. I ran into one of our old pimp partners, Johnny Valentine, up in the Bronx hooked like a dog, man."

"Really, I always liked Johnny too, Slim."

"I know you do, that's why I'm telling you about it, because I always like both of you. Damn Mitch, you're a pretty good pimp too, man, like Johnny, but I guess y'all have your reasons."

At first Mitch thinks, *reasons. What reasons? I have no particular reasons. I just like being loaded and can afford to stay that way all the time.* Then, Mitch almost reacts angrily towards Slim, because Slim obviously doesn't know who and what Mitch is now. In Mitch's mind, no one knows that he's always loaded on dog food, but he remembers how respectful Slim has always been to him, so he thinks better of it.

Within six months after agreeing to work for Don V. and Carmine, Don V poses another business proposition to Mitch. The offer is for Mitch's top shelf girls to be set up in a store front cathouse and escort service in the North Beach area, and have a regular spot in two of the major hotels in town. Don V also instructs Mitch to, "Stay off the streets high siding and attracting attention to yourself, and leave that part of the business to your dealers." Even as Don V tells him that, Mitch is thinking that he is bigger than his mentor, Fast, ever was. Mitch concurs, and under Don V's tutelage Mitch backs away from the street dealing scene by three or four layers of contacts. He has Digger, Walter and Stack to handle all those affairs on his behalf.

Don V gets Mitch suites at the two upscale hotels that will accommodate three of his girls in each suite, twenty four hours a day during conventions and special parties. Mitch will be notified prior, and there is to be only upper echelon white girls in the hotels, unless otherwise specified on an out call basis. This is where opening up two escort services will come into play.

Once they are operational, Mitch starts targeting mostly white and exotic game at the local colleges along with young runaways. Mitch's stable has grown to seventeen girls including White, Black, Asian and Mexican girls ranging from street hoes to bar hoes, right on up to hotel and escort service hoes. The latter being the class Lana and Brea are in, when they're not traveling and pillaging around the globe together playing the circuit.

Mitch has grown to understand that in the game, even a poor, broke White trash female can be dressed, schooled and groomed to produce amounts of capital many times over that of her Black and Mexican female counterparts. Mitch just reasons that life isn't fair in or out of the game, but as long as it's profitable for him, oh well, such is life. He doesn't make the rules he just intends to profit from them whenever and wherever he can. One thing he believes is for certain, *America is the land of milk and honey but a nigga can't taste it without money.*

Mitch is making over ten grand a day net from drugs, but the stress of the lifestyle, things he has to do and have others do, is driving him to use more and more of his own products, especially the heroin. He's making another five grand a day from his girls behind his new connections and police protection. Occasionally, he'll use a very select few of other pimp's white girls in the hotels, but only as a means of knocking them or if there is a big party or convention that requires more white girls than he has on call at any given time. Of course, he gets a piece of anyone else's girls that he might use. Mitch takes care of the hotel's management and Don V with a piece of the action. Carmine has become an extremely valuable asset to Mitch. He and Carmine have gotten to be like *boys* for at least two reasons. First, the cash that Mitch generates for them through drug sales and profits from his girls. Second, Mitch lets Carmine go for free with any, or as many, of his girls as Carmine wants. Mitch considers it a kind of added insurance policy. Carmine and Mitch are kicking back in a sauna one evening, when Carmine inquires, "Mitch, I gotta ask you, how in the fuck does a little fucking guy like you manage to have all these different fucking white broads doing all this shit for you and giving you the fucking money?"

"Carmine, you would really be doing me a big favor, man, if you refer to me as Big, Pretty or just Mitch, for a man's stature lies solely in his deeds." Mitch looks over into the bigger man's eyes and asks, "How would you feel if I called you a grease ball?" Carmine rolls his cigar around in his mouth, and Mitch can tell he made his point. Carmine stares back into Mitch's eyes in silence for a moment, and then acknowledges that he understands where Mitch is coming from. Mitch continues with, "In reference to your question, if you have to ask you'll never understand." From that day forward there is never another problem with short jokes or such references between Carmine and Mitch.

Mitch's automobile order comes in for a brand new, customized, royal blue, 1970, Eldorado with a blue vinyl top, blue leather interior (blue on blue), and a Rolls Royce grill along with wide whitewall tires. He has four fully furnished apartments complete with entertainment centers and all the accessories that either one or more of his girls live in them or they are used for cutting and bagging, or just for entertaining with his partners and crew when he and his game entertain other pimps, hoes and hustlers. No males are allowed in his main residence, except him and Digger. Mitch has learned that keeping your friends close but your enemies closer, doesn't mean in his main sanctuary.

Mitch has his main spot in Pacifica just outside Frisco, actually between San Fran and Half Moon Bay. The property has two big houses on two and a half acres. There are eight bedrooms in total, five in the front house and three in the rear house. The property sits on a hill with a picturesque frontal view of Frisco in the distance. The driveway on the property has a section to drive in front of the four car garage of the front house and a second driveway that leads up, and back to the rear house's two car garage. There is a lower level large pool and an upper level smaller pool, both with saunas.

The driveways are always congested with cars belonging to Mitch and different hoes. There are small walking trails, benches, walkway lights and a stairway from the front house to the back house. All total between the two houses is seventy eight hundred square feet. Lana, Brea and Mitch have the master bedroom in the front house. The girls that have been with Mitch for the longest have bedrooms there. Also, the ones among these girls that have a sufficient earnings track record with Mitch, and aspire to own homes for themselves, their kids, or their families, have homes.

Others who do not have a sufficient earnings track record are appropriately housed in apartments or other temporary dwellings. The girls in his stable whom Mitch has both a sexual relationship and a business relationship, sleep over here even more than at their own homes because this joint is always jumping, day and night. There's always some chick doing another or some combination of them indulging in some form of debauchery. Sex, drugs, jazz, R & B, and rock and roll are always in full bloom, much like a hippie commune, except this is Mitch's money commune.

Some hoes either like living in hotel suites with room service, weekly spots, or their money isn't right regular enough for them to have homes, or cars of their own. Then you have the girls like Neicy. She really isn't interested in having all that stuff. She just loves the game and being as near and as dear to Mitch as she possibly can. He'll meet them all at whatever level of competence and productivity they're at, little money or big money. Versatility is just one of many edges that Mitch has learned to use to his advantage in the game.

Margo and Lulu have a home in Sac for them and their mother, Mable. Chris has a spot in South San Francisco for her mom, younger brother and son, as do a few other select girls. All the properties are owned by Mitch as rental properties, and are in either Mitch or his company's name. Mitch figures that since he has to have someone in the rental properties and a place for his girls to live anyway, it might just as well be his girls in them. It kills two birds with one stone by housing them in rental properties in a way that the average pimp can't or won't, and ultimately if they don't work out, neither does their future ownership of the respective property or vehicle.

It's like Don V has taught him, "You must be willing to do today what most people won't so you can do tomorrow what most people can't." He also feels like it's the best form of advertisement that a player can have for big game hunting. It has become one of his edges, that thing that separates him from most of his peers.

Lana is feeling more and more threatened by all of Mitch's new found success and independence from her and Brea. With all the freaking that goes on in this spot and no matter whose bedroom Mitch is playing musical sheets in, when Lana is in town, she always makes sure that when the partying is over, he goes to sleep at her side. She is just a white girl who loves the thrill of the hunt, the game, and her man.

Kat, like so many fly by night females in and around the game comes and goes. She gets caught up with some revolutionary, *we shall overcome* type of brothers. Mitch has no time for that ideology. The only thing that Mitch wants to overcome is having too much money.

Lulu has been around a while because of Margo, but she is way too flighty. Mitch knows that she, too, will eventually move on, and he is on borrowed time for getting money out of her. Having houses and big money is not Lulu's primary purpose. She just likes freaking with anybody, anywhere and anytime. Mitch is really fond of her, and that little freakish body of hers, too. On any given day, Lulu can produce among the best of his hoes, and Mitch can have some of the best sex that he has ever had with her little nymphomaniac ass. Then, her mood swings come about, she gets full of any drugs she can get her hands on, goes MIA, and usually ends up beat up, broke, busted and disgusted when he rides up on her. Sometimes, Margo runs across her and brings her home.

Lana, Brea, Niecy, Margo, Lulu and Chris are Mitch's nucleus of main girls and have always lived where Mitch lives whenever possible. To Mitch it seems that they have been with him forever. When real live professional prostitutes find a good man they usually stay with that man, barring jail, institutions, death, drugs, or getting out of the game. They're smart enough to know their best investment is with that man, especially if they're interested in having things. Mitch's stature or their sexual preferences don't come into play, because they can always find anyone to get laid as long as Mitch gets properly paid. Mitch takes care of them all (i.e., homes or apartments, kids, families, holidays, school clothes, and other responsibilities).

That has become his greatest edge. He believes if one wants to have world class hoes that are smart and capable enough to at least spell the word 'the', then one has to have world class game and treat them and theirs appropriately. Mitch even has a few college girls at different times; supposedly, just working until they get their degree. About fifty percent of the time they either quit school and straight hoe for his service or him. The other fifty percent finish school and get offered some ridiculous amount of money per year in the real world, and come back to get back down with him. Of course, Mitch has different financial agendas for them all, individually. The right hand never needs to know what the left hand is doing, and 'everybody's business ain't nobody's business' is his motto.

One night as Mitch is prowling through the streets in the wee hours of the morning, the children of the night are out and about, and he is cruising by the greyhound bus depot right off Market Street. He sees this petite, but long legged, blue eyed blonde. She looks to be about sixteen years old with long straight hair that hangs down her back, in the hippie style. She's out on the sidewalk, and Mitch notices a white boy lurking behind her in the doorway. She's hustling people that pass by for spare change. Mitch pulls up to the curb and calls her over to his new Rado. She comes over and asks, "Do you have spare change, man?"

"I'll do better than that. How about a ten spot instead, and you and I go get a bite to eat and talk about it?"

"Can I bring my brother?"

"Sure, why not?" As they are getting in, Mitch makes Sean, her seventeen year old brother, sit in the front seat with him, so he can see what he's doing with his hands.

After the three of them exchange names, Alexis says, "This is really a nice car, man. And Pretty Mitch is an unusual name."

"Yeah baby, it is, but I'm an unusual kind of guy." Mitch meets Alexis's stare in the rearview mirror, as she responds to his comment with a little seductive smile. Mitch has developed distrust of most everyone he meets, and because of his own hidden agendas and ulterior motives, he cannot be trusted by most people he meets, either. Mitch has distrusting others and their motivations for what they do down pat. His attitude is that people are untrustworthy until proven otherwise. He reflects back to lessons he's learned over the years the hard way, so he doesn't believe most of what he hears from most people. 'What one does will speak so loudly that you won't hear a word they say' is another of his adopted mottos. So with Sean and Alexis he's thinking, *what's really going on with these two?* His alter ego suggests, *her brother, yeah right?* His calculatingly devious alter ego also assures him, *it really doesn't matter one way or*

the other because by the time we're done with them, they'll both be doing
something to get at our money.

They laugh and eat at a little hideaway restaurant where Mitch
takes some of his prospective prey when he's in this area trapping.
Mitch probes and prods Alexis and Sean, searching for the right
tune to play for each of their psychological and emotional appetites.
It turns out that Sean actually is her brother and they really are
just two naïve, gullible, young runaway flower children stranded
in Frisco. Mitch notices that Alexis is quite pretty in her little mini
skirt and tank top with no bra or makeup, and a huge rack. He
thinks tricks will eat this young bitch up alive. Mitch learns that
Alexis and Sean are from Nebraska and haven't been able to get
plugged in or find permanent residence before their little money
ran out. They have their stuff in a locker in the Greyhound Bus
Station, and she's trying to pan handle enough money to get them
bus tickets to go back home.

After eating, Mitch tells them he's got some business to attend
to and they can accompany him to one of his spots. The Frisco
for flower children is slowly winding to a gradual halt, and they
have nowhere to turn but to someone like Mitch. Alexis is digging
on Mitch, his car, clothes, jewelry and all the trappings. Mitch is
thinking, *Alexis is a pretty classy little white girl, polite, soft spoken,*
outgoing, and best of all gullible and easily excitable, how perfect for
me. He takes them to one of the apartments he has for different
transactions including tricking new prospects. He puts on some
mellow jazz, Miles Davis's *Bitch's Brew* and Lee Morgan's *Sidewinder*.
Mitch gives Sean and Alexis a joint and glasses of cognac as he's
plotting on pulling her into his web of trickery. He notices how
she keeps staring him up and down, as he's staring back at her. The
mood is set in Mitch's little spot and he and Alexis are 'feeling each
other.' There's an aura of lust going on between the two of them.

Mitch figures all Alexis needs is some proper instructions to get
her going in the right direction, so he asks, "How do you two feel
about making some cash?"

They look at each other and almost simultaneously answer, "Sure, that would be great, man."

Alexis further inquires, "What do you do, Mitch?"

"I do, the very best that I can." As Alexis looks confused Mitch laughs and she gets it. Mitch continues, "No really, I'm an entrepreneur, and I dibble and dabble in models management, real estate, and a few other enterprises. Why don't the two of you kick it here with me for the night, and I'll find something for you to do to earn money when we wake up, okay?" The apartment has two bedrooms, so Mitch shows Sean to the second bedroom and he goes back out to get at Alexis. Mitch sits next to Alexis on the sofa and asks, "How important is making money to you, baby?"

"Man, I'll do anything to keep from going back to Nebraska."

Mitch stands up and sticks his hand out to her. "Then trust me little one, and I'll show you how not to have to go back to Nebraska." She watches him lock the door to the master bedroom, put his jewelry and money inside his pillow case, and lay his 45 on the sink while they're showering.

Alexis asks, "You're something like a pimp, aren't you, Mitch?"

Mitch smiles, "No, not something like."

He and her laugh, as her face lights up. She places her arms around his waist and leans her body into his and sniffs him. "I knew it, the car, jewelry, your hair, the way you *smell.*" Mitch laughs as he realizes that she is actually excited that he is a pimp, as so many young girls are during these times of economic unrest, lack of purpose, and misinformation. It's not a matter of whether getting with a pimp's ideas and formula for success is good or not. For Alexis and Sean, it's more about the fact that they have no idea or formula of their own for living successfully. So any idea beats no idea, or so they rationalize. "Mitch, I've never done anything like that before, but I've always been kind of curious about it; but what about my brother?"

Grabbing her face in his hands, Mitch tells her, "Baby you let me worry about him, and everything else, okay? You just concentrate on doing like I tell you and learning what I have to teach you in order to partake of the lifestyle I represent, by just being my girl."

"Okay, I can do that," she replies.

Mitch generally sleeps in just pajama bottoms or nothing at all, so with no pajamas at this location he chooses nothing this morning. She has no undergarments on, so Mitch offers her his silk underwear to use as pajamas and she refuses saying she'll sleep nude like him. It becomes obvious to Mitch that her agenda is perhaps a bit different than his for sleeping in the nude, as she positions all of that fine young, prime merchandise in bed up close next to him. He's thinking, *work with me here pimp God* as he feels her body pressing hard up against his. In an effort to distract his mind from his genitalia he suggests, "You need to know Alexis, I'm going to give you my all, and I will accept no less from you in return. Are you willing to do whatever I say?"

"Are you kidding me? To be a part of all this, of course I will."

"You and your brother got real lucky baby, finding me." She keeps kissing his chest and rubbing her body against his until Mitch can't take it anymore. "Alexis, go to sleep!"

As she grabs his member in her hand, "I'm too excited to sleep, Mitch, and damn, it looks like someone else is excited too."

"Yea baby, I really want you right now too, but I want you to understand that we have priorities, first things first. We'll have plenty of time for that, but first business."

"Aw… come on Mitch," as she takes Mitch's hand and places it between her legs. "See, how wet I am for you." Then she seductively whispers, "And Mitch, I've never been with a black guy before."

"Alexis, remember, I said, 'whatever I say'?"

Begrudgingly, Alexis responds, "Okay," as she turns over and backs into Mitch as close as she can. Mitch doses off thinking how hard it is... not doing her, but he has great expectations of her. That afternoon Mitch hooks Sean up with Joey, a short Italian dealer out of New York that he's met through Carmine. Joey helps Sean become a fairly good little dealer in time, so his production is still all in the family.

Lana is becoming really possessive because she knows she is losing her control and dominance over her young lover to the very same game she has helped him to master. Now, Mitch has the application strategies from the male perspective of the game. He brings Alexis to his spot and introduces her to Lana. Lana notices Alexis's extreme attachment to Mitch. What really annoys Lana, however, is the fact that Mitch has already laced Alexis up with the game and has had her down getting money for three weeks, without Lana's input, until now. Alexis takes to the game like a fish takes to water. She is the personification of a professional prostitute.

Mitch wants Alexis fluent in all aspects of the game from hustling in the streets, which she is now becoming astute in, to hustling bars, the hotels, escort services and finally the circuit with Lana and Brea. At only sixteen and as aggressive as Alexis gets after the money, Mitch knows he's got a long term keeper here, without being told. Lana is also irritated because Mitch has never brought a new broad to his main spot so soon. So she questions Mitch's motives and special feelings for Alexis. Mitch reassures Lana that it will be him and her until the wheels fall off their money wagon, regardless of what pretty young females come and goes through his life. Still, shortly after his conversation with Lana, he moves Alexis into his main spot. Mitch is sitting in the den downstairs and Margo is doing his nails, while Chris is giving him lines of cocaine and heroin mixed. The new little blonde hippie, Alexis, is sitting between his legs teasing and playing around with him as Lana comes down the stairs.

Lana snarls at Alexis, "Bitch, don't you have something to do other than always sitting up under my man and rubbing on him?

You little freak, you'd fuck him every minute of every day if you could."

Alexis responds, "Lana, he's my man too."

Lana really gets riled. "Bitch, don't talk back to…"

Mitch interrupts them. "Both of you bitches shut the fuck up." Then he directs Lana up to their bedroom as he follows. Once the door is closed, Mitch lashes out, "Look *bitch* just because you like pussy doesn't make you a *man*. There's only one *man* up in here *bitch,* and it isn't *you*. I run this, them, and *you* too Miss *bitch,* and you need to remember that."

"Daddy, I was just trying to …." Mitch cuts her off again. "L, we both know why you did what you just did. We both also know it took me years of following you, Brea, and a couple of other bitches that I had crushes on around to different trick pads out of jealousy from those very same insecurities. L, we've come too far for insecurities baby, and believe me I understand." Lana drops her head and Mitch picks up her chin with his hand. We're on the verge of having it all. Lana grabs Mitch and holds on tightly as she trembles and sheds tears knowing he is right. This day is the passing of the baton because they both realize that he is no longer her young protégé. Even though, he is still young, and he is still her lover, he now belongs totally to the game that they both love so well. Her role as Mitch's ruler and big mama is over. "L, you have been truly more of a mother to me than my very own blood mother, my female mentor, lover, main woman, and my most trusted confidant, but now I gotta be a man and stand on my own merit."

As Mitch descends the stairs, he feels both sadness and exhilaration in the fact that he will now sink or swim based on himself, and as the only star of his show. After hearing Mitch's ranting and raving with his bottom, Chris, Margo and Alexis don't know what to expect, so they watch his face and demeanor as he enters the den and sits back down. They search for signs that they need to either get lost, or return to their posture from before the incident. He lies back in the recliner chair he was sitting in previously, knowing what the girls around him are feeling and thinking. He finally allows a smile to come upon his face and laughs aloud, as his alter ego reassures him, *it's about time we got that situation handled and L will get over it.* He smiles as he rubs Alexis's face and in a normal tone of voice says, "Give me a blow Chrissie girl, and Margo, come finish doing my nails." All goes back to as it was before the incident.

Chapter XVI

Dangerous Liaisons

Mitch is already a whoremaster, but from this day forward he is also a power monger and not willing to share the spotlight with anyone, not even his precious L. This transformation is all inclusive in his life and affairs, even down to his preferences in sexual positions. He no longer likes women in the top position, as he once did, but insists on maintaining the dominant position. He relishes in the fact that he is the only power 'that be' in his world. Even so, L is still, and always will be, his for real girl until either he or she dies. Once Lana begins to recover from her feelings about this change, she realizes that it is not the change in Mitch that is disconcerting to her, but the intensity of her feelings. After all, she has been around the block more than a time or two and this really is the vision she has always saw for her young lover. Now that it is upon them she finds that her feelings are much more involved with him than she realized. She not only loves this game and Mitch, but she finds that she now is in love with a man for the very first time in her life, and that man is her man, Mitch.

She feels like a mother that has lost her only child to adulthood, yet proud that it is her energies and efforts that have enabled it to be that way. She is able to at least simulate mastery of her jealousy, as she kicks it with Alexis and agrees with Mitch that Alexis is a gem. "You're right, baby. This little bitch is classy and sharp to be so young," she tells him one night. "Brea and I will take her on the circuit with us." True to Lana's prediction, within that first month that Alexis turns out to the circuit, she hits a lick for forty two g's. Mitch nicknames her Peaches because he's decided that both her and her work are so sweet. She is more excited about bringing Mitch the money than stealing it, and she loves playing and ripping off tricks.

With the flower child movement still in full bloom there is never a shortage of new, young, wild, gullible white girls who are looking for some direction, or a messiah to follow, and Mitch leads as many of them as he can right to his promised land of getting a pimp's dough. Haight and Ashbury Streets are booming so hard with little innocent, free love, LSD drinking white broads that it has become a mecca for a source of fresh game. Even pimps from other cities come to Frisco just to work that area for new game. Sometimes, Mitch picks up two or even three of them at a time to turn out into the game. They're homeless, hungry, lost, and disillusioned about being in the big cold world on their own. Some stay and make good hoes, but most don't. Mitch reasons that it's a numbers game, as hoes come and go as all pimps know, and ultimately, they all come to pass.

Mitch notices that there is plenty of availability of runaway flower children at bus stops, homeless shelters, free food outlets, free medical clinics, on the streets playing music, begging spare change and giving free love. One of the biggest problems a pimp has is reeducating these broad's minds, to not give it away for free. Mitch has one such experience when Casey, a young seventeen year old, cutie pie, blue eyed hippie brunette with a killer body gives a trick sex on credit, and is stupid enough to tell Mitch. Digger is driving as Mitch rides shotgun. They are rolling through the Tenderloin checking on Casey, because she is only a two to three week turn out, and her money has only been mediocre. For Mitch, mediocre money from a white girl is unacceptable.

When Digger spots Casey car dating some white guy on a side street he points it out to Mitch. "Digger, go round the block and park at the head of this street, so we can wait for her to get done." As Casey exits the car, Mitch gets out. "Case come over here and get in." Digger has such a presence that hoes and most men are uneasy around him, as even Mitch was in the beginning, which is another reason to have Digger as a bodyguard, driver and partner in crime. Mitch lets Case into the back seat, and asks her for the money. Case tells Mitch that she just broke luck with the guy in the car. "Bitch, you been out here over two hours, an all American White woman, and you just broke? Case I got big things in mind for you, baby, but your money needs to do more showing and telling first." Mitch is about to let her out when he decides to take whatever she just made on that date. "Gimme what you got anyway, Case."

"Mitch, I didn't get money from Woody yet. He'll pay me this Friday like he has for the past three weeks."

"Bitch, are you fucking nuts or just stupid? You give a trick my pussy on credit!"

"Mitch, he dates me almost every day and he pays me sometimes later."

Mitch can hardly believe his ears as he looks at Digger. "Digger, did you hear this stupid bitch, man?"

"I heard her, Mitch. I don't believe what I heard, but I did hear it."

Mitch shuts his door back and tells Digger to drive to one of the secluded spots that he and Digger have used for the purpose of performing playhouse ninety on different niggas and hoes. When they arrive out by the beach, Digger gets rope, a towel and a can of lighter fluid from the trunk. Then he grabs Case out of the back seat by her arm and drags her to a tree, as she's crying and pleading with

Mitch. Mitch walks over to Case as Digger ties her to the tree, and tells her, "Bitch, shut the fuck up." Case sniffles, but stops crying. Then Mitch takes out his 45, twists on a silencer and places the muzzle against her temple. "You give away *my* pussy for *my* money, on *credit*. I should kill your ass."

"Oh my God, Mitch, please don't kill me, I swear on my life, I'll never do anything like that again."

"I'm going to give you a break bitch." Mitch removes the silencer and puts his weapon back in its holster. "Give me that can, Digger," taking the can of lighter fluid in his hand and spraying it in a small amount over the front of Case's clothes, careful not to touch her hair or skin with any. Case knows about Mitch and Fast's infamous move from sometime back. Like all of his new girls, he makes sure of that for purposes of control and fear tactics. Mitch backs away from Case, and Digger takes out the matches with that emotionless expression of his, and looks back at Mitch.

Case's eyes are filled with terror as she cries out. Mitch instructs Digger, "Burn that bitch Digger." Digger lights the matches and throws them on Case and that ignites the fluid into that brief bluish flame that comes from lighter fluid. It goes out almost as quickly as it lights up, in only a flash. It's not enough to burn or hurt her, just scare the living shit out of her. Case pees on herself as Digger unties her and leads her back to the Lac. Digger puts down the towel on Mitch's backseat, and helps her into the car as she is justifiably wobbly and shaken. Digger and Mitch have done this rodeo act quite a few times.

Mitch can hardly keep a straight face. He knows that usually after this move a bitch will be scared straight about advocating his business correctly. Mitch takes her to the spot he has her staying in, so she can get cleaned up and clothes changed. Then, he and Digger drop her back off on the stroll. After they drop Case back off, Digger, who doesn't talk very much at all out of the blue says, "Mitch, man, you're not one of us."

"What?"

"Don't get me wrong… I mean… I have a great deal of respect for you and how you handle your business, man, but you're different than the rest of us, man. I see it in your eyes every now and then, man. You're like a little kid, man."

"Nigga, I'm like what?"

"I'm sorry, Mitch, I didn't mean any harm, but I see that same look in my son's eyes, is what I meant."

"Digger what the fuck, are you talking about, man?"

"I don't know how to explain it Mitch, I'm not all good with words like you, man. I was born into this shit, in the projects, man. I been in the dope game since I was nine or ten years old, because I always been bigger than everybody else. I'd watch for cops and carry dealer's sacks just to eat and have clothes and shit. The dealers started fronting me dope at twelve or thirteen. I did my first robbery at fifteen, and busted a cap in a nigga's ass for the first time when I was sixteen. I guess what I'm trying to say, man, is that I feel like as long as I'm straight with you, you'll look out for me, Mitch. You're a good dude, Mitch, man. Don't ask me how, but I knew that about you when I worked for Larry. Larry was cool and all, but Larry came up just like me for the most part. You don't come from all this, man. You could do anything you want to, man, outside of this shit, I mean. Hey Mitch, tell me about you, where you come from, and how you grew up, man."

Feeling Digger's words stirring something within him that he doesn't particularly want stirred, Mitch responds, "Digger, you talk too motherfucking much, you know that? But if you must know I come from the pimping, I'm about the pimping, and I intend to pimp or die being about this pimping."

"I can dig it, boss man. I didn't mean anything by all the questions, Mitch. You know I'm down with you, Mitch, for whatever. You say it, I'll do it. Just like that is just fine by me."

"Yeah, I know Digger, but enough. Just drive." As Mitch feels a lump in his throat and tears well up in his eyes he turns his face out the window so Digger can't see as he wipes a tear that rolls from his eye. It is one of those rain drenched, foggy, gloomy nights in the streets of San Francisco and inside Mitch's heart. For a brief moment, he succumbs to the feelings within, as they ride in silence, except for the sound of the eight track tape playing.

Mitch hears the lyrics of the song *Runaway Child* by the Temptations, "Runaway child, better come back home where you belong. Roaming through the city going nowhere fast you're on your own at last."

Almost without his permission Mitch hears his alter ego saying aloud, "this is our home."

Digger looks over at Mitch confused and asks, "What did you say, boss man?"

"Nothing Digger, I was just thinking out loud, man." Mitch feels troubled as he can't help thinking about Digger's words. Mitch's alter ego again interrupts his melancholy and more vigorously points out to him, *this is our home, our kingdom, and we are Lord over it. Does it not define who and what we are? Have we not arrived? We can summon three, four, five or more women at our beck and call, a fleet of cars, custom jewelry, property, bales of stash cash, and people standing by just waiting for the opportunity to kill or maim for us at our behest. What could possibly be wrong with us or any of that? Is this not all that we have ever dreamed of, and more come true?* Then, it hits Mitch, he has no idea how his family is doing. Those two old ladies, Madea and Mama Jo, are getting older by the day that he's away, if they aren't already gone. His alter ego nudges him, *we have no number for them so how will we possibly be able to locate them? And even if we could they will be more of a liability than an asset, because they will become a means of getting to us. That is yet another of our edges, we operate under the motto that anyone and everyone is expendable, before us.*

In reflection, Mitch wonders if his childhood best friend, Albert Lloyd, ever went into the military, as he had mentioned. He remembered seeing Albert on that leave in Memphis after Nam, and riding out with him and his dad to see that fine ass sister of his named Josie. They had talked of Mitch not graduating high school in Chicago, and getting a G.E.D. in the Army. Albert had told his dad that he thought it sounded like a good idea to him, but Mr. Lloyd had said, "You can always go into the military after you complete your education, son."

Mitch remembers thinking back then, *why is it that I never had anyone to give me that kind of input or direction about my life?*

As Digger and Mitch cruise, Mitch does lines of a speedball. He justifies his life as he thinks he has only an eighth grade education technically, because he never completed the ninth grade and he is still a big success. So school must not make all that much of a difference in real life. The blow and dog food mixture jar Mitch back into the moment from his momentary trek into events of his now seemingly very distant past. Mitch's alter ego rationalizes, *all that was another whole lifetime ago for us, and has no place with us in this arena. And anyway the things that really count in life are having heart, money, hoes and drugs, all of which we have plenty of.*

In the words of Francis Albert Sinatra, Mitch thinks of his life as doing it *my way*. Still, he feels that perhaps Digger is right, because there are times when Mitch really doesn't feel like he is one of these cats at all. He dresses, walks and talks like them, but he seems to have to work hard at it. It isn't easy being cool all the time and maintaining his image. He feels overwhelmed by it all at times, like he's in way over his head, so he does more lines of heroin. Mitch knows that, when all else fails, heroin always seems to give him the relief, courage, and freedom he seeks from the thoughts that are counterproductive to what's really going on in his life today. So, if he isn't one of these cats and he surely isn't one of those squares, then who is he and where does he belong? As the drugs continue numbing Mitch's mind, body, and senses, he laughs and he thinks, *who cares?*

Mitch feels like Popeye the cartoon character that always says, "I am what I am and that's all that I am." He pushes such stupid things out of his mind. He is a pimp and a drug dealer and in either there is no room for such sentimentalities. They are a form of weakness, and it has been burned into his consciousness since jump school, 'No Fear'! Women and children can be ruled by fear and emotions, but not men. Besides, he's at the top of the game. He has nothing and no one to fear.

It's 1971 and he is at the all purpose adult book store and video arcade that he operates in North Beach on Broadway Street in San Francisco. It is located right next to Big Cal's, a cabaret featuring naked seduction shows, which along with the adult store, is actually owned by Don V. Don V also has interests in a renowned club named the "Music Workshop" located diagonally just across the street. The Workshop hosts some of the most renowned jazz and blues entertainers in the world. On top of that Don V also owns at least part of the El Banger Cabaret located further down Broadway. These are just the establishments that Mitch knows about. Mitch either has open tabs or gets comps to all the aforementioned.

Mitch is technically the only black business owner on Broadway in North Beach, thanks to his connection. Mitch's joint is a combination topless shoe shine, XXX video arcade, and adult book store. In the back, behind the black velvet curtain just past the arcade booths are a couple rooms of ill repute for very specific clients that absolutely just cannot wait. Of course, most of the business is done on an outcall basis except for those very select few clients, like Mitch's partner, Carmine. Beautiful white girls giving "shoe shines" and hosting a joint like this topless, bring men in by the droves. Mitch cannot ever remember seeing a pair of shoes getting shined in his joint. The joint stays packed from open to close, because one of Mitch's out call escort services also operates out of here. North Beach is an extremely happening part of Frisco with strip clubs and live simulated sexual, nude erotica shows on stages, along with belly dancing, French sidewalk cafes, and the Playboy Club just down the street a few blocks.

As people enter this section of Broadway during special promotions, they see Go Go Girls dancing inside open cubicles elevated high above the street lights wearing bikinis and Go Go boots. Talk about an erotic sexual circus. It's all orchestrated compliments of Mitch's Italian connection, one way or the other, indirectly by Don V. A lot of influential people, celebrities, and sports figures frequent North Beach. It is nothing to see big name entertainment figures hanging out having espresso coffee at one of the sidewalk cafes. Stars like Sidney Poitier, Carl Malden or Michael Douglas are part of the street scene. He finds it ironic that these actors play cops arresting people like him while he, himself, feels untouchable by such entities. It is the good life for Mitch and he begins feeling bullet proof. While being fully shielded from the law, he's sinking ever deeper into using drugs, especially heroin. It seems the more money he makes and the more success he has, the more he uses. Then, one night Mitch meets *her*, Maria Debora Di Stefano.

Maria is Carmine's younger sister and only daughter of Don V. She and her spoiled, UC Berkeley, snobbish girlfriends enter the store one night as Carmine comes out from in back, again. Maria is about five feet seven with long, jet black flowing hair, dark fiery brown eyes and luscious full lips. She holds her lips slightly apart so her perfectly white teeth are visible. Mitch observes that she doesn't walk in, she struts in with her head held high, and her hair hanging down to her back, which makes her five seven frame in heels look even taller. She struts right past Mitch over to Carmine, gives him a hug and without even looking at Mitch asks Carmine, "Does *he* work here?" when she already has a good idea who Mitch is and what he's doing there.

Carmine awkwardly responds, "Maria, this is Mitchell, he runs this joint."

Then Maria strikes a familiar sensitive nerve to Mitch. "Oh, this little guy is Mitchell." She and her friends laugh. Mitch's blood begins to boil, so that nervous, trademark sinister smirk shows on his face. Yet even while being pissed, he can't help noticing that she is even more stunning in her arrogance. Maria and Mitch stare into each other's eyes as Mitch is thinking how he'd like to take her down a peg or two.

Carmine feels what he assumes is tension between his younger sister and Mitch, so he mediates, knowing how hair triggered Maria's temper is and that Mitch will only back down so far. Carmine is thinking that he likes Mitch and he wouldn't want to have to kill him over such a trivial incident. "Maria, you need to show some respect. Mitchell, this is my kid sister, Maria. Maria, ladies, this is Mitchell."

She says something in Italian to Carmine, and he responds, while Mitch is thinking how much he hates it when people that speak a different language use it in front of people that don't understand it. It is rude and disrespectful. Mitch is shocked when Maria asks, "Where did you get a name like Pretty Mitchell?"

Carmine intervenes with, "Where have you heard that Mitchell is called that name, Maria?"

"My darling big brother, never you mind; just around."

Mitch is a perfect gentleman. After all, this is his boss's daughter. He also thinks he'd really like to show her why and how he got that name, but he thinks it through. After carefully choosing his words he respectfully responds, "It is a name that some people very close to me gave me out of love and respect."

Maria shocks Carmine and even Mitch as she turns to face the three white girls with her. "You mean from whores close to you, don't you," and she laughs at her own dark dry wit. Carmine and Mitch look at each other in utter disbelief at what Maria has just said. The three girls with her are flushed and embarrassed at her brazen remark as well. Before either Carmine or Mitch can say a word, Maria tells her companions, "Well ladies, I guess we've slummed enough for one night." Mitch watches her leave with dripping animosity over how she talked to, and about, him, but he gets over it swiftly as he has too much at stake in this relationship with her family.

As Maria prances out of the joint, Mitch is boiling as he thinks what a fucking bitch, but oh so fine like a dark exotic wine. That first night they both feel the static cling between them that will be Mitch's undoing. It'll be a few more trips back, as Maria and Mitch flirtatiously and verbally spar back and forth, before it will happen.

It is late on a Saturday night, actually the wee hours of Sunday morning, and Mitch is getting ready to leave the shop. Everything shuts down in Frisco, in a conventional sense, at two am. Of course Mitch's other escort service operates 24/7 because it is in a more discreet location than this one. Digger is parked out back in the Rado, as usual, waiting on Mitch to do the night's receipts, put the cash in the safe, and come out. As Mitch is walking out the back door, Maria drives up in that little red 1971 Porsche 928 of hers. Digger and Mitch make eye contact, as Maria exits her vehicle looking sweet, dark, kind of tipsy and sexy as hell dressed in a black clinging mini dress that accentuates her every luscious curve with each step in those four inch black stiletto pumps. "I'm almost out of gas and you have to help me."

"Maria, give Digger your keys so he can handle that for you. Digger, we'll be inside in my office waiting until you get that handled."

Digger drives off in the Rado with Maria just standing there staring at Mitch, her legs wide apart and her hands on her hips. Mitch invites her into the office to be more comfortable while they wait for Digger. She arrogantly throws her head back. Her long hair swirls around her head, through the air, and back into her face as her head tilts slightly to one side. "You know, I have half a tank, and I could have gotten gas for myself." As she speaks she's smiling with a little devious look on her face as if defying Mitch to say or do anything, yet sultrily inviting him to engage her in this little game of cat and mouse. Mitch just studies her, not sure if he wants to accept the invitation—just yet.

Mitch's alter ego cautions him, *we absolutely cannot allow this temptress to make us go there, for it could prove hazardous to our health.* Mitch is full of coke and heroin, so he ignores the logic of such thoughts, as chemically induced abandon overcomes him with no regard for the possible consequences of his actions. He approaches her slowly grabbing her in the back of her hair and pulling her face down to his, because the stilettos make her taller than him. "You're a spoiled guinea brat, you know that?"

"Can't no nigger talk to me like that, and take your hands off of me." She struggles, but not very hard, and it forces their bodies together. Somehow in the struggle her back rests across the hood of the Porsche with Mitch pressed on top of her. He feels the heat of the engine as his left hand rests on the hood of the Porsche, but his senses are numb to the heat as is Maria's body lying upon it.

Mitch hears a guttural moan from deep in Maria's chest, and his alter ego cues him, *okay real tough bitch, we gotcha now.*

Lost in a haze of mindless lust and passion Mitch feels only the yearning to fulfill his tensions of the moment and may the outcome be damned. Maria matches Mitch's aggressiveness with that of her own, as they hungrily kiss each other's mouths and rip at each other's clothing while whispering obscenities to each other. He takes her there on the hood of her Porsche, in the hallway of his shop and on the top of his office desk just as hard and rough as he possibly can. Maria urges and begs Mitch to spare her no savagery, and pushes his chest up from her body. Then, she holds his face in her hands so she can look deeply into his eyes to see the lustful urgency that matches her own. They lie lost somewhere between agony and ecstasy as they exchange smiles and kisses of gratitude that this moment is finally upon them.

Afterwards, as they lay embraced, Marie whispers in a hoarse voice, "Mitchell, I just had an other world experience as I was thinking about all the decadence that must take place in someplace like this." As she wipes her eyes and the smeared makeup off of her face, she continues, "God Mitchell, you made me cry. I have fantasized about doing this, here, with you, like this, probably since that very first night I saw you in here."

"In this shop Maria, service is our motto Miss, and service is what we do."

As Mitch laughs at his own joke, Maria pushes his chest playfully. "You really are a dick Mitchell, you know that?"

Mitch laughs and sighs, "Yeah, well, at least you didn't call me a little dick." He and Maria both laugh hearty to that as he tickles her playfully.

When Mitch looks outside for Digger he finds him sitting in the car with a knowing smile on his face. Mitch smiles back as he reflects, Digger hardly ever smiles. He sends Digger for clothes for Maria and for another trusted comrade, Stack, to drive Maria's Porsche to another location, just in case. Mitch figures it will be just asking for trouble having her car parked there in plain sight at this hour of the morning. Yet they stay, lying together in the shop laughing and joking about how she'll mourn at his funeral if her father ever finds out about this. Maria and Mitch spend a good deal of Sunday here in Mitch's shop of services, as Mitch's alter ego shares with him, *how avant-garde, we're having sex with the boss's daughter, using the boss's sex for hire shop as safe haven.*

He and Maria laugh about the stolen moments that they share over the next several months. Mitch is so loaded on heroin and in dreamland that the severity of what would happen if his connection finds out he is doing his only daughter, doesn't penetrate his mind. After many, many of these secret rendezvous well into July of 1971, Maria tells Mitch she's pregnant. Mitch thinks, *damn I never figured on that,* but he reflects, neither of them did anything to prevent it either. His alter ego reminds him, *it's not on her. It's on us. She is but a young square broad in lust and love, and we're a young fucking idiot, instead of the man of the world that our experiences suggest. And if that's not enough, on top of that it's not her ass on the line, it's ours.* Maria assures Mitch that no one knows, yet. "Maria, exactly what do you mean by, *yet?* You mean you're actually contemplating keeping this child and telling Don V?"

"Mitchell, I'm Sicilian and I have no intention of getting rid of this baby." Mitch feels that this is a sure way to seal his death warrant.

"Maria, you can't be serious, and you do realize this will mean you'll be raising a kid without a father, don't you?"

Maria laughs and makes light of it, "Oh Mitchell, once my father finds out I'm having a child and *you're* the father, it may be *me* he kills, not *you.*" She waves her finger between the two of them to emphasize her meaning.

Mitch sarcastically responds, "Well now, Maria, I feel so much better because that just makes all the sense in the world to me."

"Mitchell, my father knows that no one seduces me, and that *I* do the seducing."

Three months after Maria gives Mitch the news on a late Wednesday night, Carmine and a couple of guys come by the shop as Mitch is preparing to leave. Carmine tells Mitch, "My father wants to see you."

Thinking nothing of it, Mitch replies, "*Mine* (his nickname for Carmine), I've got a lot on the schedule for today, but I can drop by tomorrow, okay?"

"No, it's not okay, Mitch, and this is not a request."

Mitch stares from Carmine to Digger to Pauley, who Mitch knows, and Rudy, a guy Mitch has never seen before. "No problem, Mine, we'll follow you out."

"No Mitch, just you."

Mitch becomes concerned by the climate of all this. "What's up, Mine?"

With Rudy and Pauley closely flanking Digger, Carmine says, "Come on, Mitch, we've got to go, my father is waiting."

Carmine is riding in a black on black, 1971, Cadillac Fleetwood Brougham. Mitch is about to get into the backseat next to Carmine where he usually rides when he and Carmine are rolling in that particular car. Digger calls out to have a word with Mitch. Mitch looks at Carmine and he nods to Rudy to take Mitch's 45 and then he nods for Mitch to go talk to Digger. With Carmine sitting in the back, Rudy and Pauley are standing outside the car watching Mitch and Digger. Mitch stands with his back to the three men in between them and Digger.

Digger cautions Mitch, "Make them let me come along with you, Mitch. Don't go with them whops by yourself. If they won't let me to come with you, then it ain't going down right, man, so whatever it is, let's do it right here, right now."

"Nah Digger, man, that'll really blow up everything. I'll work whatever this is out, Digger. I'm still a valuable commodity to them," he assures Digger while only half believing that himself.

"Mitch, do you know what it's about?"

"No man, but I got a pretty good idea."

"Mitch, man, let me at least follow you, man."

Mitch stares at Digger as he reflects on how Digger has always been there for him, even before Digger started working for him. He remembers back to the time before he purchased the Pacifica property when he had problems with another dealer named Sherman. In the heated discussion Sherman said to Mitch, "And, I know where you live too, Mitch." Digger slept in the hallway just outside Mitch's bedroom door on the floor for a week until the situation was worked out.

Carmine is becoming restless waiting and irritably calls out, "Mitch, come on, we gotta go."

After turning to face Carmine, Mitch turns back to Digger. "It's cool Digger, man, and everything is going to be alright. I'm telling you, I got a couple of little birds flying on my side." With that Mitch winks at Digger and turns to get into the car. Digger watches as they drive out of sight. The four men take the long ride out to the Hayward and Concord area to the home of Don V in silence. Don V has a huge spread and his parlor sits off to the rear next to the extended driveway of the big two story estate. Even full of dog food, Mitch is a bit uneasy as he walks into Don V's parlor through the rear entrance.

Mitch feels that if push comes to shove, other than the fact that he is a cash cow for Don V, he has two last things working either for him or against him, his kid growing in Maria's belly and Maria, herself. Mitch has learned that Italian men do not discuss business with women or children present. He has adopted that same rule in his own life and affairs along with several others that Don V and Carmine have taught him in their business dealings. Additionally, Italian women never, ever, interrupt closed door business discussions involving men. Mitch's eyes begin to focus in the dimly lit parlor, and he looks around for Maria or Caprice, Maria's mother. Mitch reflects that Caprice and her sister, Amadora, just love him and are always playing with his hair, pinching his face cheeks and talking to each other in Italian. Mitch smiles as he thinks, *those two old women probably have fantasies about my pretty black ass.* Mitch thinks of his Madea and Mama Jo, who he hasn't seen or talked to in over five years now and their not knowing if he's alive or dead, and now maybe they'll never know. *But Lord, I don't want to die, not now, not like this,* he thinks.

He further thinks of his granddad, Dandy, who used to regularly tell him, "There will come a time in your life when you're going to wish for these very days, Snoopy." Well, he's definitely wishing for them right about now.

Mitch figures that it won't be done here anyway, not at Don V's home, would it? He thinks whatever it is, it won't be long now before he knows. Mitch remembers well Don V's words from when he first started working for him, "You'll be the richest black guy in the ghetto, just don't even think about trying to cross me and you'll live to enjoy it." Just then Mitch's reflections are interrupted by Don V standing close to him and pointing in his face. "Stupid, stupid, stupid, what are you stupid, or using your own supply?"

Mitch thinks, *so that's it, they know I'm using heroin, and therefore making me a liability.*

Don V continues his rant, "Now, I'm going to have a nigger grandchild? No way, no fucking way!"

Now Mitch gets it. He braces himself by clutching tightly onto the arms of the chair he's sitting in, facing the window. Then he thinks, *here I am with my stupid ass going to die over some bitch's pussy.* He's screwed off a multimillion dollar opportunity and his life by allowing drugs to affect his mind and judgment in a way that hinders him from advocating his business sensibly. His alter ego isn't much help right about now as it quips, *we live by the pussy, so we die behind the pussy.* Mitch takes no particular humor in that prospect. He starts to wonder how Don V.... His thoughts are interrupted by a door opening behind him.

Mrs. Caprice Di Stefano comes walking into the room and Mitch feels a sense of relief. He thinks, *thank God, nothing will happen with her here, but why is she here?* This is very uncustomary for an Italian female, especially Don V's *wife.* Caprice sits on the sofa diagonally across from Mitch and doesn't look up or speak to anyone as she begins knitting. It is quiet, too quiet in there for Mitch, but no news is good news for him right about now. Mitch looks around at the faces of Don V, Carmine, Rudy and Pauley, all of which show the same perplexity as Mitch's own facial expression at Caprice even being there. Don V uses his hands expressively as he is noticeably aggravated with his wife. He speaks in Italian and she responds in the same, as the exchange briefly goes back and forth.

Then, she speaks in English, "I don't care—Black, White, or Purple—Maria's baby will have a father and a mother just like I did and you did." She just sits there knitting and not ever looking up. Don V finally throws up his hands and tells Caprice something in Italian, to which she nods, gets up and walks out of the room as quietly and politely as she had entered.

Don V turns to Carmine and says, "Get him out of here." Carmine taps Mitch on the shoulder and, as they are leaving, Don V points his finger at Mitch menacingly again. "For whatever the reason the Gods have smiled upon your black ass, and you better be a damn good husband to my only daughter, or else."

Mitch is thinking, *husband—right about now I'd marry the Antichrist if it'll get me out of this one.* Outside Carmine stares down into Mitch's eyes before getting into the car, and also puts his finger into Mitch's face. "Mitch, don't have my sister around your pimping bullshit or I swear... other than that I'm happy for you and my sister." He gives Mitch a hug of all things, a hug. On the ride back, there is the same silence as coming. However, on this ride, Mitch pats himself on the back feeling once more that through his cunning, manipulative people skills, and game, he has again prevailed.

Stack figured with Mitch out of the way he could slide right on in and assume the lead role with the Italians. Mitch thinks Stack should have figured that if Don V and Carmine thought he was suitable for the lead role he would've already been in it. It was Stack that let Don V know that Mitch is having a liaison with Maria. Mysteriously, of all the people, Walter finds Stack overdosed about a week before Mitch's wedding.

Mitch finds himself in a big wedding. It's like a parade of underworld figures, Blacks and Italians, and of course cops everywhere. Don V gives Mitch and Maria a house in Half Moon

Bay as a wedding gift. There is a large pool with a sauna and tennis court, four bedrooms on one point five acres, and the best part, it is free and clear. Mitch feels that he's in with this family like no other black dealer, hustler or person has ever been, even Fast, because Mitch is now just that, family, whether they like it or not.

Mitch high sides as he tells Digger, "My strong position within that family came by way of injection." They laugh and make light of it, but Mitch thinks, *what's the big deal?* Don V, himself, has at least one kid in the hood from playing across the tracks, and his son, Mine, can't get enough of black women either. Nobody sees any of that as a big deal, and in a perfect world they wouldn't about Mitch and Maria either. His ever present alter ego reminds him, *we don't live in a perfect world.* Mitch feels like whatever works. Of course, when asked by his crew how he pulled it off, Mitch lies and tells them it's the way he planned it all to work out. He figures it might just as well have been his plan, because by hook or crook, he did get out of it. Then Lana gets pregnant, and Mitch thinks *damn* when Lana halfway insinuates she wants to keep it, because it's Mitch's.

"Bitch, I don't give a fuck whose it is, I don't need another fucking kid," he informs her.

"You're having one with that guinea bitch that you married. So all of a sudden I'm not fucking good enough to have your kid."

Mitch knows he has to tone down the gist of where this conversation is headed. He knows that L is just being insecure and jealous because of this kid with Maria, but mostly because of the marriage. "L, so even bottom broads need love and reassurance sometimes too, huh baby? Come here."

"No, you're going to try to sweet talk me out of our child, you son of a bitch."

Mitch smiles and says, "Yeah right, I am kind of like your son, and you're most definitely a bitch. However, you could go to jail for what you've been doing with, and to, your son all these years, L."

That gets a smile through L's tears. Then Mitch speaks softly near a whisper. "L, come over here."

Now crying she comes. "Please don't make me give up this baby. I can handle everything else. I've looked the other way through the different flings you've had with these bitches that come and go. You've favored this one and that one over me, but I felt like they would all wear off in time, and they did, but this square *dago* bitch is different for you, I can just feel it."

"L, this marriage and this kid are good for business."

"But, it's not just business for you with her. You love her, Mitchell. Tell me that you don't."

"I cannot believe my ears, my bottom is jealous after all you've taught me about having thick skin."

"Yeah, okay, so?" They both laugh as they hold each other close.

"Lana, you're my beginning and my ending, alpha and omega forever. Remember? When all is said and done and the smokes clears, who do you think I'll be going home with?"

She smiles and says, "My God you're good, or should I say, *I* am."

"No baby, *we* are. You play men as you've taught me to play women. L, you taught me that the game is about one hoe, one square bitch, or whatever it takes, as it or they come."

"Oh, you're going to have your way anyway, Mitchell. You always do, and to think I created this monster. Don't mind me, daddy, I'm just having an old bitch moment. It's what we do, but you know when all is said and done, I'm down with you and for you. Therefore, I will do whatever you need me to."

"That's my girl, L." Mitch realizes and appreciates that what he and Lana have transcends love, sex or money. They are *folks* (family) and they have the love of the game as their common bond.

Mitch goes to buy a new Ham at a local car dealer named Arnsberger Cadillac. It is the joint that hustlers go to buy their Hogs because all you need is a chunk of cash and you'll be rolling out in a new or used one, depending on your bankroll. Mitch bought his 1970 Rado from them earlier under somewhat different circumstances than he finds himself now. He is twenty four years old looking sixteen or seventeen, still. First he goes into the dealership alone. He's looking at a model on the showroom floor, tricked out with all the extras a hustler could want at a cost of twenty five grand. As he looks around, he becomes offended and he feels it's because of his skin color and stature that no one rushes over to help him. He wonders, *didn't they see me drive up in a near new Rado that I purchased from them? Don't they know who I am?* Mitch jumps in his Lac, peels rubber leaving, and comes back with Lana, Brea and Peaches and a paper bag of twenty five k in cash just to make a point.

This time Mitch notices that everyone wants to help him because of his girls. It really pisses him off to no end. Here he is, a man of his station and clout, don't they know who in the fuck he thinks he is? Now the Arnsberger salesmen come running out to greet them. One white salesman named Carl asks Mitch, "Are all those women with you?"

Mitch arrogantly states, "You saw me drive up with them, didn't you?" As Carl introduces himself and asks Mitch's name, Mitch responds, "My name is Pretty Mitch." Carl leads Mitch and the girls into the showroom while Mitch is asking, "How much do I get off this price for cash?" "This unit is our special, custom accessorized, display model, Mitch."

"I don't think you heard me. How much for cash?"

"Mitch, we can't negotiate the price for this one, we've got lots of extras tied up in this one. However, we do have other units that we can negotiate the ..."

Mitch is now irate, so he blatantly interrupts Carl. "Who else can I talk to here?" Carl gets the sales manager named Marty and Mitch gives him a business card for his attorney, Asher Roth & Associates and tells Marty, "Call this number and ask about who in the fuck you're dealing with here."

Mitch was so pissed that he has already put in a call to Asher's office to advise them of his intentions before returning to the dealership. Mitch's attorney is also one of the attorneys of his connection. The girls are looking at each other snickering at how Mitch is throwing his weight around.

Marty leads Mitch to his office. "Right this way, Mitch." Once inside his office Marty dials the number, and Asher isn't in, but another attorney named Blain gets on the line when Marty gives Mitch's name. "This is Marty at Arnsberger Cadillac and we have a Mitchell Stone here and…"

Marty is cut off from the other end. "Yes sir, I am a manager here. Yes sir… oh… I see, okay, yes sir…that will be no problem at all," and Marty gives Mitch the phone.

Blain tells Mitch, "Mitch like I said before, you'll get whatever you want there, now. They'll kiss your black ass all over that lot. That, I promise you. Oh, and Mitch, call us back if you need to, alright?"

"Thanks Blain, man, tell Ash good looking out," and Mitch hangs up.

Marty amazingly moves much more deliberate now. "Excuse me for just one moment, *Mister* Stone." Marty steps just outside his office door and calls for Carl, the salesman. Marty tells Carl, "Prepare that vehicle for delivery." Then, Marty comes back into the office. "Mister Stone, please forgive me, we will deliver the car to you wherever you say when it's finished being cleaned and filled with gasoline."

"Nah, that's okay I'll send my girls back to pick it up."

"As you wish Mister Stone... oh... by the way, aw... Mister Stone if you'd like, we can finance the vehicle at our very best interest rate and terms, with no money out of your pocket if you prefer, sir?"

"Nah, I don't need the loose ends."

"As you wish sir, but also all of your scheduled maintenance will be free of charge, and any time you wish we will be happy to detail the vehicle for you at no charge, as well."

"You're very kind Marty, thank you."

"Yes sir, and thank you, it's the least we can do for one of our most preferred customers. You will get this unit at our absolute minimum cost for the car and accessories, Mister Stone."

"And how much is that?"

"That'll be seventeen thousand nine hundred Mister Stone, including tax and fees sir."

Mitch pours out the cash from the bag. "Lana, count out eighteen five and give it to Marty." As Mitch is leaving the office he turns to Marty and says sarcastically, "The six hundred is for you and your staff's *exemplary* service."

"Thank you sir, and if you would, be so kind as to give my regards to your lovely wife and her family....aw...your, I mean, both your families."

Mitch and the girls laugh as Mitch tells Marty, "I know what you mean, man." Mitch drives away from that dealership reflecting that it never ceases to amaze him it's not what you know, it's always who you know.

Chapter XVII

Price for Power

Now, not only is Mitch a cash cow, but Don V also has a more personal vested interest in Mitch's success. So Don V takes Mitch under his wing and teaches him about investment basics, stock ownership in growing industries, and how to get his foot in various doors financially. Universally, this is quite difficult for most black businessmen of the time. Don V explains to Mitch, "Just as cash is king, owning businesses and real estate is right up there next to it. Walk softly, talk softly, but carry a big stick. Never discuss business on residential or business phones and never frequent the same pay phone consistently to discuss business. Trust only what you see and only part of what you hear depending on who you're hearing it from. Take no photos of yourself or associates. Never include your wife and young children in your business. Maintain low visibility from the authorities, no flashy clothes, jewelry, or vehicles. All of these things attract the wrong kind of attention from the wrong kind of people."

Mitch reasons, even as he listens to Don V, that he definitely flunks a few of these principles, because the pimping is all about pretentiousness, flashiness and attracting and promoting oneself continually to maintain a competitive edge. Mitch figures, if you come from a lot, it's easy to act like you have little; but if you come from little, it's difficult not to act like you have a lot, especially when you got it like that. He knows that Don V means well, because the future of his only daughter, Maria, his future grandchild now in her belly, and the mixed unspoken son, Walter, all lie with Mitch. Walter and Mitch are like the bastard secrets of the family that are really not so secret to anyone at all, but no one dares to say anything negative about either of them out of respect for Don V.

In December of 1971 Mitch is stalking on the UC Berkeley campus and neighboring coffee shops and restaurants. Paulette is a student from Denver, Colorado, living on campus. Colbert, a six feet blonde white boy only slightly younger than Mitch, who is one of Mitch's coke dealers, is also attending the university and introduces him to Paulette. It's not the first of such hook ups arranged by Colbert for Mitch. Mitch and Colbert have a standing agreement that Mitch will pay him ten percent of the first five grand that Mitch makes off any particular girl that he sets up for Mitch, unless said girl leaves before the five grand threshold is achieved. When Mitch first meets Paulette she is doing lines of coke. He sizes her up as just another snobbish, pretty white girl, but just crazy and daring enough for him to maybe have a shot at flipping her.

Paulette is a redhead, twenty two year old, freckle faced, green eyed, hot bloodied Irish girl. Mitch notices from the very beginning that Paulette dresses very seductively and acts real slutty, especially after a couple of lines. After their first drink and a couple of lines of blow together, she openly insinuates that she is bisexual. She is considerably older than Mitch prefers, but her arrogance and defiant attitude convinces him that there is a window of opportunity here, so he offers her a job.

"Paulette, you're gorgeous, smart, you got game, you know how to carry yourself, and I can just tell thus far that you're a freak as well."

"Oh yeah, and just what makes you think something like that, Mitchell?" As she says it she snubs her nose at Mitch. It hurts his feelings, but he doesn't show it. She continues with, "That's quite presumptuous of you, Mitchell, don't you think?"

"Look Paulette, in my business there is very little room or time for tact and diplomacy. Sometimes, like that old adage goes, 'when you snooze, you lose,' there is little time for proper protocol. Therefore, I seize the opportunity when and where I find her. Can you dig it? Anyway, just for the record, you have to be the prettiest white girl I've ever seen. The average guy would grovel at your feet just for your favor. You'd be a natural, and you can just escort and entertain them with your charm, wittiness and intellect. There is serious money in it for you."

"Really, is it that easy?"

"Of course it is, baby. I mean, you've charmed the hell out of me in this short time I've known you. The level of the game I'll have you at will be all VIPs with big money and the rest is up to you." Mitch suggests a game plan for him and her to buy properties and businesses together, supplying transportation for her immediately, and after one year he'd buy her whatever kind of car she wants based on her level of productivity.

"That is a pretty attractive offer Mitchell, and I could sure use a vehicle, right now especially."

Mitch spots that window and pounces as he explains, "All the connections, clients, in call facilities and services are handled by my people, including police protection, you'll never have to work the streets or bars, and you'll have an expense account for school and your other needs. All you have to do is be your charming, seductive, gorgeous self and bring me correct checks. Your level of success will depend on your level of application and performance. I mean, unless you feel that you aren't qualified to operate at the level I'm speaking of."

"Mitch, I'm not one of your little groupies and I am under impressed with your princely trappings and pomposity, so I recognize what you're trying to do here."

Mitch doesn't understand the wording of some of what Paulette just said, but not to be outdone and to coin a phrase, if he 'can't dazzle her with brilliance then he'll try baffling her with bullshit'. "Paulette, I would have been very disappointed had you not seen where I'm coming from."

Over time she agrees to get hooked up with Mitch because, in coming from relatively poor beginnings, she needs money for school to supplement her scholarship and for no other reason. "This is just about business, right Mitch? I mean nothing personal, but you're not really my type," she tells him as they seal the deal.

Mitch feels a pang of rejection, and he hasn't even gone there with her, so he lies, "Paulette, in all due respect, you're not really my type either. But that need not have anything to do with us doing business together. So let's just keep it as we've found it, and make money together." Paulette sticks out her hand and Mitch reciprocates with his own hand, and it's on between them. Almost instantly Mitch finds that Paulette is highly self motivated and driven with work ethics unparalleled by any single hooker he has ever seen, including Lana. No single hoe of his pays him as much on any given night as she does, unless they steal a piece of cash. The one exception is Peaches. Mitch notes that the more intelligent the female, the more intelligent the money. One can only do up to their level of understanding. There are hoes of the track, and there are hoes of diplomacy and tact. Paulette turns out to be of the latter breed.

Maria gives birth to Mitchell Vincent Stone Jr. III, April of 1972, and it seems to Mitch that the time is just flying. At one point in the year, Mitch has over a million six in stash cash, the most cash that Mitch has ever had at one time that's all his. The cash is pure profit after buying cars, houses and other properties.

Some of which, are with Paulette as part of their individual business arrangement. His order comes in for a two tone, custom painted, wine on burgundy, 1972 Bentley T1 with wide whitewall tires, in celebration of his amazing degree of unheralded success, which he still hasn't shared with his blood family.

He's been telling himself that he has to go see about Madea and Mama Jo, once he gets this amount of cash, or that amount, or maybe when some last deal goes down. There is always that next deal and the next amount going down that he feels that he must be personally involved in first. For whatever reason, it doesn't dawn on him that his family may need him or that he could be of financial assistance to them. It probably never occurs to him because he feels that his life and success is based solely upon him, and him, alone. Someplace lost deep within his heart and mind, he feels that his family hasn't been there for him, so why should he even remotely consider the idea of being there for them. He views himself as a self made man, one who has pulled himself up by his own boot straps through sheer will. The streets and its people are his family. He doesn't like even entertaining such things, so he gets loaded and that pushes the thoughts out of his mind, at least for now.

There is this jeweler that a lot of pimps, hustlers and dope dealers use. He's an old Jewish cat named Ollie Weinstein that Don V has known and done business with since forever. His jewelry store on Market Street is the new spot for Mitch to make drug pickups and cash drops. Don V doesn't want it at any of his businesses anymore, even for Mitch. The amount of Mitch's pickups has been elevated, but Ollie begins systematically whacking the dope, repackaging it for Mitch's pickups, and dealing the rest off through his own sources. Greed is a killer, and since the Columbians and Jamaicans are heavily moving into Frisco's drug game anyway, Ollie figures it will be just a matter of time before the Italian's hands are so full with them that what he is doing will go unnoticed indefinitely. It goes on for a couple of pickups until one day Carmine tells Mitch that this latest shipment is stronger and will hold a four. When Mitch tries it, it won't even hold up under the normal two to three, forget about a four. So Mitch tells Carmine, and between them, they come up with one plus one equaling three, which points directly at O.W.

They decide that, on the next pick up, Mitch will make Ollie believe that if he gives back all the money and drugs he's stole, Mitch won't rat him out to Don V. It supposedly will be a secret from Don V between O.W. and Mitch. Mitch doesn't get it. He wonders what different could it make whether it's coming from him, Don V or whoever? In talking to Digger on the ride to Ollie's store, Mitch verbalizes his sentiments. "Digger, who the fuck do they think O.W. is going to tell after he's dead? I mean, what difference does it make if he knows who it's coming from?" Mitch has been going along for the pickups with Digger and Walter since Walter eliminated his brother, Stack, by means of an overdose of heroin. Mitch used to just send the three of them, but now Mitch doesn't have a third guy that he trusts enough to be this close to his business, especially with the delicate nature of this particular pick up. They do what has to be done and recoup at least some of their losses in drugs and money.

Mitch spends the next several weeks blitzed on drugs, as he's strung out really bad with a dealer's habit. He's starting to avoid his partners that don't use and some of his own joints, because of feelings of paranoia, shame, guilt, and remorse over becoming a common junkie. He feels self conscious when he's out and about, because he feels like everyone is watching him and knows what he's doing, so he prefers to just stay in and nod from the effects of the dog food. It's hard for him to even get up to go pick up hoe money. He's sending others to take care of the business for him. He's spacing appointments and even when he does remember, he fakes being sick and sends someone in his place. He's not eating very much so his body weight is diminishing, and instead of going to sleep he's passing out. His act is getting real raggedy.

Maria, Lana, Digger and Walter are helping to keep him and his act somewhat together. Through it all he reasons that he'd rather be who and what he is, even hooked on heroin, than some square with a wife and kids and working some dead end, jive job, and still broke after each payday. Mitch reflects on Milton's *Paradise Lost* in his attitudes, mind, heart and very existence, "It's better to rule in hell than to serve in heaven."

Paulette has been noticing that at least four or five of the girls that work for Mitch's escort services are also involved in relationships with him beyond just business. She becomes curious as to how and why a guy of Mitch's stature could have such power and control over so many gorgeous multiethnic females. So she approaches Lana asking, "I know that most of the women that I see in and out of Mitch's different spots are just in business for business sake with him, but my God, how many of you guys are actually doing him as well?"

Lana laughs and tells her, "Whatever your relationship with Mitch may be, that's too much information for me to get into with you Paulette, so just ask him."

Lana advises Mitch of Paulette's growing curiosity about him and the different girls he's involved with sexually. Mitch and Lana agree that all of this plants the seed of curiosity within Paulette. Mitch adds, "And L, it's like that popular old adage that states, 'curiosity killed the cat, but satisfaction brought her back.' There's a reason cats are referred to as pussy."

"You're absolutely right about that, Daddy, and I like that analogy, you fucker." They laugh and continue plotting, scheming and setting about the business of playing the game. When the smoke clears, Paulette never knows what hit her or which way it went down. Her relationship with Lana and Mitch takes a turn of a sexual nature all because of Paulette's love of doing blow, partying and freaking. It culminates with him, her and Lana in a ménage à trois. Over time, this scenario becomes more just Mitch and Paulette. Over the next six months, Mitch's drug use escalates, so he and Lana make preparations for him to secretly go into a heroin detoxification unit at the Menlo Park Veteran's Administration

Hospital for a week. They are careful to conceal it from everyone except Brea, Digger, Peaches, Margo, and of all people, Paulette, because he has been spending so much time with her. Mitch and Lana rationalize that Brea, Margo, Peaches and Digger are like her, lifers, and in it to win it with Mitch to the very end. Even Maria doesn't know just how bad Mitch's drug problem is, because during the two to three nights a week that Mitch goes home to her, he masks it very well. Mitch reasons that even though Maria is the prototype Italian housewife, loyal, supportive, and stand by your man kind of dame, there are still limits to the things he will and will not discuss with her.

Don V and Carmine are her blood family. Mitch can ill afford his Italian connection finding out about his habit for fear of what might happen ranging from cutting off his open drug credit lines to perhaps even worse, much worse. He figures he got real lucky once, and therefore is not looking to push the luck needle that far again. Once out of the VA hospital, Mitch swears off all drugs and vows that he will only drink booze, which he does, but like a lush. Booze doesn't hold the magical power for him like hard drugs. So he starts back doing lines, but only before, during, and after sex. He reasons that it increases his excitement, stamina and drive.

Lana tells Mitch that he needs to contact Paulette. Mitch reflects that he and Paulette have done well together, so he spends the day with her. After a year together, they have bought the house in which she lives. They also have another rental house along with a small restaurant and bar, all in Mitch's name only. In addition, the brand new 1972 Chevy Malibu that Paulette drives is also in Mitch's name. Paulette brings Mitch a few different new recruits from time to time, but this time she has more on her mind. She and Mitch are at dinner one night and right in the middle of the conversation she tells him, "I'll be right back baby," and ten to fifteen minutes later she comes back with a buck fifty from giving head to some broad's husband sitting a few tables over. As she hands Mitch the money and winks, she jokingly tells Mitch of the incident. When Mitch turns to look subtly at the trick, he notices that it is all over the guy's face and Mitch wonders how his wife doesn't notice it too.

Then Polly (his nickname for Paulette) breaks the humor of the moment with, "Mitch, I've been meaning to talk to you. I really love you so why can't we just walk away from all this, just the two of us, sell what we have, leave the life behind, get married and start a real life."

Mitch's alter ego is thinking, *real life? This is as real as life has ever been for us. And this bitch doesn't know it, but we already have a wife.*

Polly continues her cocaine induced jabbering with, "Then, you'll be away from around the dope and you wouldn't have any reason to snort that shit anymore. If you could put all this together, you could do whatever you set your mind to, legitimately. The money we have will give us a start. I'll be out of college soon, and I'll have a real job and we can have a real life together."

Mitch gets defensive and responds, "Polly, you snort damn near as much coke as I do heroin, so what's to keep you from doing that still, in this new life you speak of for us?" At this point neither Polly nor Mitch is aware that they both are far beyond recreational drug use, even though he experiences the sickness and withdrawal symptoms when he doesn't do heroin for a period of time. They are classic drug addicts in denial about their being addicted, as evidenced in Polly's response.

"Mitch, I'm not as bad off as you. I just do coke to stay up to work so I can make money for us and still do school all day. I can quit and never do another line at any time if I've got a good enough reason. If we leave the life together, that would be good enough reason for me stop."

Mitch realizes it's true that he has grown attached to Polly's crazy, sexy, Irish ass, but not to a point of giving up everything he's fought, scratched, and clawed to attain. So he consoles her, "Polly, I have those very same feelings for you, and I want nothing more than to marry you too, baby. I'd like nothing better than to just pack it in, run away with you and live happily ever after. In fact, I've been thinking about all these same things myself, but I need just one more year baby, so we can leave all the way splab doobie, and never look back."

"Mitch, just don't play me, just don't do it, okay?"

"Nah baby, I'd never play you like that. By that time our holdings will have matured, and we can get a grip out of them. Plus, we'll have more of a nest egg saved to get started with, now that we know this is our next move." He grabs her hands in his and kisses them. "Just hold on one more year Polly girl, you're not just one of these hoes to me, you're my heart and my woman, and eventually it'll be just you and me, and *you* know that."

"Oh Mitch, I'll work so hard, you'll see." Then, she gladly tells Mitch about a new prospect named Delane, a petite, young, sixteen year old blonde with blue eyes that wants to meet and interview with him.

He smiles to himself as his alter ego reassures him, *we've dodged that bullet for now.* Mitch hooks Delane up in the business, and between Polly pushing and him pulling, Delane comes to work for him personally. He starts spending a good deal of time freaking with her and Polly, and the three of them snort coke together, but for him, he still prefers mostly heroin.

On one occasion Polly's mom comes to town from Denver, so Mitch tells her to take a couple of days to kick it with mom. Still, Polly calls to the services to turn tricks in between entertaining her mom. Polly is just one of those broads that love sex and playing men or women. She doesn't have to steal because she just seems to be able to get tricks to give her whatever she wants. She tells her mom that she is a model, and Mitch is her manager and freelance photographer. She's having a ball showing off the houses and bar that she has acquired with Mitch. Mitch asks, "Why don't you just tell your mom you're a professional prostitute? I'd be proud to tell my mom that I'm a pimp, in fact I did tell her just that, the last time I talked to her."

"Mitch, if I was a pimp I might be proud to tell my mom that too, but I'm a whore and I can just see it now, 'mom this is Mitchell, my black pimp, and I'm just one of his many white whores'." They laugh and leave the playhouse ninety cover story in place for mom. So Polly introduces Mitch to her mom, Katie, as her manager and photographer. After Polly's mom leaves town, Mitch, Delane and Polly start hanging out, getting high and freaking together again. Polly and Delane love snorting coke when they're getting freakish, which leads to Mitch snorting blow excessively, which leads him to shooting heroin for a quicker effect to counteract the paranoia of blow. He decides to get away from Paulette and take Delane more under his wing. Between Polly's abusive use of cocaine and the seeming separation of Mitch and Delane from her, Polly becomes delusional and jealous, thinking they're plotting against her. Add to that her severe mood swings and Mitch starts avoiding her and makes Delane do the same, because he doesn't want her tainted with Polly's tripping.

Mitch never did really like the high of cocaine or crystal by themselves, because they speed him up too much. He prefers the mellow, laid back, calming effect of nodding on heroin, so he discontinues using cocaine, except in an occasional speedball. That way it helps him in the management of his affairs and running interference with different hoes and members of his crew. He reasons that the stress of it all dictates that he has to take something for his nerves. The increasing clash within the love triangle of Mitch, Delane and Polly, along with her disruptive behavior, during college break, Mitch takes Polly and Delane to Joe Conforte's joint up near Reno. Usually, hoes that are known to be with black men are banned from working brothels run by Italians. However, Mitch has an automatic in, in the personage of his connection. One phone call and Delane and Polly are welcomed with open arms.

It's like the strip casinos in Vegas where very few Blacks are welcomed to stay in the hotels on the strip. On one occasion, however, Mitch got a complimentary suite when he goes there with Carmine, Pauley and several girls, Black and White, in their entourage. While Mitch is the only Black male in the group he receives sideway looks, but no discernible difference is made in treatment towards him, and he knows it is only because he is with Carmine and crew.

One weekend Mitch is in Nevada to hang out with Delane and Polly on their day out of the brothel, and Polly cautions Mitch. "If you keep it up with this young bitch, Delane, there'll be trouble for you and her." Mitch has lots of hoes with serious mood swings and occasionally delusional thinking, but Polly is way out there even without coke. She goes from near worshipping him to threatening to destroy him and herself in a blink of an eye.

For some time now Mitch has been plotting on how to separate himself from Polly all together, even to a point of permanently. "Polly, you don't seem to get it. Bitch, if I go down you go down, and if you go down I go down, we're joined at the hips financially for years to come. Everything you own is in my name."

"Mitch, I don't give a fuck about that stuff, I want you to be with me when this is all over like you promised that you would." Mitch realizes he's on borrowed time with Polly, so he sexes her up and keeps on about his business, spending less and less time with her. Perhaps, he has forgotten that, 'hell has no fury like a woman scorned.'

Carmine lets Mitch know he has to do a job for Don V. Some east coast black dude named Pretty Pleasure, or at least that's his street handle, is making noise. He's shaking and moving in the Tenderloin and causing problems for Joey, a long time Italian associate of Carmine and Mitch. Pleasure is a six feet, light skin, dealer and pimp out of Philly, who wears a huge afro and is a known partner of a big time dealer named T, for Tony.

Mitch and Digger make the move. When T gets wind of it, he goes running scared straight to the cops because he knows where it's coming from. He also knows that it may be coming at him next. T tells the cops a whole bunch of stuff about Digger and implicates Mitch in his accusations as well. Carmine lets Mitch know that they'll handle the situation with T.

Word on the street is T's wife, two sons, and daughter is found dead in T's home with a dead rat in each of their mouths. T luckily just happened not to be home. At the shop in North Beach, Carmine tells Mitch, "It's unfortunate what happened to T's family, because something like that will just eat at a man until he dies inside, rendering him nonthreatening to anyone. Mitch, you know what I mean?"

"Yeah Mine, I know exactly what you mean."

One Saturday, shortly after losing his family, T is in the Tenderloin shooting off his mouth about what he's going to do to Digger. T is drunk and loaded standing right out on the corner of Eddy and Leavenworth Streets in front of a bar as Mitch, Digger, Walter and BJ are riding down in Mitch's Bentley. The four of them beat T down, and Mitch kicks his eye out.

Chapter XVIII

Trouble in Paradise

It's 1973, and Mitch is enjoying the benefits of having a close knit crew. Maria is now down with just about his every move, at least in the drug game, and along with Digger and Walter, there's BJ, who is a new partner in Mitch's circle. BJ and Mitch are on an equal basis in the drug business. BJ is a medium height, medium brown skin guy around Mitch's age that is a pimp and dealer in his own right and has his own people. They're handling the drugs, because Mitch has gotten busted with a couple of ounces, and is being investigated for the Pretty Pleasure thing. A new team of cops are running around with a search light up Mitch's ass and affairs, looking for any and every little thing.

In this same year, law enforcement decides to form special task forces to investigate pimps and dope dealers at all levels. Hustlers are falling left and right for racketeering, possession with intent to distribute, income tax evasion, and pimping beefs. Don V tells Mitch that he needs to get lost for a bit because he's under investigation and indictments are probably coming down for possibly four counts of pimping and pandering, the Mann Act, statutory rape, witness tampering, assault with intent to do great bodily harm, mayhem, and possibly the Racketeering Influenced and Corrupt Organizations (RICO) Act.

No sooner than Don V. warns Mitch the federal agents tape off Mitch's joint in Pacifica and confiscate cars (including the Bentley Mitch drives up in while they're there). They also take jewelry, furs, furnishings, art work, everything, including the jewelry Mitch is wearing and even the cash from his pockets. Lana, Brea and Margo are the only girls there at the time. Along with Mitch, the three girls have to walk off that hill with what they have on their backs and only non expensive clothing items that they can carry. As they flag a cab in frustration, Mitch declares to the three girls, "Ain't this a bitch!" He thinks, *it's a good thing I have stash cash and other vehicles not in my name, along with other spots with clothes and jewelry.* As for the girls, the anguish and frustration shows on their faces. Their things left back in that house represent most of the fruits of their labor accumulated over the years with Mitch. To ease the tension of the moment for all of them, Mitch reminds them, "All three of you still have your homes and belongings in them that even the feds can't take from us."

Also, with all the heat and attention focused on Mitch, he has to give up managing the escort services and the adult shop on North Beach per Don V's instructions. Since they aren't in his name, he can't be tied to them. It's like his whole world is coming to an end. The one consolation, at least so far, is that Mitch still hasn't been arrested or formally charged. He learns that the feds don't need to prove anything to keep what property they've confiscated, whether they convict him of anything or not, because it's up to him to prove how and why he has all this property. Mitch is livid when the attorney, Ash, explains it all to him, "In this situation Mitch, you're guilty until proven innocent."

Don V explains, "This will bring heat on us all. These are more than just local cops, and they will load the charges on you, knowing they won't get convictions on most of them, but they figure safety in numbers. We must distant ourselves from you at least on paper, Mitch."

Mitch begins trying to figure out which broads could be flipping on him. Who is out of pocket? Mitch starts shooting heroin and coke like his life depends on it in an attempt to keep it all together in his mind. He vows that he won't end up like some of the old school, major players that become statistics as common street hypes, up today and down tomorrow, here today but gone tomorrow and today's dealers becoming tomorrow's buyers. With charges finally coming down, Mitch is forced to leave Dee Dee (his nickname for his wife) and his son, Lil' Mitch, now two years old. He's strung out on heroin and the two cars he has left are in either his dummy company's name or his wife's. Since those vehicles are known to be associated with him, they are too hot to use for hitting the road. BJ has his mom buy Mitch a burgundy on burgundy, 1974, Cadillac Fleetwood Brougham De Elegance in her name and pay cash for it. This allows Mitch to hit the road with a few loyal chicks in a vehicle that can't be connected to him. With everything coming down around him, he has only Lana, Brea, Margo and Peaches left down with him as he's hitting the road. Like rats fleeing a sinking ship, so does Neicy, Chris, and the other females, along with even most of the crew, except for Digger, Walter and BJ and, of course, his wife, Dee Dee.

He learns from Don V that Paulette and Delane are the sources of the two counts of 266H and two counts of 266I (pimping and pandering), one for each girl. The Mann Act (white slavery) is also about these two girls. Apparently, the proprietor of one of the motels where Mitch stayed on one of those trips up to Reno to kick it with Polly and Delane has identified and placed him there with the two girls in question. Another local entity places Mitch and the girls as a unit in Frisco, which solidifies the transporting girls for purposes of prostitution. Other charges are being processed including, *who knows what?* wonders Mitch. Don V's people don't have access to exact federal charges. Meanwhile, Mitch is following his boss's directions and not sticking around to see what any of these charges are. As they cruise down Fillmore Street headed out, Mitch reflects on other pimps that he knows, who are also on the run or already incarcerated. He chuckles as he nods in and out and his alter ego suggests, *we now join that illustrious list of fugitives to be incarcerated at some point down the line.* Mitch reflects that, in just a few short years, the streets and the game have changed so much for people like him.

As Mitch sinks deeper into a heroin induced stupor he raises his head slightly, and through half open eyes assesses the four girls around him in the Lac. Driving is Peaches, a tried, tested and proven road scholar at getting dough, as taught by him and one of the very best world class white hoes to ever do it, Lana, who is sitting in the front passenger seat. Then there is Brea sitting to his right as he nods on her shoulder. She may be crazy, extremely flighty and moody, but there is none more loyal to him than her. Of course, sitting on the other side of Brea is Margo, who has been with him since she was sixteen and has been all the way down with him even to help train her blood sister to be in his service; enough said.

Mitch ponders how none of these women resemble anyone from where he comes from in Memphis, in the little racially segregated community of Douglass, but then too, he is no longer like those people in Douglass either. He is now someone or *something* else. As they head down the freeway, Mitch's alter ego reminds him, *Snoopy, we made it didn't we. We have drugs, money, property, power, women, cars, a hundred suits, fifty pairs of shoes, and custom jewelry.* Still, Mitch wonders why he feels so empty and alone inside right about now. He wishes he could go back to Tanner Street and start all over, somehow. As he begins to feel a tear forming in the corner of his eye, Peaches interrupts, "Daddy, how long we going to be in Canada?"

"Bitch, shut the fuck up, and just drive. Slow my Lac down before you kill us all."

"Well, excuse me, sir." All four women stop giggling and jabbering until Mitch has done a few more lines of smack. Once they can hear his heavy breathing from nodding back out, they resume chatting. As he nods out, he smiles, thinking these down bitches are his family and with them he's as safe as the president.

Shortly after setting up shop in Seattle, Mitch has Lana and Peaches hit the road working the circuit. In Frisco, Peaches gets popped on a robbery and murder while playing a trick. She slips this trick a Mickey and takes him off for thirty seven hundred, cash. Supposedly the trick had a bad ticker, so he dies. The DA offers Peaches a deal of fifteen years to life for second degree murder and robbery, which Mitch and her feel is really no deal at all, but Mitch leaves it up to her. She decides to fight it and loses. When all is said and done, Peaches gets twenty five to life for first degree murder and robbery. In California, a killing that isn't intentional can be treated as a first-degree murder if it happens during the commission of a felony. It has to do with some felony murder rulings. She is a true to life down ass hoe that loves the game, the thrill of the hunt and Mitch. When Mitch sends Lana to visit her and see where her head is at Peaches tells Lana, "L, tell Daddy I'll always love him, but I'm pretty much a dead bitch in here."

"Mitch, as the visiting time ended, Peaches looked back over her shoulder and smiled at me, threw me a kiss, and gave the clenched fist power sign over her heart," Lana reports back to Mitch. Mitch spends a bundle trying to keep her from going down, and when he realizes that he can't, he has his attorney send her a chunk of cash, so she'll at least have money on her books to make the journey a bit easier. After losing the appeal process, the ending of Peaches last letter to Lana for Mitch will read, "It's killing me inside to keep thinking about the streets and our people. Tell them that I will always belong to only them. Thanks for all the good looking out, but now my head's got to be where I'm at in order to survive in here. So this must be my last good bye."

Lana says to Mitch as he reads the letter, "Daddy, they don't come along like that young bitch too much anymore."

All Mitch can muster is a nod in agreement as he hangs his head and tells Lana, "Peaches is our family, L."

After Mitch, Lana, Brea and Margo cross the border into Vancouver, Mitch gets word from Walter that BJ got indicted on the RICO Act, possession of a controlled substance with intent to distribute, and murder one of a federal undercover agent. Ironically, Mitch had known that agent as just a cool white boy from kicking it with him. BJ had told Mitch that the agent was an alright dude. Mitch and BJ even did lines of blow with the agent all along, so Mitch and everyone figured he was alright, not a federal agent. It wasn't the first time he had copped from them, but Mitch and BJ had never been around when the actual deals went down, so he was waiting to nail all four of them, as he already had cases on Digger and Walter. Mitch's alter ego poses a question to him, *what would we have done under the same circumstances that BJ found himself on the night that he did that fed?* Mitch has no answer.

BJ gets ninety nine years for the RICO Act, and another seventy five for the murder of the federal agent, just for good measure. Mitch has their attorney help BJ and his kid's mama, Coco, and his mom, Coretta, liquidate BJ's assets that the feds couldn't snatch. His mother gets to keep the house that BJ has bought for her because it's in her name only. Coco and her mom, Rita, get fifteen and ten year sentences, respectively. So Coretta is left to raise BJ and Coco's three kids. There is a bit of a grip left of BJ's stash after legal costs, so of what's left, Coretta puts a stack in an account with the attorney so BJ, Coco and Rita will have at least some resources to make their numbers a bit easier. The rest of it, Coretta will need to help raise BJ and Coco's kids. Mitch is stunned because BJ is only twenty nine, which is only two years older than him, and yet BJ is gone forever, almost as if dead.

Chapter XIX

Loss of L

Mitch has barely flown back to Vancouver when Walter calls him to tell him Digger was shot up and killed in Mitch's Rado, with another cat that Mitch doesn't know named *Saw Buck*. Mitch reflects that life is a strange, bitter sweet bowl of cherries and 'what goes around comes around'. Mitch wonders, *what the fuck else can happen?* He's already running from pimping and pandering charges, the Mann Act, possibly the RICO Act and whatever the fuck else.

With Peaches and BJ locked away and now Digger dead too, Mitch thinks about what Carmine had said to him about T, "I figure after everything that's happened to T, losing his family and all, he'll be too mentally and spiritually broken to be much of a threat."

Then Mitch thinks about what Fast used to say all the time, "Never fight the same fight twice." Well, here that fight is staring back at him. Talk about timing. Just as Mitch is having all these thoughts, with the radio playing in the background, he hears an old Janis Joplin song named, *Me and Bobby McGee.* The lyrics, "Freedom's just another word for nothing left to lose," hits home.

Mitch reasons that when you take away every reason a man has to live, you give him every reason to kill or die.

He sends Lana back to Frisco to handle some of his affairs and she rips off an older black dealer and hustler named James Ives, who she has turned dates with on occasion because he spends big money with her. It was not a smart move to make, but she is so worried about Mitch's legal problems, and him possibly going to prison, that she is obsessed with getting at any and all money that she can for him. Even though dating black men goes against Mitch's basic modus operandi for his non Black girls, enough money and the docility of older Black men is an exception to that rule. However, Lana is a prostitute and thief and James is a trick, who exposes too much bounty for her not to take, so she gets him. That's what hoes do to tricks. She comes back to Seattle with James's jewelry, a few thousand, and four ounces of near raw heroin.

Mitch has every intention of flying to Frisco and smoothing it over one way or the other, but never gets around to it. James catches up with Lana on one trip back to Frisco months later. He has a couple of his boys pistol whip her in the head and leave her for dead. Walter calls Mitch and lets him know about it and tells Mitch, "Mitch I can go ahead and straighten that out for you right now, man."

"Put that on hold, Walt, until I get there, man, and pick me up at the airport so I can first go see about L at the hospital, man." After Mitch gives Walter the flight info, Mitch paces back and forth seething with rage.

The doctors do emergency brain surgery, but the main doctor, a surgeon named Dr Zielinski, tells Mitch, as her husband, "There's just too much damage done. She will have chronic migraines, blackouts, and eventually serious complications that will probably lead to her early death. She needs a very low key, stress free, lifestyle from here on out, along with minimal exposure to bright light."

They put her on meds for migraine, blackouts and other symptoms of her condition.

Mitch is furious, so he, Walter, and a guy named Laquan handle that unfinished business. Mitch has known Laquan since the days with Fast, and knows him to be a down ass right arm man to Walter. He is swiftly becoming an intricate part of Mitch's inner circle. Quan is a six one, heavy built, dark skin no nonsense kind of hustler and dealer.

Mitch and Brea get Lana set up in the house that she and Brea have in Daly City. Other than his house with Dee Dee this is the only other property he has left because they are no longer in his name. He pays for in-home nursing care and when he's away he leaves Brea or someone else there for her just in case. Brea has a hard time seeing Lana this way, so she prefers to be on the road or wherever else Mitch happens to be. Brea will visit Lana but will only stay over when Mitch does. When they do stay over, it feels almost like the old days for Lana. Mitch's intravenous heroin use escalates as he uses the excuse that an intricate part of his life is now missing. Lana urges Mitch to stop taking the risk of coming to the bay area just to see about her, what with warrants out for his arrest, but he will have none of that. "L, for better or for worse we're in this together, we are alpha and omega forever, remember?" Still, like Brea, he too grows to hate seeing her this way.

On one trip back to Frisco, Lana tells Mitch, "Daddy, you have to let me go back home to Germany to be with my family."

"But L, your home is with me. I am your family and you are my family, and I cannot have you that far from me like that."

"Daddy, I'm no longer of any good use to you. Anyway, you've long since arrived, and I can't be a burden on you like this."

They lay together embracing, laughing and talking about the good old days for hours, just like in their beginning. Lost in the moment, Lana starts to cry and tells Mitch, "I'm so sorry Daddy that all this happened."

Her tears stir Mitch's emotions until he finds tears flowing freely from his own eyes, and this time it's for real. Mitch vows to her and to himself that he will keep her with him and take care of her until death do them part, just as they vowed long ago. For the longest time he does just that, until she sees him totally lost to dope. She believes it's the stress of being on the lamb and still taking care of her. She doesn't understand, or doesn't want to understand, that Mitch is a drug addict and needs no reason or justification to use drugs. Just being conscious is reason enough.

One day Mitch goes by to see Lana and he is nodding and scratching so bad from the heroin, she cautions him, "Daddy that dope will be the death of you. You must let me go home to my family, Mitchell. You can't keep taking care of me, and I cannot continue watching what you're doing to yourself any longer. I know you won't give all this up and come with me, so please just let me go."

Lana's condition worsens as the migraines and blackouts become more frequent. Mitch goes against everything inside of him, and agrees to send her home. For days after Lana is gone, Mitch feels disoriented as she is no longer there to drive out to see, laugh with, or just kick it with. Lana is one of the few people in the world that Mitch has truly ever trusted with his all. They will talk several more times, but he feels that it isn't the same as actually seeing and being with her. He vows to go see her, and he sends chunks of cash on a few separate occasions. As far as he is concerned, Lana owns half of everything he owns.

Still, like his dad, mom, Dandy, Mama Jo, Mouse, Sonji Pak and so many others, out of sight becomes out of mind. Street life and drugs are coming at Mitch faster than his ability to maintain contact with anyone or anything, including his own sanity. Mitch makes Margo his bottom woman because he reasons she is most like Lana (a Mexican version), diplomatically firm, but charismatic, because she is Lana's creation. In addition to that, she is also younger and emotionally stronger than Brea.

His decision hurts Brea deeply, but he explains, "You are the closest and most connected to me, my family Brea, and the best girl I have left; but Margo has proven that she can manage Black, White, or any other kind of bitch right alongside me, or in my absence. She is tougher and less emotional than you, baby." Brea still doesn't like it, but she adheres to her man's wishes. Mitch is running with Margo, Brea, and a new knock named Barbara, who is a young seventeen year old, cutie pie sister.

Polly testifies against Mitch, knowing the feds will keep every possession she and he have accumulated together, including both houses and the bar. Mitch's alter ego thinks, *what a stupid bitch that shoots herself in the foot just to get at us.* So she and Mitch lose everything they have acquired together. Polly played her young lover, Delane, into signing a statement against Mitch.

However, Delane has learned Mitch's lessons well. On the stand she switches her testimony and perjures herself saying, "Paulette made me lie to get at Mitch, because she and I are lovers. I've only known Mitch through Paulette, and I have never worked for him or had sex with him."

In late 1974, Mitch takes a plea deal for one count of pimping, one count of pandering and the Mann Act, providing he gets a ninety day psychological observation at Vacaville Prison prior to sentencing. The plea deal states he will do state time *only,* if any. He also must agree to sign an agreement relinquishing ownership of cars and other property that the feds have confiscated. In turn, they agree to drop the investigation of the RICO Act, witness tampering, mayhem, attempted murder and other miscellaneous charges.

If he's determined to be completely sane and not a drug addict, after having pled guilty, he will be sentenced to one to ten years on each of two counts and the Feds will rescind their end of the plea bargain. This means the sentences on the Mann Act will kick in, and he will have to serve twenty years federal time. Dee Dee comes to visit Mitch at Vacaville Prison, and laughs as she gives him a message from Don V. "My father said for you to, 'be and do your best rendition of an insane madman and dope addict with the shrinks,' and not to worry, because he has your back."

"Dee Dee, what's so funny about that to you?"

"Because Mitchell, you must be insane doing that stuff. How bad is it really, Mitchell?"

Mitch smiles as he thinks how naïve his little Sicilian wife is as he responds, "I can quit anytime I choose, Dee."

"I just hope you're right, Mitchell. Meanwhile, don't worry baby. My father will get you out of this."

Mitch feels that he has to worry because there is chaos in the streets. The court sets a date for sentencing after his ninety day observation at the Vacaville State Prison. Vacaville is really more of a medical facility to determine the profile of different criminals who are considered either psychologically challenged, insane, or addicts trying to get a reduction in the amount of time at sentencing. Mitch feels that he will only fall in the latter category of these.

Mitch is concerned because everyone will know now that he's a common junkie. Dee Dee comes to visit Mitch again and tells him, "I've been knowing that you're messed up on that stuff, but now it'll be okay, because when you get out we're moving far away from all this and will become a real family." Mitch finally comes to realize that just about everyone that knows him up close and personal has known he is a dope fiend long before he knew they did.

Chapter XX

Everything Changes

Mitch is entering a whole new chapter of his life. While doing the ninety day bit at Vacaville, Dee Dee, comes up to visit him on one occasion and repeats to him what Walter told her, "Dealers are turning in short money or switching connections." With Digger and BJ gone, things are unraveling. Walter is loyal and down, but not competent enough to oversee the business. Just as disturbing is the news from cats that Mitch knows who are coming into the pen from Frisco. He's hearing that it's a whole new game out in the streets.

Then on one visit, Dee Dee tells Mitch that the police found Walter dead at his spot in the Fillmore. "Whoever killed him, took the drugs and money, shot him six times, cut his throat then poured Drano down it, and pinned a note on his chest ordering them to *get out*.*" Mitch recognizes it as a message to his Italian connections. He wonders who would have that kind of nerve to buck the Italians. Dee Dee sees her husband's concern and offers to help. "Don't worry, Mitchell, we don't need that business or its blood money." Mitch is distracted by the money he will lose if no one is there to pick it up. He agrees that Dee is right, but inside he wants that money that he still has in the streets. He wonders who he can trust to get it for him. Almost as if she reads Mitch's mind, Dee Dee volunteers, "I can go get what money I can for you, Mitchell."

In greed, Mitch half heartedly tells her, "No, stay out of this. I don't want you to get involved." Mitch momentarily reflects on what Don V taught him, "Don't involve your wife or small children in your business." Yet Mitch's facial expressions and body language convey something totally different to Dee. Mitch has become like Dee's soul mate and she knows him better that anyone, except maybe Lana. Dee tries one last appeal to Mitch's sense of reason.

"Mitchell, we'll be okay without that money, and it'll only lead you back to taking that stuff again once you're out of here. My family is rich, baby, so we won't have to worry about money."

While that makes a lot of sense to Mitch, he reasons that it's been a very long time since he has had to depend on anyone for anything. "I'm a man, Dee, and I must have my own. I love you and our son very much, and after I get my affairs in order we'll do what you want baby, okay?"

"You promise?"

"Of course I do, baby."

She drops her head and mumbles on the visitor's phone to Mitch, "You are my husband and your business is my business, so I will do whatever must be done."

Mitch knows, and believes that Dee Dee knows too, that he will not, and cannot quit the lifestyle that has come to define him. After all, what else can he do? What else would he want to do or be? He is a down pimp and dope dealer and is accustomed to living like a movie star, and that is as addictive as the drugs.

Mitch is in the prison laundry kicking it with a few of his homeboys, when the guards come for him. The two guards shackle him at the wrist and ankles with cuffs and chains. They take him to isolation in a segregated housing unit. He thinks someone had snitched him out because it is still business as usual selling drugs, even inside the pen.

There is easier access to drugs inside some prisons than in some places on the outside. He is smuggling drugs inside and has hooked up with the Black Guerilla Family (BGF), so he has all the dealers and protection he can use inside that penitentiary. The BGF gets a piece, so whoever or whatever Mitch needs taken care of, gets done. He has a few staff members that work there, including medical personnel and guards, on the take.

Once he's inside the small, dingy, isolation cell, they hand him the wire that has come. It reads, "Found Maria's body at house in Half Moon Bay. Attorney is making arrangements for your temporary release for services." Mitch goes numb and weak in his stomach and knees, yet for whatever reason he can't cry, even though he feels like it. He finds that he is all cried out from losing people in his life for one reason or another. In the solitude he reflects that he loved Dee, but then he's loved a lot of people. He feels the overwhelming urge to get loaded, so he sends a kite to the prison main line for heroin and a cooker (metal object to cook dope in) and an outfit (syringe). The prison authorities won't let him out for the funeral service for fear of some form of reprisals, and he is stuck in isolation until his release.

Margo, along with Brea and Lupe, pick Mitch up after he is released from court. Lupe is a young Mexican broad that Margo has knocked for him from the Mission District. He has to complete twelve psych sessions over the next twelve weeks and his probation is only for one year after their completion, thanks to Don V's connections. If Mitch catches a case within that year, he will be remanded to the California Department of Corrections to serve the suspended sentences, both state and federal. Mitch thinks, *here I am, a dope dealer that can't deal drugs, and I'd better be damn careful with pimping hoes as well. One disgruntled broad could cost me years in prison.* He gets to see Lil' Mitch for a brief bit, but it is made clear that he won't be getting him back. Mitch feels that it's probably for the best, because he can't seem to shake heroin and the spike anyway.

Don V won't see Mitch, as Carmine tells him, "My father doesn't want to ever see your face again. His message to you is this, 'you're on the stuff and I have to wash my hands of you. My only daughter is gone because of you being on that shit, and making fucked up decisions in your business.' And this is from me, Mitch, if not for my father telling me not to, I would cut your fucking body up into a thousand tiny little fucking pieces, and feed you to fucking hogs."

Carmine gives Mitch twenty four hours to get his personal belongings out of the Half Moon Bay house where he and Dee lived with Lil' Mitch. The bulk of what stash cash Mitch has, goes towards helping pay off his cases. He only has his 1974 Ham for transportation. He vows to himself and Margo to turn that page and start anew in his life, without using drugs. Secretly he vows to himself to avenge his wife's death, but for now, he will turn that page as well.

Shortly after his vow and conversation with Margo, she, Brea and Lupe run off because Mitch starts back shooting heroin. Mitch stays so loaded that, while their leaving matters to him, it doesn't matter much. In fact all that really seems to matter to him lately is having enough drugs to consume. The girls stay gone for three days, no call no show. Since Mitch's release, he and his three girls have been held up in a one bedroom suite in the Tenderloin. It's a mess in that suite with clothing, plates, and food wrappers all over the place. He has stayed indoors for the whole three days blitzed on speedballs. What little he eats, he orders to be delivered. He is so stoned that he can't even remember where he parked his car. The phone rings, "Poppy, can we come home? We've got all our money for the past three days."

"Yeah Margo, bring my hoes and my money, and come home."

They are in the suite in three minutes because they were downstairs in the lobby when Margo called. Margo walks in first, as her and the other two girls look around at the mess in the suite. They shake their heads and laugh, as does Mitch. Only Mitch is laughing out of joy to see them and more money to buy more drugs. Mitch knows that he has to deal with Margo to save face in front of the other two girls. So after getting his money he gives Brea and Lupe a hundred bucks along with his car keys. "You two hoes go find my ride and then go eat, shop, or what the fuck ever while I deal with this bitch."

Brea inquires, "Daddy, where did you park your car?"

"Somewhere close by Brea, you figure it out. Now, you two hoes get the fuck out of here."

As the two women are leaving, Brea looks back over her shoulder, "Daddy, you just really don't know how to take care of yourself, huh?" The three girls laugh and so does Mitch because like each of them he realizes that to be true.

Margo knows what time it is for her, but first she has something to say, "I know what I did was wrong, and I know what I got coming, but you won't listen to me or Brea anymore. I'm your bottom woman for a reason, and I have been one of your main women for years. You know I've always been down for you, but baby a lot of our troubles are because of you being loaded on that shit all the fucking time. "That dope causes you to make bad decisions that affect us all. I have been willing to follow you, right or wrong, but I only want what's best for you Poppy. We got lucky this time and didn't lose you to prison for a long time. Why do you think we go out and sell pussy, risk getting crippled like Lana or even killed, every night?" Before Mitch can respond she continues, "For you, and the game. I'm a hoe and, even though I once loved this game, after you Mitch, I will never work for another pimp."

Mitch agrees, "Part of what you say is true, but it doesn't excuse the way you went about getting my attention, bitch. It sends the wrong message to this new broad, Lupe. Brea is my family, and she will be with me until she or I die." Mitch pauses briefly as he ponders that Brea feels that all she has in this world is Lana, him and the game. With Lana now out of the equation, that leaves Brea with just him and the game.

After Mitch disciplines Margo and he is again on, full of coke and heroin, he freaks with her like they're two wild animals for a couple of hours. That's how he and Margo have always done it, an ass whipping for her means great sex afterwards. She loves it rough and he loves obliging her. During the session Mitch reflects about the many occasions that he was too busy in the past to see much of Margo. He laughs during sex, as he remembers Margo would deliberately do something to piss him off just to fuel the passions and fire between them for first the fight, and then the freaking.

This time Mitch's promise to stop using relocks Margo's mind for only a couple of weeks, as Mitch's using gets even worse. In a last ditch attempt to help him straighten out Margo urges Mitch into the VA hospital for one more time. When Mitch does get out, only Brea comes to pick him up. "Where's Margo, Brea?"

"She left yesterday Daddy, and Lupe left about two weeks ago. I wanted to tell you, but *Go*, (Brea's nickname for Margo) thought the bad news would worry you," and she hands him a letter from Margo.

The letter reads, "I can no longer go on watching you kill yourself on the installment plan. I've been with you almost eight years and I once wanted to be with you forever, but not with you on that shit. It kills me to see you doing that to yourself, man. For the past couple of years my heart hasn't been in the game anymore, but I continued anyway hoping to see you once again like you were when you first got me in Salinas. I really didn't want to leave you this way, but I feel like if I see you, you'll just talk me into staying one more time, just like you always do. My heart and soul for the game, working, tricks, and even you, are just not there anymore. Take care of yourself, Poppy, and please get off the shit."

As Brea notices the troubled expression on her man's face she smiles and rubs his hand, "Daddy, remember that day that I told you I'd never leave you, well, I won't."

"I know Brea, you and me are family baby. We're all we've got." They hold hands as she drives them home.

Mitch will see Margo only a few times after receiving that letter. Once at the house that he bought for her, her mom and Lulu, who is now only God knows where. Margo's mom has long since bought Mitch out of that property, and it is theirs alone. Another time is when Margo comes to Frisco to visit and see how Mitch is and they do the wild thing for old times' sake. Then, the last time will be at a market in Sac after she has her first kid with some square black dude, but she doesn't say much about him, and Mitch doesn't ask. Through the grapevine, Mitch will hear of a second kid that she has over the years after marrying that same guy.

Mitch's life spirals downward into heroin addiction as he loses his only car through an accident. Right after he finishes the year's probation and gets off that paper, Mitch starts catching misdemeanor cases from engaging in street con games. His world becomes pretty miniscule, as Brea works Powell Street, and he stays in their kitchenette apartment shooting dope and nodding out in the evenings, once he has enough money or drugs to hold him through the next day.

His life style becomes one of a street hype as he learns and plays various con games on would be tricks. One such game the police label '*paddy hustling*,' uses a small notepad to log tricks into an imaginary brothel inside different unrelated apartment building hallways and stairways by offering them imaginary girls. Then he dupes them for all their cash and jewelry, under the guise that the girls steal, so Mitch will hold their money for safe keeping. This night, Mitch is soliciting for an unsuspecting victim on a busy corner in the middle of the Tenderloin when two white guys pass by, and show time for Mitch. "Hey man, you guys looking for the very best girls in town?" he asks.

"Gee, I don't know. What kind of girls you got?" responds the taller of the two men, a blonde named Andrew. The shorter of the two is Cory, a dark haired, muscular built guy. Cory is more suspicious of Mitch's pitch than his partner, Andrew. As they introduce themselves to each other, Mitch tells them that his name is Earl. Mitch sizes the two men up and determines that Cory will be the hardest to persuade, so he concentrates his pitch mostly on him. Mitch has learned that by getting the hardest prospective victim the less difficult ones among them just seem to follow suit.

Andrew is all for it, but Cory tells him that he's not so sure about all of this or about Earl being who he says he is, as he looks directly into Mitch's eyes. Mitch notices that Cory and Andrew are wearing Military issue shoes and goes for common ground with Cory. "You know Cory, when I was in the Army I had a real tight partner who you remind me of. Man that cat and I were just like this," as he crosses his two fingers to illustrate the closeness between him and that Army buddy.

Cory relaxes a bit and begins to bite the bait, "Yeah Earl, we're in the military now and stationed here at Presidio."

Mitch laughs and pats Cory on the shoulder, "Man that's some posh duty assignment. Who did you have to kill to get that?" The three of them laugh at that. After a bit more small talk and they each confirm a tour of duty in Viet Nam, the two soldiers agree to Mitch's proposal. From there Mitch seals the deal, and takes them for one hundred and sixty bucks between the two of them. About a month later, Mitch is playing that same corner along with a young twenty year old kid named Huey. Huey is a tall, dark skin, clean cut young hustler with no apparent vices, other than hustling and making money. Mitch goes into the Zim's Restaurant just across the street for a hot chocolate. While Mitch is sitting at the counter waiting on the hot chocolate, he notices through the huge plate glass windows a guy that looks a lot like a mark that he's taken before, and is now being hooked by Huey.

At first Mitch is glad that he just missed the encounter with the guy in the Army field jacket on that corner because, with no pistol, he would have a hard time with such a big white boy. Mitch decides to have his hot chocolate inside. That will give Huey time to get the mark to the apartment building they're playing out of this night. It is Mitch's intention to rotate to another corner after he finishes his drink. Then, Mitch's alter ego inquires, *why would a mark come back to the very same corner where we beat him out of his money before to get taken in the very same way again by someone else?* It hits Mitch, and he bolts off the stool and races for the apartment building where Huey is headed. He catches up to them just in time to see them enter the apartment building about a half block in front of him.

As Mitch approaches the front glass doors of the apartment building he hears a shot ring out loudly, boo yow…and then another, boo yow… so he runs and ducks into the cover of the preceding apartment building entryway. When Mitch peeks around the doorway wall, he sees the white guy in the field jacket that left with Huey stuff something that looks like a pistol into his field jacket pocket. At that precise moment Mitch remembers the guy. It is Cory who he had conned a few weeks ago. Mitch's mind is racing over what has just happened and perhaps what almost could have just happened to him. He is thinking the worse, as Cory pulls on a knit cap and disappears around the corner.

Mitch's worse thoughts are realized as he peeks in the door of the apartment building and sees Huey lying in front of the elevator on his back in a pool of blood. Huey is not moving, and even if he is, Mitch is not about to go in and involve or implicate himself in any of it. Instead, Mitch goes to cop and shoots two bags of heroin into his blood stream.

Afterwards, under the total influence of smack and contemplating ways to get more, Mitch goes to another corner a few blocks away and continues plying his hustle. It's business as usual with absolutely no regard or thought about what just happened. When Mitch learns from another hustler later that Huey was found dead by one of the residents of that apartment building, he vows not to play marks out of that apartment building again. Instead, he will use the one right next to it; and he thinks this is a smart move.

Mitch plays this con game on a regular basis from time to time, and makes anywhere from a hundred to as much as three thousand on one occasion. He talks them out of expensive watches and other jewelry along with traveler's checks and cash. Mitch gets a string of arrests from playing this con game ranging from soliciting for purposes of prostitution, obstructing the sidewalk and under the influence of a controlled substance when the police can't get anything else on him. Brea is the only girl he has left now, and she always bails him out. Mitch also starts hustling with a network of other street hypes.

At different points in time, two or usually three of them go out *till tapping* around the neighboring communities and cities. Till tapping is an extremely lucrative con game wherein Mitch can make anywhere from one to several hundred dollars, even thousands per day. Just as the cashier opens the register to get Mitch's change for the purchase of a pack of Winston, he distracts her by purposely spilling coins from his hand over the counter onto the floor. The cashier turns, bends down to retrieve the coins from the floor with the register still open. A hype crime partner of Mitch's creeps up from next in line and quickly snatches bills from the top of the twenties and tens stacked in the register, being careful to leave just enough for the cashier not to notice the bills missing at a glance. A third hype crime partner is standing in line with an open newspaper, just behind the hype snatching the money. When the play goes down, he holds the newspaper up to block any customers standing in line so they don't see what is happening. Mitch and the two hypes then meet back at their car. They slap hands and laugh as one more time they have gotten over and are off to go shoot dope together.

As Mitch's drug habit grows, he abandons all sense of caution and restraint. He asks Brea about her regular customers that spend good money and the ones that she goes to their homes to turn tricks. She tells him, "Mitch, I've got this one guy down by Fisherman's Wharf. He never wants sex. He just gives me two or three hundred each time I date him to tie him up and spank him while I curse him. Daddy, he always has cash around that joint. The only reason I haven't robbed him already is because, I'm your only girl right now so I don't want to get busted and leave you with no money and no whore."

Mitch tells Brea of his plan and because she loves robbing and stealing a trick's money, she gets instantly excited about it. Mitch steals a car and parks down the street from the prospective victim's pad, waiting on him and Brea to arrive. Once Brea and the john are in his pad, she is careful to leave the front door unlocked. Mitch puts on a black ski mask at the door and quickly enters the house. He hears Brea talking louder than normal per his instructions. He follows the voices and bursts through the door with his 45 complete with silencer. In a calm voice slightly above normal, Mitch tells Brea and the trick, "On your knees. If either of you moves a muscle, I'll kill you both, you got it?"

"Take what you want, but please don't kill us," says the mark.

Mitch demands, "Okay, where's the cash?"

They get twenty eight hundred. It goes so effortlessly that Mitch becomes addicted to this particular hustle and whatever Mitch likes, Brea loves. The trick doesn't even report it to the cops because Mitch robs Brea along with the trick to not arouse his suspicion of her.

Mitch gets busted for grand theft auto of a car he uses to commit just such a burglary and robbery. He's having Brea, or some other hooker that he has at different times, go home with a particular trick supposedly to turn a date. Mitch and sometimes another of his hype associates follow in a stolen car and the girl follows the same procedure that Brea initially did. The tricks usually think the girl is a victim too, so they don't even call the cops. The problem with this is, hype broads have a very low threshold for loyalty to anyone or anything, except the drugs. So one night while Brea is with another date, Mitch and a heroin addict female get popped for such a situation, and she snitches Mitch out.

With a plea negotiation, he is sentenced to sixty days for joy riding and misdemeanor burglary to be served in the San Francisco County Jail located in San Bruno. The night before Mitch is released, some psycho murders Brea and a trick sitting in a parked car in Frisco. It is suspected by police that it is possibly an act of the, by now infamous, Zodiac killer. Again Mitch finds that he has mourned so much and so many that he just feels numb to the news. He feels as if he's in a trance from it all, so when he gets out he loses himself to the spoon and shooting dope once again. He has about three g's to his name that Brea has left on his books in jail. Being hooked on heroin again, that money goes quick.

Mitch always manages to have a young working girl, or two or three, during these times but, more often than not, they are junkies like him. He has no connection, so he has to support his habit as best he can by pimping and running con games when and where he sees an opportunity. He knocks a big time dope dealer named Rex for a young, 'high yellow', cutie pie named Pricilla. Rex is a small, thin man about Mitch's age and complexion who usually runs with an entourage of his boys, as Mitch did once upon a time. Priscilla is seventeen years old, and Mitch has been hitting on her for a week or so, when she finally agrees to choose him. Mitch still has a rep of sorts in Frisco, but Rex is not from the bay area and knows nothing of Mitch. Rex agrees to meet him at Powell's Restaurant in the Hayes Valley where Priscilla mostly works, and Rex brings a couple of his boys with him.

Just in case, Mitch is packing his 45 as he sits down at the table to exchange ownership of Priscilla with Rex. He notices the two men with Rex, so he sits with his back against the wall facing Rex and the two men that he doesn't know. Rex asks, "Can I get you something, Mitch?"

"That's okay, Rex, man, I'm straight. Let's just handle this business, man." Mitch wants to end this exchange as swiftly as possible because he is well aware that, in these changing times, certain codes of the pimp game aren't adhered to by a good deal of young up and comers.

Rex tries Mitch, opening with, "Mitch, I'm not a pimp, so this serving shit doesn't fly with me."

Mitch rests his right hand on his left leg closest to the weapon in his belt, and glances from the two men with Rex back to Rex's eyes as he responds, "You know Rex, my name is actually Pretty Mitch, and you'll find that name is not exactly unknown around the city and up and down the West Coast, man. You just might want to ask around about that name before we continue this little conversation."

Sensing that Mitch's demeanor does not match his baby face and size, Rex agrees. "Maybe, that's a plan for now Mitch. Give me a call tomorrow at this number, and we'll finish this business then." That's all fine and good with Mitch, because he already has Priscilla down at the cash.

"So Rex, I take it that until we finish this little business about Priscilla, I won't have to be concerned about you sweating her while she's getting at my dough?" Mitch questions. They shake as Rex agrees.

Once Rex finds out whom and what Mitch has been around the bay, Rex tells him by phone, "I checked around and got the 411 about you, Mitch. Still, like I said before, I'm no pimp, so all that meeting and serving notice shit isn't me, but we all good about that bitch, man. Quiet as it's kept, that bitch don't want nothin. That's why she gets with a nigga that ain't got nothin."

Mitch doesn't notice Rex's intended insult of him before he responds, "Alright Rex, we're straight and I take you at your word, man, because like you said you aren't a pimp. Which means you probably don't know that once a nigga is served about a bitch, it's the respectful thing to do to not fuck with that bitch while in the avocation of another pimp's business," and with that Mitch hangs up. However, as he reflects briefly on what Rex said about him having nothing, it troubles him, so he gets loaded to forget about it.

Mitch spends a lot of time hanging around the drug strolls with other hypes and street dealers kicking it about the good old days, how it used to be for him, and how big of a man he was once upon a time. It seems about as close to balling as Mitch can get now. He avoids contact with old places and associates out of shame, embarrassment, and guilt for having utterly ruined his life. Now, on top of all that, he's a common street hype as well.

There are new up and coming pimps, dealers and hustlers on and around the sets who have heard about Mitch's exploits, so they get him high just for association. They're curious about what happened to cause him to fall so far, and so hard. His answer is always the same. "Today's dealers are tomorrow's buyers," just as he remembers being cautioned.

He has a couple of hoes, Priscilla, and a new white hoe named Trina. Trina is a twenty year old fine brunette with blue eyes, an old school hoe out of Ohio. She was turned out into the game at twelve and started shooting smack a year ago, at nineteen, so all the dog hasn't come out in her just yet. The three of them share a room and one bed in a hotel flop house located at the corner of Fillmore and Fell Streets. Mitch no longer has properties, cars, jewelry or anything of value other than a few of his old outfits, and now a very tarnished reputation.

When he comes to for the day, his first order of business has to be injecting the much needed heroin into his veins. As he feels the effects of the substance that has become as essential to him as his life's blood, he vows to get help. However, as his senses succumb to the rapture of the drug, he abandons himself to the inevitability of yet another day of addiction, in which he will lie, cheat, steal, or kill, under the total possession of heroin and the pursuit of getting more heroin. As the substance surges through his blood stream, he experiences that peculiar unpleasant taste, and feels the sensation of that warm, calming veil that starts in the pit of his stomach and creeps magically through his body and senses. His nose stops running and it relieves his chills, hot flashes, and aching bones. His whole body feels like one big exposed nerve end that desperately needs insulation from everything, including life itself, until the effects of the drug begins to melt those feelings away. His entire body and mind are transformed by the miracle drug as it begins to make him feel whole again, invincible, unafraid and unconcerned about anything, except the next fix.

He then fixes Trina so she can go to work and get at the money. As Priscilla wakes up from the smell of the drugs she asks in futility once again, "Daddy, can I try some of that?"

"No bitch, and I better not ever hear about you trying this shit, you understand me?"

Priscilla pouts as she tries again, "Mitch, I just want a little bit, please. Anyway, it's part my money that pays for that shit for you and Trina. And I don't even get to have any of it, that's really fucked up, Mitch."

With Trina in the shower Mitch consoles his main girl, Priscilla. "Come here baby. Look, you are my baby and my bottom broad. I don't want to see you go out like this," he says as he points to the tracks up and down his hands and arms. "Remember the plans we talked about baby. We're coming up out of this shit, you'll see. I'll be right back up there doing it like I used to, and guess what? You'll be right up there at my side as my right arm. I can't have you in that position if you're using this shit." Priscilla excitedly hugs and kisses Mitch and jumps up. She's fired up to go get showered and dressed to go get at the money for him.

Mitch is thinking, *for the moment that pacifies my young Prissy* (his nickname for Priscilla). He knows from experience that hoes are like pimp's kids, so what they see that man do they want to do as well. That applies to whatever it may be, even shooting dope. It's not all about good intentions for Prissy, though. Mitch doesn't need another junkie in the family cutting back his own amount of daily drugs. Mitch is also aware that Prissy has been sneaking around and chipping with heroin behind his back for a while now. So he figures he will hold back her progression of use for as long as possible. He no longer has any delusions about controlling his or anyone else's using, for he has learned the hard way that heroin is the biggest and most powerful of all pimps. His alter ego suggests to him, *Prissy is a great money maker for us and we don't want that to end, because once she gets strung out, this dope will become the main pimp, not us.*

After the girls are gone, Mitch's extent of washing up is throwing water on his face before hitting the streets. Mitch wears his hair in an afro now because he can no longer spare money for processing his hair. He has the stench of multiple days without showering. His addiction to dog food has made his life one of just that, a dog's life.

As Mitch sits on the side of the bed nodding, scratching, and listening to the lyrics of the song playing on the radio, he thinks how fitting the song (originally sang by Billie Holliday) is for his life lately. As he hears Diana Ross belt out the words to *Good Morning Heartaches*, "Good morning heartache thought we said goodbye last night. I tossed and turned until it seemed you had gone. But here you are with the dawn," he ponders how these words describe his dilemma to a tee. Even though he and Billie live in different times, they are both ostracized from the game that they love so dear by the alluring charms of heroin. He wonders how many people will listen to this same song not knowing that the entity Billie sings about is not love, but the seductive powers of the poppy plant derivative, *King Heroin.*

Chapter XXI

Second Time Around

Mitch generally hangs out on the street corner nodding, drinking wine, and talking trash with other hypes while his two girls are getting at his dough. One early evening Mitch is standing in front of the liquor store in a half nod on the corner of Fillmore and Ellis Streets. He notices a big black Ham pull up, and through his barely open eyes he strains to see who is inside. As the front passenger window rolls down, Mitch can make out Spike, an old pimp and dealer who once was a partner of Mitch.

"Hey Pretty, come here man, it's me, Spike."

"Spike, man, is that you?" Mitch is embarrassed to have Spike or anyone that knew who, when, and how, he once lived to see him this way. The promise of a freebie in the form of a bag or two of heroin or a couple of bucks overrides his shame, however. Mitch approaches the window with a bottle of Thunderbird wine wrapped in a paper bag in his hand. Like most heroin addicts, Mitch finds that wine enhances the effects of heroin when he doesn't have enough of the drug in his system.

"Get in Pretty, let's kick it, man, I got something up you might be interested in. Damn Mitch, man, you smell." Spike rolls down all four windows and blasts the air conditioner on high. Spike is a medium height redbone of about twenty nine years old.

Mitch ignores Spike's comments and takes a swig of wine and asks, "What's up Spike, man?"

"Mitch, let me see your keys, man."

"Nigga what do you mean, my keys?"

"Yeah Mitch keys, you know nigga, you used to have some or don't you remember those days?"

"Nigga I got keys," he says as he reaches in his pocket and pulls out the single key he has to the room he shares with his two girls.

"Mitch, you got no business these days, do you?"

"Nigga, I got hoe business, and fuck you, pull over so I can get out."

"Mitch, come on, bro, ride with me and talk for a minute. You were once a hell of a nigga, man. What the fuck happened to you? Man, losing your wife and all those broads you had for all those years must have really screwed your head up real bad." Mitch hasn't considered the thoughts of the misfortunes of some of his girls until this moment.

"Spike, where is all this going? And what does any of it have to do with me?"

"I'm hooked up with some people that may have some work for you, Mitch. I'll tell you what. You got a gat (gun)?"

"Why, do I need a piece, Spike?"

"You need a piece Mitch so you can at least look like a nigga that's down and about serious business."

"Yeah, I got a piece, but it's in pawn right now."

"How much is it in pawn for, Mitch? Never mind, here's two hundred and two bags, get it out or buy another one, take a *bath,* get some decent threads on, get your shit together and meet me here tonight at midnight. You'll get out of this shit, and be back down doing it the way you belong, Mitch, okay?"

Mitch is so anxious to inject the two bags that he doesn't waste time getting to his room up the hill. It's a long walk or bus ride and he can't wait on either. He runs to one of the nearby shooting galleries. This particular spot is located right down the street in the Booker T. Washington Hotel, which has become a haven for hypes and dealers.

Mitch knocks softy on the door and identifies himself when asked. Once inside he hands Rock, the proprietor of the gallery, one dollar. Rock is an older, dark skin hype who was once a big time drug dealer around the bay area. Rock tells Mitch, "I'm really sick, man, so keep the buck, man, and let me get a little taste on the cotton (to leave a small bit of liquid heroin on the cotton used to filter the drugs)." Mitch notices that familiar stench of accumulated dried blood and drugs, which has been squeezed out of the syringes countless times onto the carpet as different dope fiends have cleaned them after each other for reuse. Disposable syringes are used by different addicts over and over again with no regard whatsoever for their individual health or safety, until they break. As Mitch cooks up his two bags, he looks around the room and sees a female hype named Short Line. Very few addicts and street hustlers know each other's whole or real names. Short line is hitting herself with a syringe in her inner thigh up near her pubic area, and Mitch smiles as he thinks how glad he is to still have healthy veins to use in his arms or hands. As he draws up his drugs into the syringe, he also notices another addict named Papa, a fiftyish year old, tall, light skin addict, who is lying on the bed while someone is shooting heroin into a vein in his neck.

What's really incredible about all of this is that it has become the comfortably accepted norm of Mitch's existence. He is consumed with running, gunning and getting money only to squander it on his heroin habit. He has justified all of this as just being how things are in the world of a dope fiend. What's even more pathetic is that he has come to accept that he is just that, another common street hype.

After getting back to his room, Mitch showers and puts on one of his old tailor made suits that he hasn't sold or pawned. He walks to the stroll in Hayes Valley where Prissy and Trina work, and tells them he'll be gone for awhile. Prissy tells Mitch, "You're sure looking and smelling good daddy. Where you going?"

"I'm going to handle a pimp's business bitch. You just make sure you and Trina mama stay down for mine."

As Trina walks up from turning a date, Prissy asks Mitch, "Do you want the money we got now, Daddy?"

"Yeah, as a matter of fact I do, so you two hoes break yourselves." The two women laugh, as they pull money from different stash places on their person. "Y'all stay down until I swoop back through in the morning for you, and we'll go get breakfast, alright?"

Spike picks Mitch up and they head for an after-hours joint out on Haight Street near Divisadero Street. "Damn Mitch, you still polish up pretty good, man, he says." They laugh and slap five. On the way Spike and Mitch do lines of heroin and coke. Under the bravado of the speed balling, Mitch feels invincible.

Once inside the after-hours, Mitch sees a lot of old faces, some of which he hasn't seen in over a year since he's been held hostage by his dope habit. Mitch is sitting at the bar drinking when he notices Spike walking back towards him with T and another guy, now known as One eyed T, since Mitch kicked the other eye out. Mitch starts looking around for an exit and gauging his position to the approaching men. As T and Spike walk up, Mitch's hand instinctively slides to his 45. Mitch stands up for position thinking, *damn, I never noticed before that T is such a tall dude.* T's imposing stature causes Mitch to instinctively bolt back and clutch tighter to his piece in his weight band. His alter ego reassures him, *there's no such thing as bigger or smaller with this 45 in our grasp.*

Mitch knows what his own intentions would be if some nigga had kicked his eye out. He starts trying to figure out a way to get out of this joint without having to kill T, or being beaten to death by him. T senses Mitch's discomfort, takes a step back and throws up both hands in front of his body as if to insinuate he wants no trouble and then says, "Hey, hey, be cool baby, I just want to talk." T motions Spike, and the other guy with him, away and Mitch notices that the one guy with T, who he doesn't know, is noticeably Jamaican. "Hey Mitch, I heard you were out, man," he says while sticking his hand out to Mitch. Mitch doesn't reciprocate the hand shake gesture by T and remains cool, calm and collected as he tries to decipher what's really going on with T, and what he's doing with his hands.

One thing Mitch is absolutely sure of, *I absolutely cannot and will not let this big ole nigga get his hands on me.*

T takes back his hand and continues, "How long have you been home, Mitch?" Still with no response from Mitch, T attempts to ease the obvious tensions of the much smaller man, Mitch. "Listen Mitch, just for the record, I know you didn't have anything to do with that deal with my family, man, and this wasn't personal," he remarks as he points to the patch over his left eye. "It was just about business, and that thing with Digger. Well I mean, you even lost your own wife, man. I know for a fact it was those guineas, man. So what do you say? Let's let sleeping dogs lie. Now you and I can be all about the money thing again. We did real well together back in the day, me and you, Mitch." T illustrates by pointing between he and Mitch. With that, T offers his hand again. Before grabbing T's hand Mitch stares into his eyes as he wonders why T is trying so hard to convince him that it was the Italians that did Dee Dee. So he asks, "How do you know it was the Italians that were the cause of my wife's death, T?"

"I got my sources, Mitch."

Mitch is thinking, the only possible reason this nigga, T, is trying so hard to convince him that it was the Italians is because he either did it, or knows who did. Mitch wonders, *does he not know that Dee Dee was Italian and those guineas, as T puts it, were my wife's blood family. So it couldn't have been them.* Mitch reflects that only everyone that was anyone in the game, in and around the bay area at the time of his and Dee's wedding, has at least heard about it. His alter ego quickly reminds him, *T isn't from around the bay area, and wasn't in the bay area during the time of the wedding, so how could he know? T obviously doesn't even seem to know that Dee Dee was Italian.* So Mitch decides, *yeah nigga, we'll let sleeping dogs lie until it's time for them to be awakened once again.* Mitch has that little smile on his face as he responds, "Yeah T, we both lost a lot in that deal, man" as he shakes T's hand with his left hand to keep his right hand free to get busy.

It's as Fast once summed it up, "I'd rather have a piece on me and not need it, than to not have it and end up needing it. Also, I'd rather the cops catch me with a gat than for my enemies to catch me without one."

"Mitch, I know those cases set you back, man, but I got some work that I know you'll be interested in." Between being badly hooked on drugs and dead broke without even an automobile, Mitch's judgment is clouded by his near destitution.

Then he remembers Don V's words, "Keep your friends close, and your enemies closer." Mitch thinks this is perhaps a bit too close. Still, he listens as T explains, and agrees to ride with just T to meet some people.

T gives Mitch his piece and lets Mitch search him for another, so Mitch will feel safe. Mitch still doesn't feel safe because T is big enough to kill him with his bare hands. So loaded or not, Mitch is not taking any chances and his alter ego is screaming for him not to take this ride. Even so, desperation to get something going drives him to take this risk. Mitch and T are blowing lines of speedballs en route and as always, Mitch does too much and nods out.

The next thing Mitch knows they've stopped, and there is this Spanish guy named Jesus standing by the passenger window, which is now down, poking Mitch in the shoulder, and telling him to get out of the car. T and Jesus take the two pistols off Mitch and lead him into the house. Jesus explains that it's just a precautionary move. Mitch is thinking yeah right, here he is again, but this time he sees no way out because he has no ace in the hole this time.

Inside the house, Mitch notices there are a few Spanish cats, lots of dope, and a couple of fine ass Latinas. A guy with a real heavy accent named Emiliano asks Mitch, "You know why you here?"

Mitch stares at Emiliano and responds, "No, I don't," but he's thinking, *it's for retribution.*

Then, Mitch does the most uncharacteristic of things for someone in his current position. He smiles nervously as he reflects on something a Viet Nam bud of his said to him once. While this bud of his was loaded on smack, he had said, "Even if I do get it, I'll be too high to know it one way or the other." Mitch smiles as he thinks, *I'm so loaded right now that whatever or however it goes down, I won't know one way or the other, either.*

"Your old Italian connections are pretty much done in this business. I understand they were perhaps responsible for your wife's death, and they abandoned you afterwards. We would never do that to one of our own. You have a distinct advantage of knowing a lot of people and this area, so here's the deal. You show our people, as he points to T, where, who, how, and what, you did for the Italians, and you're out of it."

"I thought you just told me that the Italians are done in this business anyway." "They are, but this will make our transition that much smoother and quicker. Plus, a good deal of their product has come from us anyway."

"What's in it for me?"

"First, you walk out of here, and none of us or our Jamaican associates will cause any problems for you or your girls."

"How can I be sure of that?"

"I give you my word."

Then T adds, "And Mitch I give you mine, as well."

Mitch is thinking, *yeah right until you get the information you want.*

There is a brief silence. Then Emiliano continues, "T tells me that you are very good at what you do, so you will have open credit lines anywhere you want with heroin and cocaína.*"

Mitch's alter ego suggests, *because of our rep and the fact that we have rolled in this area in an unprecedented fashion while being backed by the Italians, Emiliano sees the potential of cash that we can produce.* So Mitch agrees. He realizes that no matter what transgressions are between them, if they make enough money using each other, each will let bygones be bygones, at least for now.

"One more thing, you two *vatos locos* shake hands, and whatever was between you is no more."

Mitch offers his hand to T and Emiliano and says, "You have a deal." Mitch thinks, *there is no other way to explain it other than it just isn't my time and I have played my way out of another one.*

Mitch is contemptuous of Don V and Carmine dumping him after Dee Dee's murder, since the situation really stemmed from their combined involvement. Taking his son from him without even so much as visitation rights is also a thorn in his side. Of course Mitch conveniently doesn't consider his use of heroin, in concert with Dee Dee's demise, as becoming an even more glaring liability between him and his Italian connection. His alter ego reminds him, *we are actually quite lucky to just still be alive after all of that, because we know the thought crossed Don V's mind. So we ducked another bullet there, perhaps literally.* Mitch concurs with his alter ego and also thinks, *between the Columbians and the Jamaicans, the Italian's reign in the dope game is coming to an end at least in this locale anyway. The Italians need either the French or Columbians to supply them, so now I can deal direct with the Columbians, and the profit that I once had to kick up to Don V will be all mine now.*

He lost his son, but he figures that was inevitable anyway, because the game is hard on kids and family. Also, Lil' Mitch is much better off with them. He reasons Lil' Mitch would be just one more way for someone to get at him anyway and that he doesn't need. He lives for himself and the bounty of the day, and doesn't expect to see thirty five years alive anyway. Now, with a brand new connection, Mitch has started freebasing coke, which is becoming the new drug trend for getting high. A lot of his pimp partners that looked down on him for shooting heroin are now becoming base heads smoking raw cocaine. Mitch likes to smoke for social and getting high purposes, but heroin and the spike are still his main love, because he still doesn't like speeding for that long or that much. Getting the rush and speeding for a bit is cool, but right after that he has to run a half of spoon or so of high quality heroin into his veins to feel his true mellow groove.

He sees that a lot of pimps have also gone almost totally from the pimp game to the dope game. Hoes seem to be becoming even less of a commodity in most of the old places. Now, if he could just get off dog food, but that's an awful big *if,* he reasons. He couldn't do it to keep Margo as he replays that tape in his mind of what she said to him, "I gave you everything in me. I could stand anything as long as you were my poppy. I accepted other women or not seeing you for days. None of that mattered, because as long as I could see you being Pretty Mitch up there doing it big like you taught me, I felt big as well. Now you're just, another hype."

That hurt his feelings both personally and professionally, so he had responded, "Bitch, you can't talk to me that way and you aren't going anywhere. Do you know who the fuck I am?"

"I know who you used to be, Poppy. You alone were my source of pride and joy. I cared more about how you were than I cared about myself. You were my all, man, and now I go to work and I feel nothing but tired and sad. I've been with you over seven years. Come with me, I can get you off that shit if you're not around all this and we can live our lives together in peace someplace."

"Peace! Bitch I'm Pretty Mitch, I was pimping when you met me, and I'll still be pimping when you leave me. I'm in it to win it, and I'm all about pimp or die." He reflects that he loved that crazy, sexy, little Latina bitch, with a bigger heart than a lot of men. He remembers learning, 'play them bad, they come bad or end up going bad,' just like Margo. Mitch ponders how his style of pimping had helped raise Margo properly in the game and in life. He is proud that she played the game long and hard, and left it strong. She was a loyal broad to him, and he wishes her only the best. Pimping isn't personal. Over the years he will come to wonder what might have been had he left the life with her. Not many pimps or hoes get out the way Margo did, and stay out and stay okay.

With his new package from his new connection, Mitch goes to the VA hospital again and kicks heroin, and he's back in the chips. He doesn't forget his stint on 'down and out' street. He vows to do it bigger and better than ever, but this time he's playing for keeps. On holidays, he takes a case of wine to the corner that he once nodded out on with the street hypes and winos, and takes regular rides through there to remember his days of *when*. He even has a couple of the old boys from the corner in his employ.

He distances himself from Trina after he gets her on the methadone program. He leaves her on Fell Street, but in an apartment down by the freeway, fully furnished, color television and all the creature comforts. She's a good broad as long as he can keep her on methadone. One night during the Christmas holidays he is staying over at her spot when she walks in about five am. He's nodding out in front of the television and the Christmas tree, and she walks in and hands him his check for the night.

"Hey Daddy, you been nodding in that recliner all night? Here" as she hands Mitch a buck seventy five. "Oh Daddy, Fillmore Slim gave me a ride across the bay bridge, and told me to tell you hello, and he doesn't know if you would have done this for him, but he did it for you anyway, because you two are cool like that."

"Bitch what? You were in another pimp's car and presence?"

"I told him you'd be pissed, but at least let me explain." Mitch is aware that Trina knows that Fillmore and he have been cool over the years, and did it up and down the road in different spots together, but that still doesn't excuse her behavior.

Mitch has Trina working in Oakland on San Pablo Street, because police have been sweating hoes in the Hayes Valley and the Tenderloin. Sometimes he'll drive over and pick her up, and other times she'll catch the rapid transit, or have her last trick drive her home. This particular morning she is posted up at the Doggy Diner restaurant just off San Pablo Street and near the freeway exit. She is about to call Mitch and ask how he wants her to come home since there is no trick to bring her. As she's standing there, Fillmore cruises by, and sees a good looking white girl, who is obviously a hoe, so he does what pimps do, he gets right at her. She does the ignoring bit, looking and walking away until he asks, "If you won't tell me your name, then at least tell me your man's name."

Without looking at him she responds, "Pretty Mitch is my man, and you know him."

"Aw, you're one of Mitch's, where is he? I haven't seen him in ages."

"He's at the apartment."

"Look, Mitch and I go back some years, and I'd love to talk to him. Can you call him for me, please?"

"So Daddy, I tried to call you but you didn't answer, so when he offered to give me a ride home, I felt like it was cool, because he was cool and respectful of me and you about it. I mean, Daddy, you know and he knew that I'm no fresh turn out bitch that's going to fall for just any kind of okie doke."

As Mitch thinks about it he reflects back on how he and Slim have been towards each other through the years. However, his alter ego poses a question to him, *if the situation had been reversed would we have done the same by Slim that he just did by us?* There was a time when Mitch could have decisively answered that question, but at this moment he truly doesn't know. It would all probably depend on the bitch and the circumstances. Mitch vows that the very next time he runs across Slim he'll buy him a drink out of respect, and to thank him for the courtesy.

It's another of those foggy San Francisco nights, and Mitch is kicking it with his home boys at a club when he sees this super fine, light, bright and damn near white female from across the dimly lit club. Mitch goes, "Lil' Butch, man, look at that bitch over there," as she appears to be walking directly towards them. As she gets closer, Mitch notices that she is that mixture of Black and White, commonly known as a *trick baby.* Her dominant features are of an obvious white father, so it is assumed he was the trick of a black hooker. She has natural green eyes with curly, long, sandy blonde hair, a face like an angel, and a body like a sexual goddess. Sitting at Mitch's table is Lil' Butch, Mack Major and T. Cats like them are always being approached by different young girls. They're like folk heroes of the streets. Anybody that doesn't already know them or know about them wants to meet them. As a result there is always some young girl, or group of young girls volunteering themselves as new recruits, groupies, or sexual playthings.

Mitch watches as his three pimp buds get at this gorgeous trick baby female. She walks right past them directly to Mitch and smiles. "Hello Mitch." Mitch doesn't find her knowing his name out of the ordinary. It also isn't uncommon for women or people in general to know players like him, even though he doesn't know them, so he doesn't ask how or from where she knows him.

Instead he responds, "What's up, little mama?"

She looks at him curiously and defiantly with her hands on those sexy hips. "Mitch, nigga, you don't know who I am, huh?"

"Yeah baby, I know you from my dreams."

"Mitch, I'm Ellen Kaye. I used to be with B..."

Mitch cuts her off with, "Yeah, with BJ!" Then he laughs, stands up, grabs her hands off her hips, and pulls her to him, and they hug each other tightly. "Damn Kaye, I don't know how in the fuck I didn't remember your fine ass, girl. Bitch you were so fine you used to make my tongue hard."

Kaye blushes her obvious approval of Mitch's comments about her. Then a sexy little, deviously defiant smile comes over her face. "So what you saying nigga? You don't think I'm *still* fine?" She puts her hands back on her hips again, and sways her hips from side to side to display her assets for Mitch and the other three men.

Mitch's buds are cracking up, and exchanging hand slaps as they observe. "Kaye, you're still the finest specimen of female flesh I've ever observed. If God had the perfect bitch in mind when he created females it had to be your sexy ass, he replies."

Kaye unpretentiously thanks Mitch for the compliment. "You know, Mitch, I've traveled a lot since right after BJ went down years back."

"So Kaye, what brings you back to Frisco?"

"Well, this is home and you know, I left my heart in San Francisco, and shit like that."

She and Mitch laugh to that comment, as Mitch inquires, "You got people?"

"No, I'm here just partying with an old high school girlfriend of mine and her man. He's been after me to choose up with him."

"Kaye, you're still down, aren't you?"

"Yea Mitch, I'm still down, I just haven't found a man I want to be down with like that."

"What do you mean baby? Here I am."

Kaye laughs and says, "Is it okay with you, Mitch, if I go say good night to my friend, and come back over here and kick it with you?"

"What, you aren't back yet?" Again she laughs as she glides away. Mitch turns to his pimp buds saying, "You niggas need to go find some business someplace else." They each give Mitch five and laugh as they take their drinks and move to another table. It's the common courtesy that players extend each other when one gets action like this.

When Kaye comes back she looks around at Mitch sitting alone, and shrugs her shoulders as if to ask where Mitch's buds went. Mitch intuitively comments, "They went to get up out of a pimp's business."

Kaye sits in the chair closest to Mitch. "You know, Mitch, it's been so lonely and hard not having a man to be down with. I mean, I know I'm a down ass bitch whether it's selling pussy, boosting, selling dope, or whatever needs to be done to get paid on my own, but I'm still a hoe, and I want to be down with someone in everything, and not a square! I cared so much for J. He was the first and only pimp I was down for like that."

"Why is that?"

"I don't know, man. Niggas just want a bitch's money, subservience and sex. Mitch, there's so much more to me than just that. My father was my mama's pimp, and he schooled me in making sure I get something out of the game, and not just giving it all to a pimp, so I end up with nothing. I'm light, bright, and damn near white, because my mama got pregnant with me by one of her regular white tricks. But Jewel Pope is my true father in every sense of the word."

"So that's why you got a white girl name, huh?"

Her face turns red as she playfully pushes Mitch's face with her hand. "Aw shut up nigga, I'm just as black as you are in my heart."

Mitch realizes that he struck a nerve and it dawns on him that her Anglo features and complexion have probably been as much of a liability as an asset in her life as his stature has been in his own. So he looks deep into Kaye's pretty green eyes. "I know you are baby, and I was actually teasingly complimenting you, not criticizing you." Mitch waves his hand up and down her profile as he states, "In fact, how you look, your name and all of that is splab doobie with me. However, now that I see it bothers you I will never tease you about it again." He winks at her and pinches her face cheek.

She blushes again, and a look of surprise and appreciation of Mitch's acknowledgement of her sensitivities shows in her eyes as she continues. "Anyway, Jewel couldn't have done any better by me if I was his own blood daughter.

He used to tell me, 'your mama had you in the line of duty, so that makes you mine in accordance with the code of the game, which is why I gave you my name,' and he always treated me like his real daughter. Mitch, I own my home that my mama lives in now since I've been traveling. I still get money turning dates and slanging (selling drugs) a bit here and there, but I really miss the involvement of being down with a man in it all. You know what I mean, Mitch?"

Mitch recognizes that this is a situation that he needs to play at this broad's level, so he stops popping his collar, shucking and jiving as if she's just the average street hoe. He understands that Kaye is a female that requires facts, not cracks and acts, so he gets real serious. She is no dumb broad, and he has always known that. He looks directly into her eyes again, "Kaye, the *pretty* in my name doesn't come from me being just another air headed cutie pie nigga out here in these streets."

She laughs and says, "But Mitch, shit, you are a fine ass nigga though."

He laughs as well, and then continues, "The name 'pretty' actually comes from the fact that I put in such pretty pimping and work. All the people that are, and have been, really down with me in this game for the long haul will testify that I have taken great care of them as well as I take care of myself."

"Mitch I know that about you, nigga. Why you think I'm back over here kicking it with you. I've been around big niggas, little niggas, niggas with money and without, and they've all came at me real hard trying to knock me before and since BJ, because they like what they see. But I'm a down bitch, and I stand by my man no matter what. But I want a man that'll stand by me as well, and put my needs right up alongside his own.

"I've known and worked with some of your main girls, and I've seen how you've been by them. That's all I'm asking, Mitch, is for a fair shake, and nigga I'll die and go to hell with, or for, your ass, if need be. I've always been attracted to your game even back when I was with J, but I knew better than to play between you two niggas." The expression on her face changes to one of jokingly serious, "Plus nigga, I didn't want to get set on fire." Mitch continues staring into her eyes without expression or comment. She stares back into his momentarily to see if he will respond. When he doesn't she continues, "I mean, don't get me wrong, I've played niggas out of their dicks, money, weight in drugs, and shit, because all they wanted to do was fuck me. So, if a nig…"

Mitch interrupts her, "I wonder why they wanted to fuck you, Kaye?" he half questions, half states, as he smiles at her. "I mean, I'm telling you, you're only the sexiest bitch in the world and you just look like pussy and radiate sensuality."

"I didn't think you ever noticed me, because everybody knows that your exclusive hoes are *white* girls, and nigga I ain't white."

"Listen sexy ass bitch, I had to make a concerted effort not to stare at you when you, BJ, and I were in the same forum."

Kaye laughs appreciatively. "*Really*, I never knew that, you never said anything."

"You were one of BJ's main broads, so it would have gone against our understanding as partners to tamper that deep into each other's game. I mean, if you had been just one of his loose end crew, I would have got right at that ass, just as he would have with mine, before quick could get the news."

Kaye smiles again, approvingly, as Mitch is playing and saying the melody of her tune. "Mitch, if J were out I'd still be down with him, but he's not, and like life, the game goes on, right?"

Mitch slides his arm around her waist and pulls her face close to his. "Show you right when you know you right. Baby we're in a game where we bet all every day. Sometimes we win it all, and sometimes we lose it all, but win or lose we stay down for it, in it to win it and we do it until we die."

Later in the morning she gives Mitch six hundred and after sex they lay embraced. They laugh and talk about BJ, the old days, a nigga she shot once for BJ, and this game that they both love so dearly. She also explains to Mitch that the house she has she got when she was with BJ. Mitch considers telling Kaye that BJ got that game from him; that he taught BJ deserving hoes should live a lifestyle at the level of their seniority and productivity. However, he thinks better of it, because it serves no particular purpose at this point. Plus, Mitch feels that he and BJ weren't down with that back biting shit, at least with each other.

About a month later as he stays over with Kaye, she wakes him up with forty one hundred over and above her night's take, and laughingly tells him, "That's all of it nigga, I swear."

Playfully Mitch asks, "Bitch, you been holding out on me?"

"Nah nigga, I had that money already, I just needed to see what was really going on with us first before I gave it all to you like that. Now I know you're being straight with me, and you're about me like I'm about you." Then she kisses Mitch. "You really are a down ass little nigga, and next to J, the baddest nigga I've ever seen. I'll do anything for you. I got your back, and I know now that you got mine."

"Check this out baby, you know how you are about your Anglo features, well I'm the same way about words like short, little, small, honey and sweetie. You know what I mean?"

"I'm sorry Mitch. I forgot how you are about that. It'll never go there again."

She becomes one of the best dealers Mitch has in his employ. Mitch especially likes her because of one particular reason. She doesn't pester him to stop shooting heroin and cocaine. Kaye only smokes a little weed, has a couple of drinks here and there, and on rare occasions does a few lines of blow. On one occasion she tells Mitch, "Baby you'd be much better off if you'd stop shooting this shit."

"Bitch, you'd be much better off if you let me handle this, understood?"

"I got it Mitch," she answers and that is that. From that moment on, they set out about the business of 'hanging and slanging'.

Chapter XXII

Columbian Experience

One thing about having hoes and drug connections, you can go to any city in the world and its business as usual. Mitch meets Gabriella, the daughter of his new Columbian connection, Emiliano, at a party in the Mission District of San Francisco. She is tall for a Latina female, but has that trademark sexy ass like most Latinas, big legs, and is really pretty. She has these brown almond cat eyes that are about as seductive as any Mitch has seen. Mitch feels that Gabriela is high strung like most Latin *princesses*. There is instant attraction as they flirtatiously spar verbally with each other. In dealing with Gabriela, Mitch ponders that he has learned his lessons about life, women, world, flesh and the devil quite well. Lana and Fast would be too proud.

Lana taught him, "Being able to recognize women's little ploys and plots in motion will make up for your feelings about your stature being a liability."

He learned from Fast, "It's not the height of the man that's important. It's the height of the man's understanding and how qualified he is to convey it to a woman and people in general."

Mitch reflects that he has learned those lessons well, along with yet another of his favorites, 'so as a man thinketh in his heart, so is he,' and so too will he be perceived. As a result of years of OJT he can read Gabriela like a cheap novel. They hit it off and this time, with no opposition from Mitch's connection about it.

When they first meet, Mitch is introduced as Pretty Mitch. Her immediate response is, *"Cómo te llamas?"*

"I'm Pretty Mitch."

"No, what is your birth name?"

In jest and flirtation Mitch responds, "That is my real rebirth name."

"No, that is the name you have women call you because it is phallic."

Mitch finds Gabriela much too rigid, high strung and well mannered for his liking. However, he reasons that he'll fix that, as he responds, "Okay, my birth name is Mitchell Stone."

"Then, I will call you, Mitchell. It sounds more of nobility, not like this Pretty Mitch thing."

Mitch thinks, *whatever trips your trigger, bitch.*

He still notices that the Columbians he encounters in general are racist against Blacks, but Gabriela put it best when her dad, Emiliano, asks her, "Why a Negro?"

Her response is, "He's not Negro, he's just Mitchell." She always calls Mitch, "Mitchell" because she will not acknowledge any part of his street handle.

When she tells Mitch of the conversation, she has him cracking up. "It never entered my mind that you are Negro."

Gabby and Mitch start spending a lot of time together. He's been cautioned about how he treats her and interacts with her, and if he deviates from proper protocol it could be hazardous to his health. Talk about a rarity, she's a virgin, but that's not uncommon for Latina princesses. However, kicking it with her in this way, buys Mitch more clout with Emil. After sexual relations, Mitch proposes before Emil can find out and assume Mitch engaged Gabby in an affair of indiscretion. Mitch also feels that being married to Gabby gives him an instant edge, just in case. He really cares for Gabby, but it's not like he did with Lana or Brea, Dee Dee or Margo, or even Kaye.

Gabby gets pregnant and grows more and more disenchanted with Mitch pimping, because he is not around very much. So she gives him an ultimatum. "Give up the whores and the pimping, or me." Mitch finds it incredible how square broads like the thrill and excitement of getting involved with bad boys, pimps, players, and hustlers, but expect that they, or their sex, will change them.

After the baby girl, Gabriela Mitchella Jimenez Stone, is born, Gabby and Mitch travel to Bogota, Columbia with Lil' Gabi to meet Gabby's mom and family. Gabby figures that time away from the pimp game along with having Mitch around conventional Latino family settings and values, will reel Mitch into a semi-square lifestyle as a respectable drug dealer with just her and Gabi. She is very excited about showing Mitch and Gabi the place of her birth, how relationships are there, and places she liked to hang out as a kid. It amazes Mitch how they all feel like drug dealing is a respectable profession, but pimps are considered scum. Mitch thinks that if that's not a case of 'the pot calling the kettle black', he doesn't know what is. Mitch is recruiting here, even though he has no idea what he'll do with a female if he does come up, but he reasons that he is a pimp, and that's just what he does.

Gabby's family owns horses so they go horseback riding for what seems to Mitch as forever, far out into the countryside. It is truly beautiful in the Bogota countryside even if the actual city leaves a lot to be desired as far as creature comforts are concerned. There are very distinct differences in the lines drawn between the haves and the have not's. In fact, at Emil's ranch style home, it's like staying in a five star hotel with all up to date and modern décor, however the city as a whole is like one huge ghetto. As a result, Mitch and Gabby spend most of their stay at the ranch with only a few trips into the city to show Mitch around. Mitch spends most of the time nodding off on heroin, because he gets great heroin here for free. He also buys souvenirs for different ones of his crew back in the states, and it is Mitch's open relationship with those hoes that deeply concerns Gabby. They are a drug dealing family. It's how they make their living. They grow, process, smuggle, deal, and solicit dealers in other countries, especially the USA.

Once back in Frisco, Mitch manages to do what he does and keep it from her for a while. He reasons that he needs a real down bottom bitch and Gabby isn't the one. Neither is Prissy or Trina. That leaves only Kaye who is lowest on the totem pole. Mitch's alter ego reminds him, *it is our totem pole and ours is the only vote that matters. So as we say it, so shall it be written and so shall it be done.* He needed Gabby for leverage with his connection in the beginning, but now he's making himself and Emil a lot of money, so perhaps not complying with Gabby's wishes won't matter so much. After all, he was nice and honorable enough to marry her and give her child his name, but now he's out of there. *See ya wouldn't wanna be ya,* is his thinking.

Mitch has unfinished business that's never left his mind during the two years, to the date, that Dee Dee was murdered. He and One eyed T have been allies for two years while dealing, riding around getting at hoes, clubbing, watching each other's back in pickups and the whole nine yards. Like fine vintage wine, the taste of vengeance just gets better with time.

Laquan has become Mitch's new right arm. He is loyal, old school and down with whatever Mitch needs done. Mitch and Quan are rolling this night in the Mission District and Mitch tells him, "I got this thing I need to do, Quan, man."

"What do you want me to do, Mitch? I'm down with you for whatever, man, you know that."

"I have long term unfinished business with T, so we need to find him. Drive by that spot where T likes to hang out since its close by. You know the one where all those little fine ass young Mexican bitches hang out down here on Mission Street."

Mitch is riding in the back seat of the midnight blue on midnight blue, 1976, Ham d' Elegance, as Quan is driving. Their eyes lock in the rear view mirror, and Quan acknowledges that he and Mitch are on the same page by saying, "I've been wondering when you were going to get around to that."

Mitch stares out the back window as he mourns his late young wife's absence, her laughter and unrelenting loyalty to him. Without looking back at Quan, Mitch responds, "All things in good time my brother, all things in time."

Quan and Mitch have come to know each other pretty well over the years after lots of different *up to bats* (times for actions without words). "One thing Quan, it has to come from me. Just cover me with his boy, Spike, or whoever else is around."

They ride by the club and the parking lot and don't see T's Jag or his black Ham, so Mitch has Quan pull over at a phone booth. Quan goes into the Club Tequila to make sure T's not in another vehicle while Mitch calls T's spot in the Avenues. "T baby, man, I got some for real, super fly blow here."

"Is it ours?"

"Nah man, I'll be over in a few, and I'll explain everything."

"Ah Mitch, man, I got this real fine freak of a bitch here, man."

"Just for a minute T, I'll be in and out." Mitch laughs and asks, "Anyway nigga, you pimping over there or tricking?"

"Nigga, it's all about the pimping over here on mine."

"Then act like it nigga, like I said, after a few lines you're going to want in on this shit. After all, who else am I going to include in this deal, but my main man?"

"Alright, how long before you're here?"

"I should be there in twenty to thirty minutes, tops."

It's a very quiet and upscale neighborhood where a real old school player that Mitch knew years ago, ole man Mickey Cohen, had lived only a few blocks from T's house. As they pull up in front of the house, Mitch looks up and down the street both ways on his side, and Quan does the same for the other side of the street. Mitch rings the door bell and T's boy, Shorty, comes to the door. Mitch asks where T is, and Shorty tells him upstairs with some broad.

They follow Shorty into the hallway that leads to the stairs. At the bottom of the stairs Mitch shouts, "T, nigga, get your ass up, get dressed and come on down here," as Quan and Shorty laugh. Mitch continues with, "You aren't the only motherfucker that's got business tonight, nigga."

T shouts back, "Mitch, your timing is really fucked up, man. I'll be right down."

Mitch and Quan look in each other's eyes, acknowledging that whoever she is, she now knows that it's Mitch that's in the house. As T starts out of the master bedroom, Mitch hears him speak to someone and a woman's voice responds. Quan and Mitch's eyes meet again, as Mitch asks Shorty, "Is it just the three of you here, Shorty?"

Shorty looks at Mitch suspiciously, as Mitch explains, "Man, I got some real fly shit here from a new connection, and we don't want word getting out about it just yet, especially to the Columbians." Mitch leans his face near Shorty's ear and whispers, "Everybody's business ain't nobody's business. Can you dig it, Shorty?" Shorty acknowledges his understanding of it by nodding.

As T descends the stairs, Mitch asks Shorty to take Quan for a drink and T nods to Shorty that it's okay. While T is leading the way down the hallway to the study, Mitch is following making small talk with T. When T starts into the doorway of the study, Mitch looks back over his shoulder in the hallway to make sure no one is behind them. Then he turns back to watch T, as he pulls out his 45 and fixes the silencer in place. Mitch's alter ego reminds him, *T is a real big strong dude, so we can't take any chances.* Mitch speeds up his stride and just inside the door of the study before T can turn around, the muffled sounds of the silencer can be heard as he quickly puts one into T's right lower back, whoosh… and another in his left rear thigh in the hamstring area, whoosh. He only wants to immobilize him, not kill him or cause him to pass out right away. T grabs for his back and grunts, "Ugh, motherfucker," as he falls forward.

The crashing sound of T's body falling between his desk and a den chair causes Mitch to laugh loudly so as not to arouse Shorty's suspicion. It also lets Quan know that T is down. Swiftly checking the hallway and then T, to make sure he's completely immobilized, Mitch exclaims, "Damn T, clumsy ass nigga, you don't know your way around your own house."

Quan laughs loudly a brief moment later, and then Quan speaks loudly, "Yeah Shorty, I'm cool with that," as if talking to Shorty to let Mitch know that Shorty is down.

While checking T for a piece, Mitch laughs loudly and shouts back, "You guys better come and get a blow before T does it all."

Mitch closes the study door and helps T over onto his back. Mitch has a need for T to see him with that one eye and know that Mitch has known for the past two years that it was him all along that was responsible for Dee Dee and Digger, and probably even Walter as well. Mitch knows the broad upstairs won't come down, because women in or around the game know better than to interrupt men in the midst of business, unless it's a matter of life or death. Mitch smiles as he thinks that this is just such a scenario, but the bitch upstairs won't know that until it's too late. Still smiling, Mitch stares down into T's one eye and sees the agonizing pain, shock and disbelief in it, and whispers to T, "Nigga, I know it was you, and this is for my *guinea* wife, Digger and Walter."

T mumbles, "You little punk as…" He never gets to finish, as Mitch puts two in his head, whoosh…whoosh… and it is done. When Mitch comes out of the study Quan is standing next to the stairway wall, so he can't be seen by any one that might come down the stairs. Quan gives Mitch a thumb up gesture. Mitch gives him a thumb up in return, and they head upstairs for the broad, any money, drugs or jewelry they can find. Mitch figures it will look like just another dope dealer and crew robbed and killed and no one will care but him. They wipe clean and dispose of the parts of the gats in different places. Not a word is said between Mitch and Quan as they drive to Mitch's spot. Mitch is thinking, T was a big dumb ass nigga to have taken Mitch to his spots on many an occasion, and Mitch had never taken T to any of his own. Mitch wonders if that had ever seemed strange to T, or if he even noticed. His alter ego responds, *T just probably figured like most big men that we are just another little old nigga of no threat to him whatsoever.*

As Mitch reflects on the idea of 'never fight the same fight twice,' he realizes that it could have been him lying back there. So he feels that his luck and wit have seen him through, once again. He and Gabby separate because he will not abandon the hoes and the pimp game and she can't keep from nagging him about it. He thinks, *aw well, bitches come and go as all pimps know.* Her dad, Emil, doesn't say anything to Mitch about Gabby or T, except in casual conversation, so Mitch feels home free and it's on.

Chapter XXIII

Big Bust Runs

Mitch rents a pad in a nice quiet neighborhood to use as a cut and bag spot. It is a truly unique setup for his needs; a regular looking two story house, but with one special difference. It is constructed backwards, almost as if a dope dealer designed it. There is only one door on the ground level, in the rear. The front door is on the second level, and can only be reached by the front stairs. Mitch has the back ground level door closed off and reinforced. He adds a back door and stairs to the second level and has reinforced bars put on both doors and all the windows. The kitchen is actually on the second floor along with the living room and master bedroom. Downstairs are the two other bedrooms and the den.

Kaye and Quan generally handle all the business of cutting and bagging at this spot. However, this one morning Mitch stays after everything is done from the night before, freebasing and shooting speedballs. His people have picked up and gone. Mitch lies in bed wide awake and too high to do the freaking he'd previous planned to do with Kaye as she is curled up under him. Suddenly, it feels like an earthquake. Mitch rolls out of bed, grabs his 45 and rushes to the side of the living room window and peeps out. He sees cops and helicopters everywhere. He turns to Kaye shouting, "Flush the dope."

Then he hears the voice from the bullhorn, "You, inside, come out with your hands up."

Quan rushes upstairs as the jolt comes again. The police have hooked a cable to the front door bar gate and, with a helicopter, are pulling that part of the front wall out. Quan starts to aim a shotgun at the door, when Mitch gestures by waving his arm downward. "Quan, are you crazy? Put that damn gun down, nigga, they'll kill us all. Quick, go help Kaye flu…"

Before he finishes the statement a third jolt comes, and this time it pulls off a good portion of the front wall from around the living room door. As Mitch sees cops rushing up the steps, he throws his 45 across the floor. One of them rushes in and hits Mitch in the gut with the butt of a shotgun and knocks the wind out of him before he can raise his hands. Then he's slammed face down to the floor, as the police yell "Don't move you motherfucker." Another of the police hits Mitch in the back of his neck with a shotgun butt.

Mitch is gasping for air and passing out as he hears Quan yell, "You motherfuckers, he ain't got no gun, leave him alone." The policeman closest to Quan breaks Quan's jaw with the butt of a shotgun, knocking him out.

As Mitch is going out he hears the faint sounds of cops yelling something at Kaye, and her screaming back, "Fuck you motherfuckers," in the hazy distance, and then gun shots, and he slips into unconsciousness.

When Mitch finally comes to, he's handcuffed sitting inside a police car. The ride to the city jail is pretty much a blur. Mitch is charged with possession of a controlled substance with intent to distribute, obstruction of justice and the kicker, first degree murder. In the interrogation room a narcotic detective named Welles tells Mitch, "We got you, you son of a bitch."

Mitch stares silently at Welles, who is a big white guy with dark hair and eyes. Mitch rubs his bruised wrists in an effort to get his circulation back from the too tight handcuffs. He also rubs the back of his neck where there is still sharp pain. He has deep prints in his wrists from where the handcuffs were so tight and his hands are near numb.

"So Mitchell, what have you got to say?"

"I need to call my attorney."

"Sure, but first you ought to know this, your whore is dead, and your man is telling all he knows, so he doesn't get charged with murder one, baby."

"Who do you mean, dead, man?"

"Oh, so you do want to talk without your Jew lawyer, huh?"

"No, I just want to know who you're talking about being dead." The other narc named Cushing pulls a driver's license out of a woman's wallet and throws it on the table to Mitch.

Mitch recognizes that it's Kaye. "I got nothing else to say until I talk to my attorney," he repeats. Mitch's alter ego is nudging him with, *we can't allow these cops to make us believe Kaye was stupid enough to draw down on them, knowing we would have all three of us out within a day or two, at most.*

Mitch reasons that Kaye had no record other than hoe cases. She had the guts to make a move like that, but she also had the smarts not to because she was a down bitch and knew the game too well. She would never do as they are suggesting that she did. Could it be they caught her flushing the dope, and maybe she wouldn't stop when they told her to, so they just straight did her? He figures he will never know the answer to that. What's most paramount for now is bail for him and Quan, and then, what to do about these new charges?

His bail is set at two hundred large and Quan's is one hundred large. Mitch gets out that evening, and he springs Quan that next afternoon. The attorney, Asher Roth, tells Mitch, "Well, Mitch, you're a celebrity. You made the six o'clock news and the paper," and then he laughs.

Mitch is offended that Asher would laugh at such a time, but thinks, *what does this white boy care? It's not his ass that's in a sling, and he gets paid for it, either way.* Mitch's and other hustler's legal dilemmas are Asher's payday.

Asher continues, "The murder won't stick, but they found several packages with enough stuff and residue still in them, along with cutting mechanisms with enough traces of drugs in and them to make a case that you're dealing in weight for distribution. Also, to add insult to injury, they found a raw ounce each of heroin and cocaine."

"What? How is that possible, Ash?"

"You tell me, Mitch, you were fucking there?"

"Fuck, Kaye didn't have time to get rid of my personal stash that I was taking with me. I had those two ounces in my briefcase in the closet."

Asher admonishes, "Mitch, I'm not trying to tell you your business, but didn't you tell me that this house was a cut and bag joint? What the fuck were you doing hanging out there in the first place?"

Irritated with the attorney's inquiry, Mitch responds, "Getting loaded. So what am I looking at here?"

"Brother, you need to leave that shit alone. This is only a local matter so far, thank God. If we're lucky the feds won't step in and try to proceed again with filing the RICO Act; so I'd say one fifty to two hundred large, or so."

"Man, that's a lot, Ash."

"I know, but we can buy some time."

With that monetary news on his mind, Mitch smiles that little inappropriate smile, and says, "Okay, I gotta go get at this cash, man."

Later, Mitch learns that the police report discloses that the cops had followed Mitch and Quan after the pickup based on the tip of an anonymous informer and had let them do their thing. Then, they had followed the three dealers to other spots of Mitch's so they could bust all four locations simultaneously. Mitch figures, since it's only the local cops he might have action at a way out of going to prison. Mitch is also struggling with why there is no mention of a bust with his connection.

Mitch and Asher bounce the information off of each other and one plus one comes up four. After all, if the cops followed Mitch after he picked up and all the places down the line, then they must also know who is at the top of the line where the shit came from. "Now just picture this for a minute, Mitch," Asher theorizes, "what if Emil and company possibly have a license to deal from someone or some entity, as long as he feeds them a bust here and there of some magnitude? Since Mexican or Black crews are considered lower on the dealing food chain… well you figure it from there."

Mitch thinks about it and admits that he's on the outs with his inside license, Gabby. Having fallen from his connection's grace obviously means he is expendable. Would that mean fair game for the cops? What if Emil has connected Mitch to the T deal? Surely if he has, he hasn't let on that he did, and just as surely if Emil had, wouldn't his act of vengeance be more severe?

Still, Mitch reasons that Emil wouldn't still give him credit lines just to lose precious product to a bust, unless as Asher suggested, "It all ends up back in Emil's hands anyway." Mitch considers all of that to be quite possible, but it doesn't change the fact that he still has to do what's in front of him in order to stay out of prison. Mitch realizes it's now all a never ending story. The bottom line for him is, he has to pimp and deal to get money to stay out of prison, so he can continue to pimp and deal. He figures he'll be extra careful on his future pickups, just in case.

After running, dealing and pimping up on the money necessary, Asher tells Mitch that the entity downtown wants another one hundred and fifty large. That does it for Mitch. He is hooked worse than ever before and now he can't stop dealing, which means he can't stop using. He throws in the towel and takes a plea deal after shelling out three hundred large between bribes and legal expenses.

That first night in the San Francisco City Jail is okay, because Mitch has smuggled in enough drugs to ward off withdrawal sickness, for the moment. He has kicked several habits from doing different jail stretches, but this will prove to be his worse yet. The second day, as he comes out of a drug induced sleep, the beast is upon him. He is sweating heavily, yet his body is cold from the chills as he shivers. His bones ache and throb as if someone has pulled the flesh from them and is scraping them with a dull knife. His body jerks uncontrollably as he grinds his teeth and talks to himself. He moans, groans and curls his body up in the fetal position in an effort to stop the burning and the yearning in his stomach for the soothing essence of heroin.

He can almost smell it as it cooks, taste it and feel it saturating his body and mind, and numbing his senses. Even through his cries out to feel heroin's warm, sedating euphoric power, his withdrawal symptoms are unrelenting, and there is to be no relief. He prays for unconsciousness but it comes only in brief intervals. For days on end the monkey rages from within and without, churning and ripping at his insides and his flesh. He goes from laying his burning hot flesh on the hard cold concrete floor of the jail cell to wrapping himself in all the blankets he can buy as he gets the chills. Through blurred vision he can see through the bars of his cell other hypes withdrawing in the cells across from his. He hears their agonizing screams and pleas to the guards for help, but in the darkness of his despair and theirs, there will be no help for them, or him.

It is now between each of them, the devil, and the deep dark sea of agony that is kicking a heroin habit *cold turkey*. Even through all the suffering, Mitch would, if he could shoot heroin right now. The lyrics of an old James Brown's song, *King Heroin,* keeps going through his head, "Curse me in name, defy me in speech, but you'd pick me up right now if I were in your reach."

Mitch ends up getting the lesser of two evils. As part of his plea deal, instead of regular state prison, he's sent to California Rehabilitation Center (C.R.C.) for criminals with drug problems. Mitch's sentence carries five to life on the big end on down to one to ten on the little end. He can be on the streets in a year which sure as hell beats the alternative, a much longer stay in a regular lockdown penitentiary. Plus, when they threaten him by mentioning the RICO Act, both his hands go up in submission as suddenly C.R.C. sounds like a great idea to him.

Asher tells Mitch, "Mitch, you're lucky to get C.R.C. with the amount of drugs it was calculated that you had in your possession to distribute, and your reputation with local law enforcement. Other than that thing with your connection that we discussed, I can't for the life of me figure why the feds didn't file RICO, anyway. It seems that it would have been damn near open and shut on you, Mitch."

Mitch laughs and tells Asher, "I'm sure my bales of money didn't hurt either."

"No Mitch, I don't think you get it, no amount of money can buy you out of RICO because it's all about the Federal Government."

Mitch has no answer for Ash or himself, except, as his alter ego chooses to have him believe again, *it is quite simple, we have just played and parlayed our way out of another one by maneuvering our way into C.R.C.* Quan's charges get reduced to accessory before and after the fact of possession with intent to distribute, but he still gets San Quentin both on those charges and a parole violation. He had previously served a bit there for a murder. Mitch counts his own blessings and figures he'll get out in a couple of years or so, broke, but at least he'll be out. Like fair weather hoes and niggas do when the going gets tough, they get going the other way. Once Mitch is sentenced and awaiting transportation to C.R.C., his remaining people including Prissy and Trina know he won't be around to take care of them, so their productivity and support for him falls by the wayside. He's just happy to get what little shekels he can out of them.

In C.R.C., Mitch throws himself into a rigorous body building regiment of lifting weights, and doing dips and chin ups on the yard recreational bars. His thin angular frame starts to show signs of muscle tone and depth. He is clean and free of heroin, which he feels is the one redeeming quality about doing time. He usually stays clean during stretches incarcerated and at least for awhile after he gets out. Mitch vows that, when he gets out, things will go down all the way differently for him than ever before. He musters all the self will, intestinal fortitude and determination that he has to convince himself that he will, and can, come up again, and this time without the use of drugs. This next time around will be about strictly business, strictly pimping, and no drugs, not even dealing.

Mitch finds C.R.C. to be like a prison country club, with dormitory living, a baseball diamond, park, track, and best of all, conjugal visits. Drugs are plentifully available inside but Mitch doesn't touch them. Gabriella brings Gabi, now eight or nine months old, to C.R.C. for family visits. Mitch woos her into hooking back up with him, so he can get sex and money while he's locked down. It's too dangerous for Mitch to deal or do drugs in C.R.C. or on conjugal visits. If he gets caught his sentence will convert to straight hard time in a maximum security lockdown facility for a much longer period of time. As Mitch does this bit, he learns that Latinas are the best runners for their husbands, boyfriends and family while they're incarcerated. It's part of their one-man-women culture and their loyalty to their baby's daddy, no matter what.

Mitch meets this art instructor, a white guy named Flynn Davis, who gets Mitch involved with art work and oil painting. Mitch likes doing this, plus it looks good on paper to help expedite his release. Between Flynn and a couple of white broads that work in C.R.C., Mitch is able to get out even earlier to attend college. One old white broad named Rita Toney, who takes a liking to Mitch, tells Flynn one day, "Mitchell is just a victim of the women he's known." Flynn and Rita get Mitch a twelve hour pass to get enrolled in Cal Poly Pomona, which means early release. Rita is married with children, but Mitch can tell she is attracted to him, and not just as an object of good will. Mitch feels like she is just another old, bored working housewife in heat for some strange, especially some of his strange.

The mystique behind the pimping and criminality has also been known to be extremely provocative and alluring to some square females. Flynn and Rita help Mitch get financial aid and housing for his release into the nearby community of Pomona. He and Gabby fall out again and she goes back to Bogota for what will prove to be indefinitely. Mitch feels there's nothing back in Frisco for him anymore anyway, besides getting hooked, getting dead or the big one, RICO. So for now, he'll play this college game until he can knock a couple of young broads and its back on—only this time, without doing drugs.

Chapter XXIV

Going Home

Mitch is free in Pomona, California, in 1977. To him it's just another one horse town although it's only about an hour outside Los Angeles. He checks into the half way house Flynn and Rita help secure for him. One of the first people he sees is *Big Top,* a pimp he knows casually from back in the Sacramento days. It turns out Big Top is running this halfway house. "Pretty Mitch, man, I haven't seen you in years. What's going on with you, man? Man, whatever happened to all those Mexican hoes you had up in Sac, seven wasn't it? Come on in the office, man, and tell me what's been happening with you."

"Top, I just did a stretch of eleven and a half months in C.R.C. after two weeks in San Francisco County Jail, awaiting transportation. I'm in the mindset of staying clean. I'm healthy, broke, no hoes, no clothes, no cars, no jewelry, no connections and no prospects. My daughter's mama divorced me just before I got out because she figured I'm not done with the game, hoes and drugs. You know how that shit goes, man."

"Yeah, but you can get her back baby, pretty pimping ass nigga like you."

"Nah man, she left for Columbia after we couldn't work it out and took my kid, so that deal is pretty much done, I think. Anyway, she had half of it about me right, I'm not done fucking with hoes." He and Big Top laugh and slap five.

"Well, you got Carte Blanche here, Mitch."

"Thanks Top." Mitch is thinking, *I have arrived all the way down to the red carpet being rolled out for me at a half way house.* Still, he's happy to be free and drug free. He has to be because he's thirty one years old and his baby face still doesn't portray his years of wear and tear. Also, with no money and no hoes he smiles as he tells Top, "My money is funny and my change is strange, man."

First day of college is tough for Mitch. They're talking math levels that require prerequisites that Mitch quit school before reaching, let alone completing. He's uncomfortable because he misses the hero worship and the illusion of being a big shot. He feels that he's just a regular everyday nobody. He meets this square broad named Teri, who is a classy light brown skin sultry female from an upper middle class family background. She is also the Director of the facility where Mitch is staying. There is very little mingling of the races that Mitch can determine in this small town of Pomona and Mitch is not all that okay with that. However, he is okay with the halfway house hiring him as a drug and substance abuse counselor after only a few months out of prison.

With pimping always in the forefront of his mind, Mitch ponders his circumstances. How can he knock a gullible young white girl if he doesn't meet any? He has no car so he does the next thing in front of him, get at them on campus while going between classes. He has his hair in a perm in a style called *Lord Jesus* with his usual hip and slick demeanor. In his mind and modus operandi and for all intents and purposes, he feels like he's still a pimp that just happens not to have hoes, yet.

He is not exactly a poster child for what a college student looks and acts like. However, Mitch does take immense pleasure in his psychology class, B.F. Skinner's *Psychology 101,* because he reasons that he would make a really great psychologist with his hands on experiences in mind control and the power of suggestion. He thinks his experience using his wits to provide the emotional, mental and spiritual needs in respect to managing people (prostitutes) follows what is described in Skinner's text. When he reads and studies the text, he finds himself spellbound with hearing some of the same basic principles that he already uses to perfection in his life and affairs.

One day in class, his instructor, Dr. Schultz, asks the class, "What is the main unofficial reason most psych majors pursue this field?"

Mitch's hand goes up as he is sure he has the correct answer, "Because they aspire to help people master their issues and better understand themselves and their actions," he responds when called upon.

"Mitchell, that's a pretty noble answer for a first year psych major, and the reality is close to just that. The accepted theory is that confused and troubled people pursue avenues that offer them assistance in better understanding *themselves* and *their own* issues and actions through helping others towards that same end. What better way to do that than by solving those same dilemmas and issues for others?"

Until this day, Mitch has never entertained the possibility that he has been confused or troubled, just extremely uninformed about some things, maybe even a lot of things. Okay, so he's done a few things that might be considered somewhat maladjusted by some. He reasons that he has seen and done things that many have only dreamed of, living the up and down sides of life. Yet, he does feel like there is something missing.

On yet another occasion in his psych class they have to do research on sociopaths. Upon learning the definition, Mitch is further amazed that there is a description that is so definitive of him, "one who lacks a sense of moral responsibility or social conscience." He finds all this stuff so interesting that he wishes he had been able to get it when he was in school, but he figures one knows what one knows when one is supposed to know it. Right about this time Mitch woos a young Jewish girl out of L.A. named Stacie. She is very well connected with professional people, attorneys, and administrators within in the company where she works. He meets her one day on the Cal Poly campus while she is visiting a girl friend. Mitch looks really out of place on a college campus of about ninety eight point five percent Caucasians and non Blacks.

Stacie is a petite little brunette of the ripe old age of about twenty four and Mitch later learns she has graduated from UCLA. She is gullible and naïve about Black men, but far from stupid about life in general. She is too smart for her own good, and is attracted to Mitch's wit, charm, and aggressiveness, even though, every other word out of his mouth she calls "a line." In dealing with Stacie, Mitch feels the biggest hindrance in the history of pimping is the women's liberation movement. When he first sees her, he asks, "Hey, where you going?"

She turns to look and see if she knows who's speaking to her, sees Mitch and responds, "me?"

"No not me, you, I'm talking to you, little mama."

She questions, "What? I'm not your mother, and why are you talking to me anyway?" As she looks up and down Mitch, she adds, "Do I know you?"

"Well, you can."

"What makes you think I want to know someone that uses a line like that?"

Mitch rubs his chin as if searching for an answer. "Well, let's see. I'm pretty, charming, and you're still here talking to me, when you could have just kept walking, and not responded at all."

Noticeably irritated, she responds, "And conceited too, I see. I have to go."

"Hey, wait a minute, so we got off to a bad start. Can we start over? I'm Mitchell Stone, and you are?"

"I am *leaving!*"

Mitch starts laughing, "Man, you're sexy when you're riled. But if this relationship is going to have any chance of success you must learn to control your temper."

"Temper, I don't have a damn temper."

Mitch smiles and teases, "Yeah, that's the one I meant." Stacie turns back around to face Mitch, as his antics force her to smile against her will. So he presses the situation. "Forgive me. I can see you're not comfortable around black men. I didn't mean to make you uncomfortable."

Now she's beginning to stutter and her face flushes red. Mitch thinks triumphantly, *gotcha, you bitch.*

"I'm not uncomfortable being around anyone."

"Yeah, and I'll bet some of your best friends are black too, huh?"

"As a matter of fact, some of them are. Anyway, I don't owe you any explanations, you're an asshole, and I can't believe I'm even talking to you."

When she turns to walk away, Mitch asks, "So, how about having a soda or something with me?"

She spins around and puts her hands on her hips defiantly as Mitch is looking at her smiling. Stacie smiles, "No… aw… yes… I don't know, maybe. Who are you anyway and why are you here?"

"I told you my name is Mitchell Stone, and I attend this school."

Her facial expression softens a bit, as she comes around, "I only have a minute before I have to meet my friend, but I guess a soda would be okay."

"What's your name?"

"Stacie," she replies and goes with Mitch to have the soda and make small talk. They start calling each other back and forth between L.A., where Stacie resides, and Pomona. Sometimes he puts it on a basis of her helping him with his studies and assignments. Either way, they both know what time it really is between them. When she asks his age and he responds twenty five, it is believable, so she accepts it as being true.

Mitch finds that his baby face and smaller stature make it harder to gauge his actual age. Finally those things become assets for him, instead of liabilities. His alter ego adds, *young square white girls are easily manipulated by a player, especially a seasoned, vintage player like us.*

After several phone calls back and forth, they finally make arrangements to meet at a local disco in the neighboring city of Ontario named Narod's that coming weekend. Mitch keeps the halfway house he's living in a secret at first, until he has Stacie reeled in good. Then he gives her this sob story about being poor. He tells her friends of his family from Chicago, now living in Pomona and operating the halfway house, are helping him out with a place to stay while he's finishing college.

Coming from a stable background of faith and trust, Stacie believes what Mitch tells her. Why would she not? Stacie feels that Mitch just needs a good woman behind him to believe in him, and he'll be just fine at whatever he aspires to do. Pushing all the right buttons, Mitch is able to get Stacie to get real serious and fall hard and fast. Unfortunately, she begins to talk of their future, kids, and travel abroad together. Fortunately for Mitch however, she gives

Mitch money, lets him keep her car for extended periods of time, and even does some of his school papers for him.

Mitch starts thinking more and more about looking up his mom and grand mom. It's been over eleven years since he's seen or even talked to them. He realizes that, during all this time, they don't even know whether he's alive or dead, nor does he of them. His alter ego urges him, *but we can't go back now, broke with nothing. And how will we ever find them after all these years anyway?* Mitch ignores the urgings of his alter ego, that same part of his mind that has prevented him from even making the effort to find his family. Instantly, after all this time, he remembers his Aunt Martha on the little street named Tanner. He calls Memphis information and simply asks for the phone number to Martha Stone on Tanner Street. As he dials that number, he feels like he did before a firefight in Nam.

"Hello, is this Aunt Martha?"

"Yes, who is this?"

"It's Pretty, I mean… aw… it's Mitchell."

"Oh my God, Snoopy, boy where have you been?"

"Do you know where my mother and grandmother are?"

"Yes, let me give you the number, boy."

Mitch realizes that it has always been just that simple and easy to find and reconnect with Mama Jo and Madea. It never entered his mind over the past eleven years that all he had to do was call information to get his aunt or other relative's phone numbers in the little community of Douglass to find his mom and grand mom. Could it be that he or his alter ego just didn't really want him to find them? After all, how could he have remained what he had become with them in or around his life and affairs? Still, he's grateful that they haven't passed away while he's been gone, and neither has he. His mom and grand mom are living in the house just across the street from where they all once lived. So he calls. Mitch has always called her Madea, but it has been so long that when she answers, the best he can come up with is, "Hello, Mama."

There is a moment of silence and then, "Snoopy, is that you?"

"Yeah, it's me."

"Where are you? How are you?"

"I'm okay. I'm living in Pomona, California, in a halfway house."

"We have places like that back here. When are you coming home, Snoopy?"

"I don't know. I just got out of prison, and I need to get things together first."

"We'll send you a ticket to come home."

"Yeah, but I'll need to get a round trip ticket, because I'm in college here."

"We'll get it to you. Just give me the address where you are." Goldie has thousands of questions for her oldest child, like when, where, how, and why. Mitch knows that it's not the questions that will matter, but he has to be extremely selective about the answers, and just how much information he gives them about his past. Goldie and Mama Jo sound so excited as is Mitch about his homecoming. Goldie contacts Mitchell Senior and gets him to buy the plane ticket for Mitch and send it to him. Stacie takes Mitch to the airport from her apartment that morning because Mitch spent the last night with her as a brief farewell sleepover. She makes Mitch promise to call her collect just as soon as he gets to Memphis, so she'll know he's arrived safety.

As the plane lands in Memphis, Mitch is going over what he can and cannot say and how he can and cannot act. He's got on a new Petrocelli suit with matching blue gators and gator belt that Gabby brought to him for his release clothing before she split. Goldie and Mitch's two sisters, Veronica and Sierra, meet Mitch along with Mitch's new brother, Randy, who is almost eleven years old. Mitch reflects that Randy obviously came along right after he came up MIA, and lost contact with them. Madea confirms that when she says, "This is your new brother, Randy, who is going on eleven years old, almost to the exact date that you went missing." Mitch will learn that Goldie remembers both those dates all too well. Mitch notices how his mom looks at him, and he realizes that she has either heard of or at least ran across one or two of his kind in her many years of life. Between Mitch's expensive upscale outfit, attitude and mannerisms, his old mother is able to read him quite easily.

As Goldie observes Mitch's clothing, demeanor and swagger, a certain looks comes upon her face. That look causes him to reflect back to one of the times his mom had to go Englewood High School in Chicago to meet with the principal to get him enrolled back in school again after one of his suspensions. They're riding the bus down 63rd Street, and Goldie is sitting by the window, when they both observe a big black man with processed hair and dressed to kill. Some white woman was giving him a stack of money. Watching what was transpiring, Goldie spoke her thoughts aloud not talking to Mitch or anyone in particular, "I wonder what would make a woman do something like that." Mitch did not understand what that "something" she referred to was way back then.

Mitch has learned to perfection how to talk, walk, and act to convey what's really going on with him, without having to open his mouth. It's no longer an act, because it has become truly who and what he is now. Goldie reserves comments about Mitch until she and Mitch are alone. When they arrive at the house, Mama Jo tells Mitch that some white girl named Stacie has called twice, checking to see if he got here okay. He has forgotten to call her. "Snoopy who is Stacie? She sounds so sweet, boy."

"That's my girl, Mama Jo, and I was supposed to call her to let her know I got here safe." They all sit around and reminisce about Mitch growing up on that little street. There are some questions that Mitch dances around from his younger siblings, but overall it is a good reunion for everyone concerned.

As Mitch's stay continues in Memphis, he grows increasingly more restless and irritable with his situation. Pretty Mitch begins to uncontrollably emerge. Goldie is yet another female to say to him, "Snoopy, I believe you're just a victim of the women you've known. But along with your little baby face and look of innocence, there is a harshness and bitterness in your eyes."

For the very first time in his life Mitch realizes that his success with women has been because of that very same look and demeanor of innocence that Goldie describes, and not so much what he thought he had to become. After all these years, he finds that the person he fought and even killed not to be, is the very same person that people love in him in the first place.

His sister, Sierra, inquires, "Why is it that when I agree with you, your eyes shine warm and loving but, when I disagree or say something you don't like, your eyes change to anger and hardness? What's up with that?" It is those unconscious stares that he has learned to perfect in the looks that he has used for years to communicate, either his satisfaction or dissatisfaction with both prostitutes and men. Mitch reflects that he has always been able to revert back into being Snoopy when the situation called for it to charm and romance cops, women, and even other hustlers to do whatever he needed done for him. Mitch cannot identify the cause of his moodiness or his sudden bad attitude. He just knows that he feels those old feelings of restlessness, discontent and alienation from his family, partially because he is broke, busted and disgusted. Mostly however, his psyche is missing the familiar stimuli of his drug of choice, heroin. He has become dependent on it even when he's not using it.

When thoughts of heroin romance his mind, he still refuses to believe that any substance, thing, man, or woman can get the better of him. It doesn't matter the countless number of times that have provided much proof to the contrary. He truly believes, or at least wants to believe, that *he* is in control of his life and circumstances, and not some drug. He has lived by that, has been willing to die by that, or spend the rest of his natural life behind bars by that very same principle. He believes that success is about his commitment and willingness to sacrifice himself, and anyone else in his world, to achieve his goals. It is still several years down the road before he comes to start questioning that belief system and his denial about the power of drugs in his life.

Mitch has been away barely a week, yet he is already feeling the strong need to be back where he belongs, so he can again get shaking, moving and being himself. He is becoming uncomfortable because they ask too many questions here. He has told them he was in prison for selling and using drugs and left it at that, but Madea knows there is much more to it than that. His mannerisms speak so much louder than his words.

One day Goldie overhears Mitch on the phone talking to Stacie about the progress she is making to get him involved with her business connections. Stacie tells him that she hasn't made arrangements for him to meet the bosses at her job, just yet. That pisses Mitch off, and before he knows it he hears himself saying, "I don't care how you do it, but you better get it done by the time I get back. For now, send me the money I asked for through western union, and call me when it's done."

Mitch has always been loud and boisterous and in his mom's small house one can almost hear a conversation taking place from the furthest corner of it to the other. His voice carries throughout the house, even as he tries to whisper, because he is angry and irritated. Goldie walks by and looks at him with one of those looks, and once he hangs up, she asks, "Snoopy, was that your girlfriend?"

"Aw...no, that was just... someone I know."

"If that was just a woman you know, then how do you treat your girlfriend?"

What comes to Mitch's alter ego first is, *we need to get this bitch the fuck up out of our business.* Mitch disregards the urgings of his innermost self, as he recalls this is his Madea. "I'm sorry Madea if I seemed to overreact, but I was upset," he tells her.

"I could tell. Snoopy, can I talk to you privately for a moment?"

Mitch begins to question the validity of the suggestions and advise of his alter ego. It has been this entity that has protected, guided and directed him to function and survive in all the different arenas in which he has found himself since early childhood and throughout his adult life. Until this very moment, Mitch has felt compelled to carry out just about any decisions his alter ego comes up with, believing it to be for his best benefit. Mitch's face lights up as he turns on the charm, "Sure Madea, what do you want to talk to me about?"

"I know there's a lot you aren't saying about how you lived and what all you did, but sometimes I look in your eyes or hear you, and it's like you're a stranger to me."

"Well, Madea, it has been eleven plus years."

"But why are you so cold and hard, and where did you develop such blatant disrespect for women? You've got two sisters, a mother and a grandmother, so how would you feel if someone talked to one of us like you talked to that little girl on the phone just now?" Mitch sits there staring out into space, as if he doesn't hear her. "Snoopy, did you hear anything I just said?"

"Yeah Madea, I was just thinking how to answer. I really don't know." Mitch continues staring into space, even as he hears Goldie say something else until she just gives up trying to talk to him and leaves the room. Whatever illusions he might have had about going home, he might just as well dismiss them. Too much has taken place in his life for this to ever be his home again, if it ever was. A part of Mitch wishes that he could go back to when Dandy was alive and well, and live there as his home forever. He has finally come to realize how much he loved his grand dad, Dandy, but he can't remember ever really telling him that he did.

Chapter XXV

Back in Action

Arriving back in Cali, Mitch starts right back to Cal Poly and his little gig at the halfway house. He feels torn between two worlds. There's the Mitch from 'when and what once was' of his youth, and then there's the Mitch of what's really going on with him today.

While kicking around with Stacie at Dylan's Nightclub in L.A., Mitch runs into a younger player named Fast Black, who had been up and coming in the pimp game back in Mitch's old Frisco days. Black is a short, very dark skin guy of Mitch's stature and is cruising Dylan's looking for young white girls to flip. After a bit of small talk and exchanges of who is where and doing what, they hug and jump up and down right in the middle of the dance floor from the excitement of seeing each other. Stacie looks Black up and down, but says nothing, as the two men confer. Dylan's is a predominantly white club, so Mitch compliments Black on his choice of places for his hunt. He watches Black as he departs with a longing in his heart to be back in it himself.

Stacie rather suspiciously inquires, "Mitch, why didn't you introduce me to your friend, and *what* does he do?" Mitch just stares into her eyes and dismisses the question. He knows that she already has a good idea of what Black is about. Also, it serves no practical purpose for one pimp to introduce any of his game at any level to other pimps. It could prove to become a liability in the future at some point.

Stacie takes Mitch to a few of her company functions per Mitch's request. Mitch is thinking that he needs a broad that's either got money or can get at money. He has already figured out that Stacie isn't her, at least in the short term. Her boss's boss offers Mitch a sales position with the company. He blows it off and all the legitimate opportunities that Stacie lines up for him in an effort to help him.

She tells Mitch, "With your personality and that bright smile, why don't you stop acting like a loser, move in with me, and stop drinking so much and flirting with those different drugs. I'll help support you while you finish the rest of college. You could train and work part time with this company and by the time you get your degree, you could be one of the sales managers or even higher up the corporate ladder. That negativity you're involved in will only bring you hardship and more negativity. You can do this and anything you set your mind to accomplish. My God Mitchell you have so much talent and charisma. Marry me. I want to have your children and I can expose you to all kinds of leads and contacts to become anything you aspire to be through my job and my family."

Mitch is offended by her summation of him, partially because he realizes at least some of what she says to be true. What's even more disturbing to him is his fear and apprehensions about not being able to make the grade in the conventional arenas of life. For an ever so brief moment he allows himself to entertain the thought that his disdain for squares is perhaps not based so much on him being slicker or cooler than them, as it is him feeling that he doesn't possess their courage and strength of character for the real world and life. The struggling starving student bit isn't Mitch's cup of tea. It looks good to his parole officer, but Mitch recognizes that he doesn't have a car, a prostitute, a place to stay outside of the halfway house or even a watch, so he needs to do some serious coming up. However, Mitch's age is starting to bring him from under the ether of the fast lane game. He doesn't aspire to be one of those too old men he's seen still trying to come up on a young broad in the game.

In the interim Mitch knocks a cute, young, seventeen year old, medium brown skin sister named Gina. She has a nice body and is nasty and wild just the way Mitch likes them. Gina comes from a large, tough, streetwise local family from the mother on down. When Mitch meets her she already has her little toe in the game. His alter ego assures him, *we can fix all that with a little psychological persuasion and we'll have her all the way down.*

Mitch tries smoking sherm (PCP) one night with Big Top and a couple of other dudes at the halfway house, but he finds it's too debilitating to his mind and senses. However, it comes to him as he's watching all the young teeny boppers smoking sherm or free basing coke, that this is perhaps the new twist on the game for him. Gina is already selling sherm and turning a few tricks here and there to make ends meet. Mitch takes her to the next level in getting at his money 24/7. Mitch feels that his biggest mistake with Gina, who is now Mitch's bottom, is not relocating her away from family and other familiar spots and distractions. Rule of thumb for Mitch is, when he turns a broad out, it's best to take her out of that town far away to where the only person she knows is him, at least until she is totally spellbound into him and the game.

By this time Stacie knows about Mitch's pimping other women and even his escalating hard drug use. Still, she has no idea just how deep and complete this insidious insanity runs in him. Stacie hangs in there with him and he milks her for as much cash as he can. Then he dumps her, as he completely returns to the call of the wild and the fugitive kind in the fast life. In Mitch's limited scope he is a pimp and a dope dealer and that's all he aspires to be, just as he has been tutored. Mitch quits college after milking Stacie for one last bankroll and sets up shop in an apartment freshly furnished in brand new furnishings, and buys a used midnight blue, on powder blue, 1976, Chrysler New Yorker.

Mitch comes up with an eighteen year old, cutie pie, dark skin sister named Rachel, who Mitch becomes somewhat infatuated with while having fun playing with her. Mitch hasn't been 'drug free' this long in years, and he loves it. Well, he's not shooting heroin, anyway, he rationalizes. However, he's drinking too much every night and does lines of blow excessively here and there, but for the most part his thinking is centered on *come-up-ism and the money.*

With time to cruise and hunt, Mitch knocks a little Mexican broad that comes through the halfway house named Maricela. He's now working her, Gina and another little short Latina named Dawn, between Pomona, L.A., San Bernardino and Riverside. Mitch and Teri, the director of the halfway house, start producing musical shows and bringing in different groups to entertain at the local clubs. It's a fairly lucrative enterprise, for a minute. Teri has become a loyal friend and ally to Mitch since he lived at her halfway house. Mitch has a fly perm, hoes, and a corner of the sherm market in Pomona. He's making plans to buy a house in Diamond Bar, which is an upscale community in the area. Life is good as he's going through all the young girls in the area and flipping some of them at one time or another. The name of the game is still the same. Hoes still come and go as all pimps know.

Rachel comes up pregnant and two weeks later Gina is pregnant as well. Mitch doesn't want either to have a kid, especially by him. He offers to pay for Rachel's abortion, but like a good deal of uninformed young females in black communities, Rachel thinks a kid will keep him in, or at least around, her life. Mitch tells Rachel, as does his mom, Goldie, "Don't have this kid expecting it to slow Mitch down. If you decide to have this child, know that it'll pretty much be just you and the family back here, because he won't be around or maybe even alive for you or that child." It doesn't dissuade Rachel in the least and she remains intent on having his child.

Mitch makes sure Gina loses hers, so she can keep getting at his dough. Also, Mitch knocks a few different young chicks that come through the halfway house. That, along with certain other indiscretions, causes them to have to shut down the halfway house and relinquish control to a new management group. Teri and Mitch have become the best of friends and allies, so she doesn't implicate him in any of it.

Now, back down deep in the game, Mitch is cruising down Holt Street hunting new prospects to get at one night, as he's listening to Donna Summer's new disco hit *Bad Girls*. He laughs aloud as he hears the lyrics, "Hey Mister, do you want to spend some time? I got what you want you got what I need. I'll be your baby, come and spend it on me." He smiles and wonders where Donna Summer got her information for that song. He reasons that he knows where and how she probably got her information. He laughs and says aloud, "Thanks Pimp God for all hoes at all levels in all arenas, everywhere. Pimp or die!" Everything in his world is in alignment, as he is again poised to come up. Suddenly, it's as if his car goes on automatic pilot and he ends up in front of a spot where he knows heroin and cocaine are exchanging hands. He sits for what seems like forever trying to talk his alter ego out of using again. He recalls how sick he was and how hard it was, kicking that last habit in the Frisco County Jail. He has used long enough to know that he can't just shoot or snort one speedball. It always leads to the same place for him, hooked like a dog, broke and eventually jail.

He further reasons he's thirty two years old with two pockets of cash and stash cash, along with young hard bodied Black and Mexican females, again throwing themselves at his feet vying for the opportunity to do his bidding, but most important, he loves being free, of heroin. As always, Mitch loses the battle of wits with his alter ego, and again finds himself nodding and scratching after running a syringe half full of coke and heroin into his vein. He feels the rush of that familiar euphoric veil overcoming his senses that always ends in a mixture of agony and ecstasy. It seems to him that heroin never fails to lure him back into its seductive embrace. Seemingly faster than ever before, Mitch succumbs to its sweet insanity. He foregoes sex, money, women, material possessions and all else for the false sense of emotional, mental, physical and spiritual freedom that being loaded provides him. Once again he is off to the races, chasing the next bag or two.

As Mitch surrenders his will to heroin he reflects on all the props that he has put in place this time around to run interference from his using. He has avoided old places and people, but he finds that wherever he ends up he is still who and what he is there. The faces and places may change but he seems to remain the same. He feels so utterly hopeless and helpless. How can he be so good at what he does, only to find himself one more time succumbing to a mere powdery substance? He has tried to limit his using to only freebasing, snorting coke, just drinking or all three together. He purposely didn't get into the sale of coke or heroin, but even that didn't help. No matter what path he chooses they all end up leading to here.

Mitch feels desolation and despair like he has never known. It only propels him further into abusing drugs to ease his feelings of self pity, shame, embarrassment and lack of power and control. One more time, Mitch is doing a stretch in C.R.C. This time it's only for dirty drug tests in, October, 1979. Mitch's daughter by Rachel is born during this stretch. He names her Henrietta, but is too preoccupied with what he'll need to do to come up once he's out, to feel either sadness or joy about having another kid. Mitch feels like he is pretty much done with Rachel, even though, he still needs her for a place to parole out to, money and transportation.

The first thing Mitch does when he gets out is to get right back busy. He's running girls and the new drug sensation, crack cocaine, between San Bernardino, Ontario and Pomona. Still using heavily and now smoking crack, just because he has it, Mitch's first love is still the calm, mellow euphoria of heroin. At first he figures selling crack will keep him from using heroin. Wrong. Mitch finds himself once again a big fish in a small pond, and he's attracting too much attention. In 1980, Mitch falls in with a guy named Keith, who is a tall, dark skin heroin addict, and they start hanging paper together. Keith is big in the forgery game, so one day he suggests, "Mitch you got those young hoes and I got paper, so let's put them together and get paid, man."

Mitch figures that he can make more money to support his habit through Gina and Dawn hanging paper, so he puts them down doing just that. As Mitch's habit gets progressively worse, Gina becomes disenchanted under the stress of Mitch's using so she jumps ship. It's not surprising to Mitch because he has learned that most females are no longer mentally and emotionally wired for the diehard loyalty and commitment in the game as those in the days of old. So Mitch is left with just Dawn, who is a loyal, little bitty, pretty Mexican girl and Maricela, who is equally as pretty and makes good money also. Unfortunately Maricela is a heroin addict like Mitch.

Maricela gets popped on Sunset for a hoe case and old warrants kick in, which means she'll be down for a bit. Keith gets busted with a bundle of cash and stolen checks, and Dawn gets popped hanging paper in West Covina and gets a year in Sybil Brand Correctional Facility for Women. So just like that, Mitch loses not one, but both of his fast, money getting, pretty little Latinas. Mitch and Ben, Gina's brother, get busted for driving under the influence and the police find two bags of heroin, stolen checks, and credit cards in their possession. Mitch is still somehow able to bail out before the parole hold is instituted. He reasons that finally a slip by the system, but he's glad for the opportunity to get back to his first love, heroin. A parole hold does come in on Ben, however, so Mitch has to leave him there. Mitch has had to abandon his apartments to stay one step ahead of his parole officer and prevent getting violated and sent back to C.R.C. After he's out of jail, Mitch knocks a young, hot, pretty sixteen year old Puerto Rican named Sondra out of Ontario. He does what he does in order to get her to do what he needs her to do for him. Sondra is simply a young Latina girl in love with Mitch and believes only in him. She gets money and is extremely low maintenance, which is all good with Mitch. With a heroin habit again in full bloom, he has no time for drama like with Gina and the others. As Sondra diligently gets the money, Mitch is spending it on drugs just as diligently. Mitch's latest claim to fame is spiraling downward as is his addiction to heroin, again. Sondra grows weary of working ten to twelve hours a day and having nothing to show for it but Mitch's drug habit, so she leaves penniless and disillusioned. Now, Mitch runs really short of money with no dependable broads and a monstrous habit to support.

It cost Mitch all of the cash he has for living expenses and his habit. He loses his ride to repossession and has to fall back on Rachel again for support, housing and transportation. One day after having kidnapped Rachel's new Toyota Corolla, Mitch gets busted en route to hanging some paper so he can get a fix. He's also still running on parole and ends up back incarcerated.

Chapter XXVI

And the Bit Goes On

Mitch is kicking another heroin habit, but this time in L.A County Jail. After a couple of weeks, Mitch's health is coming around. He gets into a skirmish along with a couple of his young Crip partners backing his play, and all three are sent to L. A. County's High Power Division. While in solitude, Mitch's alter ego calculates, *of the five females we've even remotely been involved with most recently, only three will qualify as long term soldiers at doing this stretch with us, especially with it being for this long of a bit.* Mitch reasons that if he had his choice, he'd much rather bet on one of his Latinas doing this stretch with him, but with Dawn and Maricela locked down like him and unable to determine Sondra's whereabouts, Mitch rolls the dice between Rachel and Gina as to which will last longer running for him. They have both started coming to visit him and dropping off *ducats* (cash) since he's been locked down. So through a calculating process of elimination, he marries Gina in the court room at sentencing. He gets sentenced to four years on forgery and burglary charges, which means with good behavior he could be eligible for parole in about three years. This is the longest he's ever been down in one stretch and he's not all that thrilled about the idea, but he figures to play is to pay.

It will turn out that his calculations are perhaps correct about marrying Gina. She is now pregnant with a trick baby but will still hold up running for him for almost a year. His old friend and business partner from the halfway house, Teri, will do what she can when she can for him (Christmas packages, cash and a few visits here and there). Rachel will check in on him from time to time by sending a check here and there to see if he's rehabilitating in her favor, and of course, his mom will do what little she can when she can. Finally, Mitch knows people from all across the State of California in the game, so he has at least some connections and support wherever they send him. Bottom line, Mitch concludes that, come what may, he will do whatever he has to do to survive just like he does when he's in the streets. The fact remains however, that drugs have once again caused his undoing.

For the next three years, Mitch will be known by a C number that the California Department of Corrections issues newly inducted criminals. He relinquishes his old N number that he had from C.R.C. Mitch immediately notices that racism is amplified by one hundred percent behind the walls, compared to the streets. When there are riots involving Blacks, it seems they always stand alone against all the other races, and he figures that's just the way it is in prison.

Initially, they send Mitch to Chino prison in southern California to await placement in a permanent institution. It really reminds him of being in the Army, which had been a lot like doing time. He gets assigned to a prison as far north as one can be in the California penal system, Susanville Firefighting Camp, which is a Boy Scout camp compared to some institutions where he could have been assigned.

Ben is sentenced to the same four years as Mitch, since they are crime partners on these charges, but Ben is scheduled to be shipped to Soledad Prison. Ben has come to call Mitch his older brother since Mitch became his mentor. Mitch is a good eight to nine years older than Ben. Mitch is shipped out of Chino first, and Ben yells at him as he's going through the bar gate, "Big bro, we'll run across each other somewhere down the line, and when we do I'll be as big as a house, dog."

As Mitch gets on the bus, he laughs and yells back to Ben, "Nigga, I don't find that hard to believe Lil' bro, because you're already six two, two hundred and thirty pounds or so *with* a heroin habit." Everybody in hearing distance laughs at the exchange, including a few guards. The convicts are dressed in bright orange jumpsuits and shackled from the waist, legs and wrist with cuffs and chains and loaded onto buses in the wee hours of the morning. Once Mitch is on the prison bus along with several other convicts headed for their assigned prisons, he runs into an old acquaintance named Ward, who is the husband of Bobbie out of Seaside from years ago.

He recognizes Mitch and has to refresh Mitch's memory so Mitch remembers him. They purposely position themselves in line so they can be seated together and kick it about old times. They are scheduled to stop over at Folsom Penitentiary before continuing to other joints. Once the bus gets moving, Ward and Mitch are reminiscing about the old names, faces and places they both have in common in and around the game. Ward laughs as he tells the convict in the seat behind them "This here is Pimping Pretty Mitch, and this nigga knocked me for my wife back in the day. Now here we are seated next to each other years later headed to the same joint to do a number." All the brothers within hearing distance laugh and start introducing themselves to Ward and Mitch. It is considered that, if Mitch and Ward can laugh so openly about such an incident between them, they must be serious entities in and about the game.

Going through the large iron gates of Folsom Prison is about as depressing as anything Mitch has ever experienced. On the way to their initial housing building and tier, Mitch and Ward see an old partner of theirs, Dean, the big time dealer and ex Army sergeant from Seaside. As Dean walks along at the minimum allowable distance from the new fish, he tells Mitch and Ward, "I'll bring over some commissary for you two when y'all get settled in." Then noticing Mitch's mingled gray hair, Dean laughs, "Pretty Mitch, those hoes have damn near driven you crazy, you got more gray hair than I do, and I'm a whole lot older than you, man."

Mitch is considered fresh meat in the market by some of the older cons. Some cons consider him easier to try on for size. Before he starts to bulk up again, Kenny, who is a homey Mitch has known in Frisco tells him, "Mitch, man, you got all that long hair down your back and you're small and thin, some of these lifers are gonna try you, man." Kenny and Frank give Mitch and Ward cosmetics and a can of Bugler, as Kenny further explains, "We're all down with each other here to cover each other's backs and shit, that's how we survive. Somebody says something out of line, sexually insinuating, or disrespectful, no matter how insignificant, you must take action and we'll move with you. Also, most of these cons for one reason or another, hate pimps, so beware of talking that pimp talk in the wrong company. A few of them are gonna try you on until they find out what you're all about. But nigga, I know as crazy of a nigga as you are in the streets, you'll be just fine in here."

Lying back on his bunk with his hands clasped behind his head, Mitch thinks there are more rules in here than in the Army, and breaking one or allowing someone else to break one towards him, could cost him his life. Mitch ponders, *how did an innocent country boy like me from Memphis, Tennessee, get here?* Then his alter ego clarifies that for him, *we're no longer innocent and we have done things to belong here.* Right at this moment, Mitch isn't sure if he was ever innocent, but what has he become? He feels no discernible shame, guilt or remorse for any of the things he's done, only anger for getting caught, except of course, for using heroin. He blames using drugs and not thinking clearly for his plight.

Mitch rationalizes that he killed in Nam out of duty, because it was kill or be killed. With everyone since then, it has been about either protecting himself and his people, or to make a necessary statement. What he can't get out of his mind is the possibility that it could have been him on the other end either of those times. How would his family have taken it? How did their families take it? Again, he reflects back to Nam and his company commander telling them, "Don't look at the VC as people; look at them as targets or obstacles that must be overcome."

Over the next three years, Mitch will be shipped around to six different penitentiaries ranging from maximum security to minimum, so that helps the time pass faster for him. He grows confused and uncertain about his future in the game and concerning his past problems with drugs. He also recognizes that he's not getting any younger as his hair is becoming increasingly more mingled with silver at only thirty five. The young bucks that he knows, or who know of him, start calling him 'pops' or 'old man.'

Mitch gets out in late 1984 to a work furlough facility in Upland, California. Teri observes how different Mitch looks, "Mitchell, you look older with that mingled gray hair and all that weight you've gained, but healthier, much more muscular and clean." The world seems a very different and strange place to Mitch, at first.

His ex bottom, Gina, is a crack head like most of the hoes working the stroll on Holt Street now. He gets a few checks out of her, but the pipe is now her true master. He has a couple of interludes with Rachel, Henri's mom. Then he knocks a Mexican broad named, Carla and a sister named Jackie. Along with Keith and Ben, who are also out on parole, Mitch sells a little crack between Pomona, Ontario and San Bernardino.

Mitch again knocks Sondra, his onetime young Puerto Rican girl from before he went to the joint, and its business with her like before. Within four months however, he starts chipping with drugs again, even though he knows one dirty test and he'll be back in the joint on a violation. He's riding one night with this much older guy named Mark, who was once in the business of slinging sherm and coke with him. Now they're in the rock business together. Mitch likes Mark because he too is a heroin addict. Mark is also old school and can be trusted so this all works out great for Mitch as they hustle together.

Mitch ends up blowing Carla, Jackie and the sack (drugs to sell). To add insult to injury he gets kicked out of his baby's mama house behind shooting heroin and succumbing to the mannerisms of a street hype. This time around, Mitch experiences the darkest times of his using career. He again stops showering regularly and becomes too sick to maintain his overall appearance. His addiction takes a far worse toll on him than ever before, faster than ever before, and he loses himself totally to shooting dope.

He is homeless until he finds refuge with a using partner named Rob, who uses his grandmother's house as a crack house. After a week at Rob's, Mitch runs into an old bookie partner of his named Willis, and gets a place to stay at a house that he uses as a bookie joint. Mitch and Mark hook back up because Mark is also staying there after his square wife puts him out behind shooting dope. So it's on again and he and Mitch start running, gunning and chasing the spoon. Mitch and Mark are broke and have no hoe between them, so they find themselves hustling *slum jewelry* (fake gold, watches and diamonds) and till tapping between L.A., West Covina and the cities between the two, in order to support their ever growing heroin habits.

Mitch finds himself with no car other than Mark's little old Chevy beater they use to do their hustling. He knows if he stays in this area, he's destined to return to prison again. Then Mitch gets lucky and he runs into Peggy, a good looking sister out of East St Louis that's been around since Mitch was balling in Pomona back before he went to prison. Mitch and Mark walk into the local Elks Lodge on Holt Street one Friday evening and are in the process of buying a spoon of heroin, when in Peggy struts looking to Mitch like an oasis in the desert.

Peggy is a twenty four year old veteran hoe of ten years, and Mitch knows her rep for 'clocking bank.' Mitch leans over and taps Mark's shoulder, "Mark, you see that pretty black bitch, Peggy? Man, those white boys eat that smooth black bitch up, and damn near rip off their hip pockets trying to pay her. So our problems may just almost be resolved, at least for now." After a few minutes of wooing and wowing her, she agrees to take Mitch and Mark back to her little studio apartment, so he can hide out from the police. Peggy smokes crack, so as Mitch and Mark are shooting dope she's hitting the pipe. Mitch tells Peggy that he and Mark are headed out of Pomona in a few days, as soon as they put a road bank together.

Peggy is all for that. "Baby, I want to get the fuck out of Pomona too, because it's making my game bad. Mitch, you know I can get money and I've wanted to kick it with you on the road like that ever since long before you went to prison, but you had all those little young turn out bitches then."

"Tell you what Peg, you get down while Mark and I are doing what we do, and the three of us can get up out of here together. Mark and I will pick up a couple of bottles of methadone and kick this dope on the road. Baby, there also won't be any room for you hitting that shit either," as he points to the kibbles and bits she has left on the pipe.

"I know Mitch, baby I just do it for the extra boost to get at the cash. You know what I mean, daddy? I'll be good to you, Mitch, I swear. With a down nigga like you, I won't need to hit this shit all that much, okay, baby? You want this last hit, Mitch?"

"Yeah, let me get with that." Mitch figures, he has nothing to lose by taking a hit, as he has several times in the past just because it was there. He doesn't see what the big deal is in smoking crack, especially when there is dog food available. Still he figures different strokes for different folks. He drops Peg off to get at the cash while he and Mark go do their hustling.

Over the next week or so, Peg gets at Mitch's dough, but he knows that it could all end with her next hit of the pipe. He reasons that since Peg's clocking bank and he and Mark are shooting a good deal of it up, he has to let her take a hit here and there. Mitch figures that the three of them are way too active in and out of her little studio pad all times of the evening and wee hours of the mornings. It'll be just a matter of time before the bust runs. So he has her pack up and they get a spot in West Covina where his mug is not so well known. One night Peg calls the motel and tells Mitch that she's in Ontario with a trick that's loaded with cash, and she's already got five hundred of it. "But Daddy, I know he's got some thousands more. I just can't get at it all."

Mitch does the next dope fiend thing. "Keep him there until Mark and I get there, no matter what you have to do, give him some free pussy, suck his dick for free, or whatever he wants. Just don't let him leave the spot."

"Okay. Just hurry," Peg agrees.

He and Mark hit the freeway in the old Chevy pushing it for all it's worth. They make the move and it's for six g's, his watch, diamond ring, and a rope chain with a whole ounce of 14kt gold nugget attached. They even take the trick's car, which is a late model Volvo. Of course Mitch decides to keep the jewelry to wear since his own has either been sold or swapped for drugs. Peggy already has seven bills, so with six thousand more, Mitch and company are good to go for the moment.

The three of them get to San Bernardino and dump the trick's car at a local chop shop, and get a motel in San Bernardino to hold up for the evening. The next morning, Mitch puts in the call to his Lac dealer, drops thirty five hundred and rolls out in a 1981 midnight blue on midnight blue used Ham to hit the road. They shoot and smoke that little money off, and begin relying mostly on

Peg's hoe money again, while they hold up in a motel near Figueroa Street in L.A. where Peg now works. First, Mitch thinks they should head for Frisco, but he decides that's too close and he needs to be out of California, period. He needs to put distance between himself and a trip back to the state pen.

It's early March 1985, two months after that little piece of money runs out and he's that many payments behind on his Lac, Mitch decides they will head for the east coast and hold up there until he and Mark can kick their heroin habits. He can no longer take the chance of being pulled over without even a fake driver's license. With his luck, he'd get stopped on a routine roust, while coming and going from different dope houses. Peg has a decent night on Figueroa and they can no longer put off leaving, awaiting another good lick. They must go now, so they do just that.

Mitch can't go back to Rachel's and get his clothes and Mark can't go back to get his stuff from his wife's, if she hadn't already thrown it out. The few outfits that he and Mark each have, including the one they're wearing and the five or six that Peg has, will have to do them until they're out of the state. They pick up a bunch of slum off Fifth Street in downtown L.A. Mitch and Mark shoot two bags of smack each at one of the flop house hotel shooting galleries on Fifth Street, and the three of them hit the freeway. They also pick up three bottles of methadone in Ontario to hold them over and jump right back on the freeway, as old man Mark asks, "Where we going, Pretty?"

Mitch actually has no idea, but he figures Peg needs to think that he does. Like he has done all of his life, he fabricates and paints a picture of what he thinks Peg needs to hear to stay motivated enough to keep getting at his dough. "We're going to Denver. I had a mama and daughter team there years back. Then, we'll hit Chicago and down through the east coast where we can come up again."

Peg is driving and Mark is riding shotgun, nodding in and out. Mitch is nodding in the backseat, thinking, *one more time I'm hooked like a dog and getting run out of yet another small town*. Still, he has been in way worse shape than this, and he's Pretty Mitch. He has a ride and a hoe. That's all he needs to get going and he'll just kick this habit and put it all back together again one more time, just like he always does. He comes out of a nod just in time to see a sign that reads Las Vegas. "Peg, take this turn coming up baby."

Mark looks up and sees the sign as Peg zooms past it, and he asks, "We're going to Vegas, huh Mitch?"

"Yeah man, we'll hold up there for a minute, put together a bankroll and head east, dog."

Even as Mitch says the words, his alter ego is asking, *who are we kidding? We got one bitch between the two of us, along with two, damn near three drug habits to support.* Mitch works Peg at truck stops, gas stations, food outlets and whatever spots that look like they have a lot of men around them. She even turns a date in a public restroom with some guy who is walking his dog through one of the neighborhoods while they're getting gas. He and Mark sling slum and till tap along the way, as well. Peg is doing all the driving, because every chance Mitch and Mark get, they're nodding out on heroin and methadone combined. Mitch notices that Peg looks road hard and put away wet, so he pleads with the pimp God to help his tired bitch hold up just until he can figure ou… His alter ego interrupts with, *until we figure out what? We can sell Mark and Peg anything we want, but what are we really going to do here?*

Mitch and crew hit Las Vegas on Sunday, March 10, 1985 around three pm with an ample supply of slum jewelry and a couple bottles of methadone. Mitch is thirty seven years old and as addicted to heroin as he's ever been, running on parole, and running with the Ham behind on payments. He's pretty much worked Peg into the ground and all three of them look and are 'tore up from the floor up.' Mark and Peg are looking to Mitch, expecting him to come up with a solution to their dilemma, and Mitch is just egotistical enough to think he still has one.

Of course, Mitch still had all these grandiose ideas and theories that he'd once been able to pull off. However, this time it's very different within Mitch's innermost self. His alter ego is now asking him for direction, instead of the reverse. He's sick and tired of being sick and tired one more time. All he has left is the illusions of who he thinks he used to be and things he has once done. In reality he realizes that he has no connections, no real crew, no hope and a dismal future. Mitch feels empty of ideas as to how to pull himself up by his own boot straps one more time. They settle into a motel named Friendly Fergie's on Fremont Street. They only have money for a one bedroom motel room with a rollaway bed in order for him to maximize what money they do have. Peg is dead tired after having driven almost the whole way from Cali and working along the way too, so Mitch puts her to bed. Mitch and Mark set out to find a fresh smack connection. They hit Jackson Street and there is no problem finding the drugs that by now they both crave. They aren't sick, just *jonesing* for a fix.

After shooting the dope, they set about slinging slum to any and everyone they can hook with the pieces. Mitch gets this rib shack owner for two hundred, and three extra large rib dinners with a large rope and bracelet combo. It had only cost them about eight to ten bucks for the set. Mark hits another merchant for a hundred, so they're set for a minute. Ironically, they find a surprisingly large amount of people that apparently haven't heard of the slum jewelry game. Mitch figures they'll have a field day in Vegas as they rape and pillage for the money, then roll on east.

They buy more dope and Mitch even gets a couple of rocks for Peg. Mitch tells Mark, "With these two rocks, Peg will be well energized. Then once she's fed and fucked, she can go get the money. So Mark, you take the car and go see if you can hit a lick or two, while I go make little mama feel real cool. I'll wind that ass up, so she can soldier where I told her and get selling pussy." Mitch and Mark laugh, slap five and they each get to the business at hand.

Mitch figures it'll take a few days before the victims he and Mark sting with slum to find out they've been took. By that time, Mitch and crew will be long gone down the freeway headed to the east coast, so Mitch figures. Over the next few days, they do the tag switch and clothing apparel return game at a few larger department stores in the process of picking up a few extra bucks in preparation for heading east. Mark tells Mitch, "Pretty, we need to get cleaned up, man. These local marks have probably started waking up on the slum we got them with, and both our pistols are in pawn. Man, we can't afford to have one of these lames run up on us without our gats. Mitch, we just can't go on like this, man."

Mitch shakes his head in agreement with old man Mark, "You're probably right, Mark."

"Mitch, I found this detoxification center, man. We can go there and hold up for a few days until you figure out what we're going to do next, man."

"How do you know they'll let us in that joint, Mark? I mean, we got no money, man."

"I called and told them about our situation Mitch, and they said for us to check in tomorrow morning."

"Umm, I don't know, Mark."

"Just think about it, Mitch, that's all I ask."

Mitch picks Peg up and valets the Ham at the Horseshoe Casino. As the three of them finish picking over lunch and are walking out Peg asks, "Can I please talk to you alone a minute, baby?"

"Sure you can, mama."

Mark decides to walk back to the motel and see if he can hit a lick on the way. Peg and Mitch walk out onto Fremont Street, as Mitch asks, "What's up baby?"

"Not us. What's happened to you, Mitch? Where is that big man I used to know?"

"Bitch, what?"

"I don't mean to be out of line Daddy, but it's just me getting it for you now, so it's my place to tell you how I feel. We can't go on like this, baby. I work for the two of your habits, and so I can get a hit here and there, so I don't have to think about it all. All I think about at work is what's wrong with us, and when are you going to turn this all around for us?"

Mitch reassures Peg, "Baby stay focused. Once we put a bank together we're heading to the east coast. I'll kick this shit and we'll do it altogether different the next time around, you'll see. It'll be like the old days when we first met, you remember don't you baby?" Mitch can't even sell himself on the message in the words he hears coming out of his mouth, because he no longer believes in himself anymore.

It seems to Mitch that he has always been able to sell women and men alike on his scams and schemes, because he always sells himself first. In an almost pleading and desperate voice, through tears Peg mumbles, "You promise, Mitch?"

"Come on girl, who loves ya, baby?"

"You do Daddy. You're right, it's just this town." Before she can walk away, Mitch grabs her arm. "Peg, aren't you forgetting something?"

"I don't have much, baby." She hands Mitch eight bucks. "I only had one date and I had to buy some feminine stuff, but I'll do better now, so we can get you out of this town." Mitch takes the money and walks away thinking, *crack head bitch*. He really doesn't have the energy to say or do anything. So he sticks the money in his pocket and decides to go play poker. It will take into the wee hours of the morning to drop his last thirty five bucks including the eight Peg gave him. Throughout the night he gets drunk, smokes a few kibbles and bits with one of the other gamblers at the poker table to stay awake, and shoots his last two bags of dog food.

As Mitch walks out of that casino around five am that morning of the 17th of March, 1985, his mind, heart, body and soul are in a state of complete disdain. He has never in his life felt as empty and hopeless as he does at this precise moment. People probably think he's insane as he walks down the street talking aloud, "I'm broke, beat up, busted and disgusted." His hair do, a jheri curl, has turned into a scary curl. It's falling out in spots from lack of care and maintenance. He's lost so much weight that his slacks are excessively loose on his approximately one hundred ten to fifteen pound frame.

He is delusional and paranoid as he keeps looking over his shoulder, thinking he hears shuffling sounds behind him. He fears that one of the marks he made at some point in his life, is about to catch up to him. It's all quite comical, yet pathetic at the same time. The sounds he's hearing are actually the hip pockets of his now much too loose trousers, hitting together making the sound of someone behind him.

Even his alter ego turns on him, *we were once somebody named Pretty Mitch. What have we become? What a complete waste of all of our worldly travels and things that we have done and learned.*

He gets the car out of valet with his very last two bucks and heads to the motel to meet up with Mark and Peg. His thoughts are on what money they have, so he can shoot enough drugs to not have to think about his life. Mark and Peg are in a panic from not knowing where, or how, Mitch has been all night. Mark speaks up first, "Mitch, we gotta get to that treatment center, man."

Peg has been smoking crack, but hands Mitch enough money for a couple of dime bags of heroin. Mitch feels the dope sickness coming in his body. "Let's roll so we can cop, Mark."

"Mitch if we go cop it'll be on and popping, and we'll never make it to that center. Let's just go as we are, man."

"Nigga are you crazy? I'm sick."

"So am I, Mitch, but we got people looking for us, man. We can't even keep enough money to get our pistols back. If we go cop and those niggas run up on us, we'll be in harm's way, baby."

Recognizing the logic in Mark's words Mitch agrees, "Okay let's go." They drive to a place named Nevada Treatment Center (N.T.C).

Chapter XXVII

Can Go No Further

They've only been at N.T.C. for two days when Mark comes to Mitch saying, "Pretty, I'm too old to kick another habit, man. I gotta get outta here and get some dope in me, man. The main reason I came in here is I was so worried about you, because you looked real bad, man."

Mitch thinks, *he was worried about me? I was worried about his old ass dying on me.* Mitch wonders what he must look like for Mark to think he is so bad off, considering that Mark looks to be near death to him. Mitch tries to talk Mark into staying long enough to get at least physically well, but Mark's mind is set. "Mark, take the car, man, and go do what you gotta do, I can go no further right now."

"I'll look out for you while you're in here, Mitch."

Mitch's alter ego is thinking, *yeah right, a dope fiend looking out for something or someone other than dope.* Mitch still believes the old man will do what he can for him, as he says, "Mark, tell my girl to stay down and I'll be out in a few more days, alright?" After Mark is gone, Mitch begins to realistically assess his situation. He knows it will only be a matter of time before the repossession people locate the Lac. Peg will eventually lose all sense of loyalty to anything and anyone, except the pipe, and he'll be on his own with an old man. Soon after that, he'll be back in prison with another new case on top of a parole violation.

After a couple of days, Mitch calls Mark at the motel and tells him that he needs money so Mark drives up, bringing Peg with him. He gives Mitch fifteen dollars, apologizing as he hands it to him, "I'm sorry, Mitch, but we don't have any more. I'm still shooting dope and with you in here, Peggy's smoking more of that crack shit."

Mitch is starting to feel alive again. "Hey Mark, thanks for the fifteen, and I really do understand, man." Mitch's alter ego is thinking, *more better them than us, still out there chasing the next one.*

Then Mark shocks Mitch, "I'm catching the first thing smoking back to Cali before these niggas catch up to me here. What do you want me to do with the ride, Mitch?"

"Take it Mark, and get as far as you can before they snatch it."

Peg looks at Mitch pleadingly, and in a cracked voice, "What about me, Daddy?"

"Look baby, I'm going to be in here for awhile, and you don't know anyone in this town to watch your back, so go with Mark. He'll look out for you."

Mark looks at Mitch questioningly, "Mitch, what are you going to do, man?"

Peg is crying, "Daddy, I can't make it without you."

Mitch puts on his best face of bravado, "I always land on my feet kid. You know that." Mark leaves Mitch a few pieces of slum, and he and Peg leave.

Mitch makes a collect call to his mom to tell her how he is and about this new facility he's in. He feels a surge of intense emotion overwhelm him while he's talking to her on the pay phone. Even though he can be seen through the window of the dayroom by whatever clients happen to be in there, he finds himself in tears as he explains to his mom, "There're all kinds of people in here that are somehow just like me, Madea."

"Well Snoopy, you better get the hell right out of there if they're all just like you." Mitch doesn't realize his mom's statement implies that she thinks he and these people are insane. All he understands is a feeling that he has never felt before has hold of him. It's all so embarrassing to him and making him feel deep shame, guilt and sorrow.

"Madea, I feel so empty, sad and lost. I have never felt this way before in my life." His mom doesn't get it. In fact, Mitch doesn't even get it himself. This is his moment of truth, that truth and the meaning of his life that he has pursued with vigor and abandon for over thirty years. Against his alter ego's advice, Mitch decides it makes more sense for him to stay in here—at least until he gets healthy and strong again.

He gets in touch with his old nineteen year old Latina, Sondra, out of Ontario, California. When Sondra hears that Mitch is clean and something is different in his voice, she flies to Vegas to see him. After seeing that something truly is different about him, she gives him a grand and says, "Mitch, I'll get back down hard for you, as long as you stay off that shit." Mitch is on restricted movement at N.T.C., so he can only get away to her motel room for a couple of hours. Of course that's plenty of time for him to handle his other needs and get back to N.T.C. Sondra heads back for Ontario with the understanding that, when Mitch gets out of the treatment facility, it's back on and popping. She'll return to work Vegas for him, or he will return to California.

Mitch finds this place to be quite a bit off his beaten track. The people that come in from the outside to attend these AA and NA meetings seemingly have similar thinking and dilemmas to his. They come from somewhat different life styles and modus operandi than he does, but he hears his own thoughts and feelings in their words. After several of these meetings, Mitch remains clean of any mood or mind altering substances and with no desire for drugs. He meets this recovering heroin addict, ex biker and old timer in the twelve step programs named Paul. Paul is a stout, balding white guy in his late fifties or early sixties, and he has twenty five years clean and sober as a result of AA.

Paul pursues conversation with Mitch and they exchange dialogue whenever Paul comes to the N.T.C. to do volunteer work. Paul tells Mitch one day, "One of the things I like most about being sober and living a spiritual way of life is that I am no longer limited in my people relationships. Back when I rode with biker gangs, it would have been impossible for you and me to interact the way we do. That was such a spiritually limiting way to live. Today, I'm capable of living and learning from and around anyone, regardless of who they are, what they are, or where they come from.

"In those days, I thought I was really free, man, because I carried weapons that I had no problem using. I felt that it made me somebody to live outside of it all, an outlaw. I lived my life like I was some kind of special badass. The truth really was, I'd been running in fear all my life until I found freedom in the grace of God through AA. I came to realize that I had been afraid all my life that people would find out that a great big six three, two hundred and fifty pound guy like me had such fear and such a large inferiority complex." Paul pauses a minute, looks around and leans his face in close to Mitch's. "Mitch, I have done things to people to prove I was worthy and somebody that deserved to be loved and respected. I did things that I didn't really want to, to impress people I really didn't like, in an effort to convince them and myself that I was someone or something that I really wasn't."

As Paul starts to speak about his weapons and the things he did with those weapons, his eyes lock with Mitch's. Mitch sees tears form in Paul's eyes and he feels tears form in his own. Mitch feels the truth in Paul's words from deep within his heart, because Mitch knows on a very personal level how all that Paul talks about feels. Paul continues, "Where and what I have been is not something one can hear about, read about, or talk about and become about. You either are *one* and have been there, or you aren't, and only another *one* would know *you* when their paths cross."

Mitch thinks as he has heard several times over the past few weeks he's been in this joint, "This guy's been reading my mail." Mitch reflects that, up until Paul, he has been hearing similarities to himself in the meetings, but this Paul guy is much too close for comfort. Yet, it makes Mitch feel just that, comfortable being there and around Paul.

Mitch's mind is so filled with chatter that he can hardly focus enough to pray, as Paul and these people suggest. They say things to him like, "Ask a Higher Power each day for the strength to not use drugs, and thank that Power at night. Pray for mercy, not forgiveness, and don't take anything mood or mind altering no matter what." Mitch has lived by his wit and charm for most of his life that he can remember, so he wonders what all that means. During and since Nam, he has lived by attack before he can be attacked. How can he now turn his will and life over to the care of this 'Power' they speak of? It is he that has been the power in his life, as well as in the lives of others. This all makes no sense. Yet these people have and know something that he does not. He has a few bucks, so his creature comforts are met. He isn't giving thought to Mark and Peg, coming up on the next score, or any of the lifestyle events that have occupied him for the past twenty years.

After dinner one evening, Mitch is sitting around watching TV and chilling, when the night shift counselor named Wilma comes up and tells him, "Mitchell, I'm sorry, but there are two Marshalls from California downstairs that are here to transport you back for a parole violation."

He gets booked into the Clark County Detention Center pending a flight the following Monday. He's uneasy this Thursday night as he sits in the one man cell alone with his thinking, and there are no distractions. Paul comes up to visit him and consoles him, "This can be the last time you ever have to be in one of these cages, brother."

When Mitch gets out after doing a ninety day violation in Chino Prison in Southern California, he flies back to Vegas and resumes his Program involvement. He hooks up with a hot, little blonde named Katherine, who is a nineteen year old, pretty, green eyed, long legged temptress. Slim, as he comes to call her, is working as a high dollar cocktail waitress, and he feels that she is about as sexy as any female he's known. Therefore, she is fitting for a guy like him, who is legendary in his own mind.

It is Slim that aggressively pursues Mitch, and not the other way around, although everyone that knows them seems to imagine so. He simply reverses the old female ploy Lana taught him. He cagily allows her to chase him until he catches her. Slim is almost as vain as Mitch, and she loves the attention and notoriety they get as a gorgeous interracial couple just as much as he does. She confirms this to him once when she says to him, "We are both beautiful people, Poppy (her nickname for Mitch), so people on both cultural sides are going to feel adverse about us being an item. But for the most part, it's White men and Black women that react to us that way. If either of us were less attractive and desirable, their attitudes would be 'you can have him or her,' whichever the case may be."

Mitch knows she turns a trick here and there, but that is of little consequence to him since he is no longer in or about the game. It's like he's an apple that thinks he's supposed to aspire to be an orange, so he paints his behavior and style so he appears to be an orange. The problem with this is he still thinks like an apple, feels like an apple and tastes like an apple, even as he's masquerading as an orange. He will come to understand that, at very best, all he's really doing is screwing off the best benefits of two perfectly good pieces of fruit. As a result, Mitch will spend the next several years looking for love using his many different faces in different places with different females that he encounters.

There is Yellow, who is a real pretty, 'high yellow' sister with hazel eyes and red hair. Her name is Marie, but even though he's no longer in the game, he still gives his women nicknames. She is everything he thinks he wants in a sister; twenty years old, Creole looking, flashy, stylish, and a freak with hazel eyes. Yellow and Mitch have very minimal dialogue, they just ravage each other's bodies for their moment in time. Mitch will hear through the grapevine that she gets pregnant, settles down, and gets married. He thinks, *God bless her, she deserves to be happy.*

Mitch answers an ad in the paper for inexperienced sales people at Toyota West. He gets hired on the spot, goes through a training session for auto sales, and hits the floor ready to sell. He feels that his years as a con man, pimp, and hustler should be a viable edge for him in this new game. Even though he is unsuccessful at Toyota West and let go, he becomes successful in the industry over the next couple of years. At three years clean and free of drugs and criminality, he takes a trip back to San Francisco with a few of his Caucasian buds. Mitch experiences déjà vu in the Tenderloin, after they get settled into the motel and Mitch rents a car. The sightseeing he feels the need to do is of a different nature than that of his buds. He has his buds follow him to the stroll on O'Farrell and Leavenworth Streets where he calls over a few hoes and gets his buds hooked up.

As his buds and the working girls are loading into the van, one of the girls named Benita, a young, eighteen year old, cutie pie redbone asks Mitch, "You're going to fuck too, aren't you sweetie?"

Instinctively, Mitch snarls and responds, "Bitch, first of all, my name isn't sweetie or honey. And second, I'm doing this for my

Colby Chase

partners, so don't get me confused with what they got going with you here, okay?" Mitch's buds are looking and listening in shock at the way Mitch is talking to this girl. This is a side of Mitch that they have never seen. This is a side of himself that he hasn't seen in quite awhile either, but his alter ego is jumping up and down reveling in it.

"I didn't mean any harm baby. I can call you baby, can't I?"

"Yeah, calling me *baby* is cool. By the way, you got a man?"

"No, my man is in the joint."

"Well little mama I'm not in the joint. Why don't I pick you up after work and we talk about *it?*"

"I don't know about you, man, are you a pimp?"

"Let's just say, I'm down, but unlike anyone you've even seen or maybe ever even heard of, so can we talk?"

"Yea… I guess we can talk. I'll be done and by that restaurant over there about three am, baby. What's your name?"

"I'll tell you when we kick it later little mama. If I tell you now you wouldn't believe me." Mitch is just vain enough to think that his name is still ringing bells in the streets of San Francisco after over a decade away from the bay. Better yet, his alter ego wishes it were so. Mitch rides around through the streets of Frisco past some of his old spots and neighborhoods. He reflects that this is still the San Francisco he once knew, but perhaps it is he that is so very different now.

His alter ego inquires, *if we're so different why do we feel like we're missing out on the action, and long to be a part of this all again, chasing hoes, freaking with them in the wee hours of the mornings, hearing the stories of perverse tricks, the cars, jewelry and notoriety?* Mitch ponders that he doesn't miss the things that went along with all that, like addiction, jails, institutions, and near death experiences.

348

With all Mitch's buds asleep, he's rolling around checking out the city. He's draped in a long leather and lamb maxi trench coat with hair hanging down his back and, what he considers, low key jewelry. Without realizing it, he has dressed relative to how he's thinking and feeling, and the Pretty Mitch persona he is missing. Mitch cruises past that restaurant around two am, and there she is waving his rental car down. He pulls up to the curb, and she exclaims, "Baby, I'm done! But if I get in this car with you, are you gonna start that, 'bitch I'm charging you for getting in my car' with the pimping stuff?"

"Look, I told you I just want to talk to you."

Benita looks both ways as if deciding whether to trust Mitch or not. "Okay, I sure hope you keep your word," she remarks and gets in the car. As Mitch is driving off he feels her staring at him uneasily.

"Relax kid, if I was going to break you like that, I would have done so when you first walked up to my car. I mean look at me, what do I look like to you?"

"A pimp, nigga, shit," she admits and they both laugh. However, Mitch winces from her flagrant use of the *n* word. Nowadays, it makes him ashamed and embarrassed for the black person he hears using that term. He smiles that little smile as he thinks, *the n word was once an intricate part of my vocabulary, and now it repulses me.* It appears to him that life is not without some degree of irony at every turn.

"You know what, you're right, I am and always will be a motherfucking pimp."

"Oh shit, I knew it."

Benita starts looking for a way out of the car, and Mitch rubs her thigh reassuringly, "It's okay little one, it ain't like that, I got you, okay?" She relaxes and they joke, laugh and kick it, as Mitch starts the old interview process just for the hell of it to find out her age and background. Mitch is in seventh heaven just going through the motions of playhouse ninety playing the game again.

"I'm eighteen and my man... aw... my ex man turned me out two years ago before he went to prison. I know I need a good man, because it's so hard out here for a bitch alone. I liked you Mitch from the moment I saw you, and I'm a down bitch. I know better than to even be in this car with you nigga, but there is something different about you. I don't know... when you put me in check like you did back there, I was just feeling you."

"Yeah baby, I'm feeling you right now." Mitch wishes that he could be back in the game right then, but it's no longer his time. He reflects that he has had his fun in the sun during his days in the game. "Benita, have you ever heard the name, Pretty Mitch?"

"No, is that you?"

"It's who I used to be."

"What do you mean used to be? You're still a fine ass nigga, shit. I know you're old school, but that's what I need, a real nigga that's true to the game." "I am that."

"Shit, my man...aw... my ex man was forty eight when he turned me out. That nigga is over fifty now, but what the fuck has that got to do with anything, if a nigga is down? These young niggas out here in these streets just want to beat a bitch down and clown a bitch. I can get at the money on my own when I get my lazy ass up to go to work. That's why I need a nigga to keep me motivated. I don't do drugs... I mean I smoke a little bush, but not when I work."

Mitch can't take it any longer so he explains, "Baby the blatant use of the *n* word is a form of expression for a black person's lack of self respect and esteem. It's not okay with us for another race to refer to us as such, so it should also not be okay for us to refer to each other or ourselves as such. You feeling me?"

"Yeah baby, I'm feeling you, and then, I'm *really* feeling you, you know what I mean?" She then looks at Mitch provocatively.

"Oh yeah, I'm all over that with you too little mama."

"Mitch I ain't never heard no nigg…I mean man talking like you talk before," she says as she hands Mitch a hundred bucks in twenties. Mitch doesn't ask if there's more money, because he's just happy to be playing like he's playing the game again. They spend a few hours kicking it at a weekly she rents when she's in Frisco. Mitch learns that she actually lives in Oakland. For those few hours they lose themselves in each other for that brief moment in time, as only creatures of the night can. It reminds Mitch of the old days. Then her comments disturbs his inner thoughts, "Mitch I don't have any kids, so I can go back to Las Vegas with you, and work for you there, or wherever you tell me."

For a very split second, Mitch actually entertains how he can work that out, but then responds, "Nah baby, I got a whole different thing going on now. I'm no longer down like that."

"I can do whatever you want. I really need somebody like you though, Mitch. I can stay here and work for you."

When Mitch leaves Bee (he nicknamed Benita) around five am he reflects how, in years past, hoes were on every corner in damn near every major city, and it was just that easy to pluck fresh game. He leaves Frisco with a lot of questions in his brain about who he is, what he is, and how he really is these days.

Flying back to Vegas, Mitch isn't very talkative. One of his buds that he shared a motel room with asks, "Where were you out to so late, Mitch?"

Mitch never turns from looking out the window in deep thought. "Just went to see a few old spots I once frequented, man."

Then, he meets Jackie in Vegas, a petite, tan, little Mormon honey with dark eyes and long dark crimped hair. She looks striking, more Latina looking than Caucasian, probably because she is twenty five percent Indian. Mitch comes to love her. He feels that he's is in love with her, but what he's truly in love with, is her complete obsession with him, and the fact that she turns her will and life over to him. Even in her choice of personalized license plates, *MSMITCH*, she symbolizes her absolute surrender to him. One more time, absolute control and domination of a woman becomes Mitch's validation. The only difference in his relationship with Jackie and his past working girls is that she doesn't work as a prostitute. Jackie is extremely bipolar, which is nothing new for Mitch because Slim, Rachel, Gina, and all the way back to Brea, Lana and even Mouse have had, one or a combination of, similar emotional and mental issues as well. After all, he prefers them damaged, and nothing changes if nothing changes.

Chapter XXVIII

Life after Drugs

During the year of 1994, Jackie comes into a piece of money and they buy a new house in the upscale Summerlin area. They get married, and take a grand honeymoon through Frisco, Monterey, San Diego, and finally culminating on an ocean cruise to Ensenada and Catalina Island. Even though they have a ball, Mitch still has this knot stuck in his throat throughout the whole period of time. He cannot stop thinking about no longer being with other women at his discretion. His Program sponsor tells him, "Do the next best thing that's in front of you, Mitch," so he suits up and shows up as a married man and member of a conventional family unit; that's actually not very conventional at all.

Mitch has been in the car business for several years, and has established excellent relationships with several of the managers and staff because of his high average gross profit per car deal. While Jackie works as a senior loan closer at Primerit Bank, Mitch gets promoted to Finance and Insurance (F & I) manager. Mitch's career growth is due at least in part to Jackie's ingenuity in helping him cultivate new leads and extra sources of clientele. Jackie comes up with the idea to do a collaborated special sales event sponsored by the dealership and Primerit Bank. She arranges a meeting between Mitch and the bank president. The bank president assigns a department head to facilitate on the bank's behalf. It all goes really well and Mitch gains further notice from the dealership's upper level management and the owner of the company.

The joint venture generates over forty-five additional car deals, over and above Mitch's regular sales, on each of two separate months. It is instrumental in Mitch's successful bid for the promotion to Finance and Insurance Manager. He initially has apprehensions about the promotion when he finds out that he'll need a state license to work in such a position and must learn how to operate a computer. With felony convictions ranging from pimping, white slavery, possession with intent to distribute drugs, and everything in between, he is concerned about whether or not the State of Nevada will allow him the bond and license needed. He has heard around the Program the phrase that, 'the doors that God closes no man can open and the doors that God opens no man can close.' That principle definitely holds true for Mitch in this situation.

Jackie begins to recognize Mitch's growing disillusionment with their marriage and tries everything to hold them together. She believes that Mitch is just going through male midlife crisis and needs to go sow some wild oats. She suggests, "Why don't you just draw enough money out of our bank account, go rent an apartment for six months, do all the young chicks you want, and get it out of your system. Then, when you're over it, come back to me, and we can go to counseling, so we can get on with our lives together."

Mitch's alter ego advises him, *Jackie obviously doesn't really know who we are. If we go and do as she suggests, why on earth would we want to come back?* That seals the demise of that relationship. He leaves Jackie in late 1995, less than a year after their marriage, and he begins to do what is known as step work examining his questions concerning their relationship. He discovers that even just living in the 'playhouse ninety' version of a pimp and hoe relationship in square life, doesn't work for him. Mitch either can't, or won't, separate the two. In reflection, he recalls some that could, like Fast, but even Fast was hooked on heroin, perhaps because he couldn't pull it off clean and sober either.

Mitch moves into his new, model town home with his new toys; a pearl white 1993 Lexus ES 300 and a beige classic 1962 Chevy Corvette with the license plates *MITCTOY* (Mitch's Toy). He is quite the eligible bachelor, but only for dinner, perhaps a concert or other social functions, and a one night stand. Of course, if the respective lady happens to be special, perhaps a weekend. He is once again into the dating game for a 'reason not the season.'

One of Mitch's little weekend getaway spots has become Humphrey's Motel, which features the well known concerts by the sea. Humphrey's is one of San Diego's older motels, so it lacks the modern updated creature comforts of newer, state of the art, motels and hotels in the area. Still, the ambiance of the ocean and concert atmosphere, along with fine dining, makes up for it all. The concert venue is located next to the dock of the bay. The motel rooms and suites are located up and down this adjacent area. Mitch is sometimes able to book a suite and watch the concert from the privacy of a balcony.

On one such trip in, 1996, Mitch is out and about in San Diego with a gal he has met on a previous trip. Her name is Samantha and she is a petite, medium brown skin little cutie. Mitch and Sam are exploring a local shopping mall. While Mitch is roaming through the men's department, Sam is off elsewhere in the store. They've decided to meet back at the car. Mitch is sampling colognes when, out of the blue, someone walks up behind him and whispers in his ear, "I have a better fragrance for you."

As Mitch turns and sees it's his old girl, Sondra, he can hardly believe his eyes. He grabs her up off her feet and swings her around saying, "Hey, you sexy ass little Latina." He notices that she is as fine as ever after he gets a really good look up and down her. Just then Sam walks up, and Mitch introduces them. Then he tells Sam he'll meet her at the car, and gives her the keys to his Benz SL 500. He and Sondra walk through the mall with their arms around each other talking about the not so good old days.

"Poppy, look at you, you're still young, healthy and fine as ever. But what's with this little afro thing you got going here," she asks as she smiles and points at his short natural hair style.

"Things are way different in my life and affairs now, Sunny." He had given her this nickname because she had been the one bright spot in the darkness of his heroin addiction back in the times they were together. "But look at you little, Latina," he remarks as he spins her around looking over her body. He pinches her butt and asks, "Sunny, what is all this you got going on back here now? Junk in the trunk, huh?"

"You know, Poppy, it's not just sisters that have a reputation for bubble butts, we Latinas have the patent on these asses," she laughs as she grabs her full hips in each hand. They laugh and hug each other, as she continues. "Plus, Poppy, things are a lot different in my life and affairs now too. I'm a thirty one year young mom with a ten year old kid."

"Sunny, how and why did you end up in Diego?"

"It's a long story, man… umm…when did I come see you in that place that last time, 85… umm 86?"

"Yeah, Sunny it was April, 85."

"Okay, I left Ontario with my baby's daddy in 1987, and wouldn't you know he was another junkie, Poppy? I asked myself what the fuck bitch, do you have a fucking welcome sign on your forehead that welcomes junkies or what?" They both laugh. Mitch inquires about her baby's daddy and learns that he's doing twenty five to life for murder and robbery. His ears perk up when she tells him she is otherwise unattached.

Not that it would matter to Mitch because he feels like she was, is, and always will be, his girl. Actually, he feels that way about them all. They exchange a few more experiences for about an hour when Mitch remembers Sam waiting in his car. So he gets a phone number, plans a rendezvous for later that evening, and kisses her a passionate good bye. He hurries up and gets rid of little mama, Sam, so he can get back at Sunny. He replaces Sam with Sunny as his date for the Lou Rawls concert that next evening at Humphrey's Concert by the Bay. They have a ball and spend the rest of the weekend together. Over the course of the weekend, Mitch finds out that Sunny is a medical assistant and is in school getting a nursing degree.

When Mitch asks why she has no car, she explains, "I got hit by some old black lady and I'm just waiting on my settlement to buy another one." Mitch observes that it must be difficult with a kid, a job, and school along with no automobile. So Monday morning as he drops her off at her apartment, he gives her three hundred, and she cries. Through her tears she laughs, "This is a switch Poppy, you giving me money." Mitch arranges to see her in two weeks on his next scheduled three day vacation weekend.

Over the next couple of months, Mitch and Sunny fly back and forth to be with each other. Of course, they are both fully aware that one more time, they are going in different directions. This particular morning as they lay in bed kicking it in Mitch's town home on the eve of the day of her flight back to Diego, she reminisces on the days of old. "I loved you so much back then Mitchell, with my lovesick ass. I'd still be somewhere trying to work for you had you came back for me. Now, after all these years, seeing you and being with you like this again, I realize that I still have feelings like that for you." Mitch begins to speak, and Sunny places a finger over his lips. "I know Poppy, for whatever reason it just never seems to be our time, huh?" A tear rolls down her face, and Mitch kisses it away. He wants desperately to console her, for she was his people, his folks, and his family back then, this night, and will be forever. Having no answer to that statement, he just holds her close as she shivers, and says, "Don't talk, just make love to me, Poppy, okay?"

One afternoon at the dealership, Mitch spots a Honda Civic in mint condition with low miles as it comes into the dealership on trade. He steals the Civic for twenty eight hundred, calls Sunny and tells her, "I'll be in San Diego this Friday evening for the weekend." He feels that after all the thousands of dollars, blood, sweat and tears she's given him, it's the least he can do. Sunny cries as Mitch makes amends to her with this small token of his gratitude, "I know it's not much, kid, but thank you for my life." He reflects that in her brief tenure in the game for him, and even after all these years, she is still as humble and straight forward as she ever was with him. It's just one more little thing that he remembers really appreciating so much about her.

Mitch stays the night, to say his good bye to her. He never sees or talks to her again. There continues to be a few similar situations as he goes about the business of making amends. He really doesn't consider these amends, more as payback for what these different women have sacrificed for him that has enabled him to still be around to partake of the life he has now. He has finally come to realize that he hasn't done all that he's done, or received all that he has, alone!

In December 1997, Mitch has been kicking it with a young, eighteen year old blonde named Daisy. He comes downstairs one morning to do his ritualistic prayer, reading, journaling, and meditation. While sitting in the nook area of his townhouse, he feels as if his 'cup runneth over' with feelings of gratitude for his new life and circumstances. During this time of reflection, he thinks of a statement that his old girl, Slim, made to him once, "You only covet the attention and presence of people that idolize you, and you shun the ones that don't." Mitch chuckles as he thinks, *only when there is nothing to be lost or gained otherwise.* He continues to ponder, *here I am at fifty years old with a 1994 model Benz 500 SL, with the license plates NEWWAY, parked in the garage of my model town home, several accounts of legit liquid cash, a great career with highly viable promotional opportunities and a hot, hard bodied, young eighteen year old, blue eyed blonde lying upstairs curled up in my satin sheets. It doesn't get any better than this.*

In this moment of serene surrender, Mitch asks aloud of his Higher Power, "What stone have I left unturned in my amends process or in any area of my life, and how can I be of better service to you and my fellows today, my Lord?" Instantly, the thought of an old attorney of his comes to his mind, Ron, out of Sacramento. He calls Sacramento information and effortlessly gets the attorney's phone number and address. When he asks for Ron, he is told by the receptionist that Ron is in court. So Mitch confirms Ron's address, and composes a letter of amends. He also declares his intentions of restitution to Ron to right the financial debt from years ago with twenty percent interest for the time it has taken him to pay it.

He humbly asks Ron's forgiveness, and he explains briefly about succumbing to the disease of addiction which caused him to be so shamefully unaccountable. On top of everything else, Mitch offers Ron a weekend stay at any casino of his choice on the Vegas Strip, complimentary at Mitch's expense. Mitch requests of Ron an alternative payment amount or arrangement if the one he proposes does not meet Ron's satisfaction. He holds no reservations about fulfilling whatever alternative arrangement that Ron might suggest. He reasons that it is his debt to Ron, and not Ron's obligation to make it easy for him.

Mitch is pleased when he later gets a favorable response back from his old friend and attorney. "To hear from someone that you haven't seen or heard from in nearly three decades is great, but to have that person recall and pay off a debt that I had probably forgotten about is a wonder. When I received your second check I realized that you were serious, and well deserving of my acknowledgment and heartfelt thanks. Usually, when a client pays an old outstanding fee, it is because he has a new case. You are the exception and I might add an exceptional person. I hope we can get together after all these years. In the meantime, stay well and keep in touch." Mitch is elated because it's just one more little sign that proves there is such a thing as karma in life and in how one treats others. He reflects that he has done the proverbial one hundred and eighty degree turn in most of his life and affairs, as is spoken of so often around the Program rooms. Still, he laughs as his alter ego reminds him, *yeah, but we've gone from criminal asshole to corporate asshole.*

When Daisy comes downstairs wearing only Mitch's pajama top, Mitch laughs aloud, and it causes her to look at him curiously. She looks around the downstairs area self consciously as if expecting someone other than Mitch to be there, and asks, "Mitch, is someone else here?"

Mitch laughs and comments, "Oh yeah, there is just the usual two of me here."

Daisy sits in the chair across from Mitch at the nook dinette set. She laughs and asks, "Baby, what are you talking about? You were laughing and talking like there's someone else here."

Mitch smiles and just tells her, "It's an inside joke, Easy (Daisy's nickname)." Mitch watches the young woman tilt her head to the side smiling at him as if she doesn't have a clue as to what he could possibly be talking about. Mitch smiles and runs his fingers through her beautiful long blonde locks as he thinks, *I hope she never has to understand what I'm talking about, because if she does, it'll mean that she's already well beyond fucked up.*

Chapter XXIX

Domestic or Not

Mitch transfers to another dealership in Henderson, Nevada, and buys a much bigger home in the exclusive Seven Hills area in early 1999. He then rents out his town home, and proceeds in his quest for further 'come-up-ism' in this new city of the Greater Las Vegas area. Later in this same year, Mitch happens to meet this long legged blonde that works at the Chicken Ranch, a brothel just outside Vegas where prostitution is legal. Up to this point, he has fled from working girls as a vampire would from a cross. For whatever reason, however, when he meets her, he longs to be back in the game. He assumes it's probably a combination of off and on exposures to the game over the years, living a lifestyle in sales for over thirty five years, and being an aging player with something to prove to himself.

There is a tall blonde named Susie, with long legs, working at the dealership. Mitch has given her the nickname of *Leggs* in playfulness only, but when he meets Melanie, who is also a tall, blue eyed blonde with even longer legs, the name *Legs* seems much more fitting to him for Melanie. She has the deepest blue eyes, about five feet ten without heels, and a look of just pure perverse sexuality. When Mitch first sees her and he openly stares at her, she smiles and looks away, but Mitch will have none of that. As he approaches her, his alter ego tells him, *you know we're getting too old for the work we have to put in with these big girls.*

Mitch figures Melanie looks to be in her mid to late twenties, a bit old, but he'll make an exception this time. She has already asked his sales guy, Chad, "Who is that black guy over there?"

"That's my boss," Chad replies.

"Really, so he can negotiate this price for me, right?"

"Yeah, he'll be the one that decides on the price and everything for your deal."

When Chad brings Melanie's paperwork to Mitch's desk, Mitch positions his head so Melanie can't see his face after he runs her credit profile. He notices that she has worked a few strip joints along the way. "Chad, her credit is so bad that she'd have a problem buying a car for cash even." Chad and Mitch snicker briefly at that. Then of course, Mitch has to talk to her in person. Mitch goes over to the table and gives her the bad news in a respectfully good way. First, he sends Chad away and then tells her they can't make this deal, but maybe there is a different deal that she and he can make over dinner later that evening.

Mitch already knows what Melanie is thinking; 'older black gentleman, soft spoken, and a manager at a car dealership, money, money, and more money!' They meet for dinner at Play It Again Sam's. Mitch is driving his flip top 500 SL and she is driving an old jalopy. Over refreshments and before ordering dinner, Mitch starts the interview process as he is aware that Melanie is sizing him up for the kill also, and, *may the best cat catch the mouse this night,* he thinks.

Mitch experiences the recall of excitement, from the days of old, surge through him as he picks, prods and pushes her buttons looking for just that right combination that unlocks her vulnerabilities. He notes that this is quite different than just hunting for a mere sexual conquest. This is about the life altering use of power through intuition and persuasion. He chuckles as his alter ego conveys, *we can trick a bitch out of her pussy when we can't get anything else, but we have a different agenda from our norm as of late.*

After Mitch finds out she's never owned a home, he gets her to talk about how long she's been in the business. He finds out that she has never been with a pimp and doesn't aspire to be, because her concept of pimps is like most females these days. "They just beat you up, take your money and do nothing for you," she tells him.

He gets her laughing about his different humorous car business experiences. Then, in the middle of her cracking up at one of his jokes, he abruptly turns serious, and asks very matter of fact, "So who was it, your dad, brother, uncle, neighbor, who?"

Melanie stops laughing just as abruptly and that cocky, in control, confident side of her that hoes use to play men, especially tricks, dissipates, and the damaged, little girl lost peeks out momentarily. As the question takes her voice away she mumbles slowly, "What… aw… I don't know what you… aw… mean, Mitch."

"Melanie, if this relationship is going to benefit you at all, you need to be honest with me."

Next, predictably outraged, she asks, "Who in the fuck are you supposed to be, a fucking shrink? And, what relationship? I don't even fucking know you."

Mitch looks directly into her eyes and very softly says, "No, I'm none of those things and I can tell you something else that I'm not, the enemy. I just happen to be the guy who can fix things, so you never have the kind of experience at another car dealership or a real estate office that you just had today at my store."

Sassily, Melanie inquires, "Oh, and just how do you purpose to do all that?"

"Look, I didn't mean to upset you. To be honest, you're quite probably the most drop dead gorgeous creature I've ever seen, and I can make every other aspect of your life just as gorgeous." That gets a smirk of approval from Melanie. Then Mitch drops the subject and begins to order. "Are you ready to order, kid?"

Now her curiosity has the better of her. "Yeah, but why did you ask me that question?"

Not looking at her and beckoning for the waiter, he asks innocently, "What question do you mean, Melanie?"

"You know…aw… about when I was a little girl."

Mitch's alter ego kicks in, *we never said it happened when she was a little girl, but she certainly just did.*

Then Mitch picks it back up with her, "I asked because I want to know."

"But why, what's it to you?"

"I guess nothing, if you don't want it to be."

"You're really creeping me the fuck out, here, Mitch."

"Don't be, I'm quite harmless. I just have this sense for detecting *dis-ease* or discontentment in my fellow human beings, especially women. I can understand if you can't trust me."

"Look, I really appreciate how you treated me today. I'd been to several dealerships and after they saw my credit they started treating me like shit."

"Struck a nerve, did I?"

"Yeah you did," she admits as slight tears begin to form in her eyes.

"Melanie, what bipolar meds are you on?"

"How do you know that I'm…?"

Mitch chuckles as he interrupts her with, "I'm a mind reader." But what he's thinking is, *I'm a damaged female reader.*

364

"Mitch, I hate those meds. They make me crazier than I am already." With that statement, she laughs hard and loud. "I don't *even* believe I'm discussing all this crap with you, and I don't even fucking know you."

"Oh, you know me. You've always known me. You raised me to be here for you, when you need me to be."

She stares at him curiously, "I don't know what the fuck all that means, Mitch."

"Melanie, if you use the word *fuck* one more time." He smiles saying it, but he means it as a warning.

"I'm sorry Mitch, I know I curse way too much but....oh my God... you got me explaining myself, to you and shit, oops." They both laugh. During dinner, the information starts to come out about where, when, who and how of Melanie's past that Mitch needs to know in order to play at her, especially about the bipolar, which just happens to be one of Mitch's majors from the school of life. Over the next few dates she finally agrees to a management deal between them on a trial basis. After a couple more dates, consisting of Mitch's probing and soul searching sessions, he finds her exact tune to play.

After three months of their arrangement, Mitch buys her a 2000 red Ford Mustang GT, in his name only. In mid 2000, Legs is in a new home, also in Mitch's name, in the prestigious Seven Hill's area of Henderson, Nevada. Less than six months later, they buy a second home in Seven Hills as a rental property. Legs has a renewed vigor, attitude, and pep in her step, because of the new purpose and game plan that Mitch has outlined for them, and she's excitedly clocking bank. As the months roll by and Mitch becomes everything else to her, Legs initiates a sexual fantasy with him. One thing leads to another and they end up acting out her incestuous fantasy, where Mitch role plays as her father. Mitch's experience has been that, more often than not, many little girls who are victims of molestation come to believe the only way to relate to men is sexually. She and Mitch play games and in those games she feels free to do all the nasty, lewd things of her fantasies, incestuous though they may be. It reminds him of the games he once played with Lana, except now his role has reversed. Mitch rationalizes that, for damaged emotional creatures, where the mind and the energy go so does the money, and often times the honey. Mitch just figures he's down with whatever trips her trigger and gets him the money, and besides, he loves the role playing as well. With Legs clocking bank, Mitch becomes even more financially secure.

Legs brings a few would be *wives-in-law* to Mitch and a couple of them even last a few weeks here and there. He has them dropping his money off at his job, because that's where he is most of each day, except Sundays. However, Mitch is very careful not to arouse suspicion amongst his peers. He doesn't want it out that he's dibbling and dabbling back into the pimp game. He does have a certain professional image to maintain.

In early 2001 Mitch has a declining career in the auto industry and a lucrative career back into pimping. Legs is on auto pilot. She only comes out of the hoe house a couple of days every week or two, in between her regular clients flying in to see her. She knows what she and Mitch both want to accomplish and that is motivation enough for her. As long as Mitch talks to her by phone regularly and tosses her up every two or three weeks participating in their sexual role playing, she's good to go at getting the money. In time, Legs begins fantasizing about having a normal life and it starts to outweigh their fantasy and the game. She marries one of her regular tricks. He buys Mitch out of the house she lives in and she agrees to let Mitch keep the other rental for a nominal fee as his severance pay.

About six months later, Mitch gets a call from Legs, "How you doing, who you doing, what you doing and who's working for you now?"

"Legs, what is your major malfunction, bitch?"

"I'm bored and I need to see my daddy."

"Legs, I told you I wouldn't be playing hide the sausage with some square guy's wife."

"Please, I need to talk to you, Daddy. I got something for you."

Those are the magic words to Mitch's ears. "Alright, you crazy ass bipolar female, when?"

Once she arrives at his Seven Hills home, Mitch listens to her bitch and whine about what her husband is not, and what he doesn't do. Mitch only laughs as he finds it all quite amusing, "Aw Legs, you mean he won't play our games with you?"

She giggles in that little seductive way of hers that Mitch likes when she has had a couple of drinks and is getting freaky. "Oh yeah, I can just see it now, Mitch. Honey, could you please pretend to be my father when you fuck me like this old black man, who I call daddy, does? Mitch, are you nuts? I can't do that with him. He'd think I'm some kind of a freak or nut case."

Mitch laughs, "Well Baby, you are some kind of a freak and a nut case. You wanted to square up and get out of the life. Well now you got it, so deal with it. That is unless you want to go back to work."

Legs breaks herself for two large, then they freak and lie kicking it afterwards as she tells him, "Mitch, during those last couple of months of working, I had reached the point where I hated for tricks to even touch me. I miss the game, but I couldn't go back to doing that ever again." Mitch leaves her in his home and this tryst will prove to be the first of several in the years to come with his ex-working girl turned trick's housewife. Mitch is back on the prowl. However, he finds that society has all but eliminated the need for old school pimps, especially for smarter hoes. Mitch always had his best success with the smarter working girls, because he was raised by a smarter type of working girl. The system has created semi legit avenues where prostitutes can work in arenas protected from cops, pimps and even rogue clients (i.e., escort services, brothels, strip joints, and the internet). Street hoes are all but a thing of the past with such updated and sophisticated entities in place. Mitch decides he needs to revolutionize his game with the times to fit a faster, smarter, and less gullible female because the world is now filled with opportunities for minorities, including women.

With women being much more informed these days, it's become much harder to dupe the average female that, in the old days, would have turned out in an instant. Plus, he's past fifty and has limited time to invest in this new breed of female. He has become a realist as he reflects on what has and hasn't worked in his past in the game. Although he's had long term success in the game with some of his women, he has had to learn to create his own edge out of the psychological and emotional wreckage of their past. It hasn't been about affairs of the heart. It's been about mind control, and the therapeutic value of one damaged soul understanding and controlling another.

He becomes things to them that no one else would or perhaps even could; tutor, mentor and most important their financial planner. He's offered them the fulfillment of their desires for material success. Also, he has learned from hands on experience how to become a bipolar female's medication. He somehow instinctively knows how to psychologically pick them up when they're running in the depressive cycle, and bring them down to manageable levels when they're running too manic. He becomes the one that they run to for their sanity and direction. Somewhere along the lines of becoming all that to them, they formulate trust in him, so the money and subservience generally comes effortlessly for varying periods of time.

That's why the name of the game is still cop and blow, because hoes still come and go. It seems such a waste not to take advantage of the years of honed skills he has acquired in preying on the weak and damaged. Like an old vampire, Mitch feels the stirring of exhilaration from even the possibilities of preying on fresh new female blood once again.

Requiem of an Old School Player

Born of larceny and distrust,
for certain he is hell bent.
From the ways and days of Miles, Jimmy and Wes,
rose him to be one of the best.
Once known from Maine to Spain,
and Tokyo to Frisco,
fast women his game and claim to fame,
with revulsion at the life of the lame or tame.
His way did the gorgeous girls come,
mesmerized they did succumb.
Of lost souls in his cluster, power, money,
and honey he did muster.
As these street walkers, club stalkers and cyber talkers,
fell prey to his charms and prowess,
about them, still he cares best.
These wild creatures of the night,
sacrificed all to answer his call,
in their plight.
For his favor they did savor,
above life or jail,
that his majesty might prevail.
With twilight now falling he reflects balling,
shaking and moving and retro grooving,
when he controlled the mind of the fugitive kind.
Without regret, shame or sorrow, and from yesterday,
or tomorrow not having to borrow, thanks be to women of Black, Brown,
Red, Yellow, Bright and White,
for their treasures and pleasures
and his life of less strife.

Chapter XXX

He's Back

Mitch buys a vehicle more suitable for his current agenda. It's a 2001 Lexus GS 400 with twenty inch chrome rims. He is having lunch at M & M's soul food restaurant, on the corner of Harmon and Jones, with a few people, including a pecan tan, attractive, sister named Katherine, who is a gorgeous, somewhat muscular, five feet five. Katherine is a stripper and she supplements that income by hoeing. Mitch has known her for years, impersonally from a distance.

Katherine was once hooked up with an ole partner of Mitch named Paddy. However, Mitch is aware that she and Paddy haven't been together in a couple of years. Also at the table are Bobby, a black guy that sponsored Mitch in the AA Program for awhile, and Pepe, who is a tall, forty one year old, dark skin partner of Mitch. As the four of them are engaging in small talk while waiting for their lunch, Mitch aggressively gets at Katherine asking, "When are you going to start investing your money with me?" Bobby and Pepe get silent, waiting for Katherine's response.

"Mitch, I don't have any money, you forget I'm just coming back around the program from a crack run."

"I'm not forgetting anything. I know it would be a lot easier now if you had something put away to fall back on, or someone financially sound in your corner. What I'm talking about is proper money management through investment basics. Are you feeling me?"

"That's something I'd be interested in, Mitch, after I put some ends together." All this time the two other men at the table are just listening, shocked at Mitch's aggressiveness in getting at Katherine.

"Well Katherine, just remember one can't do much if one doesn't know much; and if one doesn't know much, then they'll never do much. It's like a vicious cycle for most of us. We start out from nowhere and generally end up at the same place because of it, nowhere." Then Mitch drops the conversation, knowing that he's planted the seed. Katherine is a straight slut by her own admission and to Mitch's delight. She has been one of Mitch's favorite female people for years just because she acts whorish and is a working girl. Until recently, kicking it with her or any other working girl was not an option for Mitch. Now, Mitch is back on the prowl for wild things. He reasons all she needs is the caliber of management that he brings to the table and she could go far.

Over the next few encounters with Katherine, Mitch probes and picks for the information that he will need to knock her. Katherine is thirty four years young and has been stripping and turning tricks for ten years. A bit old for Mitch's liking, but he's no spring chicken anymore, either. She has never owned her own home. Mitch finds that she is quite bourgeois, and different than the average sister from around the way, which could be a big plus in the game. Mitch sets up a rendezvous to show Katherine his holdings in the Seven Hills area, so she can see his level of success. He shows her his properties, and shares a few of his goals and dreams with her. Of course, she doesn't get it at this point. He finds her clueless as to what he's talking about, but he vows to keep a light in the window for this one because she could turn out to be a keeper.

Mitch is about to move back to the Summerlin area and into his old town home. He has put his primary residence in Seven Hills in Henderson up for sale, and accepted an offer on it, which will net him a tidy sum, tax free. Pepe has come in with Mitch on the purchase of a rental property in Sun City Aliante, one of the new 'Master Planned Communities,' that are being built throughout the Vegas Valley. The house is scheduled to be finished by April 2003, about eight months away. Mitch's plan is to use this property as his primary residence, for just two years so once he sells it, he and Pepe won't have to pay taxes on the profits, just as he did with his Seven Hills primary residence.

Mitch is talking trash with Pepe about how much money he has made on the sale of his Seven Hills property, and how much he and Pepe will make on this new joint venture. Mitch makes sure that Katherine is close enough to overhear it all. As Katherine hears Mitch's boasts, she comments, "Mitch, I want to invest in real estate too. Anyway, how many houses do you want, Mitch?"

"I want as many as I can buy as fast as I can buy them, because this market is getting ready to be off the chain for making just too much money." Mitch laughs as he looks at her, because this is all part of his elaborate plan to reel her in.

"I want as many houses as I can get too, then."

"Then stick with me kid, and I'll lace you up on just how to get there," he tells her. She smiles seductively at Mitch in response.

Mitch has been stalking this particular prey since she told him that she was trying to turn out some young dude as her pimp since leaving her ex man, Paddy. Mitch also knows Katherine has heard that he is an old school pimp and player from back in the day. As the conversation continues, Mitch finds an opening to drop another bomb on Katherine. While talking to someone else, Mitch makes sure Katherine hears him say, "I'm an old school player and I still love women that are down ass soldiers in the Army of getting at the money." He knows Katherine loves stripping and tricking and has absolutely no intentions of giving either up, even while being clean and in the program. So Mitch figures he might as well properly put her all the way down for it, since she's going to do it anyway. He also knows that she is extremely self conscious of it around other program females, for fear of what they will think of her. The big game hook hits Katherine right where she lives, just as Mitch intends.

At his townhouse, which has been a rental property for the past couple of years, Mitch notices that look in Katherine's eyes that he has seen in the eyes of so many like her in years past. Mitch is showing Katherine and Pepe the custom layout of this spot. Mitch observes how Katherine is looking around the townhouse and adding fuel to the fire that has begun to rage within her about playing on this big game field. "That's what I like about you, Mitchell Stone, you're a baller," she says.

Mitch smiles as his alter ego thinks, *she has no idea whatsoever who we are and what we are capable of. She has but read and heard of real down players like us.*

Mitch is having workers fix different things in the townhouse in preparation for him moving back into it until his Aliante property is finished being built. He tells Katherine to go through the house and open the garage for the workers, not because he needs it to be done, but just to get her in the habit of following his instructions. She does precisely as Mitch tells her without question. Mitch reels Katherine in almost effortlessly, so she commits to giving Mitch a certain amount of cash each week to invest in real estate with him. Mitch is thinking for the first time in some time, *gotcha, you bitch.* He watches as her excitement grows about giving him her money, and the possibilities that being hooked up with a guy like him represent.

Mitch is shocked at how much money Katherine is capable of making as a carpet hoe (girls that work strip joints). He also comes to realize that Katherine is extremely bipolar, but is quite intuitive in dealing with tricks, which enables her to have a good degree of mastery in the art of playing them for money. She has no tact or diplomacy, however, in dealing with people otherwise. So he sets out to become her mentor and subsequently her medication along with becoming that calm voice of reason in her life and affairs. Mitch has learned from observing some of her past relationships that she is controlling and loves being in control, which is why she usually always picks men down on their luck, homeless, or in need of a 'mama.' This way she keeps the ball in her court. In that respect, she is another Lana. He actually admires that in her even as his alter ego reminds him, *that dog won't hunt with us ever again.* In her own way, just as Mitch has, Katherine has learned to prey on the weaknesses of people for her best benefit, except when she develops feelings for a man. At those times, she becomes all thumbs emotionally and interactively.

Mitch recalls learning from Lana, "Women are for the most part emotional creatures, which is why we usually wouldn't make good pimps, especially if we develop feelings for the women. It's easy to send someone or use someone that you have little or no feelings for, but it becomes a different story when feelings get involved. Real pimps send them all without exception. It's not about a love thing, it's about a money thing. A pimp's love is conditional on what and how a particular female advocates his business, as in no pay no play and out of sight out of mind."

Over the years, Mitch has definitely learned to perfect those and other tools of the game to work to his best benefit, by hook or by crook. One Saturday, Mitch has a few of his partners over to his townhouse for a fight party. Included in that group is a guy from around the Program that he nicknames 'J man.' J man is a tall, dark skin pimp also from out of the bay area, Oakland, to be exact. He married his bottom broad and has two kids with her, but they are still down in the game and about the cash. J man and Mitch have been chopping it about some of the same places up and down the West Coast, and faces from back in the day, including Fillmore Slim.

He has Katherine bring the money for that week there to him, because she has this regular trick named Chuck, who is spending two to three large for a weekend with her. Chuck is in town for this weekend, so she won't be able to meet Mitch later. At this time, Katherine is giving Mitch two to three g's each week to invest, and Mitch is all good with that. For now. Katherine really turned herself out into the game ten years ago. The only exposure she's had with pimping, other than Paddy, was with a couple of young cats she's tried to turn out (the blind leading the blind). She actually knows very little about how the game really goes, other than getting at the money, and that's exclusively as a carpet hoe. Otherwise, she has a bunch of romantic ideas about what she perceives the game to be about based on books she's read and a couple of movies or documentaries she's watched. She is hungry for the game and ripe for the pimping. After Katherine comes and goes from dropping off the cash to Mitch, J man asks, "Mitch, you've knocked that bitch, haven't you, man?"

"Aw J man, what're you talking about?"

"Come on Mitch, I been in the game for years just like you, and I see how that bitch is around you lately. Her whole attitude and demeanor has changed in the few weeks that she's been fucking with you, Mitch."

Mitch laughs and says, "Yeah man, I'm putting down some serious long range game at this bitch's mind."

J man laughs and they slap five. "Aw Mitch, I'm already knowing and watching it go down." Mitch goes back to entertaining his other guests. J man wants to check out what's really going on with Mitch, so he calls a partner of his in Oakland to get a new number of a mutual old partner of theirs, Fillmore Slim. Mitch only half hears the phone conversation as J man explains to his partner on the other end of the phone, "Yeah man, Mitch and Fillmore have done the damn thing on the road together, man."

Once J man gets Fillmore on the phone, "Hey Slim, I got an old partner of yours here, man." While checking Mitch's reaction, J man hands Mitch the phone. "Mitch, I got Fillmore Slim on the line here, man."

Mitch takes the phone and asks, "Slim, is that you, old man?"

"Yeah, who is this?"

"Man, this is Pretty Mitchell, man."

J man has a moment of recall after hearing Mitch refer to himself by that handle. "Mitch, I've heard of that name before, man."

Mitch smiles and nods to J man. "I'm so sure you have heard that name before, being from the bay."

Then Slim asks, "Where you been Mitch? Man, it's been years since I've seen you."

"Slim, I've been in Vegas for the last fifteen to sixteen years, and off and on I was in southern Cali for years before that." Mitch can't hear inside the townhouse with all the noise his guests are making and the pre fight announcements, so he walks out onto his front porch. "Slim you still got hoes, man?"

"Nary a one, Mitch, the game is so different now than when we were doing it, man. Hoes are giving money to anybody these days, man."

"You got that shit right, Fillmore, we're like dinosaurs."

"What you doing up in Vegas, Mitch?"

"Man, I'm hooked up in corporate America, doing F&I for a local auto group. Can you imagine that?"

"Good for you, Mitch." "Look Slim, I'll get your number from J man, and get back at you later. I got this fight party I'm hosting right now, alright?"

"Yeah, alright Mitch, stay in touch, man."

As Mitch hangs up he remembers that he hasn't seen or talked to Slim in almost thirty years. It was the night Slim gave one of Mitch's hoes a ride from Oakland to an apartment he had her living in on Fell Street in Frisco. Now, like him, Slim is an old man. J man later tells Mitch, "You know I had to check you out, Mitch, to see where you're really coming from, and now I've heard it from Fillmore, 'That nigga, Mitch, is a nigga just like you. I remember how he used to jump up and bust a bitch upside the head, and then go shoot that hop,' he told me."

Katherine goes to give Mitch thirty five hundred for one particular week and he tells her to hold on to it because he has a little Mexican broad named Delores that he's in the process of flipping. "Katherine, I want you to get Delores on your shift at the Crazy Horse. Then, you can give her some pointers, and keep an eye on her for me." Mitch laces Katherine up with how he wants her to act and react in front of Delores when he picks her up. "Give me the money in front of Delores when I give you the signal. I want Delores to get into the mindset of what this is about right off the bat, women giving me money." Katherine is eating it up because it makes her feel like she's into the playhouse ninety of it all, which she is, but in a much different way than she thinks. She's actually more a part of it than she knows, because part of Mitch's scheme is for her benefit as well. It's getting her used to giving him the money as his hoe, not just as a business partner.

Mitch has closed Katherine on using her money and his ingenuity, hoe management skills and excellent credit to invest in real estate and other money making investment vehicles in order to come up together as business partners. It's an easy deal with Katherine for Mitch. She knows he has fifteen years of being drug free, and the credentials and reputation of being a successful entrepreneur in legitimate business enterprises, and operating with integrity as a shaker and mover.

Also, Katherine knows that Pepe has given Mitch a stack of thousands to maneuver and manipulate in various ventures for him and Mitch. Of course, Mitch's trappings and tools of the trade including cars, properties, attire, money and jewelry as well as his reputation as an old school master mack, also have a lot to do with it. J man probably put it best when he compliments Mitch earlier on this particular day, "Mitch, you did the razzle-dazzle with that bitch's mind using your properties, holdings and financial status. That's a smooth piece of pimping from your successful position that you put in on Katherine, man."

Mitch lays out the format for buying three new rental properties in his name with Katherine. One is for her to live in with her mom. The other two are rentals that Mitch will manage until they appreciate in value enough to flip and then buy up. He already has two of those three being built.

They pick up Delores and Katherine notices that she is a real pretty, little, Latina honey. Mitch has told her Delores is only nineteen years old with a fake id. He is using each of these two females to play at the other, so he can knock both girls in one clean sweep. Mitch pretends not to know where one of the stripper apparel stores is, so he can get Katherine to come along as a ploy so he can play at her head along with Delores's. Delores is trying on different outfits for Mitch to choose from as Katherine comments, "Mitchell Stone, I didn't know you were still down like this."

Mitch shares with Katherine his philosophy about ruining the best part of two good pieces of fruit, then adds, "Katherine, I have finally come to understand that I was, am, and always will be an apple. So instead of continuing to fake like I'm an orange, I'm going to be what I am."

Mitch picks a little Catholic schoolgirl outfit for Delores to work in, which is as much for his benefit later when he and Delores are back at the townhouse, as for the clients at the strip joint. Mitch decides to head for the last of three new housing tracks where he is buying for him and Katherine. He could easily have done this at a different time, but by doing it now he can further floss for Delores's benefit because he wants her to see what the possibilities are in being with someone like him. As they're riding, Mitch gives Katherine her cue, "Katherine, aren't you forgetting something, baby?"

Katherine picks up on Mitch's lead and pulls out the bundle of thirty five one hundred dollar bills in a rubber band. She hands it to him, while making sure that Delores checks it all out. Mitch laughs as he waves the money in the air at Katherine. "Looks like you're catching on, Katherine." Mitch is cracking up laughing because he realizes that neither Katherine nor Delores know that each of them are pawns in this chess game that he is playing. It is his process of pulling them both all the way in, by using one to play the other. Over the years he has learned from the very best, like Fast and Mickey. He remembers both Fast and old man Mickey Cohen telling him as if it were only yesterday that, "It's always easier to get a hoe when the new hoe thinks that you already have a hoe, just as it's easy to attract money when you act like you got money."

Dee Dee (Mitch nicknames Delores) has her first night at the club and makes right under five hundred. Mitch figures that, since he hasn't yet honed her into what her true job description will be, that's not bad. Mitch has learned a bit more patience, tact, and diplomacy in his approach to the game. It's no longer about cop and blow, snatch, grab and run. He's playing for keeps, and there is no room for error. So he figures she'll learn soon enough about laying down first and getting up last for the cash.

At his age and position in the real world and the business community, he can ill afford miscalculations that might lead to legal or business problems. In essence, he realizes that he is no longer a young buck, and now he has too much to lose and too little time left for starting all over again. Delores only works out for about a week, stripping. Like so many Latinas, especially in Southern Cali and Vegas, she has too many morals, scruples and cultural ideas about being some guy's girlfriend or wife and making babies. Mitch feels that it is such a waste. She disappears from the Crazy Horse one night and he never sees her again. However, the main trap he set is working, and that's for Katherine's fine, money getting ass. Fifty percent closing ratio isn't bad he figures, and he still finishes in the black ink with Delores. Mitch finds that Katherine knows nothing about setting the stage with bondsman and lawyers, or insurance benefits. He lays out a game plan for her to set up healthcare insurance, acquire a bail bondsman and an attorney, just in case, and begins to teach her certain dos and don'ts of the game. Katherine clings onto Mitch's every word and stories about the blasts from the past. Her eyes light up when he shows up wherever she happens to be. Mitch never even mentions sex. Of course, it does cross his mind, and has several times in the past.

It started years ago when she was newly around the program the very first time. Mitch was married at the time to Jackie, and Katherine was standing across the room from them getting a cup of coffee. Mitch's alter ego had urged him, *look at that real nasty, little black bitch over there.* Mitch thinks about it and he chuckles, as he reflects that he'd run past twenty nice girls just to get directions to which way a real hoe went. Mitch is amazed at the amount of money that hoes generate these days, starting with Legs and now Katherine, who is making white girl kind of money. He has been away from the game for fourteen to fifteen years, so he is also amazed at how well the system has made it possible for a hoe to earn that kind of money without a pimp's scrutiny. In the old days, hoes either got with a pimp or they had no protection or backup from other pimps, jails, or other hoes especially. Now a real motivated, well disciplined working girl can do it all without a pimp. However, just as he had to adjust and elevate his game to compensate for his stature in order to be competitive back then, he will adjust and elevate his game to compensate for his age and these new days and ways in the game now.

One day Katherine comes to Mitch's townhouse and brings a couple of her dance outfits for Mitch to critique. He realizes that what she's really doing is making sure that he gets a really good look at her body and how sexy she is, because he hasn't made a move on her for sex. She has also repeatedly told Mitch, "Mitchell Stone, you don't get my money and my pussy, you get either or."

Mitch never comments or shows any emotion about her comments one way or the other. However, his alter ego is thinking all the time, *bitch your life and your little affairs have not even remotely prepared you for the manner of creature that we be. We're going to own you, your money and your little pussy, along with your permission to do so.*

It just so happens that on this day she has given Mitch eleven g's, so Mitch decides to surrender to her sexual innuendos. She calls him from work to check in as he has instructed her to, and even more so this night because she is in the depressive cycle of her manic depression. Mitch has systemically maneuvered himself into becoming the voice of reason and sanity that she runs to as her stabilizing drug. "Mr. Stone, I don't know what's wrong with me, I'm mad at these tricks and these other bitches in this damn club. I'm only getting twenty or forty dollars here and there for a fucking lap dance, and not one of these bastards is biting for a date outside the club. I am so frustrated and mad right now that I'm snapping at everybody. I'm coming into my month's cycle and I just want to get out of here tonight."

"Check this out baby. You're just crazy right now because of your bipolar. You're still that sexy, drop dead gorgeous, seductive creature that you always are. It's just that you don't feel like it right now. Find a quiet place so you can hear just my voice."

"Okay, I'm leaving the floor right now. But Mitchell, why do I feel like this?"

"Listen baby, take deep breaths and lean back and relax for a brief moment and close your eyes. What is our mission statement? Why are we doing this thing together?"

She responds as Mitch has programmed her, "It's to buy properties and engage in other investment vehicles for our mutual prosperity."

"I'm proud of you girl. Now, what is our game plan for fulfilling those goals?"

"It's me getting at the money so we can."

"Perfect baby. Now remember what I told you earlier, 'we must do today what most people won't, so we can do tomorrow what most people can't.' And what's the definition of commitment, Katherine?"

"Working even when I don't feel like it?"

"There you go baby, doing the thing that you said you would do even when the feelings that you felt when you said you would do it have subsided. Essentially baby, stay down, because that's the only way to come up. Now, I need you to focus and keep your mind's eye on the prize, *aight?*"

"Mitchell, can I come over there and stay with you after work tonight?"

"Sure you can baby, but you need to be about this business first. Just remember, a down ass bitch can do whatever she sets her mind to. So what is your mind set to do?"

"Be a down ass bitch and get my crazy ass back on the floor so I can get at the money."

"Now, that sounds more like *my* bitch." With that statement, Mitch officially takes ownership of Katherine in both their minds.

Mitch is aware that way too many men have got at Katherine about sex. He will have none of that between them. When she gets to his townhouse in the wee hours of this morning she gives Mitch eight hundred. Mitch laughs and she expresses curiosity as to why he's laughing so he responds, "I see you pulled out the night, huh?"

"I was so excited when I got off the phone with you, that I just wouldn't take *no* from those men."

Mitch chuckles as Katherine gets into the shower and his alter ego, suggests, *we don't care what systems the establishment puts in place, hoes will still need pimps like us for management of their money and minds.* Mitch reasons he is somewhat re-raising Katherine properly into the game as only a real pimp can. He proceeds with the ringing of Katherine's bell this morning.

She bursts into tears when she climaxes. "Mitch, what the fuck was that?"

Mitch laughs, "Baby I think we, together, just played your tune." They both laugh and continue satisfying and exploring their curiosity of each other, which has been mounting for the past few weeks. It is the culmination of events, probing and prodding, that Mitch has done for three weeks now. Before he goes to sleep, Mitch lays back satisfied thinking, *Katherine is sprung on my knowledge, wisdom, and the game I represent at this level, along with the potential of the short and long range material gains she can have with me as her boss. Even after over a decade away from the game, this piece of work should be in the pimping, playing, and parlaying hall of fame.*

Chapter XXXI

Old Ways in New Days

Katherine has come to call Mitch, Poppy, which is all too familiar to him. Also, she asks him one day, "Why is it that you give all these other bitches nicknames, but you haven't given me one?"

Mitch laughs and consoles her, "I just hadn't gotten around to it yet, Katherine." So he gives her the nickname of Kit, reminiscent of sweet, smooth chocolate Kit Kat candy bars with crusty centers. It fits because she's smooth with what she does, yet emotionally crusty otherwise. Of course he only shares with her about the smooth part. She likes it so it's a keeper.

In late 2003, Mitch buys a gold 2003 Lexus SC 430 convertible hardtop with the license plates, *DN4MINE* (Down for mine). He buys a 2004 Cadillac Escalade Ext for Kit sporting the license plates, *IMDN4IT* (I'm down for it). The Lade is pearl white with custom, twenty two inch rims, and all the bells and whistles.

On March 17th, 2004, St Patrick's Day, Kit hands Mitch five g's in hundred dollar bills for a gift. They are in a meeting celebrating his eighteenth year clean and sober. In the Big Book of AA it states, "We will help you to create the fellowship that you crave." Along those lines, Mitch and the game become the fellowship that Katherine craves. "You do know, Poppy, the only way we can be together like this is one of us has to back down, and since it's definitely not going to be you, it must be me," she tells him. They laugh as they kid each other about being recovering addicts in twelve step programs and being in the game together as well.

"Yeah Kit, make no mistake about it, we have dual agendas going on in this relationship. It's like in one breath, I'm telling you, bitch, you need to get up and go get my money. Then, in the next breath, I'm telling you, God bless you."

Another young, blue eyed, blonde prostitute, fresh out of the penitentiary at twenty, comes along. Janice was turned out into the game at the ripe old age of fourteen. She understands the game well, knows how to interact with the pimping, and how to manipulate and maneuver her way through stables of multiple hoes. Mitch gets at her and she responds positively, so one more time, he incorporates his bottom girl, Kit, into the process, like he was taught way back in the day. As he's in the process of pulling Janice, Kit is in the process of pushing at her the benefits of being in it to win it with Mitch. It's all part of *text book* knocking of fresh game. Times are different and Mitch is no longer as razor sharp as he once was with reading multiple females interactively and separating them appropriately. He is quite pleased at how Kit is showing up in her job description, at least at first. However, Janice is showing up as who she really is just as well, by playing Kit's kindness for weakness, back stabbing Kit for position with Mitch, and playing on Kit's lack of savvy in functioning interactively in a stable.

He has Kit pick Jan up from the halfway house she's in, take her to lunches and kick it with her on his behalf while he's working at the car store, or when he's out of town. To make things even more difficult in orchestrating his girls, Mitch is transferred back to Henderson to another of the auto group's dealerships.

Three days after returning from a trip to Memphis, he gets a call from his brother, Randy. "Mitch, she's gone," Randy, tells him. Madea dies on November 25, 2003. Even while this call is expected, and Mitch knew when he left her bedside it would be his last time seeing her alive, the finality of it initially shocks him.

His first response is, "Aw man" and he hears Randy near tears. Mitch reasons that he is the oldest and expected to be the rock in these situations. So he composes himself for his baby brother's sake. He leaves Kit instructions to stay on top of Janice's mind. Then he jumps back on a jet and heads to Memphis, right in the middle of working on fresh game. Mitch flies his daughter, Henri, in from Cali for the funeral and burial services. Henri's mom, Rachel, also comes to pay her last respects and he feels that is a thoughtful thing for her to do.

When he arrives back in Vegas, Kit clues him in about her observations of Janice. "Poppy, Janice is a Libra, which means that bitch tends to be lazy, first of all. That bitch doesn't even try getting at money while she's in that halfway house and she's ghetto. If it were me, I'd at least be trying to make some kind of money for you while I'm in there. While you were gone I'd pick her up, take her to lunch and chop it with her like you told me to do, and you'd think that bitch would at least, say thank you, but she didn't. She just has no class."

As always, Mitch is amazed at how intuitive Kit is about people when she needs to be. Also, her knowledge of people's general nature based on their Astrological sign is unbelievably in depth and usually right on the money. However, he also detects animosity growing between her and Janice. Mitch starts picking Janice up from the halfway house and letting her spend a couple of hours or so at his pad after he gets off from work each day. He uses the time to finish locking up her mind in his favor and giving her a little break from the halfway house at the same time.

Mitch's mind is totally back down in the game, so doing a hoe without dough is a *no no*. Janice is down with the game, so she knows what time it is and what time it isn't about that as well. He's getting flack from Kit about spending time with Janice while Kit's at work. He should check Kit about it, but he's so empathic about her feelings that he doesn't come down hard on her in the interest of peace, harmony and money. For the record, Mitch files all of this away under things to remember. He feels he needs to get Kit intimately involved with Janice to keep the peace at least for the moment. Mitch knows with Kit's age, being a self turnout into the game, and her being a control freak like him, eventually she'll go sideways on him. She has a history of doing that with every other man she's been with when she's not getting her way.

It's near Christmas, 2004, and the first night that Mitch gets a little work out of Jan. She makes four hundred on a date, while still in the halfway house. Mitch drives her to the date and picks her back up when she's done. He knows that dog is not going to hunt for him, so he decides to buy a little get about ride for Jan to work out of once she's released from the halfway house. Now, the controversy surrounding Mitch's open antics with prostitutes in and out of the program, spurs gossip, as he's seen sitting in meetings from time to time, flanked by Kit and Janice, his new salt and pepper team. Mitch reflects back to one or more of the hoes in his stable, at any given time getting their feelings too deeply involved with him, instead of the game. That was, is, and always will be, when serious drama begins. He's been there and done that. Stable sisters (or wives-in-law) can work together, live together, care and share together as long as their caring and commitment is first to the game. Most times that's easier said than done, and of course, little things come up regardless, when there is more than one broad.

As Mitch looks back he realizes that since his first crew of broads the best hoes he's ever had and with the least amount of drama since, have been the ones where he and they did not get intimately involved at all, other than straight pimping and the game. That means no sex at all, just bonding and keeping their eye on the prize. He rationalizes that it's better to have a broad not love him and pay him, than to have one love him and cause him drama because of it. Too late, now he has double trouble.

Jan has nothing; no clothes to speak of and nowhere to stay (that Mitch wants her at) when she gets out of the halfway house. He puts her with Kit for a brief minute for economic reasons. This way her parole officer has a place to come check in on her without connection to him. As Mitch surveys his options, he realizes that the last thing he needs is a new girl living with her family and hearing all that 'be a good girl and don't hoe' bullshit. Plus, parole and probation aren't going to buy her staying in a weekly at this point with no job or visible means of support. On top of that, Mitch is an ex felon, so she can't stay with him, technically. Mitch buys a 2001 Saturn for fifteen hundred for Jan to use to get around Vegas in pursuit of his money. He figures if she doesn't work out he'll just have another car for the next broad. At the level he operates, it's essential that a hoe have transportation to get to different casinos and hotels.

Like his old Katherine, Kit gives Mitch every clue that she's reading about his innermost thoughts through his journal. On a couple of occasions Kit tells Mitch, "Mitchell Stone, you know I'm a down ass bitch and driven to get your money." Now, those are the exact words verbatim that Mitch writes in his journal. Plus, he writes, *This little pretty, money getting blue eyed blonde white bitch makes me feel like the old days again when I'm out popping it with her.*

Kit's comment is, "Mitch, she makes you feel like you're back in the old school pimping days again, when it was once me that made you feel that way. So this white bitch is taking my place?"

Kit becomes jealous and doesn't want Jan to have clothes, a car, house or anything, especially him. Mitch realizes that he has created this monster by the way he knocked Kit, but it is what it is now, so he needs to make the best of it for as long as he can. Mitch flashes back to when he was oblivious to his girl, Slim, and his ex-wife, Jackie, reading his journal and the drama that caused him.

Mitch's alter ego poses a question to him, *when are we going to get it? Just because we're not interested in reading a woman's journal that we're involved with, doesn't mean they won't sneak and read ours. In the old days it wouldn't have mattered much, because we didn't keep a journal and, even if we had, we still wouldn't care what they found out. If they didn't like it they could just leave. Quiet as it's kept, we really don't care now either, because as far as their success and future is concerned, we were the best thing going for a working girl back then and we still are these days. However, there's one small detail we're missing, we're fifty six now as opposed to being a twenty six year old cutie pie back then.*

After he gets those little tidbits of wisdom from himself, Mitch rationalizes that he still has to put Jan in Kit's house for a very short time. He figures if he's lucky, the two of them will get along long enough for him to get a bank out of Jan and get her a spot of her own. For now at least, he's got peace between them. Jan's first night out of the halfway house and out to a full night's work, she makes twelve hundred plus. She was turned out as a track hoe and has honed those particular skills down to an instinctive science. Of course, along with acquiring those skills, over time a female becomes scandalous and a master of chicanery even with her man.

Kit on the other hand is a strip club hoe and therefore more classy and stylish, but very vindictive and a hater. Mitch understands it's just a matter of time before this whole little situation comes tumbling down and he accepts that it's all on him. If he's the power that makes it what it is, then he also is the power that makes it what it's not. The buck stops with him, not only in the pimping, but in life in general. Mitch is anxious to get Jan stretched out. He figures it might help bring her and Kit closer together in what should be their common bond, getting his money. Also, sexual intimacy will aid in bringing them closer together as well. So he lets them both know that the three of them will be spending Christmas Day and night together and it'll be on and popping between the three of them.

"But for now, I need both of you down hard for my money," he tells them. They both look at each other and smile in agreement.

Kit expresses her eagerness to have sex with Jan. "Poppy, I can hardly wait to get at this young blonde pussy."

"I'm down with that," Jan adds, but Mitch notices her facial expression insinuates just the opposite. He decides to just play it by ear from now until then.

Jan's second night out, she calls Mitch around two am with eight hundred, and about to go up to a date's hotel room. Then, about an hour later, she calls back from jail. She was arrested for old traffic warrants she received before she went to prison. Mitch explains to her that he'll have her right out as soon as her parole officer lifts the hold. However, she ends up with similar warrants from Henderson as well. When Jan gets out she asks to stay at Mitch's pad and kick it with him after she gets off from work for a couple of days since she missed hanging out with him for Christmas and New Year's. After Jan stays over for a day at his pad, Kit decides to stay over too. Jan leaves and goes back to Kit's house, because she's not interested in kicking it with Kit sexually. Mitch knows they both love pussy, but if Jan doesn't want to kick it with Kit, then Mitch isn't about to force the issue. However, Kit takes it all personally and the drama ensues, again.

Kit begins having feelings of not being in control, because she and Jan aren't clicking and everything is centered around, and goes through, Mitch. Mitch reflects on Kit telling him stories about her having her man and her bitch living with her, and her running shit as the hub of that family wheel. Mitch reasons that hoes don't have hoes in his regime, unless he's the one that decides it's that way. "Well," Mitch explains, "A female running shit in my regime isn't happening with me ever again, as long as you squat to pee." Mitch has been in this stern mindset since Lana and Brea. Kit's feelings of powerlessness and lack of control in this situation isn't happening with her either.

Kit's already set in her ways and both her and Mitch's controlling natures don't, and won't, fit in the same place and space. That's why, before Jan's arrival, he and Kit never spent that much intimate time together in the first place. They were each okay with that, but now all of a sudden Kit's not, because with another female in the picture, Kit feels threatened. Kit and Mitch's control issues begin getting in the way of each other. Kit felt in control when it was just her and Mitch. Now, she tells him, "Mitch, I'm not just in this for the houses, jewelry, cars and stuff. I want you."

Mitch ponders how many times he has heard that before. He reflects back to Paulette, from years ago, who gave up everything she owned at that time just to show him. Again, he has created this monster one more time. *Hell hath no fury like a woman scorned.* Kit's inability to deal with her feelings about it all, lead her to leave. She leaves angry, resentful and hating. Depending on what day it is and how she wakes up feeling, she will stay that way for quite awhile. She goes back to doing what she was when Mitch knocked her.

He cares for her and doesn't like her leaving. He also doesn't like losing that source of income and a self motivated hoe, but he figures, shit happens. Mitch and Kit keep doing business as usual in order to maintain their collective interests and holdings. Years of manipulating and calculating people's strengths and weaknesses to his best benefit, has honed him into a meticulously cunning player. He knows the best way to get long term results out of a short term working girl is by putting as many of her marbles in his basket as he possibly can. Of course, that starts with a woman having a strong desire for having things in her life in the first place. Kit's whole material life is in Mitch's hands and control, whether she's with him or not. That isn't the way nature planned it, but it is the way Mitch planned it.

Mitch reflects that he has been in and out of lust and love with more women in his life than he can even remember their names. Out of sight is still out of mind for him. He loves them when they're doing it as he wishes, but when their compliance ends, magically, so does his feelings. Mitch chuckles as he thinks hoes really do come and go, but sometimes they come back again. Kit may become one of them, along with Jan and several others. Still, that fine ass, young, blue eyed devil, Janice, gets Mitch thirty grand out of the casinos the first month she works for him. With that kind of productivity, who cares if she flakes out at times? Mitch chops it with his pimp friend, J man, and asks him to critique the scenario from how he sees and hears it, as he shares the events with him. Mitch ponders that it's uncanny just how much the Program relates to the game and life in general. The game is a lot like the Program in as much as no matter how long you're in it pimps always need to bounce ideas off other pimps to stay on top of their own game. J man tells Mitch, "Come on Mitch, the way you knocked that Kit bitch was sweet poetry, as I watched it all going down. But like you say, man, you'd probably have gone a lot further with her had you not gotten her feelings involved with you, and you'd still be pimping her now."

"But J man, you and I both know once a man becomes everything else to a woman, the sex is just where that female's head goes, man."

"You're absolutely right, Mitch, about them being sprung on the game sometimes leads to them becoming sprung on us. Most of them at some point or another, want to fuck their pimp and that's just the way that shit is, Mitch. However, she's given up her best opportunity for coming up in the game, in you, man. So partner, trust me, you'll get another day of pimping there, sooner or later. I mean, Mitch, she knows who got her this far, which is probably farther than she's ever been before. Anyway, man, shit happens in fucking with hoes."

They slap hands as Mitch trash talks about it. "You know J man, the bottom line for me is I'd rather be me today *clean,* than be that twenty five year old loose cannon on heroin that I was back in the day."

"Amen to that, Mitch, man, I sometimes wonder what it might have been like if I hadn't got wrapped up with that dope. You know, to go back to then and know what we know now."

"That's a scary thought for me J man, because heroin actually leveled the playing field of life for me. If not for hoes and heroin, I would have quite probably died of fright or starvation." They both laugh and slap five again.

Mitch quickly determines that Jan is not a bright female at all, but she is a money getting machine. Any day that he can get her motivated and acclimated to business, she makes right at a grand. Unlike Kit, Jan is not a self motivated hoe. She needs up close and personal pimping and supervision every day. Mitch gets her a dummy job with a partner who has a plumbing business. Mitch also has a residence set up for her with another ex hoe, now squared up, named Michelle. This way, Jan has a tight straight-looking life of employment and residence on paper by day, while getting at Mitch's dough on the real, by night. She requires constant supervision, however, and Mitch is working long hours out in Henderson, leaving her too much on automatic pilot. He's usually gone to work when she wakes up and asleep when she gets home from doing her thing. She runs good and hard for most of that first year, with just part time pimping.

Mitch buys her a new 2004 Saturn coupe with all the accessories. He also starts beefing up her wardrobe and accessories, because she needs everything. He can't very well have a shabby looking female representing him. Mitch is still not down with being high profile back out in the competitive game of street life. First, he realizes that his time for that has long since passed. Straight pimping is still a young man's game at the street level of notoriety.

Aside from a few incidents the first year, Jan holds up decently. Then, she starts really slacking off with short money here and there and missing in action. While the new lifestyle being down for Mitch represents is quite attractive to Jan, she only desires the basic necessities out of life, which is evidenced by her actions. Near the completion of the house that Mitch is having built for Jan, he takes her to select the options for the house. She seems jazzed about it all, as she's running through the different sections of the KB Homes Design Center. One would think that this alone would be motivation enough for any hoe to stay down and focused on getting money. However, one day Jan doesn't get home before Mitch leaves for work, so he calls the house and her cell phone a few times from his office, but gets no answer. He leaves work to go check on things and finds Jan is home, afraid to answer the phone, because she's screwed off Mitch's money. "Bitch, where have you been and where is my money?"

"I don't have it, I lost it gambling."

Right about then Mitch loses it. "Oh, you're real comfortable about fucking off my money, huh?"

"I'll make it up."

"No bitch, you've been hanging out with that Monique bitch and gambling with her." Mitch reflects that one of the reasons for quizzing a hoe at the end of every night is to get little insights into what may be about to go down, and with who. "Bitch, didn't I tell you when you first told me about Monique to stop fucking with her and you're still kicking it with that bitch anyway. What's next bitch, you want to get with her and her man? Have at it, bitch. I don't need a punk ass bitch fucking off her own future, along with my dough. What good can you be for my future? And bitch, we got a house being built for your sorry ass. What about that?"

Her next response makes Mitch completely aware of where her head is and isn't. "I don't care anything about having my own house. Mitch, I need to live with you because you keep me focused and straight. That house, new cars and all that is what *you* want. All

I want is a roof over my head, some clothes, food in my belly and someone like you to keep me in check. I hardly see you anymore and we don't talk as much like we used to."

Mitch just looks at her, as he's thinking, to coin a phrase, "Out of the mouths of babes, children sometimes speak in their simplicity more wisely than their elders." With that thought in mind, Mitch recognizes the need to navigate a different course of action concerning this new house. He submits to the fact that it'll probably be totally on him to deal with when it's completed, because it's uncertain how Jan will be by that time or even if she'll still be around. Part time pimping begets partial success, especially with hoes like Jan. One of the main reasons hoes pay pimps to start with, is to have someone else accountable for them and their actions or inactions. "You know what bitch, I don't need this bullshit. If you wish to be a deadbeat, then do it someplace else. In fact, you don't deserve the new Saturn, so take the little 2001 Saturn and your little clothes and go get with Monique and her man if that's what you want."

Crying, Jan begs, "Mitch, I don't want that." "Bitch, I don't want a bitch that don't want anything, so either you decide to soldier where the fuck I told you, or get on before you get shit on."

When Mitch gets home from work that evening Jan is gone with her belongings in the little 2001 Saturn. After he thinks about it, he realizes that bitch isn't responsible enough to keep that car, be dependable enough to take care of the insurance, and get it registered into her own name so he doesn't have any further liability. Even if he takes the chance, she doesn't even have a legitimate driver's license. So if she isn't working for him, he doesn't feel obligated to take any further risks whatsoever. She is a classic example of why hoes need pimps. Plus, he already knows that bitch will be back, eventually. She just wants to get with a pimp that won't keep such close tabs on her, so she'll be freed up to smoke crystal meth, gamble, and run wild for the first real stretch since she's been out of prison. Mitch gets the call the next morning from Jerome, a young dope dealer and pimp around town. "Hey man, is this Mitch?"

"Yeah, I'm Mitch, who is this?"

"I'm Jerome, man, and this broad, Janice, has come around here and chose a nigga."

"I appreciate the courtesy call, man."

"What about the clothes, Mitch?"

"No problem with that Jerome, all I need is my ride and cell phone from that bitch."

"Hey man, your car is parked at the Or'leans Casino right across from the front door and I'll have your cell phone when I meet you to get the clothes, alright?"

"That's a plan Jerome. I get off from work in Henderson around ten pm, so let's say I meet you at midnight in front of the Or'leans."

"Cool Mitch, I'll see you then."

"Oh, by the way Jerome, it's refreshing to talk with what sounds to be another real pimp, man. There's not too many of us left."

"Same here, Mitch."

Mitch notes that Jerome sounds old school. He picks up Michelle after he gets off and takes her to the rendezvous with Jerome, so she can drive Jan's Saturn back to Mitch's house.

When Jerome gets out of the burgundy Lade, Michelle goes, "Mitch, how old is he, fifteen?"

Mitch laughs and says, "It looks like it, huh, baby?" *At least this baby face kid represents this game like he's older anyway,* he thinks. Mitch reflects back to when he'd knocked older pimps. When he'd shown up, they probably thought the same thing looking at him that he's thinking now looking at Jerome. Mitch also thinks Jerome is probably thinking the same thing that he used to think back in the day when he was knocking some old man. "What is this old man still doing obstructing young hoes from young down pimps like me, anyway?"

Mitch has that little smile on his face, as he extends his hand to Jerome and offers to buy him a drink. Jerome takes a rain check on the drink. Mitch is readily prepared to tell Jerome what Jan's strengths and weaknesses have been while she worked for him, but Jerome doesn't accept the invitation so Mitch figures Jerome will find out on his own. They exchange Jan's belongings for Mitch's car and cell phone, thereby completing the transference of ownership of Jan, officially. Mitch reasons that as well versed as Jerome appears to be about the game, he might also know the underlying main reason for that drink. If so, he wouldn't want Mitch to pick his brain to find out how he knocked Jan in the first place, in order for Mitch to determine what it'll take to knock her back.

Just like Mitch figures, Jan is back choosing him in a couple of weeks. She has lost a lot of weight from smoking meth. Mitch is so concerned about the potential of the money she can make, that it doesn't dawn on him that the reason she is so thin is she's been smoking dope. He is now mentally far removed from his drugging days and the effects that it can have on an individual.

What strikes him as particularly odd at first is, Jan has the nerve to tell him, "I left trying to break your heart, because you broke mine when you told me to get the fuck out."

Mitch's alter ego asks, *what heart, this bitch really does have us confused with someone else. We sold our heart for cash money, years ago. Of course she isn't the first bitch to think that the way to get even with us is through our heart. This isn't a love thing, it's a money thing.* One thing is for certain in Mitch's mind, with part time pimping, he is still on borrowed time with this one. There are people who are driven to succeed and have the commitment to that end. Jan is most definitely not one of them, but ironically she is of the same fiber of the average hoe. However, what's even more paramount is, she's a meth addict. So Mitch resolves himself to play it as it comes. Let the chips fall where they may, based on those circumstances. Jan tries to hold up, but like so many of Mitch's girls, she's a combination of bipolar, A.D.D and schizophrenia, and eventually, she will fall by the wayside too.

Chapter XXXII

Opening an Escort Service

Having been free of cigarettes, clean and sober for nineteen years and free of gambling for over twelve years, Mitch's thinking and decision making are crystal clear. On paper he's strictly legit, but under the microscope he lives way above his legitimate means. So he sets about the business of fixing all of that. He calculates that with just two hoes during overlapping fiscal years of service he has made upward of three hundred large. In the old days it took him more than three times that many hoes to make a half million in any fiscal year. He creates a company, Mitchell Stone Enterprises, as a home based retail sales business.

He pays little to no taxes that he doesn't get back. He has learned about write offs and deductions. He has a real keen ex IRS tax accountant that's handling his tax returns. With the properties, cars, cash investment portfolio and holdings, he looks squeaky clean, like *John Doe America*. His career in the car business is on the skids, as he finds himself doing four to five times more work for fifty to sixty percent less income. It started with all the corporate cutbacks and bonus adjustments a few years back and continues to get worse. There were once three to four support clerical staff to do all of what managers now do in his department. Those positions have been eliminated for bigger corporate profits. He isn't mad at them about it, he's just mad because he's not one of them.

With a refreshed taste for the game again, he's grown more disenchanted by the day with the automobile industry and all the hours involved. He realizes that at the age of fifty six, he wants to go run and play with nasty little girls once again while he still can. His emphysema has progressively gotten much worse and will only continue to deteriorate, so he needs to sow some oats, while there's still a harvest or two left in him. Mitch takes a temporary leave of absence, and at the end of that time frame, he formally resigns. In both written and verbal form he thanks the company and its upper echelon management for the opportunities they've given him over the years.

Mitch refinances all of his properties and pulls a nice size chunk from them. With the way property values are surging, he wishes he had bought more, especially in the Seven Hills, Henderson area. He snatches one hundred large out of one little property that he had left after Legs split, plus the chunk he made with her new husband buying him out of the other. Legs is quite ecstatic about the refinance of her property, which is the other of the two they bought together in Seven Hills. She gives Mitch five g's for just on the count of money. Of course, in return, he has to indulge her in role playing their little incestuous game. Mitch figures in another couple of years or so, he'll get another similar payday provided the housing market continues escalating. Even if it doesn't he's already gotten his money up front.

He paid one hundred and fifty six large for a small three bedroom with upgrades just three years earlier. After down payment, and three years of mortgage payments he owes one hundred and thirty nine grand and it now appraises for three hundred and forty

Colby Chase

thousand. To sum up Mitch's feelings and outlook on it all, *God Bless America and its capitalistic system.*

Kit proves to be a worthy business associate, for the time being, even better than most men that Mitch finds in and around his experience now. Of course the proof ultimately will be in the longevity of her responsible behavior. That will reflect her true makeup. It's so much easier to be accountable when the chips are rolling, but the true test of one's integrity is in staying the course when the chips aren't coming as easy. Mitch reflects that some females he's put in position to blow up have done just that, blew up (imploded). Plus, he figures he's got a young, fast, money getting hoe in Jan at least for now, as long as she's reasonably drug free and he stays right on top of her. Still, he reasons that time will prove the better judge of all that and either way hoes will come and go.

Mitch gets the idea to open up an escort service while talking with his partner Pepe one day. He remembers how successful he was when he had it going on like that in Frisco, back in the day. He figures it'll give him steady action at young hoes without him having to expose himself to law enforcement scrutiny. He won't need to be hanging out at spots where he can get easily made for the true nature of his business. With his record, Mitch knows that he won't be able to get the necessary state licensing in his name. Mitch's asks his partner, Pepe, "Can you imagine how the licensing board would view a convicted panderer and white slaver like me for applying for an escort service license?"

Pepe responds, "Yea Mitch, they'll give you a one way ticket back to prison just for applying." They both crack up and slap five. As he discusses it with Pepe, he loves the idea and is all in with Mitch. He knows that Pepe is seriously and happily married. Pepe will be the owner of record for purposes of licensing, and Mitch will be the CEO and CFO, and handle all the service's functions, including money and recruiting girls. Pepe has had a working girl or two in his day, but Pepe really doesn't have the stomach for pimping. So Pepe won't be down with that end of the business. Probably most

402

important to Mitch of all these factors about Pepe, is that Pepe is in the Program and Mitch feels he can trust him.

Mitch feels that even when Jan breaks wide again he's far enough ahead on her, Kit, Legs and his other enterprises that it really won't matter in the grand financial scheme of things. However, from the very beginning he runs into obstacles because he's not connected like he was in the old days in Frisco. They have to rent a spot for the service before the licensing people will even consider the license. Also, he realizes that he'll have to continue keeping a low profile, avoiding known player hang outs and hot spots. He's at a point in his life where he has no need to compete head to head with the young bucks now in the game. He's playing for keeps this time around, and without the benefit of being as ruthless and abandoned to death or his freedom as he was once. Mitch is considered somewhat of a *'spiritual pimp,'* a term that came from one of Mitch's buds around the Program, who also happens to be a car salesman.

Pepe leases a spot inside the Can Can Room Plaza building, upstairs where several other escort services are located in the commercial district on Industrial Road. Mitch and Pepe are paying for the spot and the expenses out of their pockets, but are not able to operate without a license. Mitch reflects that back in the day, one phone call from Don V's attorney and he had licenses for two escort services and a topless adult arcade in a matter of forty eight hours. Just goes to show, one more time it's not what you know 'it's who you know.' It's one of the ways the system puts up road blocks to try to deter people from going into the business. They know it's a license for working hoes and not just escorting, but it still qualifies for a legal license. It's like legalized hoeing and pimping, but actually, everything in Vegas requires some form of licensing. It's that way as a result of the days when organized criminals ran the town.

Jan is in and out of using meth until she finally gets popped. After about two weeks they release her by accident. Mitch realizes he needs to do something to enable her to get at his dough regardless of parole or warrants. In the process of figuring out a way to get cash out of her, he comes up with the idea to hit the road with her where the fear of getting popped won't hinder her from going all out getting money. Mitch figures a hoe in jail is a liability not an asset. Now that he's no longer working a conventional job, he can invest more time and energy into the pimping. Other than managing his rentals, he has nothing else to do, while waiting on the license to come through for the escort service. He and Jan knock a little, light brown skin, cute, eighteen year old named Amber one night rolling down the strip, and after a few weeks of getting money out of Amber alongside Jan, Mitch decides they're ready.

He takes them to the noon meeting, figuring that since they'll be on the road for a few days, he wants to get a meeting in before. Kit walks into the room and the tensions between her and Jan is very noticeable throughout the whole meeting room. Amber leans over across Mitch and asks Jan, who is seated on his right side, "Is there something up with you, Mitch and that girl?" Mitch tells Jan and Amber to shut up and talk after the meeting.

After the meeting, Jan explains to Amber what's going on, while Mitch chops it with his partners for a bit. That next day Mitch gets the Escalade from Kit in order to accommodate two hoes, and he hits the highway the following morning. He gets an updated number from J man on Fillmore, who is now living in Sacramento. Mitch puts in a call to Slim and tells him that he should be rolling into Sac sometime late that next evening with fresh game to put down, and he'll call him back when he's close. Mitch reflects that it's been a quarter century or better since he's hit the highway with this particular game plan as his primary agenda. Mitch recalls all the stops he used to check out for getting money along the way. He heads through Bakersfield and stops in Fresno for the night, gets at a few bucks, hits Stockton and then on into Sac. Once upon a time, this was part of the circuit that a pimp and crew could travel and put together a bankroll on the different strolls up and down the West Coast from L.A. to Monterey and on to Seattle and Vancouver,

B.C. Mitch finds these old places to be nothing like they once were for getting money, but his alter ego reminds him, *it's been right at thirty years since we blazed these old trails.*

As Mitch and his two young girls are on the freeway nearing Sac around eleven that evening, he hits Fillmore on the phone. "Fillmore, where can we hook up, man? I'm down like four flat tires on this 2004 Escalade sitting on twenty twos with a twenty one year old blonde and an eighteen year old sister *salt n pepper* team, man."

Mitch and Slim laugh, as Slim tells Mitch that he'll be tied up until after two am. "Mitch, you'll probably leave Sac with another white girl or two off this stroll here, rolling like you are, man," Fillmore says. Fillmore gives Mitch a location where he can put his game down, along with a club nearby where he and Mitch can rendezvous later.

Mitch checks out the track and finds it looking slow and dismal, but he reflects that Sac's tracks have always looked that way even back when they were really hitting. He decides to stop at the club Fillmore put him down with so he and his crew can eat. With Jan and Amber complaining about being tired from being on the road all day, Mitch laughs and says, "I guess you young hoes today aren't made as tough as they were back in the old school days, huh? I remember the time when I used to hit the road with three or four bitches in the Ham. They'd take turns driving straight into Seattle from Frisco. When we'd arrive, they'd jump right out on Pacific Coast Highway and get busy selling pussy for the rest of the night without missing a beat."

After doing all the driving from Fresno himself, Mitch decides to bed his crew down for the night with the intention of catching up with Slim later in the wee hours of this morning. Mitch sits on the side of the bed to talk to Jan before he leaves to rendezvous with Slim, and his fifty six year old body betrays him. Other than to undress, when he gets up next it's Saturday morning. He decides to drive on into Frisco, check out the tracks there and across the bay in Oakland, instead of hanging around Sac checking out dead strolls or waiting to catch up with Slim. Mitch calls J man en route to San Fran to get an overview on what spots are hitting today and a bondsman that'll do long range bails on a phone call. Then, he calls the bondsman and gets that business lined up and now down to business.

On the way across the bridge going into Frisco, Mitch is thinking, *here I am at fifty six back in the game, having come full circle three hundred and sixty degrees from way back then to now.* As Mitch rolls into the streets of San Francisco, he's flossing and telling his two young girls about the days of old and how the game was played then. They're like little children listening to nursery rhymes, mesmerized and clinging to his every word. His alter ego suggests, *it doesn't get any better that this for an aging over the hill pimp, two young hoes that worship us and love the thrill of the hunt in the game.*

J man and Fillmore have prepped Mitch for what he'll find in Frisco. The Frisco street people he once knew are but folklore. He has been back to Frisco a few times since living in Vegas, so he knows what to expect, but this time he's got hoe business again. The arenas he seeks look so different. Hoes are on the internet, in escort services, and most of the XXX arcades and old nude joints around Powell and O'Farrell Streets and the financial district have been shut down. It is no longer about rolling up on bitches on a stroll. It's damn near like hide and seek unless he's willing to hit the road and find the places that are still jumping like he did thirty years ago, but he's got too much going for that now. Plus, he reflects that even in the old days of Lana and Brea, he could just put those two superstars on a jet and have his dough wired to him from wherever it was hitting at any given time.

Unfortunately, hoes don't come along too much like that anymore, at least as far as he's seen from his somewhat limited scope of involvement this time around. Back in the day, he didn't care who knew he was a pimp, cops included. He rationalizes that these days he is a respected entrepreneur and businessman within the community, so the less people that know about this element of his business, the better. Still, he longs for the buzz of the streets, the days when the horns of Cadillacs, Benzes, Excaliburs, Bentleys and Rolls tooted at each other in that old player style, as they passed each other in the night, while checking traps and on the prowl for fresh game, which was literally everywhere. Now China Town is mushrooming over into Broadway Street in North Beach, indistinguishably from the old clubs and pubs. All the old landmark joints like the Four Leaf Clover Irish Pub, Big Cal's, The El Bangor and The Music Workshop are either gone out of business or have new management. The French sidewalk café has lost its ambiance, because now, right next to it, is a Chinese express food joint. The adult arcade Mitch once owned is a book store only now, and with no black velvet curtain leading into the back.

Out of nostalgia, Mitch goes inside and checks just to make sure. As he and his girls cruise out of the North Beach area, Mitch smiles as he reflects on that old song, "everything must change, nothing stays the same" and justifiably so. He figures he would probably be dead, crippled, in prison for life or insane had he kept on the way he had been going just before finally getting into the Program in Vegas. He is jolted back into the reality of the moment by Jan, when she asks, "Where are you putting us down, Mitch?" Mitch doesn't respond and just keeps rolling, as Jan and Amber jabber back and forth about the sights of the city, as neither of them has ever been to Frisco before now. As the big Cadillac Escalade pulls over in front of a familiar motel to Mitch, he tells his young game to get out, get down and get hoeing. It is about ten pm when he drops them off at a spot just off of Van Ness Street across from the old Cadillac dealer. He drives off thinking what a revolutionary idea the cell phone is and what it would have been like to have had them back in the day. Mitch shifts his mind from what was, and on to the pimping at hand today, as that was then and this is now, so on to sell some fresh, young pussy.

Amber is relatively new to the game, but Jan is a pro at navigating her way around the cops and other hoes and pimps getting at them. Mitch has been in Amber's head for the past few weeks and all the way up from Vegas, as to how he wants her to follow Jan's lead in the avocation of his business. Mitch is cruising through the Mission District in search of young, hot Latinas when his prowling is interrupted by a phone call from Jan. "Mitch, pick us up. We just got an old white man for seventeen hundred." After finding out where they're posted up hiding out, Mitch spins the Lade around and goes and scoops them up.

That is the only money he gets out of Frisco that weekend before they head back to Vegas. This trip turns out to be mostly of a nostalgic trek into the glorious memories of an old man's very distance past, who has been away from the game, the strolls, and the pulse of the streets, for quite a few years. He does reaffirm that, unless he's all the way back down in it, the track game in big cities is no longer his forte. He is living a legit life in middle class suburban America these days with platinum cards, mortgages, and home equity lines of credit. On the trip back to Vegas, Mitch is thinking, *from now on I need to stick with this new age pimping.*

Jan and Amber take turns driving them back to Vegas. Mitch sits in the back asking himself, *would I trade who I have become today to again be whoever it was that I thought I was way back when?* The answer comes back a resounding, *no, no, and no!* His alter ego asks, *why not, with as much as we proclaim to still love the game?* Mitch recognizes that all those years ago, the voice of his alter ego had dominion over him. Now, by the grace of God, people, Program and the principles of anonymous programs, he finally has dominion over his alter ego. There is so much more involved with who he is today beyond the pimp game, than who and how he was back then. What he became back then he never wants to be again in those other areas outside of the pimp game.

He once felt that he had to move whenever his alter ego or the disease of addiction gave the marching orders. Now the tables have turned for the most part. Obviously, at least some of the ideas of his alter ego still rule him, because here he is at almost twenty years clean and he's again back in the pimp game. Mitch concedes it is true that he would never have made it through all he has been through and done without the reckless abandon and bravado of his alter ego. Yet, in the real world, he has learned to govern his actions accordingly with his circumstances. This is no longer the wild, wild, west and the gunfighters of old have either grown with the times, or they have perished through jails, institutions or death.

Chapter XXXIII

Health Wealth and Stress

Home in Vegas, Jan is still running scared from a parole violation. Amber hangs in with Mitch for a minute, but without a leader and out free lancing, she isn't able to hold up on her own. Jan is working the escort services mostly, so that leaves Amber on the strolls and in the casinos alone. Through researching the pulse of the other existing escort services, Mitch learns that very few black girls are successful working in them. The good news is Pepe's license for the escort service comes through after almost seven months and almost twenty g's that he and Mitch are in the red already. Mitch comes up with the name of "Vegas Valley Escorts." Other services already have the exact phone numbers that he wants, but he gets close. The local number is (702) 367-4475 (For Girl) and the toll free number is (866) 284-4757(At Girls).

He feels that these numbers will get the point across. He has cameras outside the front door, buys computers, TV, VCR, DVD players, desks, chairs, phones, and advertisement cards for specific girls, as well as business cards for his young partner, Pepe, and himself. He hires two girls, one of which is a White girl named Carol and one mixed Black and Latina named Cher to handle the incoming calls and allocate the different girls for the calls. He also contracts a crew of Chicano guys to work the strip passing out the service's advertisement cards with photos of the girls and phone numbers to the service. Mitch and Pepe have spent a grip in just waiting on the license and setting the joint up with the necessary equipment to function properly, including a website.

Now, all Mitch needs is a mix of girls. That isn't too difficult because their service is located right in the middle of other escort services. So Mitch and his two phone girls begin recruiting the other services' girls. Mitch's first recruit is this light brown skin, long legged, little, eighteen year old sister named Melissa. She proves to be quite versatile and well versed at her craft. When clients ask for a brunette or dark haired escort, Mitch sometimes has Cher or Carol send Melissa and she makes it work more often than not. She has long weaved hair and fake boobs and presents herself well. Mitch's two phone girls continue recruiting other new broads to work for the service.

Since the escort service's opening, Mitch starts going to a five thirty pm NA meeting at the New Point Club, because he's up until five or six am every morning. Overseeing the service operations, along with his own personal girls, who are in and out of the service or out freelancing all night long, leaves him little extra time. Sometimes Mitch takes one or more of his personal girls that either have drug problems or have a potential for such problems, to plant the seed in them that there is another way. First and foremost Mitch is a recovered addict, and an entrepreneur and whatever else, second. If a particular girl doesn't exhibit a problem in these areas, Mitch keeps that part of his life to himself. It's strictly on a need to know basis. If they don't have the need, they don't need to know.

At the height of the service, there are approximately forty two girls on call. It is just coming into what is supposed to be the high season for this industry. Mitch is knocking different broads that come through, getting them to work for him personally. Now, he has the best of both worlds from the escort service business standpoint and his own personal profitability. Mitch uses Jan as the service's web page girl since she was the only broad he had at the time of its inception. With the site up and running, Mitch thinks, *so now bring on the clients,* just as the message in *A Field of Dreams,* "build it and they will come."

One day, Mitch and Pepe are finishing lunch and discussing Mitch's game plan for the escort service when Mitch spots his old girl, Slim, just outside in the restaurant parking lot. Mitch goes out and greets her, as he hasn't seen her in sometime. He notices that she looks like the girl next door now, not his once provocative sex kitten. She has cut her hair shorter and dyed it red, and he remembers how he hated it when she did that. He really always loved her long, beautiful, blonde locks. After the initial greeting, Mitch inquires, "Slim, why did you cut and dye your hair, again?"

"It's so much trouble managing all that hair, Mitch. And you know how I am. I get bored and change hair colors. You remember I used to cut it and dye it just to piss you off when we were on the outs, because I knew how much you loved my hair." She laughs at her own comment. However, Mitch doesn't find her adversarial attitude at all funny anymore.

Only making small talk, Mitch asks, "You don't write, you don't call, what is your major problem, female? Don't you realize we have history? You were once my dream girl."

"Yeah, and I see you're dressing younger and rolling in style. Pretty car, Mitchell."

"Yeah, I've got five or six rides, Slim, including an Escalade and here, take one of my cards." He says handing her his escort service card from his console and she happens to notice several photos of different young, provocative female escorts in the console as well, so she grabs a few of them.

As she looks at the young girls on the cards, she remarks, "Um, um, um, Poppy, when you were forty you were fucking twenty year olds, including me, and now you're almost sixty and you're still fucking twenty year olds. Poppy, that's not right."

Mitch laughs, "Tell you what Slim, why don't you come get down with your old poppy, getting at this money."

Slim laughs, "Great timing Poppy, I'm an old bitch with a bad wheel now. Baby, you should have come up with this years before now. Now, I got nothing left in the tank."

Not really meaning it, Mitch suggests, "You can still holler at me sometimes anyway, Slim. I mean, you and me are folks. We go a long way back and we do have history." They say goodbye and he jumps in his Lexus SC 430, drops the top, and leaves.

Business starts out only fair. The service is bringing in twelve to fifteen hundred a night, but expenses and the cost of daily operation outweigh that amount considerably. Mitch figures that's usually how legitimate businesses are in the beginning. It costs more to operate than it generates. Even when it's profitable right out the gate, it still usually takes time to actually get into the black, because of the cost of setting it up.

In late 2005, Jan is still in and out from her treks doing drugs. Mitch continues breaking different girls that come through, so Jan's frivolities are of minute importance to him, at best. He knows that she is at the end of her usefulness to the game because of drugs. Plus, he has to have her dodge between the rain drops at getting money, because of the warrants out for her.

In an effort to find something for Jan to do in order to maximize her profitability, Mitch heads to Seattle to a track that Jan had worked previously. So with Jan and what other game he has at the time, his game plan is to get her working up there and perhaps relocating her. There she can avoid the legal ramifications of working Vegas and be able to continue getting at his money. It's a more than sound plan, but designed for a real professional bitch, not what's left of Jan's hoe career. There are a couple of escort services in Seattle that Mitch has Jan hook up with, plus there's a small track there that she has worked with some degree of success. Mitch gets a motel near downtown Seattle, so she'll be central to all the neighboring cities for responding to calls from the services. The few days that Mitch is there, Jan gets money so he begins to think, *just maybe.*

The reality of Mitch's dealings with Jan is that Mitch is torn between two schools of thought. On the one hand, greed and gluttony drives him to try to outwit the effects of the disease of addiction that rages within Jan so she can continue to get the money. On the other hand, as a recovered addict himself, he knows deep in his heart that as written in the AA big book, "Once a cucumber becomes a pickle it can never go back to being a cucumber again." While he's there, he keeps Jan working enough to not have time to think about getting high, he hopes. However, as soon as he's in the air headed back to Vegas, she breaks wide and out to what is becoming her first master, crystal meth. So the Seattle experiment doesn't work the way Mitch hoped it would. He gets a bit of money but, he finds out one more way that won't work with Jan. He even takes her to a few meetings while he's there, but at best she's only there because he takes her. Had he really stopped and recounted his own experiences of when and how his party in drugs and street life ended, it would be more than evident that Jan's party is rushing towards its end of manageability.

Mitch believes the principles of the Program have made him more compassionate and concerned about people and what happens to them. That's a good thing, but not necessarily so in the game. That is evidenced in the interactions with hoes that he's had that aren't in the program, and do not adhere to spiritual principles. "Bitch, you need to go get my money and God bless you" just doesn't cut it with them. Mitch is learning again through practical application that having one's cake and being able to eat it too is a classic challenge for him straddling this fence. Still, he'd rather lose a hoe if it'll save the addict. He wouldn't wish active drug addiction on his very worst enemy.

The service takes a down turn from even the snail pace that it was on previously. Mitch finds two g's in an envelope in his office drawer that the service has made, and again he recognizes that he's spending more to keep it operational than he's making for himself and his young partner. He flies back to Seattle to get his partially troubled girl and returns to Vegas in two days time.

Mitch is kicking it with his phone girls one night when Cher asks, "Of all the girls that come through here, if you had a choice, Mitch, which one would you want to work for you above the rest?"

"That's easy Cher. Based on drive, skill and all systems being a go, I'd have to say that super fine ass little bitch, Jeri. That sexy little bitch was born to be a prostitute."

"Mitch, who is Jeri? I don't remember a girl that works for us by that name."

"Jeri is the name that Jerilyn will answer to once I've knocked her."

Cher and Mitch laugh as Cher responds, "But Mitch, Jerilyn already has a man."

"Cher, most real down hoes have men. That young bitch was raised by the pimping, so she's acclimated to being with the pimping. So just start getting at her head, because whoever her man is, I'll guarantee you he isn't an old school pimp like me." Mitch and the two phone girls have a personal bonus plan, as he has had with others for over forty years. Any of the girls they steer his way and he knocks them, he will give Cher or Carol ten percent of the first ten grand that he gets out of that particular girl.

One day Jeri is sitting in Mitch's office flirting with him like she always does since leaving her man. She's explaining to Mitch that the last guy she was with wouldn't let her keep any money to give her mom or even let her go visit her mom much. She had to start stealing from him in order to break her mom off a few bucks here and there. Mitch explains, "That's counterproductive, because if we're in it to win it together," as he signifies his meaning by pointing his finger back and forth between Jeri and himself, "that means you're all the way down for mine and what defines mine is inclusive of you and yours. That's all part of a pimp's job description. I mean, I really don't want to hear you bad mouthing your man to me, but since you already mentioned it, it's all good."

Mitch can tell that Jeri is surveying her way into choosing him. During the interview process, Mitch learns that she was in fact turned out by an old school pimp, just like him. He had initially figured that based upon her professional mannerisms. That's part of the reason Jeri is so attracted to Mitch's game. Jeri hooks up with Mitch and since Jan is off doing chemical research, Mitch gives Jeri the use of the new Saturn to get at his dough. Mitch learns that Jeri's mom is empathetic about her hoeing. So he tells Jeri to bring her mom by the service so he can meet her. Jeri agrees to, and it's pimping as usual.

One night Mitch is sitting in his escort service office chopping it with J man, when Jeri comes into the service and heads straight into Mitch's office as she always does. Once she sees another pimp in with Mitch, she immediately puts on brakes, apologizes for interrupting, abruptly turns around and walks out the door. "Mitch, I'll be in the conference room when you want me," she says.

"Hold on Jeri, check this out." She turns and walks back into the office. "Where's your mama? I told you to tell her we need to have a sit down, so her and I can chop it."

"I don't know Mitch. I told her what you said."

"Alright, go on over in the other room and we'll discuss it when my pimp friend leaves." With that Jeri humbly dismisses herself. Talk about a young, well seasoned old school hoe.

J man notices Jeri's respectful demeanor in not interrupting he and her man and he laughs. "Mitch, that young bitch there comes from under some real pimping, doesn't she? That hoe stopped on a dime when she saw you were in here with another pimp, man. Aw Mitch, on top of that she's a fine young motherfucker, man. Mitch, how's the pussy, man?" He and Mitch laugh and slap five. Mitch ignores the pussy part. "Yeah J, that's a real old school, young bitch there, man."

Later that week, Mitch meets with Jeri's mom named Christine. Christine is a relatively attractive, young female herself of late thirties to early forties. Mitch ponders perhaps getting at Christine to work for him. It's not like it's too far out of the realm of possibility or probability, as he's had it like that before. They talk and Christine leaves, reasonably sure that Mitch will do right by her daughter and her. Mitch reflects that it always helps to have a girl's mom or other empathetic family member in his corner in this business for extra incentive for the girl getting at his money. He begins mapping out a plan of action for buying a house for Jeri that will one day belong to just her and her mom. Of course, that is after Mitch has made his profits. Jeri's comes up MIA and out of pocket in two months.

On the way to the service one afternoon, Mitch sees this tall, long legged blonde in front of the Riviera. He toots the horn, turns down the street where she is and she comes to his car. He's in the drop top Lexus SC with the top down, jewelry *blinging* real bright and Godfather brim cocked ace duce. Noticing Mitch is older, the girl thinks he could be a potential well to do older black john.

After getting closer she recognizes the flavor, "Whoa wait a minute, are you a pimp or the police?"

"Are you a working girl?" She turns and starts to walk away when Mitch decides on a different approach. Still not saying whether he's a pimp or not Mitch gets at her. "Hey, I own an escort service right down the street. Why don't you come with me and sign up and take some calls for me. You got a man?"

"Aw... yeah... no, I'm new in town."

"Oh really, where are you from? And which is it... you do or you don't have a man?"

"Detroit. And my man is in jail awaiting extradition back to Detroit."

"So you want to put in some work and make some cash, or what?"

She looks around trying to decide whether or not to trust Mitch. "Are you serious about the escort service thing?"

"Of course I am. Get in the car and I'll show it to you." He coaches her into the car by giving her one of his cards and opening the door for her. As she slides into the car Mitch thinks, *gotcha, you bitch.* "I'll take you to the service and let you sign in with one of my phone girls, okay?" Her name is Alexis, so Mitch has Cher sign her up and get a copy of her id. Mitch inquires if she has a car.

"No, they impounded it when my man got busted."

Mitch's alter ego is warning, *yeah right, whatever.*

So Mitch inquires, "Alexis, do you have a cell phone?"

"Yes."

"Alexis is a pretty name, in fact I have another Alexis that works for me now."

"You mean for the service?"

"No, I mean that works for *me.* She's one of my personal girls. Of course, she works through the service sometimes too, but usually she just freelances. Listen Alexis, nothing will be happening for a couple of hours yet, so why don't you take a ride with me." Mitch takes her on a tour of his holdings just to give her an idea of what caliber of game she had fallen into, as they roll and he gets at her mind.

Mitch breaks her, puts her down that night and gives her what few calls the service gets, which have become even fewer and in between. Mitch goes and picks up her clothes and leaves her ex guy's things with the hotel for him to pick up if, or when, he gets out. Come to find out there is a car, but it is in his name only and it is being held, because he is behind on payments. Mitch reflects that he really knows what it's like to be running from the law and the repo company at the same time, but he never wants to be about that again.

Chapter XXXIV

They Still Come and Go

The same week he knocks Alexis, Mitch has his attorney do a check to see if she has any outstanding warrants. Then, he goes to the city jail to visit her ex dude, puts fifty on his books and wishes him well after serving him properly. He is a Detroit pimp and hustler named Darryl who is tall, dark, savvy and appreciative of Mitch's acts of professionalism. Mitch feels that it is the right thing to do. In the old days, if it was his broad and he got out and hadn't been properly served, he'd be about the business of breaking that bitch wherever and whenever he'd see her by any means necessary. This way if Darryl's a real, true to life player he's got no recourse but to accept the knock. Of course, Mitch reasons that if he's not, he'll cross that bridge if and when he comes to it.

However, his alter ego points out, *we don't have a gun and fighting definitely isn't the way for us to go, especially with our breathing being what it isn't. So exactly how would we cross this Darryl bridge if and when we were to come to it? What we need to do is go get our hands on a couple of gats… you know just in case. We would use them if we had them, wouldn't we?* In pondering a response to this question and the rest of these things, Mitch realizes he truly doesn't know what he would or could do, knowing what he knows now, and being who he is now. One of the main reasons he has purposely not acquired any form of firearm since arriving in the Program, is that he has never had any reservations about using them. He doesn't know if that has changed in him and he prays he never has to find out again.

Meanwhile, he's straight ahead about pimping with his new broad, Alexis. She's staying at Mitch's house for the sake of economics and so Mitch has a chance to see what she's doing with her hands, in the avocation of his affairs. Mitch has four vehicles, but he's got to check out the direction of Alexis's feet for a minute before he releases her with one. About a week into it with Allie, she doesn't have much of anything, so Mitch is letting her use some of the accessories that he has in his *hooker boutique*. Allie is a big boned, tall, female with deep blue eyes and a pretty face when made up and properly attired. Mitch has her dye her dishwater dirty blonde hair more blonde, with streaks of platinum. One night preparing for work, Allie is decked out in some seriously high 'come fuck me' pumps.

Mitch observes her and chuckles as he comments, "Allie, baby, you just radiate pure sexuality in those pumps. I can see why those clients through the escort service have been eating your big fine blonde ass up alive." Allie smiles approvingly of Mitch's observations. While these are truly his observations of her, it's more about pumping Allie up psychologically for tonight's work.

Mitch is driving Allie to and from her dates when necessary on service calls, but mostly she's freelancing, working the casinos and in between. Mitch figures as soon as he's far enough ahead on cash with her, he'll get her hooked up with a few other services and allow her to use one of his vehicles. Until that time he's not about to let a bitch that may at any moment be gone, have access to either of his vehicles. One night as Allie and Mitch are having dinner at the Peppermill, Jeri calls him, "Mitch, where are you?"

"Bitch, I'm attending to pimp's business, where are you?"

"I'm back in Vegas, Mitch. I had some problems. Can I please come see you and talk to you?"

"I'm at the Peppermill, Jeri, come on over... no wait. Better yet, I'll tell you what you do. Get to the service and I'll see you when I get there."

"Okay, I'll see you there," Jeri says. Mitch figures whatever games Jeri may be playing this time around, he can at least trust her to go get the money using his vehicles. He's also thinking that he'll join this new bitch to Jeri's hip, and solve two problems in one. The other Alexis, another new knock of Mitch's, is a California brunette white girl of twenty. Mitch has had her a few weeks now and she likes working freelance on her own. She gets at the dough alone and doesn't partner up well with other girls. Mitch hooks Jeri and Allie up to work together and that handles that at least for now, because drama seems to be a way of life with young hoes. Jeri asks where Jan is and when Mitch tells her, she asks, "Why do you keep fucking with that bitch anyway?"

Mitch laughs and playfully tells Jeri, "The same reason that I keep fucking with you, now get out of my office. I'll get with you later, you fucking hoe."

Jeri laughs and looks back over her shoulder as she's leaving. "And I'll see you later too, you fucking pimp." She and Mitch crack up laughing as he watches her leave. That's a little word game they play, especially flossing for other people, hoes in particular.

On one of Jan's meth runs, Mitch gets fed up with her using drama, and tells her, "Jan, it's apparent that you can no longer go about the business of the game and stay clean. Now, I'm still down like four flat tires on an Escalade; on the other hand I'm also in recovery, so I can't keep sending you knowing that it'll only lead you back to drugs. You need to go get with some young black guy, fuck and freak him real good and get him sprung on your little pussy. I mean, you're a young, gorgeous, blue eyed blonde white girl and the average black guy, square or hustler, will be more than happy to let you sit on your ass and not bust a grape. Hey listen baby, at the end of the day, you're still my people and I'll always be here for you to talk to and confide in, so go do what you must. Just remember if ever you need me, I'm here, but don't bring me that weak game and bullshit." With that Mitch sets her free and prays she gets clean and stays clean.

Mitch knows that Allie is not a long-term entity either, especially when he finds out that she smokes crack and drinks like a fish. Just as Jeri keeps Mitch up on when Jan is getting high on the job, she also snitches on any other hoes of his that she catches being out of pocket. Jeri catches Allie smoking crack on one of their double dates together, so she tells Mitch.

Mitch wants to expose Allie in a way that won't implicate Jeri telling on her. Jeri is a professionally jealous, conniving and scheming ass young hoe, who hates to be out done, or out performed, especially since she's in a position as Mitch's bottom. This particular night Allie makes more money than Jeri and Jeri tells on Allie, which is Jeri's way of exacting her revenge.

Mitch is talking with Allie in his kitchen about eight am the morning that Jeri tells on her. He mentions to Allie that he is considering firing his ex bottom, Jan, who is now in jail, once she's out.

"Why, how long has she been with you, Mitch?"

"Off and on about two years, but she's been dishonest with me about smoking dope. I don't care what problems a girl of mine may have or that develops, we can work through them together, just as long as they're straight up with me. We're in it to win it together, right?"

Mitch sees tears forming in Allie's eyes, so he looks deep into those blue eyes and explains to her as if he means it about Jan. "I told Jan, you go down, I go down and I go down, you go down. So if I can't trust *you*… I mean her, or any other bitch, then I don't need *you,*" as he points in Allie's face. "That should get my point across to that *bitch,* don't *you* think, Allie girl? I'm not going out like that behind bullshit. Does that make sense to *you,* Allie?"

As he notices the tears running down her face he takes her face in his hands and holds her face close to his, while still looking deep into those big, pretty blue eyes. "You know, I've really gotten my feelings involved with you in this short time we've been kicking it. I sincerely hope you're as down with me as I am with you, because if you're not, I'd just as soon see you gone *now,* because if I catch you out of pocket I'll fire you. I will not accept less from you than I'm prepared to give."

Now crying, Allie mumbles, "I have something to tell you Mitch, I smoke dope sometimes."

"What kind of dope are you talking about, weed?"

"Yes, that too, but I mean crack."

"Bitch, why didn't you mention this before now?"

"I was afraid you wouldn't let me be with you."

"How long and when was the last time?"

"I hit the pipe when Jeri and I had these two tricks late last night."

"Bitch, you and Jeri hit the pipe with some *tricks?*"

"No Mitch, Jeri didn't, just me. This guy and I were smoking in the bathroom after I finished turning the date and Jeri came in the door with his buddy from another room. She didn't act like she saw anything."

"And how long have you been smoking that shit, Allie?"

"My man…aw…that guy, Darryl, who brought me out here, started me smoking with him about a year ago."

"I can't fade that, Allie. I'm thinking very seriously about just letting you go right about now."

"Mitch, don't do that, please. You're all I have out here." As she waves her arm around the room she pleads, "I want to be a part of all this. I want to be part of your life and work for you. I won't smoke anymore, I swear it, Mitch."

"You know what Allie, I believe that you believe that you have a choice as to whether you smoke or not. This isn't the first relationship you've fucked off from smoking, now is it?"

Now crying hysterically, "No, it's not, but Mitch, you make me strong and I know I can do it for you."

"Baby, you can't do it for me, you have to do it for yourself." Even as he says it he knows better. He reflects on the many times over the years that he's become the sole source of self esteem and worth for different working girls and it still wouldn't and couldn't keep them clean once they succumb to the disease of addiction. He knows that from his own personal powerlessness over mood and mind altering substances of any kind.

"Help me Mitch, please."

Those words are magic to Mitch's ears. He remembers what's inscribed on the NA medallions for clean time, "My gratitude speaks when I care and I share with others the NA way that no addict seeking recovery need ever die."

Mitch momentarily switches gears, as he is moved by this addict that sits before him and not by the cash cow she has become for him. "Allie I'm a recovered addict of over twenty years clean and if you truly want to quit, I'll do all that's in my power to help you." His alter ego argues, *this bitch makes us right at four g's a week, are we crazy here or what*. Mitch explains to her, "Allie girl, I'm prepared to put you in treatment if need be, if that'll help you get and stay clean. Can you go on working without using?" Then, he thinks, *what a stupid question. Of course she's going to say she can and I'm just greedy enough to want to believe her to keep sending her at my dough.*

"I can work without using, Mitch, as long as I know you're there to talk to and now that I know you understand."

So Mitch starts taking her to meetings and she says she likes them, but the acid test is out there on the front line of getting at the money. She can't hang, so she runs off one night to smoke and leaves what little stuff she has accumulated. Mitch reflects that losing or getting stuff never stopped him from using when he was still out there, so why would it stop Allie. Even though Mitch hates losing the money, the bottom line is that he understands that driving compulsive obsession that the disease of addiction can be in calling an addict to the wild.

He's rolling around one night and runs across her. He again offers to help support her to get into treatment, out to meetings while she's in there, and on to a better way of life once she's out, if she's willing. "I don't want to stop smoking right now, Mitch, but I'll get better and come back home to you, you'll see." That leaves Mitch nowhere to go in the conversation.

Years ago, before he knew what was wrong with people like him and Allie, he would have been bitter and resentful to a point of either doing something to her, or at the very least having another bitch or someone else do it for him. Now all he can say ask is for God to bless her and show her mercy, that she may find the happiness, joy, peace and freedom that he and so many other addicts all over the world have found from active addiction. He bids her farewell and rolls out of her life. As he drives away he looks in the rear view mirror and he sees the tears of helplessness and hopelessness in her eyes as she watches him drive away. Mitch feels for her pain.

He thinks of all the family members, friends, lovers and associates who are damaged in the wake of the lies, broken promises, unfulfilled hopes and dreams of people like he and Allie; dope fiends. As he turns the corner he further thinks of all the people like he and Allie that don't have choices in the actions they take or do not take while submerged in active addiction. They cause others pain because that's all they have to share from within themselves, pain and emptiness. Mitch's alter ego reminds him again, *we probably have much too much empathy and sympathy now to be back in this game.*

The escort service continues financially spiraling downward because of lack of incoming calls for business and Mitch is throwing hoe money at it almost as fast as he gets it to keep it going. Jeri starts screwing up again, so Mitch grounds her. Right about the same time he decides to close the escort service. Mitch is already beyond what he had intended to invest in it financially. He figures he won't go beyond a fifty grand investment into the service, thirty six of which he and Pepe put up together.

Mitch figures that it wasn't all bad. He has gone through about twelve to fifteen different young broads in search of that one, maybe two keepers. It's a combination of his age, their stupidity, or the fact that some of them just don't want anything beyond living for this day, and damn tomorrow. Mitch laughs as he thinks that statement sounds vaguely familiar.

He rationalizes that some people grow so accustomed to the taste of failure that they become afraid to venture beyond it. They'd rather stay comfortable and achieve nothing, than to experience the disconcertment along the process of success. Aside from drugs, that's quite probably the main reason that most leave the game with nothing. If he has learned anything between street life and a program of spiritual recovery, it's never give up, say he can't, or deny himself the opportunity to boldly seek out new ways to approach his goals and dreams.

Mitch reflects on the difference in success in the old days at this business and lack of success with their Vegas Valley Escorts. The difference is, he had powerful connections that could fix just about anything back then with a phone call or an envelope of well placed cash. So he feels he didn't fail in the escort service business. He simply learned another way that won't work. If he were younger and healthier he'd have another go at it after a having a necessary surgery on his shoulder. Instead, he shuts the service down, chills for a bit, looks for fresh game and keeps stepping. He's not hurting for cash because he's stashed away the proceeds from several young wild horses, and he still has a few of his young concubines that run back through and break themselves from time to time.

Mitch hasn't had a conventional job in over two years and is still rolling. He signs up to go sell time shares. There is a kid named Terry Huntley, who is a tall, dark skin, muscular kid. Terry came into the program about two years or so after Mitch, and Mitch has sponsored him all these years. Terry is one of the executives at a big time share resort facility out on a new leg of the Vegas strip. Terry and a lot of others have been telling Mitch for years to get into time-share sales because of the big money, short hours, days off and the flexibility of schedule. Mitch has been hearing from a lot of salesmen who were once in the car business and have transitioned into time-share sales, that it is easier money like the good old days in the car business. Mitch takes the personality test and passes with flying colors. The test is all about seeing if one is smooth, conscientious and honest enough to be reliable, while still being slick, convincing and ruthless enough to outwit their counterparts and customers without feeling shame or guilt about it. In other words, the company wants hustlers that are in it to win it and all about the money, but at the same time great in customer satisfaction.

That's why Mitch's transition was so easy into the auto industry from pimping, because he was used to telling people what they want to hear, woo, wow and schmooze them, make money off them, and make them love him for it. America is truly the greatest country on earth and perhaps, in the history of the world. Only in this capitalistic system could a Mitchell Stone Jr., alias Earl Potter, Fast Mitch and Pretty Mitch have succeeded in both an illegitimate criminal enterprise in one life and still in that same lifetime become a successful businessman and entrepreneur with a legitimate agenda. Well, semi legit anyway.

Mitch is officially hired at Bonneville Resorts, Inc, the time share company. He must wait until the federal records check comes back, and once again, he has some concerns in these areas. He has gotten by with a finance and insurance state license for the auto industry, so he's optimistic about being hired for this job. He trusts in the principle of, 'if it's going to be it's up to me.' Also, he knows now as he knew then, if God wants him in it, he's in and if not, he won't be. The fact that one is not supposed to be able to get a license with multiple felony convictions doesn't even deter his optimism. He uses this opportunistic time frame to get the rotator cup surgery on his left shoulder done. Nothing has ever hurt him this bad for this long, even being shot or stabbed. Legs and a couple of his other concubines look out for him while he's recovering. Mitch reflects back over his life in the area of women and recalls that it's White or non Black females, for the most part, that have been there in the clutch times for him. Even after leaving him or him leaving them, they are the ones that rally when he needs them. Legs is finding that her marriage is still not as she'd expected.

"Perhaps nothing is ever as good or as bad as one expects," Mitch explains to her one day while he is convalescing from the surgery. "Real life is never like the movies or sitcoms, especially for pimps and hoes in the game or retired from the game. Psychologically, we view life differently than do our peers in society. And perhaps the biggest game we run is on ourselves in the end, as it shows up in our maladjustment to conventional normalcy, thinking and interactions." Legs still doesn't know Mitch is a recovered heroin addict, or that just about his entire approach to everything in life is from a Program standpoint. That information in their interaction is just one more of the need to know situations.

For Jan, even the relationship that she's in and out of for the past several months with some dope boy is her way of somehow staying connected to her daddy and confidant, Mitch. This other guy is named Mitch and also has the same Zodiac sign in common with Mitch, Scorpio. However, she tells Mitch, "You are like a lot of things to me, my pimp, my man, lover, father and confidant."

When Jan runs off from the dope boy and comes to Mitch, she tells him all about who this other Mitch is and isn't. "Bitch, whatever he is or isn't, one thing he is, he's your primary enabler and if I were you I wouldn't be bad mouthing him like you're doing. If he's your problem, you don't have a solution. Your attitude is, always was, and always will be, your primary problem."

With Jeri, it's just strictly about the pimping, as she is an old school young hoe. Mitch is an old school pimp and that's all she knows or cares about. Mitch views each of their circumstances and them individually with an attitude of whatever works for them, because they are, and always will be, his people, his folks, wild things of the fugitive kind, even after he or they are no more.

Mitch is laid up two to three months from the surgery and indulging in intensive physical therapy for the shoulder. During a social function Mitch runs into his old girl, Yellow. She is still married, has another kid, and is as sexy and fine as ever. Mitch curiously inquires, "Where have you been all these years, girl?"

"Away."

"Yellow, where have you been away to?"

"I've been a long way *away* from you Mitch." They both laugh.

"Yellow, are you still as big a freak and sex addict as you used to be?"

"You still don't get it do you Mitch? *I'm* not a sex addict or a freak. *I'm* a Mitch addict and I love being with you, because *you* are a freak and sex addict." To that they both laugh and go their separate ways.

After Mitch's convalescence from the rotator cup surgery, Kit runs back through and gets with him, but she only partially goes back under the ether of Mitch's charisma and prowess. She has lingering and mixed hurt feelings concerning Mitch behind the drama between her and Jan. She comes back talking about getting married to Mitch, since in her mind she's going to be "his last hoe." Mitch's alter ego reasons, *we still have a rock and roll or two left in us and we have yet to meet our last hoe in this life.* Mitch really does admire and love Kit's work ethic and focus. Plus, she's still one sexy black bitch. So he humors her for the sake of peace, prosperity and of course the money. Mitch amuses himself by thinking, *it's a small wonder I had to use heroin back in the day in order to live with four or five hoes like Kit, Jan, Legs or Jeri, for extended periods of time.*

Mitch realizes that Kit is like one of those nickel slick broads back in the old days that wanted the notoriety of being down with a pimp. Yet, they did not want to pay the total cost to be with the boss through not only money, but complete self sacrifice and subservience. At Kit's age, she still has way too many opinions of her own for Mitch's taste. Mitch reflects on that old rule he learned in the Army, "If the Army wants you to have an opinion they'll issue it to you and ask you for it only if and when it serves their purposes."

Versatility is still one of Mitch's fortes. He has managed a large array of females from different socioeconomic and cultural backgrounds over the years and at different levels of the game from the street corner to the Hilton and all in between. Plus, he readily recognizes that he and Kit can't live together. In fact, with his controlling and demanding nature, the average female would have to almost be a robot to live with him, like Jan in certain areas. Like Mitch, Kit's a dictator, who wants to run the show. Pimping, hoeing and freaking together they can do and have a ball doing it, but after that…? The true turning point in Mitch's control over Kit comes one night when she is at the Crazy Horse II and she calls him by phone for her usual dose of medicine. "Poppy, I am fucking crazy as hell."

"What's new about that with you, female?"

"No Poppy, I'm really out of it." Mitch begins talking Kit through the insanity of the depression part of her bipolar, as she tells him that another stripper gave her a Xanax and she just took it.

"Kit, why don't you just go to the doctor and get a prescription for Xanax, or another med for your particular bipolar?"

"No Mitch, I don't want to feel like I'm that crazy. I can just talk to you most of the time and that balances me out."

"Kit, you *are* that crazy, though."

"Mitch, people have been trying to get me to take that shit for a long time. The only way I'll take it is if you tell me too."

"Alright baby, stay down, stay focused, and keep your eye on our prize." When Mitch hangs up he's thinking, *if I put Kit on meds that'll take the place of me as her medication and that might inevitably erase the need of my job description in her life.*

During the brief time Kit is back, Mitch knocks a stripper hoe named Meredith through a mutual acquaintance. Meredith is a real pretty petite, twenty three year old, blue eyed blonde of French and Italian mix. During the interview process, Mitch finds she has been a housewife with two kids, now separated and living with a new boyfriend and trick. She is working at a strip club named Sin located on Russell Road. She and Mitch hit it off right from the very beginning. Of course she is bipolar, so Mitch proceeds to become her medication and treatment and teach her about the real ways of the game. She is hard headed, with way too many opinions, as well, but Mitch figures he can fix that during the getting to know each other process.

He also finds out that she and her husband had gotten into crystal meth use together, which led to the demise of their family as a unit. She has a history of being sexually abused as a child—imagine that. Her aspirations are not of diamonds, clothes, or trinkets. She just wants a house, a family vehicle (van or SUV) and to make money as an "undercover hoe, while in the public eye maintaining a lifestyle of a soccer mom." Mitch's alter ego nudges him, *this bitch can have any reasons she wants as long as we get the money. She can play being whoever she wants to be, but we know and she knows she's a hoe.*

Mikki (his nickname for Meredith) disappears for two days right after getting with him, but when she shows back up she's got two grand. Still, because of her sporadic behavior, Mitch explains to her that he will have to wait until he at least sees some degree of stability in her behavior and work ethics before he can begin fulfilling his goals for her and her kids. He's thinking he needs to be at least five to seven g's ahead before getting her situated into a more permanent housing arrangement. This amount will be enough to at least cover a six month lease on an apartment in case she flakes out. After one year he'll buy her a vehicle of her own. Until then she'll use one of his. At that one year mark, he'll either buy a house for her and her kids to live in, or he'll put her in one of his rentals, depending on her level of productivity and accountability. So Mitch assigns these things as her game plan and goals to achieve. Of course, all these outcomes rest upon how acclimated she is to getting money appropriately on a regular basis.

During this time, Kit makes reservations for her and Mitch to go to Cabo San Lucas for a big weekend, along with Kit's blood sister, Scarlett, and Scarlett's lesbian girl friend, Ginger. Mitch hasn't been there in thirty years. It'll be refreshing to see how much growth has taken place in that city with its exotic mega resorts and hotel properties now surrounding the town. Cabo was near medieval thirty years ago by today's standards. He remembers the last time he walked those beaches was with L and Brea. The four of them stay in a two bedroom suite with separate entryways and balconies overlooking the beautiful picturesque view of the pool area and the beach and ocean beyond. The poolside bars and chairs are filled with tourists, colorfully clad both in attire and demeanor. As Mitch gazes out from the balcony view, he recognizes it is apropos for such an exotic getaway.

Since stepping off the plane, Mitch has experienced quite a bit of difficulty with his breathing because the humidity affects his emphysema so adversely. When they go horseback riding along the beach, Mitch's breathing difficulty becomes extremely discomforting for him. His chest tightens, he sees black spots before his eyes and he becomes dizzy. He feels as if he is about to pass out from his inability to get enough oxygen through his body. He becomes angry, irritable and discontent. Mitch's alter ego even complains, *here we are in a resort full of all kinds of freaks and we can hardly breathe. One more time we're on the verge of seriously coming up and we're being fucked yet again by the twisted finger of fate.*

It's taking so much resolve on Mitch's part physically, that he can't enjoy the elation of just being here. His alter ego is telling him that, *all four of us can do some serious freaking together,* but Mitch's body is saying something totally different. He tries to work out in the weight room on one occasion and has to lie down for an hour before he can steady his breathing after only fifteen minutes of lifting weights. Between Mitch's alter ego and his false pride he is not about to let either of the females in his party know just how physically sick he has become. Fortunately, he has the new girl, Mikki, down back in Vegas. His excuse for spending so much time in the air conditioned suite is, he's trying to manage his business affairs with her.

The second night a white guy approaches Kit with an offer to switch with Mitch, his wife for Kit for the night. His wife is a Latina, so Mitch's mind is all over that deal, but again not his body. He manages to have sex with Kit once, but it is so difficult for him that he can't tell if he's coming or going. Mitch is so angry with his disease of emphysema and his breathing problems that he goes into a state of depression and denial. He does manage to pick up a really nice, fairly expensive, 3D oil painting while they're shopping in downtown Cabo at a local art gallery, but that is the extent of his venturing out. They all hit a strip joint that night and Mitch is too sick to even get into the flow of partying, or at any of the fine ass Latinas.

On the last day in Cabo, Kit urges Mitch to go jet skiing with her, Scarlett and Ginger. Kit wonders why Mitch, or anyone would come to an exotic resort to spend most of their time inside the suite. It's a good thing it isn't life threatening, because Mitch's closed mouth attitude about the severity of his condition would easily lead to his demise in his process of saving his face at the expense of his ass. In the air conditioning, Mitch can breathe much easier, but even then he is still weak and weary. He tells them that he doesn't wish to participate because he has to stay on top of things by phone with Mikki back in Vegas, but he is just not physically strong or well enough to participate. The three girls have a jet skiing accident from playing around unsafely and it leaves a serious cut in Ginger's leg. Mitch goes off on Kit because it is a stupid thing to do for a woman that uses her body to earn a living.

Mostly, though, his anger is really about his condition and the fact that he has given up just about everything else that he enjoys doing in life and the associates that he once did them with, so he wouldn't be constantly reminded of his limitations. Now, he finds that travel to exotic destinations becomes yet another threshold of limitations and liabilities, as a result of his impairment. He feels shame, humiliation and dejection at the very idea that he, of all people, could be physically challenged in this way. The very thought of it repulses him.

He remembers growing tired of telling his old partners, "No thanks, I'm working," or "I have other engagements." He has changed all his immediate associates to people that either don't want to do, or can't do, the things that he still longs to do. Now, even travel to exotic places and jet skiing will become yet more things that he will have to learn to live without. He thinks, *it's not fair. I'm clean, having big money and hoes again and the world has once more become my oyster. Why me and why now?*

Once back from Cabo, Mitch finds that Mikki has put together at least a decent enough bank for him to move her into an apartment. He sends a partner of his along with two other black guys to pick up Mikki and her two kid's furniture and personal belongings and move them into an apartment that Mitch leases for the three of them. The guy who Mikki and her kids had been living with prior to getting with Mitch is pretty broken up when these three black guys show up to move her belongings out. Mikki tells Mitch, "My white lover named Joel asks me accusingly, 'You're sleeping with these black guys now'?"

Mikki starts laughing as she continues explaining, "Mitch, I could hardly keep a straight face when I told him 'no honey, I'm not sleeping with *these* black guys.' Then, I couldn't help laughing, because Mitch, he thought I was lying, but I really wasn't."

"Mikki, why did you laugh, though?"

"Because silly, I was telling the truth about not sleeping with *those* black guys, but I am sleeping with *the* black guy that sent them. He had just asked the wrong question. You get it Mitch?" Mikki cracks herself up laughing at her statement and Mitch can't resist the temptation to laugh as well.

"Mikki, you're a fucking *whore,* do you know that?"

"Yeah, I know, thank you very much for the compliment, Mitch."

"Mikki, I thought you said you love this guy, Joel."

"I do love him, Mitch, but I want to make money selling my pussy, so I need to be with someone like you in the sex industry."

That statement doesn't leave a lot to speculation. Mitch just laughs as he thinks, *sweet dirty bitch, I think I'm in love.*

Chapter XXXV

Can't Outrun the Inevitable

Kit and Mikki hit it off much better than Kit and Jan did, so there's no rivalry now. Mikki is less tainted or scandalous, more laidback and less conniving than Jan. Kit also has a new attitude towards the realities of at least this part of the game. When Mitch introduces them, he and Mikki are coming out of his garage, as Kit is pulling up in the driveway in the Escalade. Mikki is wearing a little white, tight top that ends above her navel with no bra underneath, and a little pink, too short mini skirt with no panties to leave nothing to the imagination—just nasty. Mitch is pinching one of her nipples as it strains against the fabric of the halter top while she winces playfully and smiles flirtatiously. Mitch hollers to Kit, "Kit, look at this little nasty bitch here. Do you think the pussy is any good?"

Kit sticks her head out the window of the Escalade. "I'm not sure Poppy, let me get a good look at her." Mikki shyly eases behind Mitch, uneasy at being scrutinized by Kit's piercing lustful stare.

"Mikki, why are you hiding behind me?" Mitch laughs as he teases Mikki. "You weren't all that shy when you were trying to kill me this morning. I thought you told me that you like sexy black girls anyway. Here's one that's about as sexy as they come."

Mitch takes the two girls to brunch before dropping Mikki off at Meadows Mall for a makeover, and hair tint. He is very pleased at how well the two girls get along. Even though Mikki is not as contentious as Jan, today's brunch still could not have been so pleasant had Kit not adopted this new attitude of acceptance about wives-in-law.

Later in the evening, as Mikki is getting dressed to go to the strip joint, Sin, Kit calls while she's with one of her regular dates and she has talked him into a threesome with her and Mikki. "Poppy, is your bitch ready to sell some pussy?"

"Bitch, is seven up?" Mitch gets the information and he calls Mikki out from the shower.

"Mikki Mouse, come get directions from your wife in law, so you and her can get at my money."

As Mikki comes out of the shower brazenly naked with only a towel around her hair, she asks, "Mitch, what did you just call me?"

"Mikki, answer the phone about this money first, okay?" She gets directions from Kit to a suite at some hotel, hangs up and turns to again ask Mitch what he just called her. "I called you Mikki Mouse, but sitting here staring directly into your business, Miss bitch," as he laughs and points to her exposed body, "that's perhaps a bit too domestic of a name for you, *whore.*"

They laugh as they have both gotten in the habit of Mitch using the proper pronunciation of that word jokingly in teasing her and she just loves it. Mikki is standing naked with her hands on her hips and feet wide apart in the middle of the tiled living room between Mitch and his big screen HDTV. She provocatively suggests, "Mitch, since you're staring at my *business* anyway, you got something else on your mind?"

"Yeah Miss, as a matter of fact I do, you need to get your little freakish ass popping and catch up with your big sister, Kit, and get at my check."

As she walks back towards the shower she looks back over her shoulder, and says, "We have time for you to give me just a little, Mitch."

"All things in good time my lady." Later that evening Mitch picks up seventeen hundred from Mikki for that one date, so it's the making of a great money day.

Kit calls and clues Mitch in on the details of how her freaking with Mikki went. Mitch is grateful that someone or something is keeping this too hot to trot young Caucasian female off of him. He feels that as long as he's getting paid, those two hoes can lick each other into unconsciousness and God bless them.

On a Friday evening around ten pm with Mikki at work and Kit out of town with one of her regulars, Mitch is driving to the apartment where he has Mikki staying. Just as he gets to the front gate and is entering the code his phone rings. It's Jan calling from the Texas Casino. "Hello, what you doing, Mitch?"

"What's up Jan, baby? I'm doing the same thing I was doing bitch when you first met me, pimping as hard as lightening strikes a tree trunk."

"Baby, pick me up, I'm at the Texas, where are you?"

"Just so happens I'm right down the street from the Texas, so go to the front of the casino and wait there. I'll be there in three minutes." Mitch knows that, when Jan calls, it's usually to break herself so he speeds over to the Texas Casino, scoops her up, and rolls back to Mikki's apartment. He's chopping it with her on the way and feeling her out to determine what's really going on this time around, as they pull up in front of the apartment.

"Baby, what girl you got living here?"

"This is Mikki's apartment."

"Who is Mikki, Mitch?"

"Another blue eyed, blonde, young freak like you." Inside the apartment he tells Jan, "That's Mikki's picture right there," as he points to the living room wall.

"Baby, this guy that I've been kicking it with is also old school, but he's nothing like you. I get it every day if I want, and sometimes more than once." Jan giggles at her statement. "But man he won't let me go get money and he watches my movements like a prison guard trying to keep me from getting high and being with someone else. It's really a trip, Mitch, because when I first got with him, he let me have crystal meth and let me do whatever I wanted. In fact, when I told him that I smoke crystal meth sometimes, he bought me a whole ounce, so I could just stay home and do it to him all the time."

"Jan, little boys are that way about their little sexual play toys, especially if it's good to them. And who else but a real live hoe can put it on them like that?"

"But Mitch, listen, after that he starts trying to keep me from smoking meth and I'm thinking what the fuck is up with this? It was okay in the beginning but it's not now. You know Mitch, I'm a hoe and I need to be in action. I get so bored sometimes that I could just scream and you know me baby, I start running off, so I can get high and get selling pussy like I did this time." Mitch's ears perk up when he hears the "run off and get selling pussy" part. Mitch is thinking this behavior is just a part of Jan's overall makeup as a hoe that goes on meth runs from time to time.

"What does this other Mitch know about me, Jan?"

"He knows nothing about you, Mitch, and baby you know, I just really miss working." She pauses again waiting for a reaction from Mitch. Mitch just silently stares at her. When she gets no response she continues with, "I went and got high two days ago and I haven't been back since. So I got a room at the Texas and I been working, gambling and getting high ever since."

Mitch looks at her disgustingly, and responds, "And now you're a broke bitch, huh?"

Jan's pride as a money making hoe causes her to declare, "No Mitch, I got money, see," as she flashes a hand full of bills and puts them back in her rear jean pocket.

Mitch smiles as his hook question works and he thinks, *gotcha, you bitch.* His smile turns into laughter, as he thinks how very predictable hoes can be. "Come on bitch, you know better than that, break your motherfucking self." Jan reluctantly hands over the four hundred and fifty bucks. Mitch explains, "I figure I might just as well get paid now, because your boyfriend, that other Mitch, is going to kill you about running off with his pussy." He and Jan laugh at the logic of that.

"Baby, I've made right at a grand both days since I've been gone from him and all I've done is smoke meth, gamble, drink, and fuck it off. I want to get back with you and kick it like before. I was so pretty and down back then, Mitch."

"You're still a pretty white bitch, Jan. And you *were* good when you *were* hard down for mine, but when you were down for crystal meth you weren't that good at all." Mitch is thinking, *I got Mikki and Kit down clocking bank. So I don't particularly need the added drama of Jan within my crew, and loose ends with her new boyfriend right about now, unless it's well worth it.* "Jan, things aren't like they were when you first got with me out of prison. You know how this thing goes. I got other down hoes right now, so this time bitch you'll need to get up on a more serious bank before I pull this choosing trigger, again. I need to be sure you're serious about getting at my money and not using. So here's how we'll play it, you got tonight through Sunday to get me a correct check together and we'll hook up on Monday. Then and only then, will I take whatever appropriate actions that need to be taken, you got it?"

"Okay, I got it and I'll get working at it. I need you to drop me off down the street from this trick's pad over by the Texas Casino, so I can get started putting your money together."

Mitch drops her off and as he drives away his alter ego suggests, *we'll see that bitch when we look at her again.* So meanwhile Mitch gets back with the pimping at hand.

To Mitch's surprise Jan calls in the wee hours of that morning around six. "Pick me up, I'm at the Bellagio and I got the money to come home."

"Go out front and I'll pick you up in the time it takes me to get from my pad in Aliante." Mitch jumps on the 215 freeway in the Lexus and connects at the 15 freeway flying, heading for the money. Jan gives Mitch twenty four hundred, so it's on and popping again as far as Mitch is concerned.

He doesn't bother serving the other Mitch. He is obviously not a pimp and he wants to first see how Jan is going to work out and what she's doing with her hands. However, Mitch is mindful of what could possibly happen if this other Mitch runs up on her at work, or someplace else in the avocation of his business. Mitch's experience in life is what goes up must come down and what goes out usually comes back around. It's just a matter of gravity and inertia in life and the game, as well as on the spiritual plane. He doesn't want to upset the harmony he's got going between Mikki and Kit, so he decides not to keep Jan around his crew, but on the down low.

With Kit being a self turn out and approaching her late thirties she is constitutionally incapable of holding up under the traditional pimping for very long. Mitch talks to his pimp crony, J man, as an empathetic ear about sending Kit to get on bipolar meds. "J man, getting Kit on the bipolar meds will be helping an addict get a better handle on her sanity, recovery, and mood swings. However, my alter ego is telling me, *'the only crutch we want a bitch to have is us'.* Those meds will become the thing that she relies and depends on for emotional and mental balance, instead of on me, and this pimping." Mitch and J man laugh and bump fists on that. "J man, it's like, do I save the addict or adhere to the common sense of the pimping? Then too, I know that the only reason I'm still alive, clean, reasonably sane, happy, joyous, and free is because of the grace of God, and the Program."

"Yea, yea, Mitch, that shit's like a catch twenty two, man, for players like us, man, damned if we do and double damned if we don't. But at the end of the day, we have to do what we have to do to help save the addict, man."

"Yeah, I know bro, I'm right there with you," as he points two fingers to his eyes. "I got to do what's best for this broad, man."

"Well, there it is there, Mitch. You said she'd only go get on them if *you* send her," he says as he points to Mitch's chest. "I mean, man, if we talk with another addict in recovery long enough about what's really going on, we generally come up with the answers and solutions we're seeking to our situations."

"You got that shit right, J man, that's part of 'how it works'."

Mitch instructs Kit to go to the shrink and get on bipolar meds, and start taking them as prescribed. She offers no opposition, and while the meds can't cure her secondary disease of bipolar they do make her functioning capacity with it much more manageable. That's independent of Mitch having to help wind her up or wind her down when needed. As a result, Kit's late night and wee hour calls to Mitch progressively diminish over time.

Mitch reasons when Jan is free of drug problems she's damn near a poster child for a model hoe at being with a pimp, (gullible, down for the cash and other bitches, and can get money when pet milk and gas is on strike). That's how she got it, so that's how she knows to do it. She'll sacrifice herself or anything else to get money for her man. It doesn't get any more old school than that.

That is definitely not who Kit is, and never will be, at this stage of her life. That doesn't make her a bad person just a female that'll never be able to cohabitate with the kind of man she thinks she wants, let alone marry one. However, it won't do any good to tell her that just yet. It'll only rock Mitch's boat with her sooner than it's going to be rocked again anyway. In time she'll wake up to this on her own. Still, Kit has served both their purposes quite well, given the capacity he initially knocked her to do. She stays another couple of months or so, before the inevitable end. She again goes back to doing and being her true self.

With Kit gone, Mitch turns to Jan. He knows that she will be in and out of smoking meth and back and forth with her boyfriend, so he breaks her when he can, for as much as he can, wherever he can. Mikki is a soldier when she's clean from meth, and Mitch learns to give her a lot of rope to do whatever she wants, as long as she keeps paying him. Jan's house is completed, but with her being out of pocket more often than not, Mitch decides to include his bud, J man, in his next profit making real estate venture. Mitch is known to have gotten a few people handsomely paid from his different real estate and entrepreneurial ventures over the years. So he and J man go in on the new house with the intention of flipping it in two to three years and buying up.

As Jan runs through and breaks herself on occasion, Mitch takes her to show her the house she could have had, that she literally sent up in smoke. She reacts the same way each time, she cries and swears that this time she'll do it differently. Mitch gives her the same response each time. "Baby as long as you think you've got power of choice over whether you smoke or not, do things differently or not, you're going to continue to smoke. That's what drug addicts do, we use. Trust me. I know as well as any the validity of that fact. It took me twenty years of running and gunning for drugs to finally become humble and teachable enough to accept help when it came my way."

Meanwhile, Mitch goes on with his own personal financial game plan for his life and future. Part of this game plan is to work full time in the time share game until age sixty five, before drawing the full grip on social security, if his old body and lungs can hold up that long. At sixty one, he thinks this doable. All things considered, many of his financial ducks are in a row for one day at a time.

Kit's credit is okay again, so she refinances their house, which she lives in, putting it into her name only. Mitch could step in and help orchestrate that process for her, but she is too stubborn to ask. He figures she needs to do it on her own anyway, even if her inexperience does cost them an extra chunk of cash. Mitch knows that like him, Kit is very prideful and egotistical, so she doesn't ask for his advice. Even if she had, he would've still let her do it on her own just for the experience.

Kit has picked up on at least the *cop* part of the cop and blow game Mitch has taught her, including; 'fuck me once shame on you, fuck me twice shame on me.' Mitch knows, however, it's one thing to know something or learn how to do something in theory, but practical application of that knowledge is a totally different animal. People generally rise up to or sink down to, who and what they are, regardless of what they know or learn.

Mitch has also learned that wanting something is sometimes more fulfilling to him than getting it. Therefore, what her retention and application of the *blow* part of the game is, remains speculative. If one can't learn to follow they'll never be able to lead. One of Mitch's principle adages is, 'a man has got to know his limitations.' Mitch takes that adage a bit further in practical application; a man also has got to know the limitations of his people. Kit loses her enthusiasm for stripping and turning tricks, so she starts her own exotic hair business after leaving Mitch.

Mitch observes Kit's attitude, timing and tenacity *(AT&T)* in maintaining her financial commitments to him concerning their holdings, and her preparations in setting up her new business. Since she is one of his best protégés, at least during these times, he lends her twenty five grand to help jump start her business. All things considered, he can't think of another person that he'd do that for these days in the game that's not incarcerated. He feels she may be successful, but then again she may not. What's most important to Mitch is her level of commitment when she's acting on sane positive information that's not too far left. He is confident that if she doesn't make snap decisions based on the mood swings of her bipolar and researches her choices carefully before she leaps, she should be okay. He would've straight given her at least a fraction of that amount to help her out somewhere down the line anyway if needed. He reasons that he would, and has with any of his soldiers in need who have served him for extended periods of time. She's one of his people, his folks of the fugitive kind. As he learned from *Giants* in the game years ago, that twenty five g's didn't make him when he got it, so it won't break him if he loses it. Part of the reason that Mitch feels this way about Kit is because she still steers a few different broads his way, including her own cousin. On one occasion Kit picked up a working girl Mitch had recently knocked, and put her in a position to get at some dough for him. Kit knows from her own personal experience in the process of becoming Mitch's poster child hoe during this time that she is a testament, not only to the finesse and pedigree of his game, but her determination to succeed as well.

The housing market in Vegas takes a turn for the worse, as it does everywhere with property values plummeting. This starts to affect the whole economic forecast not only locally, but worldwide. The entire economic climate takes a serious downturn. All the news and financial information sources are predicting doom and gloom in all the different markets. Mitch, however, recognizes buying opportunities on the horizon towards the end of this dismal forecast of the world economy. He knows towards the end there will be properties for the stealing, as long as he stays the course now and maintains the properties he has. Also, he realizes his eight hundred and thirty plus credit score, along with his cache of stash cash, won't hurt either. Meanwhile, he supports himself and his personal expenses with money from his legitimate time-share sales job. His mortgages and other major bills are covered through his other entrepreneurial pursuits, of which a portion of those proceeds go directly into his stash cash. He figures to pick up a minimum of eight to ten more properties for pennies on the dollar when the right time comes.

Early 2007, Mitch runs into his old girl, Yellow, at a social function of mutual friends. Having only seen her once or twice in the past fifteen years, Mitch is giving her the once over from head to toe. He finds that, like him, she is older with an extra pound or two here and there, but still as fine as vintage wine with that perfectly smooth cocoa butter complexion and flawless skin. She notices Mitch staring at her, and returns his stare just as if it were the old days. Mitch knows the very same passion and lust in his own mind from just seeing her are also still in her mind. He notes that even time cannot dispose of the attraction between wild things and, if Yellow is nothing else, she is a wild thing.

Yellow makes her way to Mitch and asks, "Hey sexy, what's up?"

"*You,* sometimes *me,* and all the time *we,* are what's up. I thought you knew."

"I do know, and you're looking good."

"So are you, and how are you, Yellow? It's really good to see you. Where have you been all these years?"

She bursts into laughter. "Trying to be a good wife and mother when I'm willing to be."

Mitch laughs along with her. "Yellow, you're a coward."

"No, I'm just married with children, and doing my best to stay out of your kind of trouble."

"Have lunch with me Yellow, and we can talk about what it was like, what happened, and what it's like now."

"Mitch, do you mean that in the context of the Program, or personally?"

_w, between you and me, everything is personal. Come on ...id ride with me."

She laughs, "Same old Mitch, huh? No, I believe I'll be a lot better off just following you in my *own* car."

Over brunch they laugh, and recount the old times of their brief but frenzied love affair. With Mitch being back in the game, he is again unscrupulous concerning women, and what he wants when he wants it. "Yellow, I didn't realize just how much I've missed you until I laid eyes on you back there just now." He grabs her hand, and asks, "You know, you're still my girl, don't you?"

"Mitch, I'll always be your girl, and I'll always feel what I feel when I see you. That wasn't the problem with us back then. What the problem was, all of the *others* that will always be your girls too."

"That didn't stop me from kissing and caressing you from your head down to your toes, did it?"

"Yea it did, Mitch, because that blonde (Slim) was talking about running me over with her vehicle. I figured back then that things were getting too out of hand, so I just split."

In a moment of compassion, Mitch appreciates her point of view. "Yellow, I wish it could have been different between you and me." They continue reminiscing and chopping it jovially over brunch.

As they are about to get into their cars in the parking lot, Mitch grabs her, and pulls her body gently into his and she sighs as they embrace, each of them feeling as if time has stood still. Ever so briefly, they each savor the aroma and touch of the other, that scent that once tantalized their senses. They realize nothing has changed between them, and quite probably never will, except her ability now to not act on the animal magnetism between them.

In March 2007, Mitch's breathing takes a turn for much worse. He goes to a specialist as his primary care physician concedes that he is unable to maintain stability in Mitch's breathing. Mitch visits a Pulmonologist for the first time in over fifteen years of treating and dealing with his emphysema on the run. They begin to try different, stronger steroids on him. A cat scan confirms what his deteriorating lungs have already been suggesting to him for years. He only has approximately thirty three percent lung capacity remaining. The first diagnosis suggests that in four to five years, as his lungs continue to deteriorate, he'll need a lung transplant.

Mitch shows little to no reaction to the information, but once in the privacy of his home, he finds himself pondering the diagnosis. He already knew what his future held because of emphysema. After all, he's only been on a rampage for the past eight years in an effort to either outrun Mother Nature, or die from indulging in just too much reckless fun, abandon and debauchery in the process.

He begins calculating, and he thinks, *okay four to five years, I'll be about sixty five. That's thirty to thirty five years longer than I once planned on being around anyway.* Never let it be said that Mitch does not possess sufficient will and determination to do just about whatever he sets his mind to within physical limitations, of course. In spite of this dismal diagnosis, Mitch reasons that he just needs to step up his efforts and energies toward fulfilling the game plan that he shares with several others in and around his life.

He continues to work at time-share sales all day, and he is still up in the wee hours consulting with different members of his constituency, who are around at various times. He continues eating on the run, and sleeping very irregularly, so his stress level remains as it has always been throughout his two lives. Yet, he is happy, because he lives absolutely every moment of everyday as if it is his very last. All of these years Mitch somehow felt that if he refused to be stopped by emphysema, perhaps he wouldn't succumb to it, even as his physical capabilities continued to decline. He figures to do all he can in the next few years. When the time comes, he plans to have left no profitable or pleasurable stone unturned, so he can live as comfortable as possible for whatever remaining years have left at that time. Like anyone else, he doesn't want to , out he doesn't fear death because he knows he has been blessed by God with all the things he's seen and done in these two lives in one lifetime he's lived. He ponders that what he fears most is pain, suffering, or long term disability. Still, it has been said now by his Pulmonologist, a West Indian named Dr. Kumar, that his condition is deteriorating from the same disease that his Madea died of and exactly what his dad also currently suffers from, severe emphysema/copd.

His alter ego thinks, *we always figured that all this stuff for us was all about much, much later.* Mitch doesn't realize at this time that it is his way of coping with a notice of finality about his mortality. On the nights that Mitch has one of his concubines coming by to kick it with him after they get off from work, he gives them instructions to call him when they turn off the 215 freeway onto Aliante Parkway headed to his spot. Then, he diverts them to go pick up some beverage item or another for him before they get to his house. Doing this gives him time to do a breathing treatment, and use all his steroid inhalers in order to pump his lungs up to the task of entertaining them. He laughs about it thinking, *they still don't know just how bad my breathing has gotten.*

Mitch really doesn't accept how bad it is at this time either, for he is still in a form of denial. It works for several months. Actually, it has worked for years, because he started experiencing this impairment to varying degrees as far back as those last times with his old girl, Slim. Over the years, he has usually managed to will his way through it, but it's progressively gotten worse. He figures, well it is what it is, so he'll just have to use smoke, mirrors, and obfuscation with the girls for as long as he can.

In late July 2007, Mitch comes down with what he believes to be another case of sinus infection, cold, or flu with a throat infection either related to his disease or side effects of the medications. He's taking stronger steroids that help support his lungs to function better, but these steroids also lower his immune system. Finally, one day he's walking from his Explorer into work and he begins experiencing chest pains. He wills himself to keep on walking. With each step his vision becomes more blurred, he begins sweating heavily, and it feels as if his chest is about to explode as he gasps for air to breathe. He sees spots in front of his eyes and his limbs grow weak and heavy. He wonders, *is this a heart attack, stroke, or is this finally just my number coming up?* All his inhalers are ineffective, so he leaves work to get to his primary care physician. By the time he drives to his doctor's office he can only take a few steps at a time before bending over from piercing chest pain, and desperately gasping for air. Dr Mc Hale, his primary, makes a call to get him admitted into Valley Hospital immediately.

Mitch resists going directly, stating that he has six thousand cash in his pocket and over one hundred thousand in jewelry on his person, so he has to go home first to drop these items off. Even possibly near death, Mitch thinks of his money, jewelry and material possessions, first. Dr McHale submits as Mitch won't back down.

After dropping off his items of value and picking up the necessary personal items he'll need while in the hospital, Mitch is admitted into the hospital. When the staff puts him on oxygen at his bedside he feels instant relief. The pounding in his chest stops, his labored breathing becomes normal, he stops sweating, and his vision comes back into focus. They put him on IV with a couple of super antibiotics. He is informed that he has pneumonia, and a bacterial lung infection.

He remains in the hospital for a week as they do every test known to man, heart, liver, lungs, kidneys, angiogram, cancer, hepatitis C, aids and sickle cell. He is put on even more powerful steroids. When he is released from the hospital, it is under the condition that he be on continuous oxygen twenty four seven. His alter ego figures, *the pneumonia and lung infection ran down our lungs and energy levels, so we'll be up and running in a few days or so.*

The doctor tells him differently, however, "It could be days to a few weeks, or even months before you get off the oxygen, Mitchell." Mitch thinks this cannot be. He has so much yet to do.

As the days roll into weeks Mitch refuses to use the oxygen when he goes out to take care of whatever business that he has to in public, except for doctor's appointments. He now sees only his new Pulmonologist exclusively, Dr. Nehru, who is the director of the pulmonary center. Mitch keeps a portable tank in his car preferring to experience the discomfort of the lack of oxygen in his lungs and body as opposed to his feelings of humiliation from the looks and whispers from people, when he's carrying a portable tank in public.

It's enough that he's sixty years old and rapidly approaching sixty one still trying to hang with young working girls more than thirty five to forty years his junior, but he absolutely will not submit to having this contraption attached to his nose in public. He simply won't do it, no matter what. So he pays the price of being extremely uncomfortable while out shopping, in meetings, and other social settings. So much so that, when he becomes faced with the choice of either wearing the oxygen nose piece when he goes out, or stay home, he picks the latter. Still, he has to go out to handle his and his people's affairs. He is in denial, sullen, angry and depressed as he sits at home, and awaits the day he'll be off oxygen, and he can get back to the business of shaking, moving, and chronic come-up-ism.

It especially kills Mitch inside to see the looks in the eyes of the girls that run back through his life to see how he is, and to assist him. He ponders how pimping is about the illusion of invincibility, courage, and strength under fire. If the general panics, so will the troops, but he's growing increasingly more visibly frustrated with his situation. He begins to doubt he'll get back physically to even where he was before the bout with pneumonia, and that thought depresses him even more.

In early November, 2007, Mitch continues to expect to be removed off oxygen and able to get back to his great life as it was. His alter ego, however, poses a few questions to him; *don't God and Mother Nature know that we have great and important things yet to achieve? Why not let someone of lesser impact potential in life succumb to this debilitating disease?* Of course, last but not least, *Why us, and why now?*

Finally, a different set of questions begins to formulate within Mitch's heart in mid November, which is three months after being placed on oxygen, *why not me, and why not now? Do I not realize that I am and never have been any more or less than any other human being? Do I not realize that everyone succumbs to some form of physical or medical dilemma along their journey through life, because not one of us is going to get out of life alive, anyway? It's just a matter of when, how, and where that differs in us all?* Reasoning that he has lived somewhat of a spiritually faithful, drug free, and fruitful life as a productive member of society for the past twenty three years, he finally begins to remember that a day above ground is a blessing, whether on oxygen or not. The standard rule is that guys like him don't even make it this far. They're usually buried deep in the ground or locked away for life long before they reach the age of sixty. Given where he comes from and the life he's led, he has truly been living on borrowed time. All of Mitch's basic needs are met and a great deal of his wants and desires within realistic proportions, are also.

He has come to a place inside his soul where he believes, come what may, if life takes him to it, God will see him through it, whatever it may be. Mitch understands that this doesn't mean that God will fix whatever it is that confronts him. It just means that God will walk at his side, and comfort him in times of sadness, disappointment, trials, and tribulations.

Mitch is sitting in his little home in Sun City Aliante and he begins to shed tears of joy and gratitude as he reflects over his life, a life that includes twenty years of street credits and twenty years in corporate America along with twenty three years clean of heroin addiction. He is a recovered heroin addict that everyone expected would die loaded, in prison, or in an insane asylum, which are the normal ends for the kind that he once was. By the grace of a Higher Power, he has been spared those fates. He realizes that he has had more than his share of being in harm's way.

There was a time in his life when carrying a 45 was as common place as wearing underwear. There was also a time when using it was second nature for him. He hasn't owned a weapon in twenty three years, nor has owning one been in his thoughts. For a guy like him this is only one of the many miracles, big and small, of his story. With all of this in mind, he realizes that he has no right to be sad, remorseful, or exhibit such a gross lack of faith. It is at this exact moment that his anger, frustration, and depression subside. He is propelled into a state the Big Book of AA refers to as "rocketed into a fourth dimension" of happiness, joy, peace, and freedom. He feels a warm, reassuring sensation overcome him as he relinquishes his life and circumstances to an attitude of gratitude. Whatever happens he will be the best him that he can be, based on whatever his circumstances are at any given time.

For the first time in Mitch's life it is no longer about finding who, what, where, when, or why, to blame for his life and affairs. Neither is it about feeling sorry for himself. He ponders, *after a lifetime of searching for a place for me I have finally found it in the most inconspicuous of places, within my own soul.* It's now about the buck stopping with him, and only him, and since it's his buck, he figures he and he alone is responsible for it.

A short time later, Mitch learns from Dr. Nehru that he was misdiagnosed by Dr. Kumar. His death is not as imminent as he'd been led to believe. He could be around another fifteen years or so, with these very same lungs. Mitch figures those years might just as well be as fruitful, positive, and spiritually free as he can possibly make them through God's grace. "Sometimes, going left is the only way to get right."

Manufactured By: RR Donnelley
Breinigsville, PA USA
June, 2010

"Sel"

702

6898204